DUELING IN
DEATH'S
BACKYARD

THOMAS JAY BERGER, MD

STORY MERCHANT BOOKS
LOS ANGELES
2015

THE STORY MERCHANT

http://www.heartofyourcase.com

ISBN: 978-0-9909436-4-8

Cover art & interior format by IndieDesignz.com

Story Merchant Books
400 S. Burnside Avenue #11B
Los Angeles, CA 90036
http://www.storymerchant.com/books.html

THIS NOVEL IS DEDICATED TO:

MY MOTHER, HELEN J BERGER: THE KINDEST AND MOST
UNSELFISH PERSON I HAVE EVER KNOWN.

AND TO:

THE REAL LIFE GIRL OF MY DREAMS; BETH ("RED") BERGER:
BY MY SIDE THROUGH SCARY THIRD WORLD PORTS, PIRATE
INFESTED WATERS, STORMY SEAS, AND LIFE.

REGARDING "THE SOUTH"

The sometimes rather harsh comments in *Dueling in Death's Backyard* about the people and culture of the southern states of America reflect how I felt after only two years in Birmingham, Alabama. By the time I completed seven years of training and research in the Deep South, I had learned to appreciate, respect and admire the Southern life style. In fact, I am now proud to say that I consider myself a Yankee by birth but a Rebel by choice.

DUELING IN
DEATH'S
BACKYARD

CHAPTER 1

BY 5:00 A.M., we had been operating for about thirteen hours and maybe thirty units of blood. Most of those units had gone into the patient, bled out again, and were now soaking our sterile gowns and shoes or dripping onto the floor.

I don't know how many times I'd given the old farmer up for dead, how many suture lines had pulled through his soggy tissue-paper arteries, how many "hissin' bleeders," as my Alabama associates called them, had finally been controlled.

Even a New England Yankee like me had to admire the Technicolor clarity of Southern expressions like that one. Blood can pour out of a major vein or artery at an alarming and life-threatening rate without making a sound. But when it's coming so fast it actually hisses at you—well, that's a hissin' bleeder.

Dr. Holt McDuff and I had replaced just about the entire descending aorta, from upper chest to lower abdomen. The previous afternoon, that huge artery had dissected, torn partway through its wall, for nearly its entire length. Any point along that weakened wall could have fatally ruptured at any moment. Emergent surgery was required to replace it. This meant clamping the aorta high in the chest and replacing it, segment by segment, with a long tubular Dacron graft.

Each important branch of the aorta had to be sewn into that graft. Each of those suture lines seemed to present us with another potentially fatal hissin' bleeder. We had just barely managed to get each bleed stopped in time to save the old man's life one more time. More precisely, Dr. McDuff got them stopped with my help. Back then, I was just a lowly general surgery resident, laboring towards my dream of becoming a heart surgeon.

Finally, against all expectations, or at least all of my expectations, we were nearly done in more ways than one. At the point of total exhaustion and a depleted blood bank, it looked like Dr. McDuff was going to come up with yet another dramatic, blood-soaked save.

Some of the residents thought Holt had more than his share of these nightmarish nocturnal dances with death. It just seemed to me that his patients, often poor blacks or rednecks, seemed to be sicker and to have worse tissue than the classier clientele of the other staff surgeons. Holt had a reputation among the disenfranchised and never turned anyone away, regardless of ability to pay. Somehow he even got the hospital to accept the uninsured.

As laudable as this was, it meant that many of his patients lived difficult and unhealthy lives, resulting in what we residents called, "PPP," or "piss-poor protoplasm." Patients with PPP tended to have dramatic operations. This was in contrast to the choreographed displays of surgical virtuosity seen in the heart room with celebrity patients, who came to our cardiac unit from all over the world.

Choreographed virtuosity meant nothing to Holt. He didn't care how beautiful or messy the operation was. To him, the result was all that mattered. Since his patients slept through the OR part anyway, I guess they agreed. Anyway, they worshiped Holt, and, to my mind, with good reason.

Finding his ass in alligator pits so often, Holt was a master at getting it and his patients out of them. When I started on his service, I was determined to learn the secret of this mastery. Now my time with Holt was nearly over, and the secret seemed pretty simple. It was nothing more or less than a pit-bull refusal to grant Death a victory, even if you just about died yourself from exhaustion and frustration in the struggle.

Holt seemed to see Death as a personal enemy, a malignant Macbeth, calling out, "Lay on, McDuff, and damned be he who first cries hold enough." To which I always imagined him brandishing his scalpel like a switchblade knife and muttering, "Come on, then, you sum-bitch."

We finally completed the last suture line in the lower abdomen and subdued the last hissin' bleeder. All that was left was to return to the top of the chest and unclamp the aorta for the final time.

I put the rib spreader back and cranked open the chest portion of the huge thoracoabdominal incision, exposing that one last cross-clamp. Holt removed it with infinite tenderness. For a moment, all the suture lines held and everything looked good.

I began to calculate how long it would take to get the patient settled in the ICU. If he was stable (fat chance), I just might be able to get my working rounds done before eight. No time to sleep, but that wasn't unusual for one of my every other nights on call.

Chronic sleep deprivation was a simple fact of my existence back then, an inevitable result of the total immersion in surgical training required by all first-class programs. That was before residents were unionized and mollycoddled, with limits on their working hours and care taken not to damage their fragile self-esteem. Back in my day, the only right a resident had was the right to sweat.

Just as we were breathing a sigh of relief, the suture line between the upper end of the graft and the aorta exploded. In Holt's words it "came half in two." Nearly every drop of blood in the old farmer's body had gushed out into his chest before we could even begin to react.

Our tacky gowns were freshly soaked scarlet, right through to underpants and socks. I'd throw them away after another sad shower in the dressing room, washing the sticky redness from my chest, forearms, abdomen, and the front of my thighs.

The subtly acrid ozone aroma of large amounts of sterile blood in a small air-conditioned room and the shameful silence of failure bludgeoned us into a stunned submission. Not for the first time, I contemplated the difference between the living human being on the table before us a second ago and the pile of decomposing organic junk now occupying the same place. If that difference was a soul, it had slipped unseen through our fingers.

"It's over," Holt croaked bitterly. "He's day-ed."

The Pakistani anesthesiologist chirped his heavily accented disagreement. "Heart beat normal," he argued. "Sinus rhythm."

Holt turned towards the head of the table. There was an edge to his voice as he repeated, "I say-ed, he's day-ed."

"Sinus rhythm," chirped the Pakistani, gesturing at the briskly beeping EKG monitor and its spurious green tracing.

"The may-an is day-ed," Holt reiterated in a tone as final as death itself.

"Sinus rhythm!"

Holt let out a low moan and reached deep into the gaping chest cavity.

Grasping the open end of the graft still welling over with blood in his left hand, he tore it up and out of the chest. With his right hand, he lunged to pull down the drape between us and the anesthesiologist.

"I am holding the fucking aorta in my hand," he explained in an even voice, enunciating each syllable with chilling clarity. "That is incompatible with life. Now, turn off the fucking monitor."

"Incompatible with life" was one of the many colorful phrases that peppered Holt's language. He applied it equally to conditions that could not be survived and to people who didn't deserve to live, as in, "That bastard is incompatible with life."

The gas passer nearly fell off his stool as he groped for the Power button, scrambling to save his crisp green scrubs from the splatter off Holt's bloody glove.

Holt paused, pulled his hand back into the no-longer sterile field, and took several ragged breaths with his eyes closed.

"Gimme some heavy suture to close this thing," he mumbled, with one hand extended towards the horrified young scrub nurse.

The incision went from a few inches below the armpit to just above the pubic bone. It would take half an hour to close.

"I'll close him, Holt," I offered, working the sucker to clean up the blood still filling a third of the chest cavity.

"If I can do it, I can close it," Holt said without much conviction. "You get you some sleep before rounds."

"You can, but you don't need to. I'm not going to sleep, anyway." I said.

"Fine," Holt spat, stepping back and extending his arms as the circulating nurse stripped off his gown and gloves.

I circled around to Holt's side of the table, stretching and feeling about ninety years old at twenty-seven. I wondered how old Holt felt at forty-something. He was in pretty good shape with heavy shoulders and the squat solid build of a fullback. Only his thin gray hair and a deeply lined Marlboro Man face bore witness to too many nights like this one and whatever else he'd been through in his life.

I closed silently, except for condolences from the nurses and mutual assurances that everyone, especially Holt, had done everything possible. There had certainly been no chance for survival without surgery, and I was surprised, as always, at how little comfort that provided.

In the dressing room, I showered, shaved, and changed into a fresh set of scrubs.

Someone had foolishly left a pristine white coat on a hook. I exchanged it for mine, which was due for cleaning. Then, properly costumed as the Grim Reaper's messenger boy, I went to tell the family that Grampa was dead.

Holt had gotten there before I did. The waiting room held only a somber nurse with an autopsy permit and a group of weepy loved ones arguing over whether to sign it.

"He's done suffered enough. He don't need to be cut on no more." This from an angry thirtyish farmer type in worn overalls—probably a son.

"But if it might-could help someone else, he'd a-wanted it, and he can't suffer no more." This from a shapeless daughter in a faded flowered dress.

The obvious wife, as desiccated and tough as her dead husband, was stunned to an oblivious silence. Her cornflower-blue eyes damply contemplated an inconceivable future without her lifetime companion. Pursing my lips, I took a deep breath to keep from smothering in the suffocating thickness of their grief. Back then, I thought I'd grow accustomed to such scenes. I never have.

There was no real need for an autopsy, but we had to get one in every case—for teaching and research papers, the cause of death had to be proven. Feeling like a sleazy encyclopedia salesman, I cajoled, bullied, and finally lied them into agreement. *Well, who knows? Something might always be found that would help someone else.* So maybe it wasn't really a lie, and at least I spared Holt that final chore.

With paper-cup coffee and a stale cruller eaten on the run through empty early- morning hallways, the day began.

I made rounds and did the scut work: changing purulent foul-smelling dressings, debriding gangrenous toes, starting IVs with psychic subcutaneous perception on people with no visible or palpable veins, ordering and reviewing lab work, and formulating plans to diagnose and treat a mix of the curable, incurable, and everything in between.

I saw patients in the clinic and ER and, finally, consultations. Consults from medical doctors to surgeons were always a challenge in diplomacy—not my strong point.

It was hard, not just for me but for any surgical personality, to tolerate the overly cautious, indecisive approach of the medical types. They always wanted to do more tests and explore other possibilities before taking any action. That was fine for them. They could debate their decisions for hours over coffee cups in conference rooms, quoting the literature at each other like orators. We surgeons often had to decide and act in seconds, with life or death in the balance and hissin' bleeders to distract us. We called the medical guys "fleas" because they swarmed around dying bodies, taking blood samples.

At some point, I ate a dozen or so salt-free cookies (for heart-failure patients), washed down with sugar-free juice (for diabetics), all liberated from the back room of the post-intensive care unit. After this hearty repast, I fell asleep at a desk in the ICU nursing station. My head was slumped into my arms, which were folded into a chart, when Holt paged me to his office. It was late afternoon, but I doubted that he'd been home. Holt was a confirmed bachelor; his patients were his family.

Holt was a vascular surgeon, not a cardiac surgeon. He operated on blood vessels, including big arteries, like the aorta, but not on the heart itself. Alabama University Medical Center was famous for heart surgery, which was why I was there. If you weren't a heart surgeon, you were a second-rate citizen. So Holt's office was adequate but far from grand. It was also a long walk through dreary administrative corridors from the patient rooms and wards where I'd been working.

Holt's phone started to ring just as I arrived. He waved me into a lumpy but comfortable chair of indeterminate color across from his cluttered desk. The standard display of diplomas was restricted to the space behind his chair. All other walls were obscured by overloaded shelves of surgical journals and what Poe might have referred to as quaint and curious volumes of forgotten surgical lore. Holt was in clean but wrinkled scrubs. He had probably permitted himself an office nap after the exhausting all-night surgery.

The only picture on his desk showed a young Holt in the cap and gown of med school graduation. A more leathery version of the new graduate, presumably his father, was shaking Holt's hand. Holt was smiling tentatively up at his father's face, but the old man ignored him, glaring sternly at the camera.

The only nonsurgical book in the room was a leather-bound volume of *The Count of Monte Cristo*. The large book sat by itself on a small but solid mahogany table easily within Holt's reach. The classic novel was a favorite of mine. Like Dantes, I was reinventing myself after my own past adversity, and I liked the way the bad guys got it in the end. The epic story gave me hope and reinforced my sense of justice. I wondered what the novel did for Holt.

Shortly after I flopped into the chair, Holt gave me a nod and put the call on speakerphone. If the patient came in I would have to admit him, so it was good to hear the problem first hand.

"Is this Docta Hope, his own self?" At least a third of his patients, white and black, called Holt "Docta Hope." At least initially, they would talk to no one else. They had heard about Docta Hope from friends and relatives and wanted to be sure that he and only he would be in charge of their care.

"Yes, ma'am, this is me. How can I help you?"

"Well, it's my husband, Docta Hope. It's his lay-egg."

"Yes, ma'am," Holt encouraged. "Is something wrong with his leg?"

"Why, Docta Hope, you know I wouldn't be calling you if they wasn't something bad-wrong with his lay-egg." She sounded perplexed, wondering if this Docta Hope was all he was cracked up to be.

"Yes, ma'am. Now, could you tell me just exactly what it is that's the problem with his leg? That would help me decide what is needing to be done."

"The problem? Why, Docta Hope, the problem is, his lay-egg; well it just turned black as a nigger."

Holt looked at me with an embarrassed half smile, gently shaking his head back and forth. He never made fun of his patients but was not above having a little fun with them.

"Well, uhh, in that case, the first thing I need to know, ma'am, is . . . is he a nigger?"

I grinned perfunctorily, resisting the feeling that I should protest the word, even as a joke. I knew from the patients he cared for and how he cared for them that Holt was anything but a racist. Nevertheless, the word put me off. I thought of black teammates I'd wrestled with in high school and college and how they would have felt at my silent, perhaps cowardly, acquiescence.

"Why . . . why, Docta Hope, it's my husband, Douglas, I'm talking about. Of course, he ain't no nigger."

At this point, the woman was clearly questioning Docta Hope's reputation.

"I see," Holt said in a reassuring tone. "Well, in that case, I think you better bring him to the emergency room and right quick. When you get there, they'll be expecting you and they'll call on my associate, Dr. Cooper Logan," he glanced at me, raised his shaggy eyebrows, and nodded. "Dr. Logan will come right down and see Douglas. Then Dr. Logan, he is gonna report directly to me. Now, what did you say your husband's full name was?"

Details were ascertained, and I wrote them down on my scut list. Holt's other resident, Bo Randolph, was on call that night but had been drafted by Trauma to help in the OR. It was already late afternoon and supposedly my night off, but I couldn't leave the hospital until Bo was cut loose. Anyway, since Holt had given the wife my name, I would have to see the leg, whether Bo was free or not. If anyone else were to welcome Douglas to the ER, it could shake his trust in Docta Hope. I was not about to let that happen.

Replacing the phone silently, Holt closed his eyes and pressed the fingers of both hands against the lids, rubbing them deeply. His tired eyes, under luxuriant brows, were gunfighter gray. When he opened them to stare at me, pursing his lips, I knew something was up.

"Am I in trouble again?" I asked with a sigh.

Holt chuckled, favored me with an avuncular smile, and lit an unfiltered Camel with a silver lighter.

"Not with me, son," he said gently, "but I am worried about you. You know you ain't ever-body's cup of tea down here, don'cha?"

"Yeah, well . . ."

I wasn't sure how to respond to that. I couldn't deny it. Most of the residents and staff had been born and raised in the Deep South. I had what they called "North-East Personality Disorder," and it seemed I had a bad case. I was aggressive and driven, even for a Yankee who went to college and med school in Boston. The move to Birmingham had been a culture shock.

I don't know how many times I was asked why Northerners in the South were like hemorrhoids, but I definitely knew the answer: they come down, they're a pain in the ass, and they won't go back up.

"You won't begin to get along down here without you start trying to understand the folks you're dealing with," Holt said kindly. "They're mostly good people. They may not seem that way to you, but they are. You just got to start looking at them a tad bit closer.

"Like that woman who just called about her husband. She said 'nigger'; and you been taught that means a whole lot of things about her—all of them bad."

I started to protest but realized he was right. Her prejudice, or maybe it was mostly her syntax, had given rise to my own prejudgments. I decided for once to just shut up and listen. The man was clearly trying to help me, not start a debate. I had once been sure I could get through this program, in spite of the alien environment. Now, towards the end of my second year of residency, my battered ego knew better. I would need all the help I could get. To become a heart surgeon, I had to survive two more years of general surgery training and two years of cardiac fellowship after that. Maybe Holt's advice could help.

"I understand that woman," Holt said, "because I understand how she was raised up. I understand that because I come up the same way. My daddy was the sheriff of Jefferson County, which includes the city of Birmingham." Holt pronounced it, Bumminhayem.

"Daddy was the sheriff from the time I come into this world until well after I got my MD. Now that might-could tell you something about my upbringing. Daddy was a good man, a hard man, and a brave man. And he was mostly a fair man. But he also was the product a how he was raised up. In my daddy's eyes, right was right and wrong was wrong, and it was Daddy's job as sheriff to help God out by seeing that wrong was punished. Daddy allowed as how God could reward the good his own self. So between the two of them, Daddy and God had the Universe pretty much covered. As a boy—and I guess still to this day—that's the world I live in. Evil must be punished, even if God sometimes needs a little help getting it done."

Holt looked over at that big volume of *The Count of Monte Cristo*, reached out, and touched the book briefly before settling back in his cracked leather chair. He rested his elbows on the faded brown arms and let his fingers come together and touch just under his nose. There was a mildew smell in the room, and I thought it might be coming from that chair. He closed his eyes again for a long moment, then opened them and continued.

"One Sunday morning—September 15, 1963, to be exact—I was on duty in the ER of this hospital when four little black girls were brought in. They'd been taking part in the Youth Day service at the 16th Street Baptist Church, when some sorry bastard blew it up.

"I watched those little girls die. I'm not gonna say nothing more about that day, except that it changed me forever. There's things that had been part of my life, and part of my daddy's life, that I just left behind me from that day on. But still, I know how that woman on the phone was raised up, and I know she can be a good woman and still say 'nigger' without a thought to all the evil that word implies. It's just the way she come up."

Holt lit another Camel, sucked in the smoke, and blew it towards the ceiling.

"Now, the point a all this," he continued, "is that just like I see that she can be a good woman in spite of saying 'nigger,' I see that you can be a good man in spite of your rude Yankee ways. That's just how people up where you come from act towards each other ever day, without meaning nothing by it. Those ways don't necessarily mean no more about you than saying 'nigger' necessarily means about her. That's just how you was raised up.

"More important, in the last two months I have seen that you are well on your way to becoming one very damn fine surgeon. That is, if you can avoid having your Yankee ass kicked out of this program by pissin' ever-body off. It's been a real pleasure these last two months to have a pair of hands helping me that are ever bit as good as my own. Hell, let's face it; they're better than my own."

He waved off my protest with an impatient gesture and sighed. "How'd you end up down here anyway, Cooper? You want to be a Kirkwood trained heart surgeon that bad?"

"Yes, I do," I answered, nodding. He knew the rest. While at the Mayo Clinic, Dr. Joseph Kirkwood became the first man ever to do a series of open-heart operations with a heart-lung machine. When Dr. Kirkwood came South to start the Birmingham program, his leadership made it the best in the world. But before I could train under him in hearts, I had to complete the general surgery program.

"Your next rotation is VA Hearts, right?" Holt asked.

Cardiac patients, from the Veterans Hospital, were brought across the street to the University Medical Center for their surgery. Post-op, they stayed at the U for the first day or so of care. Then, hopefully well enough to survive the VA, they went back across the street.

The general surgery resident on VA Hearts admitted these patients over there. He got them ready for surgery, brought them to the University OR, and scrubbed on their cases. He also helped care for them post-op, in the University ICU. Then, under the loose supervision of the Cardiac Fellow, he handled their day-to-day care back at the VA. The VA and the U were connected by a skyway over the intervening street. Part of the job, on VA Hearts, was to actually physically push the patients back and forth on a stretcher.

"You know you got you a big problem over at the VA with Dr. Jefferson, don't you?" Holt asked.

Dr. Lloyd Jefferson was chief of surgery and chief of staff at the VA. He was a scion of Southern aristocracy, tracing his roots back to long before the Civil War. Jefferson County was not named after Jefferson Davis, president of the Confederacy. It was named for a distant relative of the VA surgery chief. Dr. Jefferson's family money made the low VA salary irrelevant. By local VA standards, his medical ignorance and technical incompetence were not much of a problem. A certain skill in bureaucratic imperatives, such as shifting blame to subordinates, had assured his success.

"I locked horns with him last year over an incompetent nurse, Shaleena White. She runs the night shift in what they call their ICU," I admitted. "But I had to say something. Half the time she was asleep at the nursing station. The other half, she was bouncing off the walls, yucking it up with her pals or screaming at any new nurse on the unit. She runs off anyone who doesn't fit in with her gang of hardcore screw-ups. She should have been fired or at least transferred out of the ICU." I knew it was virtually impossible to fire anyone from a civil service–protected VA position. "She and her crew have caused at least two patient deaths through sheer negligence."

"How do you know that?" Holt asked. He crushed out his second cigarette, picked up the pack, thought better of it, and tossed it back on his desk.

"I know because twice on morning rounds I found corpses at least six hours dead. It happened once my first week on the rotation last year and again near the end. Normal vital signs had been charted in each case, until just before I came by. Both bodies were stiff with rigor mortis and cold as ice. There was no way they had any blood pressure when the charting said it was normal.

"Neither of those patients were terminal. Both could probably have been saved if I'd been called when they first got in trouble. I documented everything, wrote up a formal incident report and made sure Jefferson saw it personally. Instead of coming down on Shaleena, Jefferson defended her. And, as you say, he's had it in for me ever since. I don't know why." I shrugged my shoulders, and was surprised to see Holt respond by shaking his head and chuckling.

Mimicking my indignation, he asked, "You just can't imagine why he defended her and come after you. Can you?"

"No, I can't," I said.

"Try this then," Holt said with a wry grin. "He's been . . . well let's call it keeping company with that nurse for over a year now and if he don't keep her happy, she just might-could have a talk with his wife. Ever-one around here knows about it. Why do you think the other residents tolerate her bullshit and don't dare say a thing? If you had any friends, besides me, you'd a known it too."

"Keeping company with her? But she's . . . she's . . ."

"Yeah," Holt agreed, "She's a right pretty high-yeller, coloud girl, and Jefferson's as white as his KKK pajamas, but she's his piece on the side just the same. And that's another old Southern tradition. 'Specially where the black girl got a ass on her like that one and Lloyd's wife's butt belongs on Bear Bryant's front line."

"Well, that's just great," I said, nodding and grimacing at the irony of the situation. "Jefferson's out to screw me because he's screwing her and I'm not even going to get kissed. And all because of Shaleena . . .

"Damn!" I said, punctuating the thought with the slap of my right fist into my left palm. "I'd like to . . ."

"It's already been done, more than once," Holt assured me. "Her regular man, when he's out a prison, which ain't but rarely, is the jealous type. He beats on her pretty regular. I've tended to Shaleena in the ER myself and gone over it all with the city cops. As I said, my daddy was the county sheriff. The old-timers on the city force remember him well and they know I am his boy. I got talking to one of them one time, after patching Shaleena up. He gave me the whole story on Eightball White."

"Eightball White?" I asked. There was something vaguely familiar about the name.

"Eightball is Shaleena's husband, or boyfriend or whatnot." Holt said. "She uses his last name but my cop friend said they never made it legal. Either way, she is his property and, if the story's true, has been since they were kids."

"The story?" I asked.

"The story of how he got the name Eightball," Holt chuckled. "According to the cop, Eightball's given name was . . . I don't hardly remember for certain but I think it was Malcomb or something like that. Anyways, let's say Malcomb and a bunch of his buddies and some gals, including Shaleena, were at a little bar and pool hall. One of the boys and Shaleena was sitting at a table while Malcomb, he was shooting pool. The boy started flirting with Shaleena and he give her a little kiss. Malcomb, he don't say a word. He just picks up the eight ball, licks his finger and carefully marks its spot on the felt. Then he walks over casual-like and mashes the boy's skull in with the eight ball. Then he saunters back to the table, wipes the ball off, puts it down where he marked its spot and sinks it to win the game. The kid he hit was in a coma for a while and finally passed on. Since then, Malcomb's been known as Eightball."

"If the other kid died, how come Eightball didn't go to jail?" I asked.

"He was under eighteen at the time, so all he could get was juvenile detention up to the Youth Center at Kilby. Law said they had to turn him loose when he was twenty-one, and they done it."

"I'm sure he was completely rehabilitated," I said.

"You bet he was," Holt guffawed. "He stayed rehabilitated for about five minutes and then begun a lucrative life of crime. At some point he sent Shaleena to nursing school. Maybe just to keep her out of trouble. Maybe she wanted to go enough to do what it took so he'd let her. Maybe he figured to retire and for her to support him. If that was it, he never needed the money. Within a few years, he was running all the black crime in Birmingham."

Holt started to chuckle again and shook his head.

"What's so funny?" I asked.

"Me having to tell you about Eightball is what's funny," Holt said. "Fact is you know him your own self. You been closer to him than me, that's for sure."

"What do you mean, I know him? His name does sound familiar but . . . how do I know him?" I said.

"Well, maybe, 'know him,' ain't exactly the right way to say it, but you did kick his scrawny black ass down to the ER last year."

So that was why the name rang a bell. I had nearly forgotten the incident, but now it all came back. I'd been seeing a hot appendix in the ER when angry voices came from the waiting room. I stopped to listen and heard someone yell for security. I was staring at the door to reception when a frightened nurse came through. She grabbed me by the arm and said, "Come on, we need your help."

"Where's security?" I asked, as she pulled me along.

"Same 'where' they always are when you need them," she said. "Else-where."

A small wiry black man with oily slicked back hair was raising hell about something I can't even remember. He radiated the capacity for cruelty and violence like heat from a red hot wood stove in a small room. As he cursed the nurses, much larger men in the waiting area pretended not to notice.

When I tried to calm him down he took a swing at me and missed. I swung back and didn't and that's about all there was to it. He had a pint bottle of booze in his back pocket and when I knocked him down he sat on it. He ran out of the ER with blood and whiskey soaking the seat of his pants.

It was funny at the time but I didn't really like talking about it. It was bad enough being a rude Yankee. I didn't need a rep as a brawler. "Look, Holt, I didn't have much choice. A nurse ran back into the treatment area, from the waiting room, grabbed me and pulled me out there to help. I don't know why she chose me. There were plenty of other docs and techs around."

"It's no mystery why she chose you," Holt grunted. "You look like Clint Eastwood as Rowdy Yates. The other residents resemble Richard Chamberlain as Dr. Kildare? Who would you want by your side in a fight?"

That comment touched a sore point. People were always telling me I didn't look like a doctor. I would sometimes come back with, "I am a doctor, so I must look like a doctor. What I don't look like is your idea of a doctor." Usually I'd just let the comment slide or pretend to take it as a compliment.

If Holt noticed my discomfort, it didn't slow him down. "You're what, about six two?" he went on. "And you still got most of the muscle from being a big wrestling star at that Nawthun college you attended."

I was surprised that Holt seemed to know all about my wrestling career. Apparently he'd taken the time to check out my personnel file. I wondered if he did that with all the residents on his service.

"Holt, it was Tufts. The league we played in had mostly girls' schools. Radcliffe was our toughest adversary. It didn't take much to do well against those teams." I hoped the joking would end the discussion.

"Yeah, sure," Holt said. "But I did hear them Radcliffe girls have some pretty tricky moves. Not like our sweet and innocent Southern gals."

"I wouldn't know about those kinds of moves," I admitted. "Radcliffe girls aren't much interested in boys like me."

"Well, I guess not. So how come you didn't press no charges against old Eightball?" Holt said. "I know the police must a asked you."

"I didn't have time to go to court," I said. Then I added, as a joke, "And I'd already helped God out with the punishment, like your father used to do." I smiled but Holt didn't smile back. He didn't seem to think it was funny. He stared at me with a look on his face that I didn't understand.

I was about to apologize when he said, "Well, it's good you didn't push it. And it's even better that Eightball was back in prison, a few weeks later. They busted him on some kind of drug charge. It had nothing to do with you. But the way you embarrassed him that day; he wasn't the type to forget it. You woulda heard more from him if he'd a stayed on the street."

"So Shaleena was Eightball's girlfriend and then, with him in prison, she somehow got hooked up with Dr. Jefferson? How did that happen?" I asked

"Drugs, most likely," Holt responded.

"Shaleena had easy access to them on account a living with Eightball," he said. "From what you just said about her behavior, she's been using on the job."

It occurred to me for the first time that drugs could explain Shaleena's incompetence. Her nodding off in the unit could have been narcotic related and her levity and anger fueled by coke or amphetamines. "So why don't they drug test her?" I asked.

"They have tested her more than once," Holt said, "and she passed with flying colors." There was a smug smile on Holt's face and I knew there was more to the story.

"But . . . ?" I prompted.

"But, just guess who is in charge of drug testing over at the VA," Holt said.

"Jefferson," I groaned.

"Now, you just must be psychic, Yankee Boy. Drug testing there is supervised by the chief of staff and, in addition to being chief of surgery, that just happens to be Dr. Lloyd Jefferson. Whether he and Shaleena had something going on before she had her first test or whether Jefferson used her drug problem to force her to be his girlfriend . . . I don't know. I guess it don't matter anyway, except maybe to Eightball . . . if he knows about it . . . which he more'n likely does."

"You think he'd hear about it in prison?" I asked.

"Hell, yes," Holt said. "He's still running the black crime from in there and no doubt his boys keep him well informed."

Holt pointed his finger at me and said, "Never you mind about that. What matters to you is that Jefferson can't have anyone calling attention to what's going on in that ICU. He's gotta make an example of you, Yankee Boy, so that other folk learn to look the other way."

"I guess it was lucky I didn't file my complaint until after I was back at the U," I said. "But this next rotation at the VA will give Jefferson another shot at me and . . . I suppose he's going to make the most of it."

"You got that right, son," Holt said laughing, "It ain't over yet, not by a long shot. If he can do it, he's gonna snap you up faster'n a frog flickin' a fly." Holt slipped his tongue out of his mouth and sucked it back in with a slurping sound.

"You give him just one excuse, boy, and what Jefferson's going to do is; he's going to pull your privileges at the VA." Holt raised his heavy eyebrows, cocked his head and nodded to emphasize the point. "Now, Kirkwood likes you. He's a Yankee too, so your ways don't bother him none, and he's noticed how good you are. He told me as much before you come on my service. Kirkwood wants to see you finish the program. He knows you'll do him proud, but . . ." Holt left it hanging.

"But, the VA patients are part of the heart Fellowship, as well as the general surgery program. If I can't function at the VA, as a Cardiac Fellow . . . if I can't supervise the general surgery resident assigned to VA Hearts . . ."

"Now, aren't you the smart little Yankee boy. If Jefferson bars you from the VA, you'll have no chance for a Cardiac Fellowship. You'll be out of general surgery, too. Wouldn't hardly be fair for you not to rotate through the VA like ever-one else. And there won't be a damn thing Kirkwood can do about it. He's King o' Hearts over here, but he got no clout at the VA. That's a gubment bureaucracy, and Kirkwood's no part of it. Jefferson is The Man across the street. If he says you're out, you will be out." Holt leaned forward and pointed at me. "And there ain't but one thing you can do to save your sorry Yankee ass."

He paused for dramatic effect.

"And that one thing would be . . .?" I prompted glumly.

Holt enunciated his answer clearly and slowly. "Don't give the sum-bitch any excuse."

CHAPTER 2

LEAVING HOLT'S OFFICE, I stopped by the operating room to check on my relief. Bo Randolph was a short, trim third-year resident, one year ahead of me though he looked much younger. His ready, boyish smile and country charm made him a favorite of the nurses. Being unmarried, Bo made full use of his popularity.

Since early that morning, while I was in the OR with Holt, Bo had been helping trauma with a train wreck. It wasn't really a train wreck. That's just what we called any event that sent us a bunch of badly injured patients. Some high school kids on the way home from a kegger way out in the sticks had bounced off a deeply rutted dirt road and into a tree. I couldn't help but think that if any of their parents had let the kids party at a house and held on to car keys until the next day, they'd all have been fine. But that was not an option, not in the Bible Belt.

The trauma team was really stretched thin, so I found Bo first-assisting. Two nurses hung onto retractors in a gaping midline abdominal incision. I squeezed by the somnolent gas passer and peeked over the drapes. Bo was lifting a shattered spleen while the trauma chief applied clamps to its last few branches. I caught Bo's eye, and he shook his head to give me the bad news.

"Blood welling up behind the liver, Cooper," he said. "Could be the hepatic vein. I don't know. If it is, I'll be here a good piece more. Rest of the trauma crew's in with cases as bad or wors'n this'un. They'll relieve me when they can, so maybe—"

"Holt's got a dead leg coming into the ER," I said. "I'll start getting him set up and admitted. Give me a beep when you get free, okay?"

Bo just nodded and adjusted his hold on the spleen. I left the OR and took an elevator to the residents' sleeping quarters on the top floor of the hospital. I was hoping to get a few minutes of sleep before Douglas and his dead leg hit the ER. I pushed the Up button repeatedly, like a mouse in a Skinner box. I knew the elevator wouldn't come any sooner but could not resist trying.

I called them Southern elevators because they were so slow. When one finally arrived, I got in and cursed with frustration while it sat silent and motionless. Finally a bell rang. Nothing else happened; the bell just rang. This was the Southern elevator's way of saying, "Y'all get ready now. I'm a-fixin' to move." An eternity passed. The doors closed, and the Southern elevator began its interminable climb.

On the very next floor, a tribe of redneck teenagers, obviously experiencing elevators for the first time, shouldered each other aboard. The girls giggled and the boys jostled each other, competing for the thrill of "mashing" the button for the first floor.

"It's going up," I said.

"Well, what goes up gotta come down, don't it?" their husky pig-faced leader demanded, much to everyone's amusement but my own.

He guffawed and proceeded to push or "mash" the buttons for every floor on the way up. I should have switched elevators but simply couldn't bear to start the process all over again.

With every stop and start, the teenagers joked and laughed moronically about leaving their stomachs on the previous floor. I wondered if they could have known the kids from the accident. If so, they didn't seem to be overcome with grief.

As nearly fifteen precious minutes of potential sleep time was squandered, I closed my eyes to deliciously dangerous fantasies of walking out of the elevator leaving broken and bleeding bodies behind. By the time we reached the top floor, the vision had become so real I had to look back as I exited to make sure the kids were okay.

The elevator opened into a short narrow vestibule. A prominent sign limited access to authorized personnel. To the left, running perpendicular to the vestibule and parallel to the street out front, was the floor's main hallway.

By a quirk of architecture, and only on that very top floor, a right turn out of the elevator dead-ended in a concrete and brick aerie. A single waist-high railing was all that kept one from stepping off into infinity. Just for a moment, trying to calm down enough for sleep, I leaned on the railing, took a breath or two of fresh air and looked out over the grey blandness of Birmingham. Turning away, it occurred to me that I'd lived there for two years and didn't know the town at all.

There were three resident sleeping rooms. Each contained eight narrow cots lined up on either side of a barren, high-ceilinged space. By each cot, was an unfinished plywood table with a phone and a cheap lamp. The only other furnishing was a single bare sink with a small mirror behind it. Had there been an exposed toilet in the middle of the floor, the ambiance would not have noticeably suffered.

I collapsed onto a cot with a thin mattress and squeaky springs and took a deep breath. Before falling asleep, I knew I should call Katy. Let her know I'd be late . . . again. I wasn't looking forward to it. I closed my eyes just for second, trying to decide what to say.

Two hours later, my beeper went off. It was seven PM and Douglas had hit the ER. Struggling awake I tried to remember whether I had called Katy before falling asleep. I didn't think I had. I knew I had to talk to her before getting involved with Douglas and forgetting about it completely.

"Hello." I could tell by her voice that she was angry. What else was new?

"I'm sorry, baby. The trauma guys had a train wreck and Bo's tied up helping them in the OR. I've got to get an admit started in the ER, but Bo'll relieve me as soon as he gets free. I—"

"I don't want to hear about it," she snapped. "You could at least have called. It's Saturday night, in case you've forgotten."

Of course, I had forgotten. I was lucky if I knew what month it was.

"I got steaks for dinner, to cook on the barbeque," she continued. "I was even stupid enough to think we might go out after dinner and do something together. See a movie. Anything. I've got to get out of this apartment. I'd have gone by myself, but I had to wait to pick you up."

We only had one car, her VW beetle. There were no cell phones back then, so she'd been waiting at home for my call. We'd driven the little yellow bug down to Birmingham from Boston, where we'd met and fallen in love. I'd been a medical student at Tufts and she was an ICU nurse at the Tufts New England Medical Center.

"I'm really sorry, Katy, I—"

"I don't want to hear about it. Just call when you're ready for your taxi service. That's all I am to you anyway."

She hung up, and I held onto the phone quietly for a minute or two, thinking how tired I was of saying I was sorry. How tired I was of being sorry. How tired I was of being tired. But none of that mattered. I would do whatever it took, sacrifice whatever had to be sacrificed—yes, even Katy—if that was the cost of becoming a heart surgeon. If she really loved me, she'd tough it out. If not, might as well find out sooner rather than later.

That's what I told myself, but part of me wasn't so sure. I didn't want to lose Katy. Just the thought of it made me feel cold and hollow inside. I tapped my forehead lightly with the earpiece of the phone, stood up, and walked out of the sleeping room.

Katy and I had met over a sick open heart, in the ICU at Tufts. I was in my last year of med school and she was a very young charge nurse. We kept the patient alive all night and by morning he was out of danger. The cardiac fellow had looked in on us only once or twice. He was mostly tied up with other cases or napping while we worked.

We stood by as he gave report to the staff man on morning rounds, taking full credit for what was mostly our save. I'll never forget how Katy rolled her blue eyes and bumped hips with me as we listened. I wanted her then but she insisted on keeping things professional. The warmth of our friendship finally burst into flames a few weeks later, when saving another patient nearly got me expelled from med school. No future lover could ever understand what we shared back then. Losing Katy would be like losing a part of myself or my story.

Halfway to the Southern elevator I stopped and rubbed my eyes hard with thumb and first finger. The colors exploding behind my closed lids were caused by chemicals in the retina called phosgenes, released by the increased intra-ocular pressure. That was just one of the millions of useless facts I'd learned in med school. I cursed, went back to the room and picked up the phone again.

"Listen, Katy, you're right. You need to get out and you can still catch a late movie. If you want to, go ahead without me. I can sleep here tonight." I'd been on the previous day and up all night operating. Sleeping in the hospital now, on my night off, and then when I was on again the next night would mean at least 80 continuous hours in the Belly of the Beast. I wanted out of there like a drowning man wants to break the surface for one last breath of air. But I was far too tired for what Katy had planned and would need to start it all over again at 4:30 the next morning. She would enjoy the evening more without me. I felt noble, giving up my few hours of freedom and expected Katy to appreciate the grand gesture. In other words, like most men, I didn't have a clue.

"Fine, then," she said, "Stay there if you want. You don't have to ever come home as far as I'm concerned."

"Katy, it's not what I want. It's the last thing I want. I just thought; if you needed to get out and I'm going to be— "

Click. She'd hung up on me again.

I could smell Douglas's foot before opening the door to the ER exam room. The gangrene was so bad, he must have procrastinated for weeks before calling a doctor. Ironically the amputation might have been avoided if fear had not delayed treatment.

As I walked through the door, Douglas quickly turned away, spit thickly into his palm, and surreptitiously stubbed a cigarette out in the saliva. He was a big, beefy, red-faced guy with a belly hanging over his belt and the red-veined mushroom nose of a devout alcoholic.

The chubby nurse by my side started to lecture him about smoking. I waved her to silence. I told Douglas it was okay and pulled a couple of paper towels out of the dispenser. Using one towel to take the squashed butt from his hand, I dampened the other one and gave it to him. Embarrassed but grateful, he washed the ashes off his hand. I took the dirty towel from him and threw it into the trash.

The foot was dead from the ankle down, but the gangrene was limited, so far, to the toes. Femoral pulses, in his groin, were strong but the popliteals, behind the knee, were absent. So were the dorsalis pedis and posterior tibeal pulses in the foot. He'd need an amputation for sure. The only question was whether it would be above or below the knee. That would depend on how far down he had enough blood flow to heal the stump. There was no way to know without arteriograms, X-rays of the arteries, taken after injecting dye.

I called radiology to set up the A'grams for first thing in the morning, got IVs, antibiotics and pain meds started, drew blood and ordered lab work. Then I brought his wife, Lula, in to hear the bad news.

The first reaction was anger.

"I done told you to call Docta Hope last week," Lula wailed through hands spread over her tear-damp face.

Then denial.

"Ain't nobody takin' my lay-egg. Come on Lula we're clearin' on out a here."

His acquiescence was inevitable. The pain and stink of his own flesh would eventually convince him. I tried my best to guide him gently towards the ultimate decision.

"Douglas, I'm sorry to have to tell you this," there I was, sorry again. "But just listen to me for one minute. Then, if you want to sign out AMA, against medical advice, you can certainly leave. No one's going to try to stop you."

"Ain't nobody cuttin' on my lay-egg," he said with equal parts of aggression and fear, as if expecting me to attack him with a scalpel and saw at any moment.

"Douglas, does your foot hurt?" I asked.

"Hurt? Damn right it hurts. It's sore as a raisen." A raisen was Southernese for an abscess. "Sore as a raisen," was the highest level of intensity on the redneck scale of pain.

"Can you smell it?" I asked.

He paused then, "Kinda got used to it by now but, yeah. It stinks. I know it."

I got eye contact and held it, kept my voice soft and reasonable. "Okay, look. If you go home, it's just going to keep hurting worse and smelling worse until you'll have to come back. Let us clean up the foot, trim off the dead skin, treat the infection with antibiotics and give you some pain medicine. If you refuse amputation, we'll treat you that way for a while. It's your leg and your decision.

"What's going to happen though is this. The pain's still going to get worse, in spite of all the pain pills we can give you. The infection, which is gangrene, is going to get worse no matter how many antibiotics we give you. And worst of all," long pause, "The longer we delay, the more of your leg is going to die. That means the longer we wait the more of your leg you're going to lose."

We went back and forth like that for a while. I didn't argue with him, didn't become impatient with him. I told him how well folks did with modern prosthetic legs, especially with amputations below the knee. Not as well with those above the knee.

By the time Bo paged me, Douglas had agreed to have the arteriograms and see if it would be above the knee or below. He claimed he'd decide about surgery after that, but by then we all knew what would happen.

When Bo showed up, he agreed to get Douglas admitted. He would do the initial debridement of his foot, opening up any pockets of pus and cutting away what superficial tissue was infected or dead.

Leaving the ER, I was once again swallowed by the now-empty Southern elevator. I endured another interminable ascent to the Spartan luxury of a cot in the resident's dormitory. I was literally asleep before my head hit the pillow.

CHAPTER 3

I NEVER HEARD Bo come in but at five AM, when the phone shrilled our wakeup, he was comatose in the cot next to mine. We went together to make rounds on Holt's patients and do the morning scut work. Then we rounded all over again, this time with Holt, when he arrived at seven.

Holt told Douglas and Lula exactly what I'd told them, but in his own inimitable Docta Hope style. The amputation was scheduled for early that afternoon. Bo and I would review the arteriograms with Holt later that morning. Hopefully a BK, below the knee, amp would be possible.

With a few rare hours of leisure ahead, unless an emergency came in, Bo and I went for breakfast in the cafeteria. By then it was nearly 9 AM and the morning rush was long over. Large, sullen black women cooked and served from behind a glass counter. They were reminiscent of water buffalos but not nearly as friendly. Moving with the speed of rust, they ladled up watery scrambled eggs and a few limp slices of grease-soaked bacon. I supplemented these culinary delights with a fresh-baked cruller, orange juice from a carton and watery black coffee. The cruller, dunked in the coffee, would make it all worthwhile.

We'd just sat down and started to eat when Ben Rogers, a fourth year resident, finished his meal and swung by our table. He was an elegant

Virginian, with a cultured accent nothing like the coarse Alabama dialect. He'd been my senior resident the previous year on the head and neck service. Casual condescending sarcasm was his most endearing quality. Leaning onto our table with both hands, in his immaculate white coat, snowy shirt and expensive tie, he was all smiles. Ben worked as hard as any of us, but somehow his clothes were never rumpled and he never seemed fatigued.

"Good day to you, Beauregard," he said, with feigned formality, to which Bo responded with a wary nod. "I do hope you are enjoying your morning repast."

"And you Double D," he said, clearly addressing me. "Do you know why a Northerner in the South is like a hemorrhoid?"

"Yeah, I know, Ben," I said. "I've heard it before."

"He comes down. He's a pain in the ass. And he won't go back up," he recited pleasantly. "You can't hear a really good joke too many times, now can you?"

I didn't answer and Ben glided out of the cafeteria with the grace and dignity of a Southern Senator stepping down from a filibuster. I guess it was genetic. His father was some kind of state legislator.

"Double D?" I asked, turning to Bo for an explanation.

"You don't know about that, huh?" Bo looked down at his food and shifted uncomfortably. He was a compact athletic little guy, with a round face and straight sandy hair. His soft brown eyes were studiously avoiding mine. Katy once met him, at a hospital function and told me she thought he was cute. The nurses apparently agreed with her.

"Shit, why do I . . .? That's what they call you." Bo looked back at me with tight lips: embarrassed and unhappy.

"They call me Double D? Who calls me that? What does it mean?"

"The in-group. You know. It stands for Different Drum. They say you march to the beat of different drum." Bo said. "'Course, they don't have much more use for me than they do for you, if that makes you feel some better."

"Well I guess maybe they're right about me," I said. "But the actual quote is 'distant drum' not 'different drum.' Anyway don't worry about it. I don't care what they call me or what they think of me," I lied. "I'm a Yankee and that's the way they're going to feel about me. Nothing anyone can do about it. But what do they have against you? You're as Southern as grits."

Bo chuckled. "Yeah, I suppose I am. But the in-group, they're Southern gentleman and I'm just poor white trash." It came out po white trash, like Edgar Allan's last name. "Barely one step above a nigger, if that." Bo paused, smiled broadly and added, "At least I am still several large leaps above a Yankee. Praise the Lord."

I let the "nigger" remark go, but resolved to confront the issue later. At times, it seemed like Bo could become a friend, but, before that could happen, it was something we'd have to deal with.

"Poor white trash? What does that mean, Bo? Your family doesn't have money, so that's supposed to make you trash?" As Bo considered his response, I forced down the last of my eggs and bacon, and cleansed my pallet with a swig of OJ, to prepare for the *pièce de résistance.* Carefully dunking bite-sized pieces of cruller, I devoted my full concentration to optimizing flavor-enhancing sogginess while avoiding disintegration.

"I'm the youngest a six kids," Bo finally said, "Four boys and two girls. I come up on a little produce farm outside a Tuscaloosa. Our house was an old share-cropper's cabin. My daddy fixed it up some, but as a carpenter he was one hell of a farmer. No kin a mine ever gone to college. Damn few finished high school. If there was ever a book in our house, other than a school book or the bible, I never seen it. Hell, my momma could barely read, best I can recollect. Never read to me leastways. She died when I was young." He paused and then added, shaking his head as if he still couldn't believe it, "Died of a ruptured appendix.

"Well . . . long story short, I surprised myself and ever-body else who knew my family by scoring high on some test or other at the school there. A teacher, Miz Simmons, she didn't have no kids of her own. Well, she took an interest in me and, with her hep, I got me a full scholarship to UAB, the University of Alabama in Birmingham.

"Daddy said I could go. The farm was small and he and my brothers could work it just fine without no hep from me. When the time come, I packed one little bitty suitcase and we headed for Birmingham. I'd never been in Birmingham, nor any city near that size before, and my daddy hadn't neither, his own self. Not but once or twice. Anyways, we just followed the highway signs, took the exit for Birmingham and drove around aimlessly for a bit, gawking at the big buildings.

"Finally we had to admit we was lost bigger'n shit. So, we just waved down the next fella we seen and yelled, 'Hey Mister, where's the college at?'" Bo raised his hand and his voice as if hailing a passing pedestrian and I couldn't help but laugh.

"The rest is history." Bo smiled and finished off his coffee. He asked if I wanted another cup and, since mine was thick with dead cruller sludge, I thanked him.

Bo came back to the table with the coffees, sat down, leaned back in his chair and said, "So what's your story, Cooper?"

"I'm just . . . I want to be a heart surgeon, like most of us, I guess, and . . . Since Kirkwood came here from Mayo, this is the best heart program in the world." I smiled and added, "So here I am, a hemorrhoid on the ass of the South."

Bo slid back his chair and I thought for a moment he was just going to get up and leave. Then he looked at me, with his face closed down and said, "I don't want to be no heart surgeon, Cooper. Just a simple country practice a general surgery, that's all I want. Maybe back around outside a Tuscaloosa where I come up. Maybe if I can do just that, maybe some poor white trash kid like me won't have to grow up without a momma – leastways not because a something as simple to fix as a hot appendix.

"But when I asked for your story, that's not what I meant and you know that," he said. "Now I showed you mine. You gonna show me yours and maybe have you an actual friend around here? Or are you really happy just being Double D, the hemorrhoid?"

I thought I was doing okay and didn't really need or even want a friend, but I didn't want to hurt Bo's feelings either. At least that's what I told myself.

"Well, I lost my mom when I was young too," I admitted, "if that's the kind of thing you mean."

"That's a start," Bo said and just sat there waiting.

"She didn't die," I said. "Just took off one day. It hit my father harder than me really . . . He changed and . . . everything changed." I looked away, hoping for a distraction to change the subject.

"He take to drinking?" Bo asked.

My head snapped back as if I'd been slapped and I shot Bo a look. "That's kind of personal don't you think?"

"Yeah, I guess it is . . . the kind a personal stuff friends tell each other. Like about being poor white trash and all. That kind a personal," Bo said evenly.

I took a deep breath. Other than Katy, I'd never talked to anyone about this before. "Okay, yeah, he took to drinking, as you so delicately put it. I was fourteen years old when he drank himself right out of a good job and drank us both right out of Lexington, Mass., an affluent suburb. We ended up in the lovely community of Medford, where I got beat up for my lunch money the first three days in my new school." The old anger welled up in me . . . anger at my mother, for deserting us and my father, for falling apart. Maybe at myself for not somehow holding them together.

"Why would you ask me that, Bo? Why would you even think that?"

"Just took me a guess," Bo said softly. "And . . . I seen it before . . . with other friends. Alcoholism, its causes and consequences, is not unknown amongst us poor white trash."

There was an uncomfortable silence, finally broken by Bo who asked, "What about the fourth day?"

"What fourth day?" I asked, although I knew what he meant.

"You said you got beat on the first three days in your new school," Bo said. "What about the fourth day?"

The story of the fourth day would test this nascent friendship, but Bo wasn't about to let up. I couldn't stonewall him and I didn't want to lie to him. "You're not going to let this go, are you?"

"It ain't likely," Bo assured me.

"Okay, it was two punks that were harassing me. Sammy Sizzorio was the leader. I don't recall the other one's name. We called them hoods back then but they were punks. Both had been left back in high school long enough for a PhD. They weren't just older than me either. They were also bigger and stronger, and they were experienced street fighters. I had no chance against them . . . in a fair fight. But I couldn't let things go on the way they were. So . . . I decided to even up the odds a little bit."

"Couldn't you a told your daddy or a teacher?" Bo asked.

"My father had enough on his mind. Teachers couldn't do anything and . . . It was a new school. I didn't want to be known as a snitch." Bo nodded in understanding and I went on.

"Fights at Medford High were practically an official school activity. They traditionally took place on the pitchers mound of the school-yard baseball diamond. Sammy and his friend dragged me there each day and half the school gathered for the show. The night after the third beating, I snuck out of my house and buried a baseball bat in the loose earth of the pitcher's mound."

I snuck a quick peek at Bo's face, searching for signs of disapproval. I didn't see any, so I took a chance and continued.

"On the fourth day, after the obligatory pre-fight shoving and taunting, I managed to get myself knocked down right about where I'd buried the bat. I pulled that Louisville Slugger out of the ground and . . . well, let's just say I ended the fight. And, I never saw those guys again. So that's what happened on the fourth day."

"How much damage did you do?" Bo persisted.

I took a deep breath and let it all hang out. "I broke Sammy's leg when he tried to kick me after I went down. I don't think he ever even saw the bat. When his tibia snapped, it sounded like a gun going off. When he fell on it, the bone came right out through his pant-leg. I had to chase the other punk a few steps before breaking his arm. Maybe I shouldn't have done that, but . . . I just wanted to be sure it was over. I couldn't bury baseball bats all over the town."

After a moment or two of silence, I asked Bo, "Do you think I was too . . . I don't know . . . Do you think my response was . . . disproportionate?"

"Not to my mind, it wasn't," Bo said, much to my relief. "I never have had me no use for a bully. My daddy always said, if a fella opens the door to violence, he ain't got nothing to say if violence comes through that door and carries a ass-kickin' with it."

We both laughed and I said, "Bo, you just forget about that poor white trash bullshit. Your daddy was a philosopher."

Bo snorted and said, "Maybe so. Anyways, what happened after that? You get in trouble with the school or with the cops?"

"I think the cops and the teachers knew I'd done it but the two punks had been terrorizing the school for years. They'd hurt some younger kids pretty badly and their victims were always afraid to testify against them. They questioned me. I denied it, and they didn't push it too hard. Anyway, all the kids who saw what happened were too scared to rat me out, so nothing could be proven. The main result was I was typecast as a bad-ass. No one would associate with me except the juvenile delinquents so . . . I didn't have much choice but to become one of them. At least, after that, no more kids were shaken down for lunch money, not when I was around anyway." I flashed on a mental image of Andy Rose, a kid who had often needed my protection.

"How'd a juvenile delinquent get into college, let alone med school?" Bo asked. "You must a been a longer shot than me."

"Wrestling scholarship," I said, and just then my beeper went off. The arteriograms were ready. I thought I was off the hook but, as we walked down to X-ray, Bo continued.

"So you were a good enough wrestler to get you an athletic scholarship, even coming from a little Podunk town like . . . what was the name of the place?" Bo asked.

"Medford," I said, "or Mefud, as it was known locally. The thing is; Tufts College is in Medford. They offered a few scholarships to local kids, athletic as well as academic, for community relations I suppose. My grades were only average but my SATs were a little better and, most important; Tufts' wrestling had been an embarrassment for years." Again I thought of Andy who had gone to Tufts on a music scholarship.

"How about med school," Bo asked.

* * *

"Well the wrestling got me into college and I took some pre-med courses and liked them and . . . I was a Medford success story, a local PR bonanza for Tufts, so . . ."

"So you got you a free ride through Tufts Med?"

"Well, I had to work to supplement the med school scholarship, but that about sums it up," I said, and then, we were in radiology. Douglas' X-rays were up and Holt was already viewing them.

What I didn't tell Bo and what I'd never told anyone, not even Katy, was that I hadn't wanted to take the college scholarship. I was afraid I wouldn't be able to hack it academically. When I told my dad I was going to turn it down, he was already working on his second fifth of Wild Turkey. He tried to change my mind. First he got upset. Then he got angry. Then he had a heart attack right there in our little kitchen.

My father died literally in my arms, but not before I had promised to take the scholarship and try to do something good with my life. He might not have been worth much after my mother left, but I loved him anyway. I never realized how much until that moment . . . that moment when I knew I had killed him.

CHAPTER 4

THE CASES THAT day, including Douglas' below the knee amp went smoothly. No late train wrecks or midnight emergencies materialized. I might have gotten a few hours sleep had it not been for Oatis Cottonfield. Two weeks after his surgery, Oatis was still in the ICU and still hammering on Death's door. It wasn't the first night I'd spent in a chair by his bed, dozing off and waking up to handle the latest life-threatening crisis.

Oatis was a middle-aged black man who'd accidentally shot himself while hunting a pack of wild dogs through the thick swampy lowlands around his little chicken farm.

"Hunting wild dogs?" I had asked, as we scrubbed for his surgery. "We didn't see a lot of that up in Boston."

Holt and Bo explained that, in rural areas of the Deep South, packs of feral dogs were not uncommon and far from harmless.

"They'd a gone after Oatis' chickens, for one," Bo explained. Holt said they were also a danger to young children.

Oatis and a neighbor had been tracking the dogs, when they came to a low barbwire fence. Before crossing the fence, Oatis had leaned his shotgun, barrel up, against the middle wire. As he pressed down on the top strand and began to step carefully over it, the wire slipped off his hand and a pointed barb twanged up to cut through a thin patch in his denim overalls. It tore through the sensitive skin of his inner thigh, causing him to slip. He fell onto the shotgun, which went off, with the business end of the barrel pressed against his side. The entire energy of the blast was discharged into his body.

I'll never forget what we saw when we opened Oatis up. Most of his bowel and nearly every abdominal organ had been devastated. And that wasn't even the worst of it. A shotgun shell contains pellets which are intended to fly out of the barrel and into the target. The shell also contains paper wadding which normally travels a few feet before falling to the ground. Oatis' abdominal cavity absorbed all the pellets and all the paper wadding. There was no way to get every little shredded piece of paper out of the abdominal cavity. This virtually guaranteed that the wound would become infected.

It had taken all three of us, Holt, Bo and myself, to get Oatis out of the OR alive. Neither Holt nor I thought he had any chance of lasting the night. Standing around Oatis' bed, in the ICU, we looked and felt like mourners at a funeral.

"He'll do just fine," Bo assured us, with complete confidence.

Holt and I looked at each other and then at the EKG, which was irregular; the blood pressure readout, which was low in spite of high dose epinephrine; the urine bag, which was empty, because of renal shutdown; the huge surgical dressing which was again becoming soaked with blood, because all the transfusions interfered with clotting; and finally at Oatis himself, who was clearly moribund.

"Excuse me?" Holt asked Bo, with ominously raised shaggy eyebrows.

"He'll do just fine," Bo said smiling and nodding.

Holt rarely lost his temper at any of us, but it could happen and I took a couple of steps back, away from ground zero.

"Now just what-all makes you think this man will live through this night?" Holt asked Bo. Then he added, "And this better be good."

"Y'all see his gums?" Bo said. "They're blue."

"Yeah, so?" Holt asked.

"Well, he's from Louisiana," Bo said. "I seen it on his admit sheet."

"Yeah, so?" Holt repeated.

"So," Bo explained patiently, "That means he's a Louisiana Blue-Gummed Nigger and they don't never die. You'll see." Bo smiled and nodded confidently. "My daddy has kin in Louisiana and they told us all about the Blue-Gummed Niggers from there. I mean, I guess they must die eventually, but not from any sickness or injury that would kill normal folk. I heard all kinda stories 'bout stuff they survived. Ever-thing from getting a leg chewed off by a Bush Hog, to falling head first off a Silo, to . . . Well you'll see. Oatis'll be alright. I'm telling y'all."

Holt glared at Bo and said, "Oatis is not going to be alright. Oatis is going to die. Oatis is going to die tonight. And when he does, you are going to present this case at the next Mortality/Morbidity conference. And when you do, you are going to repeat to ever-one at that conference ever-thing you just said. You will repeat it word for word. You will look like a complete, blithering idiot, in front of Dr. Kirkwood, and all the other surgical staff, and all of your fellow residents, and a large number of nurses and technicians. And for your career to survive that humiliation, will require mystical powers even more bizarre than those you attribute to Louisiana Blue Gummed Niggers." Upon which Holt turned and stomped out of the ICU, muttering to himself under his breath.

Two weeks later, Oatis was still alive. He'd had every lethal complication known to modern medicine at least once and several of them twice. This time it was septic shock which, given his overall condition, should have been 100% fatal. I'd spent the night at his bedside, fighting to maintain his blood pressure. Now he was stable and probably looked a little better than I did.

As I gave my report on morning rounds, Holt just stood there shaking his head in wonderment. He glared pointedly at Bo, who was smart enough to avert his eyes and keep his mouth shut. Then, since I'd been up all night with Oatis, the two of them went off to the OR and I started in on the scut list.

By early afternoon, I'd changed the last dressing, started the last central line and dealt with yet another Oatis crises, which should have been fatal but wasn't. There was a surgical resident's lounge up next to our sleeping room complete with coffee and candy vending machines and the most recent copies of major surgical journals. We were expected to keep current with these and were frequently quizzed on their contents. Familiarity with the literature was essential to survive the next round of resident cuts at the end of the year. A dozen of us had started together, at the base of the program's pyramid. Seven years later, only one was expected to stand at the top, with a cardiac surgery fellowship.

The lounge consisted of a bunch of old easy chairs and puffy sofas strewn around a scuffed wooden floor. No two pieces of furniture had any discernible relationship, of color or geometry, to each other or to anything else in the room. Journals and textbooks were stacked high on rickety tables and the floor, or were displayed on metal shelves. An ancient TV with a crippled rabbit-ears antenna squatted forlornly on the floor, in a corner. It hadn't worked in my memory or, as far as I could ascertain, that of any living human being. Someone had scotch taped a Playboy centerfold over the broken screen.

As I entered, the single occupant of the room was Roberta Coss. Roberta was the only female surgery resident in the history of the program. At that time, she was one of only a handful in the entire country. Even back then, it wasn't unusual to see women residents in the various medical fields, especially pediatrics. But surgery was still an almost exclusively male club. If not for intense federal pressure, with the new big stick of Medicare reimbursement, it would have remained that way indefinitely. Everyone knew that women simply did not have "surgical personalities." They couldn't make decisions, especially under stress, and depended on emotion rather than logic. If you'd tried to convince anyone back then that, some forty years later, Roberta would be the first female "chairperson" of the American College of Surgeons, they would have assumed you were deranged.

Roberta and I were both in the usual surgery resident's uniform—rumpled green scrubs and bloodshot eyes. Her well-worn, less than pristine, white coat was on a hook by the door and my own frankly dirty one soon joined it. With a sigh, I flopped down into the claustrophobic embrace of a pillow-strewn sofa across from Roberta's Naugahyde Lazy Boy.

"Hey, Roberta," I said, reaching for the latest copy of Surgical Clinics of North America.

"Hey, Cooper. By the way, I've been meaning to ask. Have you officially apologized about the War of Northern Aggression yet, or are you still insisting that you had nothing personal to do with it?"

"I have sworn on my carpetbag that I am not now and never have been a card-carrying member of the abolitionist movement. What more do you Johnny Rebs or Joanie Rebs, in your case, want from me?"

Roberta chuckled. She claimed to be from Texas, although she had no discernible accent. Her family history was an enigma. One day she'd claim her father was a sea captain on an ocean freighter; another time he'd be rancher or a fighter pilot. It was many years before I learned her parents were divorced and she used her mother's maiden name. Had she used her father's name, we all would have recognized it immediately. He was in Denton Cooley's inner circle and was one of the top surgeons at the prestigious Texas Heart Institute. I suppose she remained anonymous to avoid any hint of favoritism.

We all did know that Roberta was unmarried but shared living quarters with a man. Whoever he was, he did not accompany her to hospital or resident social functions. No one had ever met him and their relationship was a complete mystery. As far as I was concerned, it was nobody's business but Roberta's and his.

Roberta and I, a woman and a Yankee, were both outsiders among the other residents. I had always felt that, like Bo, she had the potential to become a friend. She had a good sense of humor and we often interacted by joking around. But, when I asked what service she was on, Roberta's mood darkened.

"Crispy Critters," she said, without looking up from her Annals of Surgery. That's what we called the burn service and also burn victims. Not very sensitive, but treating major burns was so depressing it required some kind of humor and dark humor was the only relevant type. Without sick jokes to hide behind, no one could get through Crispy Critters without committing suicide.

"Did you hear about Annie Anderson?" Roberta asked, still with her nose buried in the journal.

Annie was a senior nurse on the burn unit. She'd worked there for decades and was a huge help to all of us residents, especially on our first Crispy Critters rotations.

"What about her?" I asked.

"I admitted her late yesterday afternoon," Roberta said, still without looking up. "Seventy percent body surface area third degree burns." Anything over fifty percent, back then, was 100% fatal.

Victims wouldn't seem too bad off at first. Third degree burns were deep enough to kill the local nerves, so there wasn't much initial pain. The burned areas were black and charred or pale marbled white. The grotesque swelling didn't set in for about twelve hours and the infections not for several days. After that they'd stop looking or, I'm sure, feeling human and the weeks of agonizing misery leading to certain death would begin. Swollen and swathed in bandages, suffering from multiple attempts at skin grafting, inevitably infected and semi-comatose from pain and pain medication, forced to endure agonizing dressing changes in whirlpool baths; these patients prayed for death long before welcoming its release.

The irony was too obvious to deserve comment. I was stunned. Annie was a classic grandmotherly type. The patients loved her as much as we residents did.

"How did it happen?"

"I'll tell you but you won't believe me," Roberta said, and immediately I knew.

"Tell me it wasn't charcoal-lighter fluid on an open flame."

"I wish I could, but that's exactly what it was," Roberta said, and now her voice sounded a little hoarse. The Annals of Surgery blocked my view of her face.

"How could she?" I jumped up from the couch and threw the journal I'd picked up across the room. "How many patients has she seen die agonizing deaths from exactly the same thing? How could she do it herself? How could she be so fucking stupid?"

Maybe a quarter of all the really serious or fatal burns we saw had the same cause. I'd seen at least a half dozen cases myself, in my two rotations on Crispy Critters. Annie must have seen hundreds of them. People who didn't know any better did it all the time. The charcoal fire would be dying down and they knew that just a little extra squirt from the can would get it going strong again. At least 99% of the time, that's exactly what would happen. But 1% of the time, or probably much less, the flame would follow the squirted fluid back up into the can. The can would then explode like napalm, sentencing the holder to certain death by prolonged and horrible torture.

I walked to the room's single dirty window and looked down at the street below and the VA hospital on the other side. My eyes stung and I swallowed hard as Roberta went on.

"The worst part," Roberta said, "was when her family came in: her husband—of over thirty years—grown son and two daughters, both nurses, and an infant grandchild. She had them sit down around her bed and explained it all very calmly. Told them all that, if they loved her, this would be the last time they would ever see her; that when they left the room, if they loved her, they would consider her dead. She explained to them, in great detail, what she was about to become—the hideous swelling; the stink of infection; the raving with pain and drugged confusion. She didn't want them to see her that way, to remember her that way. She made them each kiss her goodbye and swear to God that, no matter what, no matter what, they would never visit her again; that as far as they were concerned, if they loved her, she was dead the moment they left the room. She never shed a tear until the last one was gone."

Unable to speak, I got up and left the room, heading for the bathroom to splash some water on my face. Just then my beeper went off. Holt and Bo were still tied up in the OR and one of our post-ops, from the previous week, was in the ER with a wound infection.

Fortunately it turned out to be superficial and was likely to heal with no problems. Still, with a Dacron graft on the artery below, it was best to take no chances. Admission and intensive in-hospital treatment was indicated. If the infection reached the graft, where it was sewn to the artery, the suture line could break down. If that happened outside the hospital, the massive bleed would be fatal. By the time I'd gotten the wound debrided and dressed, and the patient admitted, Bo and Holt had worked their way through the operative schedule.

Bo and I made late afternoon rounds, grabbed a quick snack, saw a couple of consults and then made rounds again, this time with Holt. By then it was after six PM and Bo was on call for the night. I had spent my last off-duty night in the hospital, so Katy could go to the movies. The nights before and after that, I'd been on call and had to stay in. That meant I hadn't left the building for three nights and four days.

Leaving Bo with the scut list, I called Katy to come pick me up. Still in my dirty white coat and green scrubs, I trudged through the big ornate reception area and out the huge front door of the hospital. On top of the big stone front stairway, I paused and looked around. The outside world seemed unreal.

CHAPTER 5

IT WAS A CRISP spring evening. Compared to the re-circulated hospital miasma, even the smog and exhaust-laden city air smelled fresh and felt clean. Summer was threatening, but its nearly unbearable heat and humidity were still a few weeks away. There was a cool breeze and the street lights glowed like carnival lanterns; the chattering, laughing pedestrians seemed like celebrants. They were oblivious to the world of pain, fear, suffering and death in the building behind me. At the bottom of the steps I sat down and leaned back against the ornate stone balustrade, closing my eyes for just a moment.

Seconds later, or so it seemed, Katy was shaking me roughly, waking me out of a dreamless sleep. As soon as I stirred, she turned and walked back to her VW, parked illegally at the curb, disassociating herself from me with what seemed like disgust. She'd complained before about having to publicly shake me awake and drag me into the car after finding me, as she put it, "Sleeping in the gutter with the bums."

Katy was an Irish girl, tall and willowy. She had a pixie face framed with long, straight, flaming red hair. Mischievous azure eyes reflected her rebellious childhood in a series of Catholic girl's schools. The nuns had paddled her frequently but broken neither her spirit nor her propensity for pranks. A few freckles only enhanced by contrast the ivory radiance of the silkiest, creamiest cheeks I had ever kissed. But the softness was only skin deep. Katy had the stubbornness and the temper to go with her red hair and Hibernian heritage and, exhausted as I was, I was in no shape to challenge either one.

She'd come to pick me up in jeans that fit like pantyhose tucked into red leather cowboy boots. Her silky white shirt was bound by a hand-tooled leather belt, which matched her boots and accentuated her narrow waist. Even in my exhausted state, she looked great walking back to the car. The high heeled boots exaggerated the sway of her hips and her rich ruby mane bounced along in time against the silky shirt. The athletic muscles of her bottom and thighs were bunching and relaxing in ways the Southern Baptists would have liked to make illegal. They had already sued to cover the butt of the apron-clad Vulcan statue overlooking the city. Vulcan's metal buttocks were bare but Katy's firm cheeks, inside those tight jeans, posed more danger to the pure thoughts of Baptist men. Back then all Baptist men—in Birmingham at least—were militantly heterosexual.

Slumping into the passenger seat, I closed my eyes again, then opened them quickly so I wouldn't fall back to sleep. Finally getting to see me and then having me pass out on her was another of Katy's sore points. After only a few blocks, we were out of the city and into the densely treed, blue-collar neighborhood where we lived. Katy parked in front of our rented house and I stumbled out of the car. We walked towards our long narrow porch in silence. The porch ran right to left along the front of the house, forming a T with the path from the street. It was backed by a long row of windows and had separate entry doors, positioned on opposite ends.

The door on the left opened directly into a shabby formal dining room, which led to the left side of the living room. As always, we used the door on the right. Katy led the way, into a screened-in vestibule and then U-turned to the left and through another door, into the living room.

Katy flipped on the overhead light, sat on the threadbare couch facing our fake fireplace and gestured for me to join her. The house was an ancient wooden structure, tilting at about the same angle as the Tower of Pisa. It had been built on inadequate stilts hovering over a scrubby hillside, so at least, unlike the Tower, it had an excuse. Because of stresses from the tilt, there wasn't a true right angle in the entire place. The other-worldly geometry, like something conceived by H. P. Lovecraft, was further emphasized by an aberration common to all the inside doors. Sometime in the past, someone had replaced thin wall-to-wall carpeting with heavy shag. The new rug must already have been laid by the time they realized it was too thick for clearance under the doors which could no longer be opened. They'd solved the problem by removing all the doors and cutting several inches off of each bottom edge. The doors could then swing freely because of the two to three inch gap between them and the floor. The effect on the décor was noticeable and, in my experience, unique. "High-water doors," we called them.

The back of the house dropped all the way down to the bottom of the hillside. This left one floor of living space at street level and three stories of open basement running down the back. Huge air ducts radiated up through the cavernous cellar space, like the tentacles of a giant upside down octopus. Each room had its own air duct for heat in the winter and blessed central air conditioning in the summer.

We'd barely entered the living room before I heard the most ominous words in any relationship. "Cooper," Katy said, "we've got to talk."

I personally thought I needed food and sleep more than conversation, but she was right. Issues had to be resolved. We couldn't continue the way we were going.

"Katy, look I know things have been hard for you but I don't know what I can do to make them better. I don't . . ."

"Forget it," she snapped. "It's not your fault, at least not all of it. I know I haven't been fair. You can't help the way things are with the residency. It's a lot tougher here than it was for the residents at Tufts. They whined about being overworked but it was nothing to what they put you through down here. Let's face it. Neither of us knew what we were getting into. I know you'd never quit and I'd never ask you to. You can't change what you're doing but I can. I've applied for an ICU job at the hospital." She looked up at me from behind straight red bangs to see my reaction. I looked away from her to hide it.

"Working again will keep me busy and, if I'm on shift when you get off, the car will be in the hospital parking lot. You'll just have to drive yourself home. You'll drop the car in the lot when you come in and leave it there for me. I know it's not what you wanted but . . . Look, I've been a bitch and I don't want to be a bitch. But this waiting around for you to get off—every other night if that—just so I can pick you up, feed you and watch you fall asleep without two words of conversation . . . It's driving me nuts. If I'm working again, I think I'll be okay and if I'm okay things will be better for both of us." I started to talk but she held up a hand to silence me. Katy had obviously decided what she was going to say. She wanted to get through the whole speech before I could react.

"Cooper, I know we discussed this when we first came down here and you didn't want me to have a job. I went along with you then but I should have known it wasn't going to work. I was a top ICU nurse and I loved doing it. I don't know what I was thinking when I agreed to quit. Maybe the idea of being a 'doctor's wife,' a lady of leisure, getting up in the morning and doing whatever I wanted all day long . . . I don't know, I guess it had a certain appeal. But it's making us both miserable. I'm an ICU nurse and a damn good one and I'm not going to be happy unless I'm being who I am, just like you're being who you are. Cooper, you're just going to have to deal with whatever male ego problems you have about your woman working. You've got to go along with me on this. I mean it."

I had to admit she'd put her finger on the problem. When we came down from Boston to Birmingham, the idea of Katy working seemed an affront to my manhood. If she worked, it meant I'd failed to provide for her. A man should be able to support his woman and I would be making all of $6,250 per year. How could any couple possibly need more money than that? Compared to the scholarship stipend on which I had been surviving, we would be living large.

Before starting the residency, I was sure I knew best about everything. But now, nearly two years later, things just weren't going the way I'd planned. If Katy and I were going to make it, something would have to change. She really was a brilliant ICU nurse and that was part of why I'd fallen in love with her. I'd been a fool to ask her to give that up.

"Okay, Katy," I said, looking into big Caribbean-blue eyes, which softened at my capitulation. "If that's the way you want it, fine. You're probably right. You usually are."

"Damn right, I'm right," she said. "We've been through too much together, Cooper. I'm not going to let us lose it now." Katy pushed me gently back into the plush embrace of the sofa and cuddled under my arm, her head against my chest. After a while, she straddled my lap and kissed me hard. Before I could grab her and pull her down onto the couch, she had slipped away and darted into the kitchen, laughing at me over her shoulder. I was beginning to think that those nuns, with their paddles, might have known best what girls like Katy needed.

I knew one thing she needed for sure and I needed it too but, in my exhausted state, was I up to the task? I took stock of my physiological status and came up with enough hard data to make what you might call a firm diagnosis. There was one thing, in addition to food, that I needed more than sleep.

I followed Katy into the kitchen and hung out with her there on the pretext of "helping" her cook. My culinary tastes weren't very sophisticated in those days and she was whipping up my all-time favorite: meatballs and spaghetti. She didn't really need any assistance. This was fortunate as my "help" involved fondling and nuzzling the chef and ignoring the food.

Katy was playfully slapping my hands away and squirming out of my caresses, pretending to be annoyed. Fortunately my psych rotations in med school, had attuned me to the hidden meanings and subtle nuances of human behavior. I persisted and Katy's token resistance softened right along with the boiling spaghetti. It had been too long and she was as randy as I was.

By the time the meat sauce was bubbling, Katy wasn't watching it because she was pinned against the refrigerator. I had her hands locked over her head and my body pressed hers firmly into cool vibrations of the fridge's door. Her wrists were so delicate that my fingers and thumbs locked easily around them and she was all mine through a long deep kiss. When I eased my body back from hers, I kept her wrists trapped against the humming door and stared down at her upturned face. Her eyes were closed and her pale skin flushed pink.

I let her go and turned off the stove. When she began a half-hearted protest I spun her around and slapped her bottom hard, propelling her into the bedroom.

"No, no, no," she said, with a teasing laugh, as I pushed her back onto the bed, pulled off her boots and shucked her out of her jeans. "What about dinner?"

I tried to silence her with kisses, but she kept twisting her head and murmuring, "No, no, no" right up until she started to scream "Oh, oh, oh." Afterwards, we lay together as one for a long, loving time. When I began to pull away, she wrapped her legs and arms around me, holding me tight, saying "no" again but with a different tone of voice. Finally she let me go just enough for us to become two again, but still in each other's arms, waiting for breathing to slow and hearts to calm.

After a while she nuzzled my neck, squirmed against my thigh and said, "The sauce will be all dried out now and the spaghetti will be glop. I'll have to cook a whole new batch." Then she pulled away, angled up on one elbow and looked into my eyes smiling as I lay on my back. "Haven't you ever heard that no means no, Cooper? If this was a date, you'd be guilty of 'date rape.' Maybe I should call the police and press charges."

"Well I admit I am a little confused about that," I said. "Did no mean no when it meant, 'No, don't put it in,' or when it meant, 'No, don't take it out.'"

With a high-pitched scream of laughter, she called me a sexist oinker, threw a leg over my exhausted, supine body and proceeded to press charges.

CHAPTER 6

THE LAST TWO weeks of my rotation with Holt were fairly uneventful. The Lousiana Blue-Gummed miracle slowly regained consciousness, overcame all of his infections and other complications, and was transferred to a physical therapy unit to regain his strength before discharge. Bo had a healthy instinct for self-preservation. He avoided any gloating in Holt's presence, but bragged freely about his prognostic triumph to all of the other residents.

The damp heat of impending summer was building relentlessly. We all knew that it would soon be oppressive and debilitating. Life would become a series of races from one air conditioned space to another. As the world heated up, so to did our tempers.

On the last day of the rotation, I approached the half-open door to a sleeping room and heard Ben Randolph's aristocratic drawl coming from inside. Bo must have been bragging again about Oatis' survival. Ben said, "I suppose, my dear Beauregard, that you understand these nigras so well because, being just po-ah white trash yourself, you are so very close to them . . . on the evolutionary scale, so to speak."

Everything inside those sleeping rooms, from the furniture to the beds to the walls, was constructed of thin, fragile ticky-tacky of one kind or another, basically plywood, plastic or plaster. The doors were the only exception. They were made from heavy slabs of solid oak.

From just outside the entrance, I could see Bo, on the far side of the room. He was facing me and it was clear that he was absolutely stricken. He usually took whatever jibes came his way in stride. This one had been mean-spirited enough that, along with the racist culture in which he'd been raised, it had pierced his defenses. Bo was stung, and he could not help but show it.

Ben was a step or two inside the door, facing towards Bo and away from me. As he turned to leave the room, I caught a sidelong glimpse of his supercilious smirk. He was just turning away from Bo and moving swiftly towards me. After savoring his last glimpse of Bo's dismay, Ben turned quickly and smoothly, smashing the side of his face into the swinging edge of the heavy oak door. I hadn't pushed it very hard but my timing was perfect. Between the momentum of his body moving towards the door and the torque of his face turning into its edge, the impact was stunning to observe. I can't even imagine how it felt.

Ben crumpled and I grabbed him before he hit the floor. "Ben. Sorry, man. I didn't see you there. You okay?" I was pleased with myself and ashamed of what I'd done, somehow both at the same time. I honestly hadn't intended to do that much damage. Most of the force had come from Ben's face turning into the impact.

Roberta Coss had been in the resident's library next door. She had heard Ben's remark through the thin walls and came to check out the commotion that followed. Roberta had been the butt of Ben's sardonic wit as often as Bo or I. "Tell me, Roberta darling," I'd once heard him ask, "Which do you think is more pathetic—a woman falling down drunk and regurgitating in the gutter or a woman trying to do surgery?"

Roberta was used to that kind of crap and, as usual, had a pretty good comeback. She just smiled and observed that the snipping and sewing of surgery was obviously woman's work to which Ben's long, delicate fingers and limp wrists seemed very well suited.

As Roberta came to the door I was struggling to keep Ben from completely collapsing onto the floor. In view of their history, I wasn't expecting Roberta to show much sympathy. She gasped audibly and clapped a hand hard over her open mouth. Whatever spontaneous reaction that stifled, was replaced by expressions of sympathy. She hardly chuckled at all as she hustled over and helped me support Ben.

His face was already swelling and a shallow cut on his cheek had angry red edges. His eyes were unfocused and he kept saying, "Ohh. Ohhh. Ohhh."

We tried to get him to lie down on a bed but he struggled loose and went staggering towards the elevator. Head in hands he muttered imprecations in which "Yankee Bastard" and "Lesbian Slut" figured prominently.

"I'm afraid I haven't heard the last of this," I said. "He's going to go straight to Ditman." Gill Ditman was chief of the burn service, which was convenient since skin grafts didn't require much surgical skill. He was also in charge of discipline problems among the residents.

"He'll go to the ER first, I think," Roberta said, keeping her giggles under control. "Anyway, I saw the whole thing and it was definitely an accident. Wasn't it, Bo?" Bo was standing where he'd been when Ben's face met the edge of the door, stunned and speechless. "I said it was an accident, Bo." Roberta repeated. "Cooper obviously didn't mean to swing that door right smack into Ben's smug face. The arrogant fop just wasn't looking where he was going. It was just an accident. I know you do agree; don't you Bo?"

Bo seemed to be coming out of a trance. "Yeah, yeah, oh yeah. For sure it was an accident." But Bo wasn't laughing. Roberta's pager went off and she hurried down the hall escaping with no audible chuckles.

"You shouldn't oughta done that," Bo said to me seriously. "That was not a Christian thing to do."

"Well, I'm not a Christian," I said, "but you're right. I shouldn't have done it. It just happened before I could stop myself. I'm not proud, but I'm not planning on confessing either. You will back me up that it was an accident, right? I know Roberta won't change her story."

"I'll back you up all right," Bo said. "In fact, I owe you for what you done, I guess. I don't know why you done it but . . . well, because we're friends I guess and you could see . . . I don't know why it cut so deep that time. I . . . I wasn't expecting it, I guess, and it . . . well it stung a lot more'n usual. I owe you, Cooper. I surely do."

"Then I want payback right now, Bo, and there's only one way you can cancel the debt . . . one way to make what I did feel right," I said.

"You name it," Bo said looking at me and shaking his head in affirmation.

"All I want you to do is to just think about something, Bo. That's all. Will you promise me you'll do that?"

"Think about something? Sure. That's easy enough," Bo said.

"Maybe not so easy as you think," I said. "I want you to think about how terms like 'nigger' and 'poor white trash' are just two sides of the same coin. You can't spend one side of that coin without paying on the other side. Whenever you say, 'nigger' from now on, you're going to hear Ben saying, 'poor white trash.'"

There was a long pause, while Bo stood there thinking. Then he put out his hand and we shook on it. I never heard him say nigger again.

The day before I left Holt's service, he took me aside, for a brief private chat. He reminded me that Dr. Jefferson would be looking for any excuse to bar me from his hospital, which would force Dr. Kirkwood to fire me. This would effectively destroy any chance of my ever becoming a heart surgeon.

Shaleena White was still head nurse on the night shift in the VA ICU. She was still under Jefferson's protection, and he would still make sure that she passed any drug tests. Even if I caught her with a syringe hanging out of her arm or found more long-dead patients on morning rounds, there wouldn't be a thing I could do—not if I wanted to finish my training.

I'd been agonizing for weeks over how I could protect the patients without ending my career. So far, I had come up with nothing. Apparently, the other residents just did the best they could, without self-destructing. They accepted an occasional "DBS," or "Death by Shaleena," as an unavoidable risk factor for VA heart patients. I tried to tell myself I'd have to do the same, but I knew damn well I couldn't. In the abstract, I might be able to live with it. When an actual dead person made it real, I knew I'd lose control. I'd make a scene, say something memorable and demand that action be taken. Action would be taken alright: action by Jefferson in support of Shaleena and against me.

Even without the kind of special protection Shaleena had from Jefferson, this sort of injustice was and is not at all uncommon. A nurse can kill a patient with gross negligence, but if a doctor reacts with politically incorrect language, the doc will be disciplined and the death will be whitewashed. This is truer today than ever before and not just at VAs.

As usual, Holt came to the rescue. "I been cogitating about your little VA problem, Yankee Boy," he said, in the empty stairwell he'd chosen for our talk. "I can't see but one way for you to survive the next month."

"What's that, Holt?" I asked.

"The problem is mostly the night shift, right?" Holt asked, "When Shaleena's in charge and no one's watching the patients like they should?"

"That's about it," I agreed. "Care at the VA is never up to University standards, but for most patients it's adequate. After a day or two at the U, even the open hearts usually do fine, but they can get unstable and they need to be watched. They can't just be ignored all night, while Shaleena and her cronies snort up and party down . . . if that's what's really going on." I had never seen actual drug use in the unit, although I had to admit it would explain everything.

"Umm Hmm," Holt nodded his head sagaciously. "So if somebody needs to be up all night watching them post-op hearts and if that somebody ain't gonna be Shaleena and her crew, then guess what, Yankee Boy?"

"What?" I bit, but I could already see where Holt was going.

"Won't nobody else be doing it, boy. So it's gonna have to be you. That's what," Holt said with a big smile. "From what I hear, that ICU is just about never full. There's always at least one extra bed in the unit and usually more. Ain't that right?"

I nodded.

"Okay. Now, how does that extra bed get used, if say you have a bad-sick patient up there?" Holt asked.

"Same as in any ICU with an extra bed and an unstable patient," I said. "The resident sleeps in it, so he's right there every time a problem comes up. That way he doesn't have to keep running up and down from the sleeping rooms. I've even slept on a gurney in the unit, if there were no extra beds and I had a sick patient."

"Well, then, that's what you're gonna have to do ever night you have any post-op hearts in there, Yankee Boy. And what's more, you're gonna need you an alarm clock so as you can be sure to get up ever hour on the hour to check on your patient's vital signs your own self. Somebody's got to do it and it, sure as shit, ain't gonna be Shaleena and her gang." Holt smiled and handed me an alarm clock with a red ribbon tied around it. "From me to you, Son. And I'd recommend that you place this here alarm button on the 'loud' setting."

"Wait a minute, Holt." I said. "You said Jefferson didn't want anyone calling attention to what's going on in that unit. Won't my sleeping there every night do exactly that? Maybe I should just sleep in the VA resident's rooms and walk over to check the unit every hour or so. I'm just afraid that sleeping there will be like a red flag for Jefferson. It might just escalate the whole thing, when I'd be safer to cool things down."

"You trust me, Yankee Boy?" Holt asked.

"Well . . . of course. You know I do, Holt. I just don't want to make things worse than they are. Maybe if I just keep a low profile—"

"Then you do like I say," Holt said and extended the brightly decorated timepiece towards my face. "If he tries to make you quit sleeping there, you hold your ground. Just be sure you curb your natural Yankee tendency to be rude and offensive. Pretend you're a Southerner and be respectful as you tell him to perform unnatural and anatomically improbable acts upon himself. Be polite but firm. Even Jefferson can't get away with firing you for being too conscientious."

"Katy's going to love this," I sighed, taking the clock. Her application for a job in cardiac care at the U was still in the works. It would be weeks before all her credentials arrived and the red tape untangled. Things at home had been better but still tense at times. Working nearly every night, instead of every other night, was not going to help. Katy was beginning to mutter about going back to her old ICU job in Boston. I knew that, whatever plans or promises were made, if she went back up North without me; that would be the end. We had never married, naively certain that "commitment" was all that counted and no "piece of paper" could matter. Now I saw that without that "piece of paper," our so-called "commitment" was a butterfly in a hurricane.

There was no point in thinking about it. I would do what I had to do. Katy would stand by me . . . or not.

CHAPTER 7

MY SLEEPING IN the VA ICU did not go unnoticed. I was as welcome there as an orthodox rabbi at an Aryan Nations convention. When my calloused Yankee feelings proved immune to her rejection, Shaleena called for help. The chief of nursing, a hatchet- faced retired army colonel named Christine Dugan, came by to pay me a visit. Chris, as she was called, was reputed to have girls' names tattooed on her arm. She warned that if my insulting lack of confidence in the nurses persisted, she would have to, "Bring this matter to the attention of a higher power."

"You're going to tattle on me to God?" I asked with a show of horror. She spun around in her comfortable shoes and marched out of the room.

Shaleena did not laugh and I was forced to conclude that she had no sense of humor. A couple of her cronies could not suppress grins, carefully hidden from their Fuhrer.

Jefferson shook me roughly awake the following morning around 2 AM. I was racked out on a gurney near a fresh open heart, just back from the U. My earlier complaints about Shaleena and the unit had only been in writing. I knew who he was but had never spoken with the Chief of Surgery before. Nevertheless, with the sleep rubbed from my eyes, there was no doubting his identity. The long horse-face, pale eyes and supercilious bearing were unmistakable.

Jefferson did not waste time on pleasantries and neither did I. He curtly ordered me out of the unit and I flatly refused to leave.

"How dare you disobey me? Do you know who I am?" he demanded.

"With all due respect, Dr. Jefferson"—emphasis on the word due in spite of all my best intentions—"I believe that I need to be here for my patient's safety." Shaleena and her gang were watching, of course: as bloodthirsty a crowd as you'd find at any cock fight. Maybe, in a way, that's pretty much what it was. Following Holt's advice had made the showdown inevitable. Now that it was here, I couldn't back down.

"You will leave this unit immediately, young man," Jefferson responded, "or you will leave this hospital and nev-ah return. The choice is entirely up to you." Jefferson was several inches taller than me but much slimmer. He made the most of his height advantage by standing close and looking down at me, sighting along the ridge of his long aristocratic nose.

I thought about Holt's advice. Call Jefferson's bluff, but do so politely and respectfully. I tried, but I am a Yankee after all, and Holt should have known I couldn't control myself. Maybe he did.

"Do you really want to expel me from the VA for being too diligent and conscientious in caring for my patients, Dr. Jefferson? Are you that eager to call attention to what's going on in this unit? Do you really want people to speculate on why I wasn't comfortable leaving my patients here without me at night?" I could see surprise and, yes I was sure of it, fear flicker behind his eyes. It was only there for moment, but that was enough. I knew he was going to cave and I couldn't stop myself from grinning at him.

To my chagrin, after a moment, he smiled back serenely.

"Well then," he said. "Stay of course, if you believe it to be a patient care issue. But do keep in mind that you still have three weeks left on this service, young man. In that time, I have no doubt that other issues will arise and I am quite certain the nurses here will so advise me when they do." Upon which, he turned and sauntered confidently out of the unit.

I tried to sleep but a sense of dread kept me twisting on the narrow gurney. Jefferson, the consummate politician, had played it smart. A better excuse to bar me from the VA was bound to come along. Goading him as I did had been dumb. Now he was more determined than ever to eat my lunch. It belatedly occurred to me that I could have defused the whole situation by submissively leaving and returning later when Jefferson had gone. Of course, that would only have put off the confrontation, but why couldn't I at least have been respectful? As far as I knew, no one had ever died of ass kissing; but

Jefferson's ass? . . . I just couldn't do it. And then there was the ultimate question; why couldn't I just let the patients take their chances like the other residents did? Those were not thoughts on which one slides gently into sleep – especially on a bed with wheels in a room full of enemies.

About two weeks later, I admitted a patient named Billy Sugg. Billy was a skinny rat-faced Vietnam vet with dirty-blond hair straggling limply to his neck. He had watery blue eyes, acne-scarred skin and a strong family history of coronary disease. Billy also had a crippling cocaine addiction. At the age of twenty-five, bad genes and worse choices left him facing open heart surgery.

Billy's parents were both dead, his father from a heart attack in his forties and his mother from alcoholism. His only living relative was a hulking uncle with a broken nose, never properly set. The uncle had colorless eyes; set close and buried deep in dark fleshy tunnels. You could barely see them without a direct face-to-face stare—not a pleasant proposition.

His head was round as a basketball and nearly as large. It was anchored by simian slabs of sinew sloping from ear to shoulder. His skull was hairless and shiny as chrome on a showroom Cadillac. He had no eyebrows. A sleeveless T-shirt exposed the ripped outlines of heavily muscled arms, also devoid of hair. I tried to remember a genetic syndrome with absent hair and colorless eyes, but couldn't come up with a name.

Shaking the uncle's hand was a competition. Between my wrestling background and the manual demands of surgery, I was just able to hold my own. I noticed a crudely tattooed swastika on the back of the hand gripping mine. When I glanced up to shoot him a disapproving look, I saw two blue tears leaking from his left eye. I knew what the tattooed tears meant; he'd killed two people in prison. Charming.

Having survived the handshake, I introduced myself.

"Tiny," was his only response.

"Of course," I said nodding, unable to suppress a grin.

Those dead eyes gripped mine for a moment, then shifted abruptly to his nephew, "You done good to come here, Billy. You do like the doc says now; you hear?"

"Sure, Tiny," Billy agreed submissively, but the big man was already headed for the door.

Tiny turned back, at the last minute, caught my eye and said, "You been highly spoke of and you'd best live up to it." Then he was gone. I couldn't imagine who might have spoken to this character about me. Holt, with his low-class clientele was most likely, but surely he would have told me about it. I dismissed the speculation and turned my attention to my patient.

Billy was severely malnourished. Cocaine inhibits appetite and addicts don't eat while they're high. He needed to be in better shape for surgery, so I started Billy on a high calorie diet with protein milkshakes. For the first few days, his angina was bad enough to keep him from running.

He tried to sneak out once but crumpled with chest pain within a block of the hospital. Following that episode, he was ashamed and apologetic.

"I'm sorry doc. I just . . ."

"It's okay, Billy. I understand. But, do you get that if you try it again, all you're likely to do is kill yourself?"

No response.

"Billy, you do know that don't you?"

"I know it, doc," he finally whispered, turning his head away to end the conversation.

Billy drank his milkshakes, ate his weight-gain diet and responded dramatically to medications. Within a week he was able to walk around the hospital without chest pain. I worried about another escape attempt but soon learned what kept him from running.

Rounding on Billy's ward one morning I saw that his bed was empty. A nurse said I'd find him in the rec room down the hall. There was a piano in the room and someone was playing as I entered. A sudden sense of *deja vu* stopped me at the door. "Andy?" I actually said it out loud before I realized the pianist was Billy.

Andy Rose was the kid I'd protected from bullies back in high school. He was skinny and small with stringy blond hair worn long like Billy's. From behind, on the piano bench, Billy looked just like Andy. Andy's musical talent won his scholarship to Tufts as I'd won mine with wrestling. One academic, one music and one sports scholarship were offered each year to Medford townies. The year Andy and I got ours, no one qualified for the academic. Freshman year, Andy and I took a Far Eastern Thought class together. We saw it as an easy way to fulfill a philosophy requirement. Much to our amazement, we were both fascinated by the subject matter. Zen Buddhism had special meaning to Andy through his music. Takuan Soho, the Zen Priest of swordsmen resonated with me through my wrestling.

Andy and I met every Thursday night to talk about Zen over dinner. We always ate at a Pizza place, until Andy discovered sashimi. There was only one restaurant in all of Boston back then offering this exotic delicacy. It was a no-name hole in the wall near China Town not much bigger than a closet. Nothing so fancy as sushi rolls was offered, just raw fish, rice and wasabi. We learned to use chop sticks and drink hot saki as we talked about gaining enlightenment. Andy worked towards it by losing himself in the flowing Tao energy of his music. Wrestling, like sword-fighting or any martial art, was to be my gate to satori.

The music dorm was on the way to the bus into town. When I picked Andy up there on Thursday nights he was always in the lounge playing the piano. He studied the classics to keep his free ride but rock and roll was Andy's first love. He could do Great Balls of Fire just like Jerry Lee Lewis and the girls all loved it. I'd always find Andy at the piano with a crowd of coeds around him.

Billy wasn't playing rock, but his classical chords filled the room with equally compelling power. Power enough to entrance the nurses gathered around the piano. From that moment on, Billy and Andy melded in my mind.

When he finished the piece, I tapped Billy's shoulder and the nurses left so I could check him. His color was much pinker than when he first came in and, with the weight gain, he wasn't so scrawny. With the more rounded features and a less dour expression, he no longer resembled a rodent. I walked Billy back to his room and warned him not to tire himself with too much playing. He lay down on his bed and I pulled up a chair. The scut list could wait a while.

"So, tell me about your music," I asked him.

Billy said Tiny, the brawny uncle I'd met, was a football hero in high school. Billy admired Tiny but was too small to follow in his footsteps.

"I knew I couldn't play football but figured in the band I'd at least get on the field at half time," Billy explained. "I tried out with a coupla instruments and playing them come easy to me. Before long the band teacher was saying I was some kinda prodigy or something."

The teacher got Billy to forget the band and start classical piano lessons.

"I got to like that kinda music a whole lot and I was good at it. Being no good in school and too little for sports, it was the first thing I shined at my own self. I worked hard at the lessons and in my senior year had an audition in New York City. I won me a scholarship to go up there and study at some famous school or other."

"So how did you end up in Vietnam?" I asked.

Billy grinned ruefully, shook his head and said, "My ass just got drafted. There wasn't no deferment for that music school. Not like a regular college."

"I guess your music didn't help much over there," I said and Billy's eyes moistened.

I handed him a tissue from the table by his bed and waited while he blew his nose and got himself together.

"It did help some," Billy said. "I always carried sheet music with me. I ain't no fighter, doc. I wish I was brave and strong like Tiny but I ain't. I guess I'm just a coward. When it got really bad with explosions going off and guys getting blown up around me, I'd curl up in the dirt and read me the notes. That would drown out the screams and the mortars."

"How did reading the music drown out the sounds?" I asked.

"I could hear it as I read it," Billy explained. "Could turn the music in my brain up as loud as ever I wanted." He paused for a while and said, "Mahler's Ninth was the best. It could always drown out the . . . horror."

"Did you get hooked on cocaine over there?" I asked.

"No," he said. "Over there it was heroin. The sergeant, he caught me with my sheet music one day, right in the middle of a battle. He tore up the music, put my rifle in my hands and said to shoot it or he'd shoot me. I ain't saying what he done was wrong. By not shooting I was letting down my buddies. After that I found the needle and just stayed high all the time. I wasn't the only one done it neither. By the time I got back to the world, I'd forgotten all about my music. I tried cocaine to get off the heroin. You can see how well that worked out." He paused and forced an embarrassed smile. "The piano here is the first I played since getting kicked out of the army. I deserved that too. Like I said before, I ain't no fighter. I'm a coward."

Billy's eyes started leaking again and I told him all about Andy. I explained about Zen and how Andy and I had been into Eastern religions.

"Andy went to New York, like you did," I told Billy. "Some kind of audition, like you had. It was our second year at Tufts and when he came back, he was all excited. Couldn't wait to tell me." I paused.

"Tell you about the audition?" Billy asked.

I said, "No. Not about the audition."

"These guys I met in New York," Andy had said. "They showed me a quick way to satori. There's no need for years and years of meditation or martial arts or music or anything. You just take a drug. It's called LSD, lysergic acid diethylamide. Mostly they just call it 'acid.'"

That was back in 1964 when LSD was just coming out of the closet. I had never heard of it and neither had most people.

"When you take the tiniest amount of this stuff," Andy had assured me, "you just effortlessly become enlightened. You look at a chair and you are the chair. You don't just see colors or hear music; you become one with the colors and the music and through them one with the universe."

"It didn't really sound right to me," I told Billy, "but I was willing to try it.

We couldn't find any LSD around at first but we did find some marihuana. I had heard that would lead to heroin." I smiled but Billy did not smile with me. "Andy assured me that wasn't true and said it would 'alter my consciousness.' He went on and on about all we could learn from both drugs and eventually I tried them."

"You smoked weed and dropped acid, doc?" I now had Billy's full attention.

"Weed a few times and acid once," I admitted. "and I did learn something from each experience."

"What did you learn, doc?" Andy sat up in bed.

I said, "The grass taught me what it's like to be stupid and the acid what it's like to be crazy. Not wanting to be stupid or crazy, I didn't continue with either."

Billy laughed. "I know what you mean, doc. But what about your friend? What ever happened to . . . Andy?"

"Andy followed Timothy Leary's advice to, 'Tune in; turn on and drop out.' I tried to stop him but Andy wouldn't listen. I guess I could have tried harder." I paused remembering how little effort I had put into helping Andy. "I was busy with my premed courses and didn't have much time for my friend. We drifted apart and within a year he was flunking and dropped out of college."

"What happened to him?" Billy wanted to know.

"We lost touch completely after he dropped out and I saw him only once, about a year later. His head was shaved and he was wearing some kind of robe, begging and chanting Hare Krishna. I was with a girl on a date. Didn't want her to realize I knew him. Andy saw me, waved and came towards us. I turned my back on him and walked away." I paused for a moment to feel the shame of that betrayal.

"Maybe I could have helped him," I told Billy. "I certainly could have tried much harder than I did. So I guess, in my own way, I'm a coward too. But I'm not giving up on you that easily."

"Don't beat yourself up, doc," Billy said. "There's no way you coulda done nothing for Andy. People don't quit 'till they're ready. Andy wasn't . . . and . . . maybe I ain't either."

"We'll see about that," I said standing up. "It looks like both of us are going to be tested."

CHAPTER 8

NO MATTER HOW busy I was, I talked with Billy daily. After the first time, we kept it light, just friendly conversation. Some days it was only a few words on rounds but a bond grew between us. Finally Billy was ready and surgery was scheduled for the next morning.

By then the night shift had grudgingly accepted my presence in the unit. They knew that, if any heart patients were there, I'd spend the night there with them. When there were no spare beds, I used the gurney in the linen closet alcove. That's where I spent the night before Billy's surgery, watching a fresh post-op heart just back from the U.

My alarm clock went off at 5AM, a half hour later than if I'd been home. Ah, the joy of sleeping in. My post-op had been stable but I'd been up every hour, just to be sure.

I was the only resident on VA hearts. A cardiac surgery Fellow, Allan Handley, was technically responsible for my patients. Allan supervised me but didn't do any actual work. All-night vigils in the ICU, morning rounds and scut work were not in a Fellow's job description.

So, after dragging myself out of bed and enduring the sullen glares of Shaleena and her crew, I made quick, uneventful morning rounds alone. Then it was time to bring Billy over for his surgery. Orderlies were not allowed to do this, in case of an emergency on the way. The resident on call had to personally push the gurney from the VA to the University OR.

The nurses on Billy's pre-op floor were friendly and dedicated. The head nurse, Bertha Henshaw, was nothing like Shaleena. Bertha was a round black woman with decades of experience. Her wise yet subtle guidance was valued by nurses and residents. She had a way of giving advice that didn't threaten one's ego and her floor was no less efficient for its easygoing ambiance.

Bertha looked on as a couple of younger nurses helped me get Billy onto a gurney. Then we transferred his IV drips and medical records. A portable defibrillator was also attached, in case he arrested on the way over.

Most VA patients were older men, often depressed and depressing. Billy's youth and daily piano concerts had made him a favorite. Bertha's nurses had adopted him like a lost kitten. As we got ready to go, Billy was mildly sedated but awake enough to be scared. Sharon Bronson, the pretty young brunette who mostly cared for Billy, was already tearing up. She squeezed his hand and told him it would be okay. Then Bertha and the rest wished him well, as they sent us on our way. They were sweet and caring, like worried big sisters, and they had good reason for concern. Cocaine abuse leads to severe blockages all up and down the coronaries. Such diffuse disease increases the risk of bypass surgery.

Once around the corner from the nursing station, Billy and I were alone. We would be alone for the twenty minutes it took to reach the University OR.

Alone with the whirring of the gurney's wheels, one of which wobbled adding a back-beat to the echoing monotone.

Alone in the dim gloom of labyrinthine hallways, with only low output night-lights to mark our way past the darker shadows of looming, open doorways.

Alone with the low moans that emanated from unseen gray men in gray hospital gowns in gray beds under gray covers, inside gray rooms.

Alone with the sickly-sweet aromas of cleaning fluids and bodily fluids and alcohol swabs and benzoin and infection and Fear and Death.

Whirring along in syncopated rhythm, we clanked over bumps in the linoleum floors, speeding up and slowing down over ramps where floor levels varied.

Laboring upwards in a Southern elevator, empty but for dusty detritus half-hidden in shadowy corners.

More gloomy corridors.

Finally we reached the halfway mark: the sky-bridge between the VA and University Hospitals. It was three stories high and spanned the chasm between entrenched institutional mediocrity and cutting-edge excellence. I stopped for a moment with Billy, halfway across that bridge, and looked out through glass walls at mostly empty streets. They would soon be glutted with rush-hour traffic. The Alabama summer was finally upon us and the cars' air conditioners would be more important than their engines. Staring out the window-wall of the sky-bridge, I knew with sudden clarity that I was losing Katy. A great desolation swept over me.

"Am I gonna die, doc?" Billy startled me, breaking the silence.

I moved around the gurney to look down at his pale, pinched face and saw how scared he really was. He'd been a soldier in Vietnam, although not a very good one. He had survived but only to be defeated by a more subtle enemy. Cocaine had robbed him of everything – even his music.

I usually answered even hard questions, like Billy's, honestly. I would provide the odds on survival and the chance of serious complications - a statistical analysis of what Dr. Kirkwood taught us to call "the risks and imponderables" of surgery. But Billy needed hope not hazard functions.

"Dr. Kirkwood's program is the best in the world, Billy. We'll get you through this, I promise. But after you get well and leave the hospital, the rest is going to be up to you. Can you promise me now that you'll do your part? If you go back to cocaine, this will all be a waste of time. You won't last a year. You have to know that don't you? Some part of you must feel it. Never mind what I say. Just listen to what your body is telling you."

A long pause and then, "I do know it, doc. I been knowing it my own self, for a long time now. But . . . I'll try, doc. I'll try. I promise I'll try." The way he said it, he had already failed. Billy knew it and I knew it and that didn't change a thing. I would refer him to a rehab program, but I knew he'd never show up. Or maybe he'd surprise me. All I could do was give him the chance and hope it wouldn't go up his nose, along with everything else he ever was or might have been.

We whirrrrred on across the bridge and clanked over a bump into a brighter, cleaner but equally convoluted new labyrinth: the deserted corridors of the administrative and research wing of University Hospital.

Dr. Kirkwood's suite of darkened rooms was the last office we passed. At that hour, he would be making stately morning rounds with his entourage of Cardiac Fellows, residents, students, nurses, technicians and visiting dignitaries.

Then we were through the final door, up another Southern elevator and down a short stretch of bright hallway, into the tightly controlled and highly organized pandemonium of the OR suite.

In the reception area, Billy was sucked into a whirlwind of nurses, anesthesiologists and technicians wearing the freshly laundered scrub suits, caps, masks and paper booties required for passage through a pair of large, automatic, double doors. Beyond those doors were corridors and scrub sinks and sterile rooms, and knives and saws and blood and Fear and Life and Death and moments of Truth where knowledge and courage and skill were tested daily.

Thirty minutes later, I was also in scrubs and standing at a deep sink, just outside the cardiac OR. With powerful disinfectants on the rigid bristles of a sterile plastic brush, I painfully abraded my forearms, hands, fingers and even the tender flesh under each fingernail. One instant, I was alone and totally absorbed in my ablutions. The next, Dr. Kirkwood, like a ghostly apparition, was scrubbing next to me. He was always appearing like that, impossibly out of thin air. All of us residents knew he had mastered the art of invisibility.

With his presence, as always, everything changed.

There are men who have an aura of power or charisma about them almost like an electric or magnetic field. Much later on in life, I met an Israeli general and an American president. Each of them had that same magical quality. Many of the great men of history must have had it, from Abraham to Abraham Lincoln and Moses to Martin Luther King. Dr. Kirkwood had it. One could no more be with him and fail to respond to his energy than one could stand in heavy surf without sensing the surge of the sea.

He was a small man, lean as a whip with iron-grey hair curled fiercely into his scalp. Because of his wiry hair or his wiry build or the way he had every operation "wired" to perfection, one of our nicknames for him, never used to his face, was, "The Wire."

The Wire's pale eyes were ray-guns, shooting laser beams of incisive and uncompromising intellectual energy. Every look was a test. And if those lasers found you lacking, they pierced you with an amused disdain that cut deeper than any angry glare. Worst of all was the knowledge that Dr. Kirkwood did not want to see you fail. He wanted to be pleased with what he saw. When he was not, it meant that you had disappointed him.

The Wire had a bulbous forehead, allowing ample room for a massive brain. His nose and mouth were prim and sharp, almost fox-like. There was a Spartan tightness about his thin dry lips. I can't imagine those lips going slack even in sleep. Dr. Kirkwood often stood with his hands pushed hard, elbows straight, deep into the pockets of his starched white coat.

His posture was perfect. Always.

In addition to The Wire's immense personal power, was the simple fact that he was the foremost pioneer in the history of cardiac surgery. For years, at the Mayo Clinic, he was the only person in the world doing open heart surgery on a routine basis with a heart-lung machine. Dr. Walt Lilliheigh, the only other heart surgeon in the world, at that time, was using a doomed technique called "human cross-circulation." Instead of a mechanical heart-lung machine, Dr. Lilliheigh used another living person's heart and lungs to pump and oxygenate the blood of his patients. Virtually the entire surgical world believed that Lilliheigh's method would prevail. Dr. Kirkwood told me that a colleague had once called his method "unfashionable."

By the time I began to study with Dr. Kirkwood, Lilliheigh's "human cross-circulation" had already hit the dustbin of surgical history. Dr. Kirkwood's "unfashionable" use of the mechanical heart-lung machine had triumphed and was employed by every cardiac surgeon in the world, including Lilliheigh. The machine allowed much more precise control of blood flow and oxygen levels, and only one life rather than two was risked with each operation.

Many years later, Lilliheigh-trained journal editors and surgical society officers would conspire to re-write history. They stole Dr. Kirkwood's crown and placed it on the head of their own mentor. As a result, Dr. Lilliheigh is wrongly remembered as, "The Father of Cardiac Surgery." Such historical injustices are, I suppose, not uncommon. Just compare the music of Elvis to that of Jerry Lee Lewis and tell me who was the real "King" of Rock and Roll.

"Good morning, sir," I said.

"Good morning, Cooper." Dr. Kirkwood responded briskly, with what I thought was the ghost of a rare smile.

"Did the University case cancel, sir?" I had expected Dr. Kirkwood to do that case and Allan Handley, the Cardiac Fellow, to operate on Billy with my help. The Fellow usually did the VA cases and the resident on VA hearts would first assist.

"No," Dr. Kirkwood said. "I decided to let Allan do the University case. It's pretty straightforward and I think he's up to it, don't you?"

"Certainly, sir." The question had, of course, been rhetorical but still required an answer. "That's great and I'll get a chance to first assist you, which is . . . also great." I smiled and hoped I hadn't come across as overconfident. Many of the residents, especially the wannabe heart surgeons, were terrified of assisting The Wire. Dr. Kirkwood often said that first assisting was, "a continuous intelligence test." With him it was all of that and more. Failure to measure up, either in technical ability or knowledge related to the case, was punished with rapier-like slashes to the ego. Such wounds were not only painful. They could prove fatal to one's career.

Dr. Kirkwood's tongue could be sharper than any scalpel. I had seen it reduce even Fellows to near tears. Some powerful surgeons were cruel because it was their nature. Not Dr. Kirkwood. His reprimands were given to teach, not because he took pleasure in the putdown. To me, that made all the difference.

I was eager to risk his wrath in return for the privilege of proving myself to him. Other times I'd first-assisted The Wire, I knew I had done well. He had even given me a few precious compliments. This was almost unheard of and I can still remember every one of them.

"No," Dr. Kirkwood said, staring at his hands as he scrubbed them vigorously, "I don't think you'll assist me today."

I was crushed. Devastated. No other surgeon or surgeon's assistant was scrubbing, so he must have been planning to have a nurse first assist him in my place. I would end up hanging on a retractor in the second assistant slot. This would be the ultimate humiliation. But why, why . . . ? What had I done to kill the goose that laid the golden eggs?

I continued to scrub in a dazed numb silence until Dr. Kirkwood abruptly left the sink and strode into the OR. I trailed miserably along behind, like a whipped puppy.

CHAPTER 9

ENTERING THE *SANCTUM* sanctorum of the primary open heart operating room, Dr. Kirkwood and I stood with our arms bent, hands in the air, soapy water dripping from our elbows. Scrub nurses handed us sterile green towels to dry with: hands first, then forearms, then elbows, before flipping the towels onto the floor. The sterilely attired scrub nurses then helped us into our own sterile gowns and gloves. Glasses with protruding magnifying scopes, called loupes, were placed on our faces and powerful spotlights were strapped to our heads, in the manner of coal-minors.

I was surprised that the smiling nurses were fitting me out with loupes and a headlight. These were usually reserved for the surgeon and first assistant. I only expected to second assist and wondered why the nurses seemed so pleased at my disgrace. I thought I had gotten along well with them but obviously I was wrong. My Northeast Personality Disorder made me *persona non grata* even here, in the one place I thought I had been accepted.

Dr. Kirkwood moved to the supine patient's left side and gestured for me to assume the position of primary surgeon, on the patient's right. I quickly followed his instructions and stood confused, waiting for his next order. There was nothing a second year resident could do on the primary surgeon's side of the table; not on an open heart.

"Well, what are you waiting for?" The Wire snapped impatiently. "I told you, you wouldn't be assisting. Do you want to do this case or not?"

Something like an electric shock buzzed through my body. The room pulsed around me, but I held myself together. My eyes on Dr. Kirkwood's, I put out my hand to the nurse and answered him with a single word to her. "Scalpel," I said, accenting the second syllable, just like The Wire. She snapped the knife into my palm and I made my opening incision—down the midline of the chest, from the bottom of the neck to the top of the abdomen—in one bold stroke. At that stage of my training, I should not have been ready for my first open heart. Dr. Kirkwood knew I was ready . . . and so did I.

From the very first time I ever watched The Wire operate, I had kept a written account of every move he made in every type of surgery. More than that, I recorded in detail every nuance of his gestures; the precise wording and phrasing and tone he used in his orders; the way he reached out his hand for each instrument; which ones he expected the nurse to anticipate and which ones he asked for by name; what he did with his right hand and what he did with his left; even how he used each finger. I wrote it all down but never needed to look at those notes again. Every word was inscribed on my soul, like a well memorized poem.

Learning prolonged and complex procedures in such minute detail may seem incredible. It was, in fact, what The Wire demanded. It helped that his cases were impeccably choreographed. In every case, every move was made the same way every time. If he decided another way was better, he would make that the new way. Then he would do it the new way every time. We could learn every detail because, lacking anatomic abnormalities or emergent mishaps, every detail was the same in every case.

In the brilliantly illuminated three inch circle of my miner's headlight, magnification magically enhanced the reds and browns and yellows and blues of the moving heart. That multicolored microcosm in the headlight's beam became my solar system. The rest of Billy's heart, around that lighted circle, was the rest of my universe. Dr. Kirkwood explained it as becoming a tiny man in the world exposed by the headlight. Flying, with SCUBA gear, through caverns of multicolored coral is a little like being that tiny man. But that doesn't really come close to the world the heart surgeon works in.

For a dive to approach the intensity of a cardiac operation, it would have to take place in the River Styx. Unlike any other type of surgery, open hearts are always done in that mystic borderland between Life and Death. I'll never forget the transcendent moment when, after exposing and preparing Billy's heart, I spoke these words for the first time;

"On bypass, gentlemen."

That was the order for the perfusionists to start the heart lung machine pumping – draining tired blue blood from Billy's body and returning it red, vibrant and singing with oxygenated energy.

My one departure from a perfect Dr. Kirkwood imitation, was to add the word "gentlemen" to the order to go on bypass. That single ad lib was my gesture of respect for the perfusionists. Their cooperation, or lack of it, running the machine, could help or hinder my performance. I wanted them on my side.

"He means you, boys," Dr. Kirkwood quipped and everyone gave a brief chuckle. It was unusual for The Wire to joke during a case and doing so showed he was relaxed and comfortable, confident in my competence. It remains the most cherished compliment in my memory.

Once on bypass, I dropped Billy's body temperature by cooling his blood as it went through the heart lung machine. Then I placed a large clamp across his aorta and injected a frigid, potassium rich solution called cardioplegia. The cardioplegia would flow into Billy's coronary arteries, stopping the heart and chilling it to 17 degrees centigrade. The relaxation and refrigeration would minimize the heart's need for energy and, therefore, minimize its need for blood. This cardioplegic arrest was what allowed us to safely deprive Billy's heart of blood, while we placed bypass grafts around the blockages in his coronaries.

As the cardioplegia went in, we watched Billy's EKG flat-line as his heart stopped. By any definition more than a few years old, Billy was dead. I would fix his heart, placing grafts to bypass his cocaine corroded coronaries. Then I would bring him back to life.

Of all medical specialists, only a cardiac surgeon walks this feather edge between Life and Death, with every single patient.

The unique opportunity to duel daily with Death was why heart surgery was the only field of medicine to interest me. If I couldn't be a cardiac surgeon, I would have been something like a fighter pilot before any lesser medical specialty. I needed the challenge of working with grace, precision and clarity of thought, in spite of Death's icy breath on the back of my neck. I knew that anything else would eventually become boring.

Like most cocaine addicted heart patients, Billy's coronaries had not just one or two easily bypassed blockages, but diffuse disease all along their lengths. Opening into the wrong spot would expose an inoperable vessel choked with plaque and clot. The Wire helped me manipulate the heart and examine each of the coronaries. We found relatively healthy spots for grafting on two of the three target arteries. Each of these opened easily to the first stroke of the scalpel and suturing grafts into them presented no problems.

The third coronary was rigid with calcified plaque all along its surface. Dr. Kirkwood and I agreed on the least diseased spot. Many cardiac surgeons use the point of the scalpel to perforate a coronary. Dr. Kirkwood's technique was to stroke the surface of the artery with the curved side of the blade.

"Gently, Cooper," he cautioned, as I began to slide the more than razor-sharp edge of the scalpel along the diseased vessel parallel to its course. "Caress her. The coronary is a woman. Never try to force her. Caress her with the scalpel and she will open herself for you."

My first stroke was perfectly centered in the middle of the 2mm vessel, following its course along the surface of the heart. But since this artery was thick with disease, the single stroke was not deep enough to open her. I would need to stroke again along precisely the same line. If that next stroke was not right on top of the previous one, there would be two cuts instead of one. Multiple cuts would shred the coronary, making a good graft impossible. Without a good graft, flow to the muscle beyond would be blocked. Without flow, that part of the heart would die . . . and so would Billy.

My second caress was exactly along the same line as the first, but still the artery did not open. "You're doing fine," The Wire assured me. "Don't rush it or force it. Just caress effortlessly along that same line until she opens herself for you."

The next stroke did it. The rigid wall parted and the edges spread to allow placement of sutures for the graft. Suture placement was not easy in this rigid, diseased coronary. It required some force to push the delicate needle through the tough wall and, if the needle bent, it could tear the tissue irreparably.

Finally the last graft was sewn into place. Checking each suture line, we found no leaks and the grafts lay smoothly without kinks or angulations. Measuring devices showed that blood flow through them was excellent.

Now it was time for me to take Billy's hand and walk him away from Death's backyard to rejoin the world of the living. I began warming his blood and, when the time was right, I took the big clamp off the aorta. With the grafts in place, blood no longer had to squeeze its way into Billy's heart through cocaine constricted conduits. Now blood could bypass those blockages, through the grafts' pristine pathways.

For the first time in years, Billy's grateful heart was flooded copiously with blood-born energy and revivifying warmth. It responded by squeezing and churning vigorously, dancing spontaneously as only a heart can to the rhythms of life. But at that point the heart lung machine was still doing most of the work. Would Billy's heart be strong enough to take over when it had to pump his blood alone? Slowly, progressively, I decreased the flow through the machine, gradually allowing the flow through Billy's heart to increase accordingly. Finally it was time for the moment of truth.

The order to stop the heart lung machine was not, "Pump off," because that sounded too much like, "Pump on," and the two could be confused. The order was, "Pump, O, F," pronouncing the letters, as in, "Pump, Oh, Ef."

I said it.

The perfusionists did it.

And Billy's heart took over, as Bo might have put it, "Slick as snot on a door knob."

Billy was stable enough that I didn't really need to spend the whole night at his bedside. But I did.

Carter Whitney, The Wire's surgeon's assistant, didn't need to stay either but he was there with me for most of the night.

Except for being extremely black, Carter Whitney looked like a classic illustration of Ichabod Crane. Carter Whitney had been with Dr. Kirkwood at the Mayo Clinic and was a part of the team that gave birth to the miracle of open heart surgery. Being from up north, he was different from the southern blacks, and may have been as much an outsider as I was.

Everyone, including Dr. Kirkwood, called this dignified black man, of indeterminate age, Mr. Whitney and treated him with the respect he deserved. Mr. Whitney had been taking care of post-op open heart patients longer than anyone in the world, except for Dr. Kirkwood. With Mr. Whitney and me at his bedside, Billy's nurse was free to help with less stable patients. The curtain around us and Billy's bed was pulled closed providing some privacy. Mr. Whitney was a man of few words, none of them personal. I had often tried unsuccessfully to mine his memories of the pioneering days at Mayo. His answers had been polite but evasive. He never discussed anything unrelated to patient care.

Never . . . until that night.

"Doctor Kirkwood never gave a heart case to a second year resident before," Mr. Whitney said. His remark ended a long silence, broken only by the beeping of Billy's monitors and ambient noise from outside the ringed curtain. The comment was so out of character I thought I might have imagined it. I just looked at him and, after a while, he continued.

"Don't know what he sees in you," Mr. Whitney said, "but it must be something—him letting you do this case, with you so green."

"I don't know either, Mr. Whitney," I said. "I'm just trying not to disappoint him."

Mr. Whitney started to laugh, another first in my experience. I didn't get the joke but he kept laughing and, after a while, I couldn't help but join him.

"That was the one and only right answer, doctor," Mr. Whitney finally said. "You not as dumb as most of the white boys scrambling around here, fighting over the keys to the kingdom. Maybe Dr. Kirkwood is right about you. He usually is."

"Thanks, Mr. Whitney and . . . you know, I'd be pleased if you just called me Cooper."

"No sir. I think not," he said quietly. "I'll call you doctor, like I call all you boys doctor . . . and you call me Mr. Whitney."

"Okay, Mr. Whitney. I didn't mean any disrespect or . . ."

"No, no. None taken. It's just better that way."

There was another long silence. After a while the nurse came back and shot a cardiac index. She used the green dye technique, now obsolete but then state of the art and unique to our program. She recorded the index and some other data on her flow sheet, did some busy-work and left. Before passing through the curtain she asked, "I didn't hear you laughing in here before, did I Mr. Whitney?"

"Have you ever heard me laugh in here, young lady?" he asked.

"Well, no," she admitted, with a mischievous smile. She was a warm, maternal woman, just slightly chubby with a 1950s hair-style and gentle brown eyes.

"Well then I do believe you just answered your own question," Mr. Whitney said, with a rare smile of his own for her.

More time passed in silence after she left and then, "See to it that you don't disappoint him," Mr. Whitney said. "He doesn't show any feelings . . . but he has them."

I waited patiently, knowing there was more but that it would only come if I kept my mouth shut.

"In the early days, back at Mayo, we lost a lot of patients. Most of them were kids back then; that's the kind of heart surgery we started with. There were no artificial valves or bypass operations back then, only kids with malformed hearts. We were doing operations no one had ever done before, operations Dr. Kirkwood made up in his own head. And all the time he was doing them in ways everyone else thought was wrong . . . but he knew was right. It was all on him you see. All on him. Not like it is now. What you boys think is stress is crème soda next to that."

There was another long pause. Mr. Whitney sat with his angular elbows on his stork-like knees, hands folded under his chin, looking down at his long narrow feet. He seemed to be talking to his feet. I could barely hear him.

"We were at an American Heart Association meeting in Chicago, one time. It was way back in the beginning. We'd lost two children in the two days before we left for that meeting. When we lost them, he was like he always was, like you always see him now. An ice-man, no fear, no doubt, no regret, no remorse, no emotion at all, just cold logic and cold facts with a cold knife.

"I didn't know anyone in Chicago and couldn't afford a fancy restaurant or a cab, so I walked out of the hotel looking for fast food. I found a McDonalds and, on the way back to the hotel, I passed a rundown movie-house with one of those old-timey theater names. I think it was The Stanley. I'd never heard of the movie that was playing and I can't think of it now. It had already started, but I'd only be missing the first ten or fifteen minutes so, on impulse, I just went in. It may seem funny to you, me going to a movie by myself like that, but that's how I am. I got my reasons." He paused and I waited, silent as a hunter in a blind, afraid that any sound or move I made might end the flow of his memory.

"It was a crummy theater," he finally continued, "It smelled like sour butter from old popcorn. There were only two or three folks there, each one far from each of the others . . . isolated islands in a dark sea of seats. I couldn't see any of them when I first came in. It was pitch black and I felt my way to a seat before my eyes adjusted. When they did, I saw there was a man just two rows away and directly in front of me.

"The movie was boring and I decided to leave before it was half over. Just as I started to get up, I thought I heard something. It sounded like sobbing, sobbing soft and low. Sobbing to break your heart. It was coming from that man, the one sitting alone two rows in front of me . . . his shoulders were shaking. He was crying. Because I came in late and quiet, he must not have known I was near him. The two or three others in the theater were far away and they were between him and the screen so they couldn't see him or hear him cry. He was sitting there alone in the dark, in that near empty theater, just quietly sobbing . . . sobbing . . . hopelessly sobbing . . . on and on." Mr. Whitney wiped his eyes with the lapel of his white coat.

"That man was Dr. Kirkwood," Mr. Whitney said, and then he got up and left the unit.

* * *

Billy's course at University Hospital continued to be uneventful. By the third post-operative day, I was out of excuses to keep him from the VA. I worried about every post-op heart I took back there, but especially Billy.

I came to pick him up at the U around midday. Looking for any excuse to put off the inevitable, I decided to grab some lunch at the cafeteria. I had just sat down, alone at a table for four, when Bo and Roberta clattered into the cheap plastic chairs on either side of me.

"Now that is disgusting," Roberta said. She was pointing to the concoction of ketchup and mayonnaise I was stirring vigorously on my plate, between a greasy cheeseburger and soggy fries.

"It's called Russian Dressing," I said. "When the great chefs of Europe have mastered the Bearnaise and the Hollandaise, they're ready to attempt this." I had never actually tried either sauce but I had heard of them. I completed my display of culinary virtuosity with a dazzling blizzard of salt and swamped both the burger and the fries with the resulting orange goop.

"I think I'm going to be ill," Roberta said, as I stuffed the burger into my smiling mouth, allowing escaping grease to run freely down my chin.

"How's Billy doing?" Bo asked.

I grabbed for a napkin to save my tie while Roberta laughed.

Everyone knew I had done Billy's case and no one could quite figure out why. No other second year resident had ever been given an open heart. The prevailing opinion was that Dr. Kirkwood favored me because we were both Yankees. Bo and Roberta were happy for me and Holt had offered his congratulations. The other residents and Fellows, and even some of the staff, were jealous. The Wire was our father figure and the sibling rivalry was intense.

"So far, so good," I said.

"Yeah, but now comes the tough part," Roberta responded. "He gets booted back to the VA pretty soon, doesn't he? And I know your good friend Shaleena is going to take extra special care of little Billy."

"Well, you know I'll be there every night, like I am with all my post-op hearts," I said. "There are no other VA cardiac cases on the schedule this week, so I shouldn't need to come over here either. If Shaleena and her gang want to mess with Billy they'll have to go through me."

"Well, you better make sure they don't," Roberta teased. "Anything happens to Billy and that golden-boy aura you've been walking around with will turn to egg yolk all over your Yankee face."

"Yeah, you best watch him close," Bo agreed. "What The Wire giveth, The Wire can taketh away."

"Okay, all kidding aside, my butt's on the line," I admitted. "I am well aware of that. But it's more than my butt or my career. Billy's just about our age. Did you ever think of that? We thought medical school was tough, but it was nothing to what he went through in Vietnam. I've talked with him about it and . . . well just look what it did to him. I only missed getting drafted because of my scholarship and a college deferment. What if he'd had the deferment and I'd gotten drafted . . . or volunteered?" They both looked at me as if I was crazy but I had seriously thought about enlisting back then. I still sometimes wonder how I would have been in combat. Would I have done my job or been a coward like Billy? Now I'll never know.

I got up to leave and cleared my stuff off the table.

"I figure I owe, Billy," I said, "We all do and I'm not going to let anything happen to him."

Then I went up to the CICU, got Billy and wheeled him back over to the VA.

CHAPTER 10

BILLY WAS STABLE at the VA that night. I slept on one of the narrow ICU beds and checked him every hour. By that afternoon, his fourth day since surgery, Billy was already pushing to be discharged. He wanted out of the ICU and out of the hospital. The siren song of The White Lady, cocaine, was overpowering the attraction of the rec room piano, the appeal of the nurses and even the personal connection that had grown between Billy and me. He promised to stay off of the coke but neither he nor I believed him. If I tried to keep Billy, he would sneak off at the first opportunity. His pre-op escape attempt had been stopped by chest pain. Now there would be no angina to hold him back.

I hated the thought of discharging him so soon. Medicare had not yet forced us to trade quality care for cheap care and we kept patients hospitalized for a week after heart surgery. With Billy, that was just not an option. Visions of white lines were dancing in his head and I knew he'd be out the door the first chance he got. Better to discharge him early with medications and instructions than to let him bolt early with nothing. He'd probably take all the pain pills at once and throw the rest away but I had to give him the benefit of the doubt.

After considerable thought, I came up with a plan that would keep Billy inside at least one more day. I ran it by Allan Handley, the Cardiac Fellow nominally in charge of VA hearts, and he agreed. Some risk was involved but less than any alternative we could imagine.

"You see these wires, Billy?" I asked, pointing to where they burrowed into his body, through the skin below his rib cage. The wires had been hidden under a dressing. He hadn't seen them until I removed the bandages and dangled them before his eyes.

"Holy shee-it, doc, what are them things? How deep they go?" Billy asked. "Hell, I look like one a them talking dolls. Like, you know, you pull you the wire and the doll says, 'Momma,' or something?"

"They go all the way to your heart, Billy," I said. "All the way to your heart and you cannot leave the hospital with them dangling out of you like . . . uhh, like one of those dolls." I explained to Billy that, except for their exposed tips, the pacer wires were covered with a thin layer of clear plastic. One bared end of each was bent over and sewn directly to the heart before closing the chest. The other ends were brought through the skin, where they could be hooked up to an external pacemaker. Early after heart surgery, it was often necessary to increase the heart rate. Temporary pacer wires, like those hanging out of Billy, let us do that quickly and reliably.

I was glad Billy was impressed that the wires were attached to his heart. If he bolted with them hanging out, they'd become infected and the bugs would follow their tracts right down into his chest. Then I'd see him in the ER, with his incision leaking pus. We'd have to operate to drain the purulence and bathe his heart in antibiotics. But, even with proper surgery, infections like that were often fatal.

"I'll tell you what. Billy," I said. "Usually these wires don't come out until the sixth day after surgery and then you'd go home the day after that. I'll take them out today, just your fourth day post-op, and let you go home tomorrow afternoon, if everything is okay in the morning. But only if you promise me you won't leave before then. Do we have a deal?"

"Hell yes, doc," he said.

"And you promise? You really promise? If I take them out today, you won't try to leave until I give you the okay tomorrow afternoon?"

"I promise, doc. I surely do promise." His head was bobbing up and down and I believed him.

There was always a small risk of tearing the thin-walled atrium, to which the wires were sutured, no matter how gently they were pulled loose. That risk would be increased slightly by early removal, before potential bleeding points were well stuck down with adhesions. Allan Handley and I agreed to accept that risk. As long as Billy bled in the hospital, we could get him to surgery fast and solve the problem safely. If he took off with the wires in place, a fatal infection would be almost inevitable.

I made morning rounds, worked through the morning scut list, saw consults, attended meetings, made afternoon rounds, saw an ER patient, and worked through the evening scut list. It was nearly 2AM before I got back to Billy with enough time to remove his pacer wires.

Painting Billy's skin, where the wires came through, with brownish-yellow Betadine, I wasted my breath lecturing him about cocaine and coronaries. I practically begged him to come to the outpatient clinic in a week and keep the drug rehab appointment I'd made for him. I listed danger signs of a bleed, like dizziness, shortness of breath or cold clammy skin, on a piece of paper, along with my name, beeper number and home phone number. I encouraged him to call me with any problem or even just to talk, any time, day or night. But the rapport of our earlier talks was gone. Billy was preoccupied, not really listening and providing only perfunctory responses.

After cutting the sutures that held the wires to the skin, I pulled with gently increasing pressure on first one wire and then the other. Each one slid through easily at first, coming taut as I took out the slack. Then I began to feel Billy's heart tugging against the wire from the other end. With my eyes closed to increase the sensitivity of my fingers, I gradually increased the pressure on the pulsing wire. When the weak suture holding the pacer wire broke or the bent-over end under the suture straightened out and slipped through, the tension came off. After feeling the release, I easily slid the freed up end out through the skin.

I watched Billy for a while looking for signs of an atrial tear. Billy lay quietly offering nothing. Finally I had to say it.

"Billy, I just feel like you're so eager to get out of here because you can't wait to go back to shoving your life up your nose again. Am I wrong?"

He wouldn't look me in the eye and was silent for a while. I waited him out and finally he turned to me and said, "All I can say honestly, doc, is . . . if I do manage to stay off . . . it'll be because of you."

"If you feel tempted, Billy, and you will," I said, "call me and we'll talk you through it."

He nodded, a little teary-eyed, and I figured that was the best I was going to do. Then I headed wearily for my own ICU bed, just a few yards from Billy's.

Shaleena was charge nurse that night, as usual. She glared at me and I ignored her, pulling off my shoes and slumping onto the thin mattress. I set my little portable alarm clock for one hour and fell immediately into a troubled asleep. I dreamed that Billy was tottering on a high ledge outside the window of a skyscraper, threatening to jump. In my dream, I climbed out on the ledge to stop him when a sudden high wind came shrieking out of nowhere and blew us both off into space.

The shrieking wind turned out to be my alarm clock and it jerked me out of bed just as we began to fall. I must have yelled because the nurses looked at me strangely. Slowly overcoming my vertigo, I released a death grip on the edge of the bed, rubbed the sleep out of my eyes and dragged myself over to Billy's cubicle. Feeling for his pulse, in the dark, I noted that his skin was cold and clammy. Turning on the light, I saw that he was pale and restless, awake but confused and babbling.

His blood pressure was only moderately low but decreased with inspiration instead of increasing as it should – *pulses paradoxus.*

I didn't need a chest X-ray or an echocardiogram to confirm that there was fluid under pressure, surrounding and compressing Billy's heart - *cardiac tampanade.*

The fluid was almost surely blood from the pulled wires. This was the risk Allan and I had considered and accepted. No one would fault me for the bleed and Billy would suffer no harm, as long it was handled promptly. He wasn't in serious trouble yet. The blood pressure wasn't too bad. But confusion meant cardiac output was low and the brain lacked adequate blood flow.

If the bleeding wasn't stopped, it would squeeze the heart more. Blood pressure and brain flow would drop lower. Billy would go into shock and finally cardiac arrest. This must have been an "upper" night in Shaleena's ICU. She and the other nurses were laughing and chattering in high pitched voices. If I hadn't slept in the unit and checked on Billy myself, I'd have found him dead on morning rounds. Like the others I'd found, the chart would show normal vital signs that had to be bogus.

I had to get him to the OR as quickly as possible, re-open his chest and find the bleeding point where the atrium tore as the wire was pulled out. It would be a tiny tear with minimal but persistent bleeding. A simple stitch or two would stop it and Billy would be out of danger.

The operation to cure him would be nothing. Getting him to surgery in time was everything.

Adrenaline pumping, I hurried out of Billy's cubicle and ran for one of the gurneys near the ICU entrance. I yelled for the nurses to call the Cardiac Fellow and the OR and tell them I was bringing Billy to re-open emergently for cardiac tampanade.

A younger nurse, not one of the usual crew, rushed over to help me. But Shaleena's order pulled her back like a jerked leash on a small dog.

Very slowly, Shaleena sauntered forward with a satisfied smile. She spoke clearly and distinctly, trying to project authority. Only a touch of her usual shrillness crept through.

"I just checked that patient and he doing fine. Maybe his blood pressure a tiny tad low but that no big thing. Din't I just check him?" she asked, looking back at the other nurses. All of them nodded except the new girl who flushed with embarrassment.

"I think you pulling some kind of stunt to make our unit look bad, pretending we missed something and then pretending to fix it," she said. You not taken that boy nowhere – not until all the proper forms be filled out and I get an okay from the Cardiac Fellow."

I knew that she was intentionally goading me, hoping I'd say something she could report and use to get me in trouble. Unfortunately, the knowledge didn't do me a damn bit of good.

I snapped and was appalled to hear myself say, "Listen you stupid bitch, get on the fucking phone and make the calls or this man is going to die right before your horrified eyes."

Then she actually chuckled, picked up a pen and pad and said, "I am writing down what you say and I can't wait to see what Dr. Jefferson say about it."

The new nurse made another attempt to help me with Billy but Shaleena once again stopped her in her tracks. "And you, girl, better get away from there quick less you want the nursing supervisor to hear how you gone against my orders."

The ICU regulars giggled and whispered to each other; enjoying the Shaleena Show; watching her put the smartass young doctor in his place.

I had to pick Billy up in my arms and move him to the gurney alone. The cocaine had melted him like a candle on a hot stove. In spite of the pre-op improvement in nourishment, Billy weighed no more than if he'd been wax.

I wheeled him out of the unit, at a dead run, repeating my order to notify the Fellow and the OR. No one tried to get in my way and, over my shoulder, I saw Shaleena finally pick up the phone.

I made the twenty minute trip in under ten, almost losing Billy around one corner. It was lucky I moved fast. I found out later that Shaleena had not been on the phone to the OR. She had called VA security about the crazy resident kidnapping a patient. I never saw them and don't want to think what might have happened if I had.

Arriving in the OR reception area, I expected to find a team of nurses waiting to rush Billy into surgery. Instead, there was no one at all. "Fuck," I screamed, realizing that Shaleena hadn't made the calls. I looked at Billy, who was paler than before and dripping with cold sweat. The pressure around his heart needed release or Billy was going to die, but I couldn't do it alone.

Just then, the big double doors to the sterile area swung open and out walked Billy's salvation and mine, in the form of Holt McDuff. Holt was just finishing up one of his all night emergencies. He was as surprised to see me as I was delighted to see him.

"Whachu doing here, Yankee Boy? They starting hearts at 3 AM these days?"

Holt wasn't a heart surgeon, but he knew about cardiac tampanade and the OR staff knew him. I filled him in and, in minutes, he'd organized everything and everyone. Then we were in an OR, rushing to get Billy prepped and draped for surgery.

Holt insisted that I be the primary surgeon. He assisted as I slashed through Billy's healing incision and subcutaneous sutures with one firm cut all the way down to the bone. Then I quickly snipped and yanked out the wires holding his sternum together. With the chest opened, Billy's heart was no longer compressed and his blood pressure rose to normal. Minutes later, his pale skin turned pink and the cold sweat dissipated. Billy was going to be just fine.

By the time the Fellow was located, changed, scrubbed and rushed into the room, it was all over. We'd found the bleeding site easily and I'd stopped it with a single stitch. Allan stood with the anesthesiologist, at the patient's head. I gave him my report as Holt and I closed Billy's chest.

"Congratulations," the Fellow said. "Dr. Kirkwood's going to be very pleased. You made the diagnosis and took decisive action to resolve the problem. And don't worry about the decision to pull the wires early. I'll make it clear to Dr. Kirkwood that you discussed that plan with me and I approved it. If there's any question about it, I'll take full responsibility, but there won't be. We figured that, if there was a bleed, it could be handled safely, and we were right. Any problems getting Billy over here?"

"Just what you'd expect," I said. "Shaleena tried to stop me and never called you or the OR to say we were coming. If Holt hadn't been here, when Billy and I rolled up, there might not have been a happy ending."

"The situation in that unit is a disgrace," Allan said. "But this incident should put an end to it. I don't care what her relationship with Jefferson is. There's no way he'll be able to protect her after this. She nearly caused this boy's death and that's a fact no one can deny."

"You don't think so?" Holt snorted. "Just watch and see. Shaleena will come through this without a scratch. That's for sure. That's for shit-sure. It's our Yankee Boy's skin that I'm worried about." But Holt didn't look worried. He was smiling and I couldn't understand why.

"No way," the Fellow said confidently, "She nearly killed the patient and Cooper saved his life. He'll be a hero. Okay, VA nursing jobs are civil service so they can't fire her, but she'll be out of the ICU for sure. Maybe someone new can finally get that unit in shape."

The chest was nearly closed and Holt backed off from the table as I finished up alone. He was shaking his head as he removed his gown and gloves. "You boys are about to learn a hard lesson of life. I just hope it's a lesson you survive, son." He spoke gravely but a secret smile still flirted behind his eyes.

After Holt left there was a moment of uncomfortable silence.

"Don't worry, Cooper," the Fellow said. "You did everything right. There's no way this can come back to bite you on the butt." Then he followed Holt out the door.

I placed the dressing on Billy's incision and helped get him onto the gurney for the trip to the University ICU. One of the nurses was Holt's regular scrub. She and I both knew Holt better than the Fellow.

"So, are you worried?" she asked me.

"Hey, was Custer worried about a few Indians?" I was trying for casual bravado but I think my voice cracked.

"Yeah, well it might be okay. Dr. McDuff isn't always right. And you really were a hero." She squeezed my arm and gave me an encouraging smile, but her eyes were saying what she really thought, which was, "You are so screwed."

CHAPTER 11

BILLY WAS WIDE awake and breathing on his own within a few hours of surgery. We spent the rest of the night at the U but had to return to the VA the next morning. Billy didn't need more ICU care and he certainly didn't need Shaleena. I placed him where he'd been pre-op, with Bertha Henshaw and her team. They had doted on Billy before his surgery and were delighted to have him back. Sharon Bronson, who'd cried when I'd taken Billy for his bypass, greeted him with a sisterly kiss on the cheek. With his fresh sternal incision, Billy needed hospital care for at least a few more days. If Bertha and Sharon Bronson couldn't keep him inside, at least no pacer wires were dangling out of his chest. After this minor procedure no pacing would be needed.

No sooner did I get Billy settled than I was called to Dr. Jefferson's office. I'd never been there before. I was surprised to find that not one bit of furnishing was VA issue. There was wall to wall carpeting, mahogany furniture, velvet curtains, recessed lighting and antebellum oil paintings of mounted confederate officers. The decorating had clearly been to Jefferson's taste and at his expense.

Jefferson sat rigidly erect, enthroned in a maroon leather executive chair. Flanking him was the CEO of the hospital, a bald bespectacled gnome of a man, and Christine Dugan, the butch ex-army colonel chief of nursing. It occurred to me that, if Jefferson was trading negative drug test reports for Shaleena's sexual favors, Colonel Dugan might well have been an enthusiastic participant. Her cooperation, at least, would be needed to falsify results.

Isolated in a solitary straight-backed chair, I faced this triumvirate across a desk not quite as large as a small aircraft carrier. The absurd old adage popped into my mind, "When rape is inevitable, relax and enjoy it." For some bizarre reason, the idiotic thought gave me comfort. The result here was certainly a foregone conclusion and there was no point in fighting.

The CEO and Dugan stood silently frowning as Jefferson sat erect in his chair for a long dramatic pause. He then proceeded, in aristocratically modulated tones, to carve me a new anal orifice.

"Nevah in the proud history of this institution has any resident evah been so crass, rude, abusive and offensive as to refer to one of ow-ah devoted nurses as a . . . ," he paused here to refer to Shaleena's incident report, "a . . . 'stupid bitch.' Do you deny using such language, young man?"

I just said, "Nope." Damned if I was going to, sir, him. It wouldn't do any good anyway.

"And do you deny that you contravened that nurses rightful authority by removing a patient from the intensive cay-ah unit and the very premises of this hospital, without completing the appropriate forms and without the approval of the Cardiac Fellow or any responsible staff person?"

Enough was enough. "Look, Dr. Jefferson, if I hadn't taken Billy straight to the OR, he would have died. You can check with Dr. McDuff and the Fellow. I'm sure they'll both . . ."

"You did not an-sah my question, young man," he interrupted, yelling and leaning forward with both hands flat on the desk. I suddenly realized that his accent was a precise match for that cartoon congress-chicken, "Senator Foghorn Leghorn." Unfortunately I could think of no way to turn this insight to my advantage. "Did you ow-ah did you not," Blah, Blah, Blah. I think you get the idea.

It ended up, of course, with me being expelled from the VA and told, in no uncertain terms, never to darken its doors again. Pausing as I left his office, I turned back to face Jefferson one last time. I didn't want to say anything that could be used against me later, but I didn't want to just meekly slink away either.

"You probably tell yourself it's a big secret, Dr. Jefferson, but everyone at both hospitals knows and, sooner or later—too late to help me but sooner or later—it's all going to come crashing down and bury you in shame and disgrace. I just wish I could be there to see it." I turned and walked out, making a conscious effort to keep my shoulders back and head high. He came to the door of his office sputtering and yelling threats. My only reaction was a smile he couldn't see, because I just kept walking.

As I was leaving the VA, wondering what to do next, my beeper went off, ordering me to Dr. Kirkwood's office. Marge, his primly efficient and very protective secretary, greeted me with sympathetic eyes. She let The Wire know I was there. He came out immediately, shook my hand, patted my shoulder and led me, with funereal gravitas, into the room where the corpse of my career would be gently embalmed.

His office was larger than Jefferson's but geared for efficiency, not ostentation. There was an unadorned conference table, where a half-dozen people could work on documents or specimens; a long bank of wall lighting for viewing X-rays; and a projector for the heart films taken by cardiologists. The walls were mostly hidden behind extensive shelves laden with well-worn texts and current journals. Meticulously organized mounds of scientific papers, charts and reports swamped the surface of a sturdy oak desk. A wide sofa would double comfortably as a bed for prolonged hospital vigils.

The Wire's swivel chair was of graciously aged and oiled brown leather, spider-webbed with stress lines and polished pale with use. It exuded a dignified air of faded elegance, far from the flashy arrogance of Jefferson's shiny throne. The office was the comfortable command center of a born leader with no need to impress.

The Wire led me to the sofa, offered coffee which I declined and sat heavily beside me. He took a deep breath, frowned sadly, turned towards me and said, "I'm sorry, Cooper. There's nothing I can do."

It was the way he taught us to break the news to grieving families. Express your sorrow. Give them the bad news. Wait for them to regain their composure. Then provide the pertinent details. At least he didn't have to talk me into an autopsy. The cause of death, in my case, was as cryptic as a small puckered hole between the eyes and a head with the back blown out.

Where Jefferson's antagonism had left me defiant, Dr. Kirkwood's compassion opened the gates of my anguish. The truth is I nearly lost it. My eyes began to burn and my throat closed up. He saw me blinking and, to my eternal shame, handed me a handkerchief from the coffee table.

"I've talked with Holt and with Allan and, for whatever comfort it gives you, there is no question in my mind that you handled an urgent situation in the optimal way. You did use some intemperate language but, under the circumstances, even that is understandable. You saved that boy's life. Unfortunately, it must be at the cost of your career."

He repeated what Holt had pointed out several weeks before. The VA rotations were an integral part of the general and cardiac programs. Expulsion from the VA precluded my completing either one.

"I'll try to place you in another program, Cooper, but I don't want to hold out false hope. At your level there is a huge surplus of impeccably qualified applicants with no blemishes of any kind on perfect records. No matter what I say, it's highly unlikely that any program director will take a chance on a resident barred from any hospital for any reason. They're going to feel that, where there's smoke, there must be at least a small fire. In their shoes, without my personal knowledge . . . frankly I'd feel the same.

"If the situation changes so that you can again participate in the care of the VA patients, I will gladly take you back into the general surgery program. I will also guarantee you a cardiac surgery Fellowship. You have the technical ability, the intelligence, the dedication and even that rarest quality, the energy, to become a fine heart surgeon. But . . ." He looked away and shook his head.

Of course, his compliments made me feel even worse, if that were possible. I could think of nothing to say but, "Thanks for everything you've done for me, Dr. Kirkwood, and . . . tried to do. Not many people ever have the chance to be part of a team like yours . . . even for a short time. It's been a great honor."

We left it that I would go home that day and wait to hear from Dr. Kirkwood. I would obviously have to skip my last week on VA hearts. The Fellow would tough it out for a week and actually care for those patients. He was responsible for them anyway and had operated on most.

Meanwhile, Dr. Kirkwood would decide whether I'd work the next two rotations. They would end in September with the academic year and then my career would be over.

When I called Katy, she couldn't believe I was leaving the hospital so early. Since our single night of lusty reconciliation, we had drifted steadily apart. Her job at the U remained on hold awaiting the clearance of some credentials. With frustration over the delay and too much time for Katy to brood, our love was melting like asphalt in the Alabama sun.

I thought the latest crisis might help heal the rift between us. We would have to work together on a new plan for our future. If Katy ever loved me, she would surely stand by me now . . . now, when I needed her the most.

"I should have known something like this would happen," Katy said. We were sitting on the living room couch when I gave her the bad news. She slammed her balled fists onto her bare thighs, jumped up and began pacing. She was wearing cut-off jeans and a black T-shirt. I couldn't take my eyes off of her but wished I could mute the volume.

"You pulled the same kind of crap that time in Boston and nearly got your ass kicked out of med school then and there," Katy said. "You always have to be the big hero, don't you? You never take the time to think for two seconds what your latest grandstand glory play might mean in practical terms."

"Katy, you were with me that night in Boston. You know I had to put that tube in that old woman's chest. You know she would have died without it." I spoke quietly, trying to use reason. But reason means more to a charging rhino than it does to an angry redhead.

"And you knew that medical students were not allowed to place chest tubes," she spat back. "But, even back then, even when you were just a med student, you were so damn cock-sure of yourself, so sure you were right. And you just had to do the right thing whatever the cost." She made quotations marks with her fingers when she said, 'the right thing.' "You haven't grown up a bit. You're just as arrogant as ever. But this time it's both our futures sacrificed to your giant ego."

I couldn't believe what I was hearing. Three years previously, back in Boston, we'd been taking care of a fresh post-op heart. The patient was an elderly woman, doing well until her blood pressure plummeted and wouldn't come up, even with massive doses of epi. We repeatedly paged the staff man, Dr. Orkey, but he wasn't responding. Orkey was an obese bully, known for verbally abusing nurses. He had a high Porky Pig type voice and was known as Dr. Porky.

There were no breath sounds on the right and the old woman was a heavy smoker. She had severe emphysema and I knew just what had happened. A torn lung was pumping air into the chest: a tension pneumothorax. The pressure from the leak had collapsed the right lung and pushed the heart to the left. This acutely bent the big veins leading to the heart and blocked cardiac filling. The empty heart had nothing to pump, which was why the blood pressure was crashing.

All the epi in the world would not help. There was only one way to save her. A tube through the chest wall could suction off the leaked air and relieve the high pressure. The lung would re-expand. The heart would resume its normal position, fill with blood easily and pump effectively. Blood pressure would be promptly restored.

Katy had been the nurse in charge and she was the one responsible. It was against the rules for me to do the procedure, but I had seen it done and was sure I knew the technique. Katy resisted at first but, when the old lady was clearly dying, she agreed to help me put the tube through the chest wall. It hung up on a rib for a couple of extremely scary seconds but finally slipped in, much to my relief.

We were elated when the blood pressure quickly came up and we knew the old woman would be okay. Then Dr. Orkey showed up. A lowly med student and a nurse had saved his patient's life while he was out of touch. That didn't make Dr. Porky look too good. He preferred the theory that the tube had never been needed. He was screaming at Katy, with his finger in her face, when I physically stepped between them. I wouldn't back off and unfortunately I think I scared him a little. I took full responsibility for the tube and that only made him madder. He swore to see I'd never get my MD and, for a while, it looked like he'd keep his word.

Fortunately the torn lung continued to leak for several days. The escaped air bubbled harmlessly from the tube instead of staying in the chest under tension. Those bubbles vindicated me and saved me from expulsion. But leaving the ICU that night, with Dr. Porky screaming, it seemed to me and Katy too, that my future was circling the drain. She also knew I was on scholarship and dead broke without my stipend.

Later that night, we met outside the hospital for the very first time. Katy joined me at Jacob Wirth's, just a block from the medical center. It was the oldest restaurant in Boston, famed for its sawdust covered floors and German sausages. When Katy took my hand across the table, an unexpected jolt of sexual energy nearly knocked us both out of our chairs. We looked into each others stunned eyes and couldn't get out of there fast enough. Without waiting for the food to come and without a word, we jumped up. Hand in hand we slipped on the sawdust trying to get through the door. Grabbing onto each other we barely managed to keep our balance. We laughed hysterically all the way to Katy's car.

Bursting into her apartment, we left a trail of clothing on the path to Katy's bed. The sex was primal and unrefined. Our orgasms were seismic events, registering on Richter scales throughout the Northeast. We fell in lust that very first night. Love followed shortly. I couldn't believe Katy was now saying that I'd been wrong back then.

"Look, Katy, if you're saying the two incidents are similar and that they both say something pretty basic about me, I guess you're right. But isn't that part of why you fell in love with me? Wasn't the guy who broke the rules—the guy who ran out of Jacob Wirth's with you that night—wasn't he the guy you fell in love with? Wasn't he the guy who did the right thing and said, fuck the risk?" I mimicked her by making quote marks with my fingers around "the right thing." In retrospect, that might not have helped.

"Yeah, well this time the risk fucked you and it fucked me too and how do I know you were even right this time? I do not believe, for one minute, that they could or would kick you out of the VA and Kirkwood's program if you didn't do anything wrong." She made that statement in a clear firm voice, leaning over and looking down at me as I sat on the couch. I looked up into her fiery eyes and believed she really meant it. She thought I had screwed up and gotten what I deserved.

Her words stung like a frozen whip. My mouth opened but nothing came out. I swallowed whatever it was I had thought to say, stood up carefully like a drunk, and walked unsteadily out the door. I kept hoping she'd come running out to stop me, say she hadn't really meant it . . . but she didn't. I slumped into the car and headed for The Recovery Room, a bar and restaurant across the street from the U. It was a resident's hangout and about the only place I knew, outside the hospitals.

Behind the bar was a huge salt water aquarium. There was a yellow ribbon eel, a giant black ghost, two huge lion fish and something disgusting sucking its way around the inside of the tank. It's big round mouth had the apparent function and approximate size of an industrial vacuum cleaner. I sat there silently, brooding and drinking boilermakers of cheap bar Scotch and Budweiser on tap. Other residents came and went. I avoided looking at them and they pretended not to see me. News of my disgrace had spread like a plague. No one wanted to be infected. That suited me fine. I was busy wallowing in self pity and wanted no distractions. All that was missing was a raven to croak "Nevermore" each time I asked if I would ever be a heart surgeon

Lacking a raven, I focused on the aquarium fish, ceaselessly searching for a way through the glass, never understanding that escape meant death. My prospects back in high school had been as dull, predictable and pointless as a fish circling a tank. Thanks to the wrestling scholarship, I had broken through the glass, only to flop around for a while in air I couldn't breath and finally . . . to drown. Poor, poor, pitiful me. I was starting to understand how my father drowned in booze and misery after my mother left. There was definitely a seductive sweetness to the combined escapes of excessive alcohol and morbid self-pity.

Eventually I got so drunk I actually forgot to feel bad. At that point the fish analogy seemed less profound than funny. *"In vino veritas?"* perhaps. But what was the Latin for, "In boilermakers bullshit?" The more inebriated I got the more humorous it seemed. I was actually laughing out loud when I noticed Bo at the bar beside me. I turned my head and there was Roberta. They had me surrounded.

"Glub, glub, I'm drinking like a fish," I said, and rocked so hard with laughter I nearly fell off of the stool.

"Come on now," Bo said. "It's time to get gone, buddy. Roberta and me'll carry you on home."

"You got no sensa humor. You know that? And anyway I don't wanna go home," I said, with some difficulty. "I'd just be a fish outa water there." This started me laughing again. I downed a shot, finished the mug of beer in front of me and tried to order more.

Bo waved the bartender off and Roberta said, "Really, Cooper. You've had quite enough. Katy must be terribly worried about you."

"Katy thinks I fucked up," I said. "Maybe she's right. None of the other residents would flush it all down the crapper like I did: not for someone like Billy."

"If Katy thinks you screwed up, she's wrong," Roberta said. "And you're not the only one who would have done right either. Although others might have done it in a more judicious manner."

"Oh, yeah?" I shot back. "Well I haven't seen anyone else stand up to Shaleena or Jefferson. Have you?" There was no answer to that and I took the opportunity to try for another shot and beer.

"Come on, you gotta get on home now, Cooper." Bo started trying to help me off of the bar stool.

I shrugged him off. "I'm not going home, Bo. What I do not need right now is Katy telling me how badly I have screwed the pooch. I am already well aware of that." Actually I got stuck on the "well aware" part which, for some reason, seemed very difficult to enunciate.

I vaguely remember Bo and Roberta half helping and half dragging me off of the bar stool and later pulling off my shoes after maneuvering me onto a couch. In the morning, nothing had changed except that, in addition to all my other problems, I had managed to poison myself.

All the brain cells I had killed the night before were sailing around in flames behind my eyes, like a fiery fleet of tiny Viking funerals. My acid-singed esophagus, ulcerated gastric mucosa and distended large bowel were competing to see which part of my GI tract could make me the most miserable.

A note on the floor by the couch informed me that I was in Bo's "luxury bachelor pad." Katy's car, which I'd driven to the bar, had been dropped off at my house so I wouldn't wake up and try to drive it. Katy had been told not to expect me until the following morning.

I stood as long as I could in the icy spray of Bo's makeshift shower-bathtub with its moldy plastic curtain. It's not that I wanted a cold shower; it's just that Bo's water heater, if he had one, wasn't working. After the shower I found some instant coffee and a pot in the roach-infested kitchenette. The coffee gave me enough strength to eat some stale bread with peanut butter and butter. Peanut butter is a good thing anytime, anyplace, anywhere and, contrary to prevailing opinion, it is not improved by jelly. It may have saved my life that morning, for whatever that was worth, which didn't seem much at the time.

Bo's living room was small and square. Warped wood and cement block shelves lined the walls. Three mismatched folding chairs almost surrounded a card table. A large bright yellow plastic bag bled beans from under a duct tape wound dressing onto the linoleum floor. The ceiling was claustrophobically low. Less than a foot in front of the hemorrhaging beanbag chair loomed an ancient wooden TV. It must have weighed as much as a compact car with a screen the size of a driver's license. On top of the TV was a surprisingly decent turntable, two speakers and a stack of vinyl records. Several of the album covers featured two hillbilly looking guys with the unlikely names of Flatt and Scruggs.

I sat at the card table and used a telephone on the floor to call Katy. The phone rang and rang, but no one answered. I watched some daytime TV, missed a chance to win a small fortune on Dialing for Dollars, and tried calling Katy again. Still no answer.

I paged Bo and he called back nearly an hour later.

"This is my phone so either it's you or the po-lice is calling 'bout a dead idiot, with turrible bad breath, in a pool of puke on my living room floor." That was how he greeted me.

"Bo . . . Bo thanks for . . ."

"Forget it, Cooper. I'm busy as a small dog in a big yard. Whaddaya need?"

"I called Katy to come get me and there was no answer. I don't know where your house is, so I don't know where I am and I don't know how to get home." Realizing how pathetic I sounded, I added, "Look, I'm sorry. I'm just not thinking too clearly right now."

"There's a beat-to-shit bicycle leaning against my back porch," Bo said, and proceeded to give me directions from his house to mine. It was nearly mid-day when I left Bo's and the damp heat must already have climbed to over one hundred degrees. My shirt was soaked by the time I got the bike to the street. Thank God, the trip was mostly downhill but even the breeze generated by coasting did little to help. The sticky-wet, sauna-like air was barely breathable.

It seemed incredible that even a single, human being voluntarily lived in the Deep South before God blessed mankind with air-conditioners. It should have been an uninhabited wasteland, like the great deserts of North Africa, but history assures us that people actually did live there. No wonder the resulting society talked slow, moved slow, thought slow and found its ultimate cultural expression in the creation of the Southern Elevator. Well, that was how I felt at the time.

Arriving home, Katy's little VW bug was conspicuously absent. This should not have been surprising. She hadn't answered the phone so there was no reason to expect her to be home. Logically the big empty space on the curb out front meant nothing.

As soon as I saw it I knew.

Katy was gone for good,

CHAPTER 12

THE NOTE WAS taped to the fridge.

I called Boston and they said I could have my old job back. We need some time apart to think where we're going if anywhere. We could have talked about it last night but you decided to get drunk instead, ASSHOLE! I want a man who puts me first in his life. You don't. You never did and you never will. Don't call me. When I'm ready to talk I'll call you.

Katy
PS - I took all but $200 out of our bank account. You can have the furniture and all the other stuff.

The tone was harsh and that didn't surprise me. Katy had never been the touchy-feely type. At least her message was clear. Whatever we'd had together was as dead as my dream of becoming a heart surgeon. Going after her or trying to change her mind would be pathetic and futile. Katy was gone and I swore I would never be dumb enough to fall in love again. If I ever felt a need for that kind of pain, I'd just slam a car door on my hand. That is if I had a car door, which I didn't, because Katy had taken the VW.

I thought I could get along without love but I needed transportation. Bo's bike had gotten me home, but that had mostly been downhill. After two years of sleep deprivation, cafeteria food, and no time or energy for exercise, I wasn't in the shape I'd been in as a wrestler. Bo's antique bike was your basic kid's model: heavy metal tubing with foot brakes and no gears. The uphill stretches felt like I was climbing an endless sand dune. Even Sisyphus couldn't have kept that up through the eternity of an Alabama summer.

On the positive side, it was just barely possible that I could afford a car. I would keep getting paychecks, at least until my vacation and sick time was over. If The Wire let me work the last two rotations of the year, I'd have income right up to September. By then I hoped to have a plan for the future, other than abject poverty.

Meanwhile, I had about twenty dollars in my wallet, beer, cold cuts, cheese, milk and mayonnaise in the fridge, and a half a loaf of Wonder Bread and HiHo crackers in the pantry. Along with the rest of what I found in the kitchen, I figured I could survive on sandwiches, tuna fish and hot dogs until the next payday. That meant I was free to blow the 200 bucks Katy had left, my entire life savings, on a car.

Let the good times roll.

I showered again and changed into worn jeans, a white sleeveless T-shirt and sneakers. Milk and the broken remnants of some stale sugar cookies helped to settle my stomach as I checked out used car ads in the last Sunday's Birmingham News. By the time the cookies were gone, I had reviewed nearly every ad without finding a single car even close to my price range. I tried to convince myself that a good bicycle – one weighing less than Mount Rushmore and with actual gears – just might be adequate. Then suddenly, there it was. The address was only twenty minutes away by bike and, best of all, nearly all downhill. The main part of the ad read as follows:

1962 Ford pickup. Looks Rough Runs Good. $150 or best offer.

My luck was finally starting to change.

A half hour later, I was staring in awe at what appeared to be a fossilized pickup truck entirely encased in concrete. It squatted obscenely, in a barren front yard, among several large rusting hulks of unidentifiable machinery. The house itself was of indeterminate color and about the size of a large shoebox. A fat Basset Hound looked on mournfully from a patch of shade by the front porch.

"The truck seems to be entirely encased in concrete," I said.

"Well, she is a tad dustsome," said Mr. Rutledge, the proud owner. He was a small, middle-aged man with buzz-cut hair and a neatly trimmed, pencil-thin mustache. He wore threadbare overalls, glazed with concrete to match the truck, no shirt and a John Deere baseball cap. "But, don't fret yourself. It's just on accounta I been hauling concrete in that there truck since it were new boughten. That's why I said she 'looks rough,' but don't fret yourself. She do 'run good,' like I also said. You got my word on that, as a white man and a Christian."

"Could I look at the engine, Mr. Rutledge?"

He smiled at me, as if he could tell I knew nothing about engines, and proceeded to pop the hood. I never had the money to buy a car of my own and neither did the guys I hung with in high school. Most of them did, at least, take automotive shop, but my schedule was always too full of academic courses. I was not preparing for college. Before the scholarship, college was out of the question. I was just driven, for some reason, to be or at least appear to be an educated man. I was determined to make the most of what high school offered and get as far as I could beyond that on my own.

I became a voracious and eclectic reader: everything from H.P. Lovecraft and Robert E. Howard to Ayn Rand and Saki. Although it was not a taste I shared with my hoodlum friends, I particularly loved poetry and memorized extensively from such disparate works as *The Lays of Ancient Rome*, *Barrack Room Ballads* and *The Spell of the Yukon*.

When the scholarship did come through, it had one string attached. I had to take and do well in a number of college level courses. This left even less time for classes like automotive shop. The one semester I might have managed it my best friend set the school's garage on fire.

So, as I pretended to study the engine, I really had no more idea than the Basset Hound about what I should look for. I was pleased to have something intelligent to say when I noticed that the engine was coated with oil.

"Uh, Mr. Rutledge, how come the engine is coated with oil?"

"Don't fret yourself on that," he said. "It's just on accounta I just changed the oil to get her all ready for her new owner and I done spilled some on accounta . . . I couldn't find my funnel."

Well, that made sense but, even to me, something about it just didn't ring true. I had a gut feeling that oil all over an engine could not be a good sign. But what did I know? I did need a car and this was the only one in Birmingham within my price range. Also, since the bike ride from my house had been mostly downhill, the ride back would be uphill. My shirt was already soaked through and stuck to my skin. It wasn't even noon yet and the day was getting hotter and wetter. The appearance of the truck didn't matter and the spilled oil story was perfectly plausible. I also thought it would be kind of cool to own a truck. Most important, I knew Katy would have hated it.

I glanced over at the Basset Hound. He shook his big wrinkled head vigorously, as if to say, "no." Exuberant jowls swung to and fro and elephantine ears flopped back and forth. Spittle flew and the dog whined to emphasize his warning, but I wasn't sure I could trust him. A Labrador would never lie but a Basset Hound? Maybe he just had a grudge against his owner.

I took the pickup for an uneventful spin around the block and wrote Mr. Rutledge a check for $100, which we agreed was likely to be his best offer. With Bo's bike in the back, I drove off proudly, thinking about a rifle rack for the rear window. At Bo's house, I wheeled the bike around back, dusted some concrete off its seat and left.

Pulling away, I noticed in the rear view mirror what looked like a large pool of oil by the curb in front of Bo's house. I hadn't noticed the oil when I arrived. Possibly some continuing drip-off from what Mr. Rutledge had spilled on the engine. I decided not to fret myself about it.

By the time I got home, the truck's temperature gauge was reading borderline high, the exhaust seemed a bit smoky and occasional ghostly wailing noises were emanating from under the hood. I decided to call Mr. Rutledge for reassurance and advice and was reaching for the phone when it rang.

It was Roberta.

"Cooper?" she said.

"Yeah, hey Roberta, thanks for last night. I . . ."

"No time. I'm due in the OR but you gotta hear this. Don't talk. Just listen. Richmond McDaniels is on general surgery at the VA this rotation," she said. I knew Richmond. He was a top resident and a good guy, just a year ahead of me. "He was presenting a case to their Mortality and Morbidity conference this morning, when Dr. McDuff came storming into the room. He must have just heard about you getting fired and he was . . . well you know how Holt gets sometimes. He was . . . Richmond said he was like a wild man.

"He interrupted the meeting, ignored everyone else in the room and went right for Jefferson. Richmond said it looked like Holt was going to tear Jefferson's head off and eat it. Jefferson must have thought the same. He jumped out of his chair, when he saw Holt coming, started backing up and looked like he wanted to run out of the room. But Holt was between him and the door." Roberta paused to catch her breath.

"Holy shit!" I observed thoughtfully.

"Exactly," Roberta agreed. "But that's not all. Holt got right in Jefferson's face and started yelling at him for firing you. Then Jefferson sent everyone else out of the room, but Richmond went into the storage closet next door, where he could still hear some of it. Richmond says, once they were alone, it wasn't even about you. First, Jefferson started saying how Holt's father, the sheriff, could be bribed for two or three chickens. Then Holt really lost it and asked Jefferson exactly what it was that his nanny did, when Jefferson was a little boy, to make him so 'fucked up in the head about women?' Jefferson's tone got all indignant but Richmond couldn't quite make out the words. Then Holt said, 'Well than how come you never could get a date with the same girl twice in spite of your family's money?'"

"Somehow that doesn't surprise me," I chuckled.

"Shut up," Roberta said. "I told you I don't have time. So then Jefferson said something Richmond couldn't hear again – he must've been talking low and Holt was yelling - and then Holt said, 'Well then why has your family kept that poor woman's black ass locked up in a private mental hospital ever since?'

Then Richmond couldn't hear anything for a while, until the door slammed open and he peeked out of the storage room. By then Holt was stomping off down the hall and Jefferson was watching him go. Just as Holt was about to turn the corner, Jefferson suddenly got brave. He started ranting about what an inept Sheriff Holt's father had been and finally said something like, 'We both know your precious daddy was too dumb to make a case against anyone with a brain. I believe we all did prove that.'

"Richmond said when Holt heard that, he suddenly stopped, and those big shoulders of his just hunched up like a bull about to charge. When Holt spun around, Jefferson muttered something under his breath, ducked back into the conference room and locked the door. Richmond could hear it latch. Holt came actually running down the hall and hammered at the door but the lock held. Holt slammed it with his fist, rammed it with his shoulder and called Jefferson a dirty yellow coward. Then it got really weird."

"Like it's not weird enough already," I said.

"Not like this," Roberta said. "Holt told Jefferson that no one gets away with anything and that Judgment Day was coming for him and coming soon. That's what he said, 'Judgment Day' was coming. Then he walked away a couple of steps, turned around and came back and hammered on the door again and said, 'I've seen the sign, you bastard. Your time is coming soon. I've seen the sign.' Then he stalked off down the hall."

"Holy shit!" I repeated, in case Roberta hadn't gotten the full significance of my observation the first time.

"Exactly," Roberta said again. "Richmond just told me and I thought you ought to know. I gotta go." And she was gone.

The phone rang again. Thinking it was Roberta calling back, I picked it up.

"Roberta?" I said.

"Ain't no Roberta here, asshole. You Cooper Logan?" the voice on the phone said.

"Yeah, I'm Logan. Who're you?"

"Never you mind who I am." The voice was high-pitched and effeminate with a hint of a lisp. "You best be thinking of me as your fairy fucking godfather."

"You don't sound like a fairy godfather, more like a godmother, and I don't think either one says fuck."

"Yeah, well who else would be giving you a present like a bunch a dirty pitchers a your ole pal Docta Lloyd Jefferson?"

"Why would I want dirty pictures of Dr. Jefferson?"

"Well they ain't just a Jefferson his own self. They's a him and his little pet nigger cunt. The two a them and that dyke nurse from the VA, and not just regular fucking. Not even just fancy fucking nor simple rug-munching neither. There's real kinky shit. Whips and chains kinda stuff." He laughed and I almost hung up, but I didn't. I understood right away why he was calling me. Jefferson would do anything to keep pictures like that secret. People speculating about him and Shaleena without proof was one thing. Pictures of the two of them actually doing "kinky shit" would be something else.

Using the pictures to save my career would technically be blackmail, but I wouldn't be doing it for money. Could it be wrong to use any means, even blackmail, simply for self defense?

Well, of course it could be wrong. It *would* be wrong. I knew that and I knew that this was one of those little tests that Life gives us now and then. A sort of moral and ethical pop-quiz that would show the kind of man I was and perhaps define the man I would be from then on.

I could do the right thing by hanging up on this sleazy bastard. And then everything I had worked for, hoped for, dreamed of and lost would stay lost. Or I could do the wrong thing by turning dirty pictures, racism, and Jefferson's hypocrisy to my personal advantage. A little defensive blackmail, or maybe I should call it whitemail, and my future would be pretty much guaranteed. Dr. Kirkwood had promised that, if I got back in the VA, I would have a place in his program. And not just general surgery either. He had guaranteed the golden ticket itself: a Fellowship in cardiac surgery. With Kirkwood's training, I knew I could become a first class heart surgeon.

I thought about how I'd felt doing Billy's operation. I could feel like that regularly for the rest of my life and help a lot of people. Okay, I'll admit that altruism was not my main motivation. What I loved, what I needed, was the act of doing open heart surgery. Helping people felt good. Helping Billy still felt great, even in spite of all that followed. But my driving compulsion was to walk that razor-edge between the worlds of the dead and the living. If I just wanted to help people, I could join the damn Peace Corps. And even more was at stake than my personal obsession. There was also the promise I had made to my dying father. Becoming a heart surgeon would certainly mean doing something good with my life. That would fulfill his hopes for me as well as my own dreams for my future.

Or . . . I could let those hopes and dreams stay dead; let Jefferson win; let everything I had lost, including Katy, all have been for nothing.

"Well," prompted the high-talker, "you be wanting them pitchers or you ain't?"

I'd like to say I agonized over this moral dilemma for more than a few seconds . . . but I did not.

"Yeah, I want the pictures," I said. "How do I get them?"

Minutes later I was back in my pickup, speeding recklessly to meet the man with the lisp. "Ten minutes," he had said. "Ten minutes in the front yard of the big white house behind the VA parking lot. It's nearly ten a noon now. Be there by twelve sharp or I'll be gone and so will them pitchers. You be one minute late and you won't never hear nothing from me no more. I bet Jefferson would give plenty for these pitchers his own self."

"What do you want for the pictures?" I asked. "I don't have much money."

"I'll tell you what I want when you get here, if you get here before I get gone. Now you got you nine minutes." Then he hung up.

Halfway to the hospital, steam started coming up from under the hood of my truck. I ignored it. The moaning and wailing sounds from the engine became louder and more persistent. I didn't let that slow me down either. Cars honked as I cut them off and left them behind, wallowing in a wake of choking black exhaust and whirling white waves of powdered concrete.

Approaching the hospitals with minutes to go, it looked like I just might make the deadline. Nearing the final stretch, I turned onto the busy street between the facing front walls of the VA and University hospitals. This was the street with the sky-bridge, over which I'd wheeled Billy. The U was on my right and the VA on my left. I'd have to go under the sky-bridge and take the first left after the VA. That road would take me up alongside the VA and the parking lot behind it. The next left would put me on the street with the big white house.

I never made it.

Just before the sky-bridge, Looks-Rough-Runs-Good bled its last drop of oil and screamed its death agony as pistons seized up in red-hot and swollen, un-lubricated cylinders. The pickup slammed to a stop as violent as if I'd hit a brick wall. My face smashed into the steering wheel breaking my nose which began to bleed profusely. Stumbling out of the car, with traffic screeching all around me, I saw a cop look up from writing a ticket on a car under the skyway. It was the driver's lucky day. The cop threw the folder with the unfinished ticket through his cruiser's open window and ran towards me, yelling at me to stay right where I was. I had no time for that. I'd pay a fine later or they could even put me in jail. Kirkwood would still have to honor his promise. There'd be a spot for me in his program whenever I got out.

I ran through the front door of the VA, knowing I could easily lose the cop in its confusing corridors. Pinching my nose with one hand to slow what seemed to be a massive life-threatening hemorrhage, I sped along a circuitous route past startled staff and frightened patients. Finally, I exploded out back onto a loading platform and leaped down onto the smoldering black asphalt of the parking lot. Never slowing down, I ducked low, zigging and zagging along between the rows of parked cars. By the time I reached the street behind the lot, I looked over my shoulder and saw no one in pursuit.

Glancing at my watch and gasping for breath, as I jogged across the street, I saw it was nearly noon. I would make the meeting with less than a minute to spare. There was a fence, backed by a thick hedge, around the front yard of the big house. The gate at its center was open. Plunging through the entrance, I let go of my nose. The bleeding had slowed but it ached and throbbed with a pain that made my eyes water. Wiping blood and tears with the back of my hand, I looked around for the man with the high-pitched voice and the dirty pictures.

The house had obviously been empty for years and was badly deteriorated. A sagging front door was secured with a huge rusty padlock on a broken chain. White painted walls were peeling to reveal rotten wood beneath. Ground floor windows had been boarded up and upper ones shattered by kid-thrown rocks. The front yard was a checkerboard of knee-high green weeds and brown cracked earth. The broken remnants of a lichen-covered flagstone path divided the space in front of the house into two equal segments. Each square had a large weeping willow at its center. The trunk of each tree was hidden behind a tangled curtain of hanging limbs, like the face of a madwoman behind a furious bedlam of lice-ridden hair.

Between the tree on my left and the front of the house, lying face down on blood-soaked earth, was the body of a black woman in a nurse's uniform. Approaching slowly, I saw that the back of her head was a ruin of mangled scalp, blood-soaked black hair and gelatinous grey brain matter. The macabre mess had congealed into a ghastly pulp and was pierced with thick white splinters of shattered skull. A hammer by the blasted head was matted with dark clots of blood and gummy grey goo. It was obviously the murder weapon. Her hands rested palms down on either side of her head. She must have thrown them up as she fell, trying to shield the back of her skull from the hammer.

My eyes were drawn to a watch on the back of one wrist. I had seen it before. It was the first I had seen with one of those V-shaped bezels that were popular for about fifteen minutes in the seventies. The band was heavy with bright gold and thick for a woman's wrist. The first time I saw that watch, I wondered how she could afford it on a VA nurse's salary.

Squatting beside the dead woman on the balls of my feet, I took a closer look at the exposed side of her face. Even with the skin gone plastic and waxy with death, there was no doubt of her identity. It was, or had been, Shaleena White. My very first thought was that everyone would think I had killed her. For just a second, I wondered if maybe I had smashed in her skull and then completely blocked out the memory.

I had reason to hate Shaleena and VA heart patients were safer with her dead. How many had died because of her negligence and incompetence, as Billy would have died if not for me? Assuming a competent replacement, how many lives had Shaleena's murderer saved by taking hers? I felt no remorse at her death, not even at the brutal manner in which it was accomplished.

But I knew it wasn't in me to kill her, not even in a moment of amnesia-inducing psychosis. Jefferson maybe . . . but not Shaleena. Holt had told me about her abusive husband and I could only imagine what her childhood had been like. Now Jefferson and Dugan were probably using her drug tests to force her into their pet perversions. All her life, Shaleena had been a victim herself. Maybe even Jefferson had an excuse, if Holt was right about that childhood nanny.

Squatting there next to the body, I sensed heavy movement close behind me. I turned my head, lifting my chin, as a huge man burst through the curtain of willow branches. He wore a brand new, long-sleeved camouflage suit, a stocking over his face, and was on me in less than a second. A beefy right arm snaked around my neck under my upturned chin.

The lethal choke sank deep and I knew it would be virtually unbreakable. The rubbery bulk of a massive bicep trapped the right side of my neck and the bony ridge of a forearm pressed like an iron bar on the left. Although the hold was not legal in wrestling, I knew it from my street-fighting days. My attacker's right hand would be gripping his left bicep, just behind my left shoulder. I could already feel the palm of his left hand on the back of my head. In spite of my struggles my throat was forced deeply into the vice of his bent right arm.

This choke has been called the "sleeper" hold because it compresses the carotid arteries. Blood flow to the brain is cut off and the victim quickly becomes unconscious. The hold was banned by most police departments after lawsuits over death and brain damage.

My attacker stood up, lifting me with my back pressed to his chest. He must have been a giant because my feet were far too high to stomp his. Hanging there, I certainly had no leverage to throw him.

With awareness fading fast, I kicked back hard slamming my right heel into his shin. I felt solid contact but my sneakers cushioned the blow and there was no weakening of his hold. I tried elbow strikes to his lower ribs but, my shoulders were arched too far backwards. The angle was all wrong and instead of cracking bone with the point of my elbow, I only connected with the back of my upper arm. I doubt he even felt it. With blackness looming, I tried gouging his eyes, but his face was pressed tight to the back of my neck. I just couldn't get to them.

I was losing the fight to maintain the final shreds of consciousness. I felt rage at being choked out after all my years of wrestling training. A primal fury rioted through what was left of my awareness, turning me into something between a ravening beast and a Viking berserker.

Any rational consideration of this move or that was gone. I was reduced in those final seconds to an insane grasping and clawing behind me. I felt the sharp edge of a fingernail break and pried up the pain-weakened finger. I levered it back violently and it snapped like a firecracker.

A high-pitched almost girlish scream stabbed my left ear. It was the sweetest sound I have ever heard. Then I was falling as the muscular noose around my neck went slack. I knew I had won and finally accepted the persistent embrace of oblivion.

CHAPTER 13

ACRID STINK OF smelling salts. Reflex head jerk. Spike of pain in base of skull. Snatches of conversation.

"He's awake. Haul his ass up,"

"Not till I check him."

"This is my fucking crime scene and this asshole is my fucking prisoner."

"Until I check him, this asshole is my fucking patient."

Supine on the ground; wrists trapped behind me; can't feel fingers; eyelids forced open; laser light burns one retina, then the other. Blurry paramedic face floats too close to mine. Twist away. Bump nose. Searing agony forces focus. Someone's sorry. Distorted fragments of orders and questions like a vinyl 45 at 33 rpm.

"Follow . . . finger . . . eyes . . . your name . . . year is it . . . month . . . country . . . state . . . president?"

Cranial nerve function tests. Orientation to person, place and time. Ignore all that. Think what happened. Flashes of memory.

Wrecking the truck. Breaking my nose. Cop chasing me. Shaleena murdered (I'll be blamed). Choked from behind. Breaking the finger. Surviving.

I was on my back, hands cuffed behind me. My shoulders ached and my weight forced the metal cuffs into bruised flesh. I needed the pressure off my wrists. "I'm okay," I said. "Let me up."

"You see, he's just dandy." A blocky balding man in a cheap brown suit, white shirt and no tie, shouldered the paramedic aside. He stuck stubble roughened jowls in my face, hooked his hands under my arms and jerked me to my feet. He was short but powerfully built: Grumpy the Dwarf on steroids. He smelled like the ghosts of dead cigars in a small cheap hotel room.

Shaky on my feet I looked around. We were by the entrance to the yard, nearly out on the sidewalk. My struggle with the killer must have carried us there from where he first grabbed me. Glancing behind me, through the open gate, I saw a clutch of the curious: nurses, techs and residents. Roberta was there, calling my name.

"Cooper! Cooper!" She was trying to squirm her way past a cop standing guard by yellow crime-scene tape. "Cooper, what can I do? Who should I call? Do you have family or . . . or a lawyer?"

"Roberta, call Holt, Doctor McDuff. Tell him I need his help. And tell him I didn't kill her." I don't know what made me ask for Holt. It just came out. He did tell me that his father had been a sheriff and that some of the city cops knew him. I was sure I could count on Holt, for good advice if nothing else.

Grumpy spun me around and shoved me hard towards Shaleena's body. Still woozy and off balance with the handcuffs, I stumbled and nearly fell. Two uniformed policemen grabbed my arms and held me roughly between them. I recognized one as the traffic cop who chased me when the truck died. He must have tracked me down, seen Shaleena's body and called in the others.

Suddenly a hand was pulling down on the back of my neck and Grumpy the muscular dwarf-cop was pressing his face against mine. I could feel his spittle-flecked breath on my ear as he whispered at me with a sandpaper voice no one else could hear.

"You best fess up, boy. We know you kilt the nigger. Neighbor seen you hammering her head in. Maybe you had you good cause. Was she getting uppity, given you attitude? NWA was she? Nigger With Attitude? Shee-it, I'd a kilt her my own self. Can't hardly blame you. Or maybe you just wanted you a slice of dark meat and she done fell in love? She want you to bring her home to Momma? Now, wouldn't that make Momma proud? Or was she gonna cause some other kind a trouble? Look at her, boy!"

He released my neck, moved his face away and pulled me towards the body by my bloody shirt-front. "You done a fair to middling job on her head; I'll give you that." He laughed. "Now, who is she? What's her name, boy? Why'd you kill her?"

He started getting angry when I didn't respond and louder as I jerked my head away from his sour breath. I didn't know whether to talk to him or not. It's easy to say I should have demanded a lawyer, but I was afraid that would make me look guilty. I had no money so I'd have gotten a public defender. Probably some kid fresh out of law school. He'd know just enough to piss off the cops and make everything even worse. Then I'd be stuck in jail while the wheels of Alabama justice ground away at the speed of a Southern elevator.

If I told the truth and they believed me, maybe they would let me go, just with orders not to leave town. But could I tell the whole truth? How about the part where I went to the scene of the murder for sex pictures of the victim so I could blackmail a prominent surgeon from a distinguished local family? That part of the truth probably wouldn't lead to a speedy release.

But if I didn't mention the pictures, why was I running towards the murder scene with a broken nose and a cop chasing me? Even if I came up with a plausible story, I couldn't lie well enough to sell it.

Saying the wrong thing could cost me my freedom or my life and I had little reason, just then, to trust my powers of persuasion. Talking to Katy led to her walking out of my life for ever. Talking to Mr. Rutledge left me with a moribund truck that broke my nose and died screaming. Even the Basset Hound knew I shouldn't have bought that stupid truck. And the thug on the phone was probably dumber than the dog but he still managed to con me into a blackmail scheme and frame me for murder. Yeah, I was a silver-tongued devil but maybe I had talked enough for one day.

I decided, for the moment at least, to keep my mouth shut.

My stubborn silence infuriated Grumpy, who seemed just about to get really unpleasant when a second plainclothes cop intervened. This one was as lean and laconic as Grumpy was beefy and blustery. He was also older, with a bad toupee, parted in the middle. There was a slate grey tinge to his skin, and the phrase "terminal cancer" popped into my mind. The diagnosis was consistent with his mournful expression. He wore a dark blue suit, white shirt, shiny shoes and a skinny black tie. He looked like an undertaker or maybe the funeral's guest of honor. Either way, he was clearly the one in charge.

A gentle hand on the shoulder was all it took to make his aggressive junior partner back off snarling like a well trained pit bull. The taciturn detective just stood there looking down at me for a while and finally introduced himself. "I am detective Owens," he said very slowly, as if introducing himself to a kindergarten class.

Owens waved off the cops holding me, spun me and personally removed my handcuffs. Then, with a firm grip on my upper arm, he walked me out the gate and over to a patrol car parked in front of the house. He had one of the uniforms start the engine and turn on the air-conditioner. After a few minutes of silence, while the car cooled down, he gestured me into the back seat and slid in beside me.

Relief from the steam-bath outside made the cop-car a welcome refuge. Detective Owens and I sat silently for a while. We savored the air conditioning as I rubbed my wrists, flexed my fingers and wondered what was next. I started to think that if jail was this well air conditioned, it might not be so bad. If I got locked up and it wasn't air conditioned, I could always kill myself. Hell couldn't be much hotter and was surely far less humid.

My nose was still throbbing and blocked with clotted blood. I had to breathe through my mouth. After a while, it became apparent that Owens was waiting for me to speak first: some kind of interrogation strategy. Eventually it worked.

"Am I under arrest?" I sounded like a bad actor in a cold pill commercial.

"Not yet," he said in a deep, lugubrious monotone.

There was another long silence. This time he spoke first.

"Did you say, McDuff . . . to that girl at the gate?"

"Yes sir." The sir seemed like a good idea. "Dr. McDuff is a staff surgeon at the U and I'm one of the surgery residents." Well, it was true. I was still a resident, if not for much longer.

"Your Dr. McDuff . . . related to Sheriff Ephraim McDuff?" Owens asked.

"I don't know if his name was Ephraim," I said, "but Dr. McDuff told me his father used to be Sheriff of Jefferson County. Would that be Ephraim?"

"Wait here," Detective Owens said and got out of the car. He talked for a while on a radio. With the air-conditioner on and the doors closed I couldn't hear a word. A few minutes later, he came back to the car. This time he sat in the front passenger seat. Grumpy dropped sullenly behind the wheel and Owens introduced him as Detective Barnes. Barnes growled in my general direction, fired up the engine and pulled away from the curb. A few minutes later we arrived across the street at the U's emergency entrance.

"You will have to come to the station," Detective Owens said, "But first we'll see to your nose." He led me through the ER and into a treatment room. We passed nurses and residents who knew me but were too busy to see me. I couldn't really blame them. I'm not at all sure what the proper greeting is for a murder suspect, covered with blood and in police custody . . . especially if you think he's guilty as sin.

The treatment room had two exam tables. Drapes like shower curtains around each one could slide closed for privacy. I was the only patient in the room, so the curtains stayed open. My clothing was removed and carefully bagged and labeled by Barnes. I was given an open-backed hospital gown and helped onto one of the tables.

The two detectives stayed as an Asian ENT resident I didn't know cleaned up my bloody nose and got a couple of X-rays. The fracture was displaced. He infiltrated the area with local anesthetic and manipulated bone and cartilage back into proper alignment. He seemed light with the anesthetic and heavy with the manipulation. It hurt and my reaction could not be described as excessively stoical. Barnes enjoyed the show and muttered something under his breath. I couldn't catch it all but the word "pussy" was clearly audible. This really was turning out to be one miserable day.

Just as the ENT guy finished a splinted dressing, Holt walked into the room and the two detectives stood up.

"You look like your daddy," Detective Owens said to Holt, as the two men shook hands. "Now you do like your daddy. Help us find the truth." Then he backed off, pulling the privacy curtain closed around Holt and me.

We heard the door to the corridor slam and Holt helped me sit up. He raised the head of the exam table so I wasn't facing the ceiling. Then he grabbed a chair, spun it around, straddled it and rested his arms on the back.

"Let's hear it," he said and I told him everything from buying Looks-Rough-Runs-Good to having my nose set by a sadist. Holt chuckled about the truck and frowned at my falling for the blackmail scam. He said nothing until I was finished and then just sat there for a while, looking down and shaking his head.

"Son," Holt finally said, "It is ever man's God-given right to make a dumb-ass move now and again. But I simply cannot comprehend how even a Yankee could make so many dumb-ass moves in such a short period of time."

"It's a gift, Holt," was the best I could come up with.

Lame as it was, Holt's deep guffaws rolled over me like waves and before I knew it I was laughing with him. The release of that levity made me feel a whole lot better.

When Holt was able, he took a deep breath and got down to business.

"Smart as you are," Holt said, "I suppose you have figured out that the luckiest dumb-ass thing you done today or maybe ever done in your entire life was buying that piece of shit truck." He paused to take in my blank expression and snorted in disbelief. "You haven't even figured that much out, have you? Maybe you're not as smart as I thought."

"What was lucky about buying that truck? I lost $100, which was half of my life savings, broke my nose, got chased by a cop . . . Okay," I said, suddenly getting his point.

"If I had gotten to the rendezvous on time by myself, there would have been no cop to run off the killer," I said.

"Right," Holt said, "and didn't you say the killer screamed when you busted his finger?"

"Screamed like a little girl," I said grinning. "If that cop was anywhere nearby he would have heard it and come running."

"You were grabbed near the house, where the body was at, but woke up by the gate to the sidewalk?" Holt raised his luxuriant eyebrows.

"Yeah."

"So he musta been by that gate when he screamed and dropped you. He most likely looked around and seen the police heading his way. That's why he run off before he finished setting you up." Holt explained patiently.

"Finished setting me up?" I wasn't sure what he meant. It seemed to me that I had been set up pretty well.

"Come on now and think, Yankee Boy" Holt said impatiently. "The blood flow should a returned to your brain by now, such as it is. If you had bashed in Shaleena's head, her blood and grey matter woulda been all over you. Now will the police find them any a her blood or brains on your clothing?"

"My shirt was soaked with blood," I said. "but it was my own blood, from my nose. My blood type is rare, AB negative: in about 1% of the population. It's not likely to match Shaleena's." I thought back and tried to remember if I had touched the body in any way. "I might have gotten her blood on my shoes, but that would be all."

"And I certainly do hope," Holt added with a smile, "that even a Yankee would not have been dumb enough to touch that bloody hammer."

"Right. That was one stupid thing I managed not to do today."

"Course, the killer had her blood on him and woulda got some on you when he grabbed you. But that would have been on your back since he grabbed you from behind an . . ."

"No, Holt," I interrupted. "I got a glimpse of him just before he slipped that choke on me. The image is clear in my mind. He was a huge, heavy guy, with a stocking over his face and a long-sleeved cammo jump suit. I can picture it in my mind and I'm sure that jump suit was perfectly clean. In fact, it looked brand new."

"Of course it was," Holt said. "This frame was carefully thought out. The blood woulda been on your back, if he'd a grabbed you before changing. That would a supported your story a being held from behind by the killer. They wanted her blood on your front, like it was on him before he changed into that outfit. Like it woulda been on you had you killed that girl with that hammer."

I was finally starting to catch on. "Okay, so let's say the killer hadn't been run off by the cop who was chasing me. Then he would have had time, after choking me out, to get blood and brains on my arms and chest. He probably would have just left me lying on the body. That would have done it."

"And he woulda got your fingerprints on that hammer," Holt smiled. "Now just let me think for a bit."

I was quiet as Holt closed his eyes for maybe a full minute. Then he got up, pulled back the curtain and revealed the two detectives. They were standing by the exam room door, which they had shut from the inside. I hadn't known they were in the room because of the closed curtain.

"Sorry, son," Holt said, "but that was the only way they would let us talk before your formal statement. They couldn't a used nothing bad you said, since you ain't been read your rights yet." Holt looked a little guilty for having tricked me, but I figured it was for the best. If I had held back anything, they would have found out sooner or later.

"It's okay, Holt. I understand," I said. "You knew I didn't kill her, so there was nothing to hide."

Holt turned to the detectives and said, "I know I'm not any kinda police officer but I can see clear enough what happened here. If you'll just give me one little minute . . . ?" He paused and looked at Detective Owens.

"We're listening," Owens said, as Barnes rolled his eyes and took a deep breath.

Barnes annoyance was not lost on Owens who turned to him and said, "I told you that Ephraim McDuff saved my life my very first year on the force. If his son has something to say to us, we are going to listen."

Barnes gestured and shrugged in submission. "I didn't say nothing."

Owens pulled up a chair and sat down. Barnes planted half his butt on the other exam table, with one foot on the floor and arms folded. Holt stood facing them and held forth without hesitation. It was almost as if his speech had been planned before he arrived in the ER.

"The murdered girl was having an affair with a married staff surgeon. That's generally believed, although not known for sure, around both hospitals. It may have started with him covering her drug use, and forcing her sexual favors. Even so, once things got going, he would have needed her silence. If she threatened to go public, the surgeon had a lot more to lose than Shaleena.

She risked losing her job but he could be charged with rape or extortion. She may have been blackmailing him and that is a motive for murder."

"She had an expensive watch," I chimed in. "Way too much for a nurse's salary."

"Who is this surgeon she was having the affair with?" Owens asked, as Barnes pulled out a notebook.

Holt looked at me expectantly. He wanted me to name Jefferson.

"Dr. Lloyd Jefferson," I said. "He's chief of surgery and chief of staff at the VA."

"Now let's just say," Holt continued, "that Jefferson was being blackmailed. He mighta wanted to kill Shaleena, but until Cooper come along he couldn't."

"Why's that?" Barnes broke in.

"Because until then," Holt explained, "Jefferson was the only one with a motive. He'd be accused and even if nothing got proved, ever-one would think he done it. At the very least, in all the fuss, his wife would find out he'd been cheating.

"But then, just the day before yesterday, ever-thing changes. Dr. Logan, has himself a bad run-in with Shaleena and Jefferson escalates the incident to where it destroys Cooper's future. This boy was doing good in Dr. Kirkwood's program. He was gonna be a heart surgeon. Now he's about to get fired . . . and it's all because of Shaleena."

Holt explained about Jefferson barring me from the VA and how that forced me out of the heart program. Then he went on.

"So now Cooper seems to have the best motive to kill Shaleena. Now, if she gets her head bashed in, Jefferson's not the prime suspect. Dr. Logan's grudge is fresh and clear and ever-one's talking about it. What's more, there's no speculation involved, like with Jefferson's affair with Shaleena. Ever-body knows for a damn-sure fact Cooper's career has been wrecked by Shaleena. With that motive, if the frame had been complete, you'd never have looked beyond Cooper."

Holt paused and waited for a nod of agreement. He didn't get one but they didn't deny it either, so he just went on.

"Somehow Jefferson or this thug he musta hired got Shaleena out to that fenced yard. The murderer waited for her there and bashed her head in with a hammer." Holt paused again, this time I think just to add to the drama.

"Then the killer changed outa his bloody clothes and called up Dr. Logan. There's a payphone just outside the door in the VA parking area. So he lured Dr. Logan to the murder scene with the hope he might-could save his future by pressuring Jefferson with dirty pitchers a him and Shaleena. Dr. Logan . . . he was desperate and he fell for it."

"I was hung over," I said under my breath. Holt shot me a look then continued.

"Now, if it hadn't been for the truck exploding and the cop scaring off the killer, Cooper woulda been left on the body with blood and brains all over him. Not only that but his fingerprints woulda been on the hammer. Then y'all woulda gotten a call at the station, that a murder in that yard was in progress." Holt paused and looked Owens right in the eye.

"If you'd a found you a man with a motive to kill that girl, with her blood and brains all over him and his fingerprints on the hammer . . . you'd a hung that frame right proud on the wall and Dr. Logan with it. Now ain't that the God's honest truth?" This time Holt waited.

"Maybe," Owens finally admitted. "Maybe we would have bought it."

"He still looks damn good for it to me," Barnes insisted. "Having a strong motive to kill that girl might a tempted someone to frame him. Or it just might-could mean what it usually means; he had him a motive to kill her and he done it. And wouldn't it seem kinda strange, in this perfect frame job you imagine, that the killer would be found taking himself a nap at the crime scene?"

"Well you found him unconscious at the scene and you just said he still looked guilty," Holt pointed out. "Anyways, hammering a girl's head in and taking a bath in her blood and brains could make a feller pass out. And, a course they'd a tried to time things so as he'd be waking up just about as y'all got there. You only found him sooner because that traffic cop was chasing him. That's why he was still out cold."

"What if he done woke up and run off before we got there?" Barnes argued.

"How much time do you think that would get him?" Holt asked. "Enough time to destroy all the evidence? All the blood and brains on his body and clothes and truck and what about the hammer? He likely woulda left it behind, not knowing his prints were on it? And if he ran you would have been more sure than ever he was guilty."

Barnes hopped off the other exam table, "Well what's all this crap about some mysterious choke hold? Why risk his getting out of it just like he done and messed up all their planning? Why not just hit him upside the head and be done with it?"

Holt just smiled and looked at Detective Owens. "You want to explain that point to your junior partner?"

"If he'd been hit there'd be a bruise to back up his story about a third person at the murder scene," Owens explained patiently, as if talking to a child. "Choking him out left no evidence, nothing to support his story."

Holt had me show them my neck which revealed hardly any bruising.

Being talked down to by his partner, in front of Holt and me, seemed to infuriate Barnes. "By Gawd, having a strong motive and nothing to back up his story usually means a suspect is guilty. They're trying to turn this here thing around back-asswards to say it means he ain't."

Before Owens could respond, Holt raised both hands in a calming gesture. He said, "Now let's just be fair here. Detective Barnes has him some good points. It coulda happened different." Holt was addressing Owens now. "It is possible, I suppose, that Dr. Logan here coulda killed Shaleena with that hammer. He coulda done it so careful that when you look at his clothes you won't find you one single drop a her blood nor one strand a her hair, nor even one little teeny bit a her brain anywhere on them. Then, he could a got in that truck from Hell and, for some unknown reason, sped around the block to head back the way he started from."

Holt quickly turned towards me and asked where I lived. When I gave him my address he continued.

"Yes, sir. That's just right. He started out towards his house, then went around the block in a half-circle so as he was going back in the precisely opposite direction. Then, when his truck blew up and a policeman was chasing him, he ran straight to where he had just murdered a girl, who was lying on the ground, in plain view. And finally, I suppose, it is also possible that he then passed out for no reason. Or maybe he just took him a nap until he was found by the body."

Holt turned, at that point from Owens to Barnes and asked, "Is that your theory of the case, Detective Barnes?"

Barnes was speechless but Owens stepped in and took some of the wind out of Holt's sails.

"You wouldn't much mind seeing Jefferson go down over this, would you Dr. McDuff? You and him do have a history of your own. Isn't that the truth?"

I recalled Roberta's description of Holt's door-pounding flare-up with Jefferson . Whatever all that had been about, Detective Owens seemed aware of it.

"What're you saying?" Holt asked, with an edge to his voice.

"I'm saying that the Jefferson estate is right here in Jefferson County, where your daddy was sheriff. And I'm saying that there is bad blood between his family and your family. . . bad blood going way back," Owens responded calmly. "Are you saying that's not true?"

"When I grew up, the Jeffersons thought they were above the law." Holt said. "My daddy did not agree. There were some incidents between the families. Jefferson was about my age and, no, we did not get along either. So no, I won't mind seeing him brought down by this, but that don't mean that this-all didn't happen just precisely the way I said."

"No it doesn't," Owens admitted. "Nothing proves it did happen that way either. We will talk to Dr. Jefferson and we will find the big man who was running from the scene."

"So, the officer who chased Dr. Logan has confirmed that much of the story," Holt pounced on this admission.

"I have given you latitude here, because of your daddy," Owens said to Holt. "Do not abuse it."

Holt raised both hands and actually took a step backwards. "Alright, sir. You are right and we appreciate it."

"And while we're talking theories of the case here," Owens went on, "how about a theory that brings Eightball White into the story?"

Holt looked uncomfortable as Owens continued. "Once we had the dead girl's name, we soon learned she was Eightball White's common law wife. I'm sure you were aware of that as well. Where you not, sir?"

"I was," Holt admitted.

"So how come you didn't mention it?" Owens persisted and went on without letting Holt answer. "What if there really are dirty pictures of Jefferson and Eightball White's woman? Someone who didn't have much love for Jefferson might have gotten those pictures to Eightball. Might have figured he'd fly into a jealous rage, like the one that earned him his street name. Maybe this person hoped Eightball would have someone murder Jefferson, not Shaleena. Maybe Shaleena's murder and the frame around your friend was a big disappointment to whoever sent Eightball those pictures."

Detective Owens kept staring at Holt, maybe waiting for a confession. But Holt just stared back silently. Owens blinked first.

"So who, besides you and Dr. Logan," Owens said to Holt, "might want to see harm come to Jefferson? Jefferson was the one that fired Dr. Logan, not Shaleena. If we find photos like that in Eightball's cell, whose fingerprints will be on them? Maybe Dr. Logan's. Maybe yours. Anything either of you want to tell me?"

"I don't know anything about any pictures," I said and Holt just snorted.

Owens turned to me and asked, "Any grievance Eightball White might have against you? Any reason he might choose you for the patsy, other than you having a motive?"

Of course there was: the scuffle last year in the ER. I'd knocked Eightball down and embarrassed him in front of a roomful of people. But, before I answered, for some reason, I looked over at Holt. He moved his head back and forth, just once and just barely enough to notice. But the message was clear, Holt didn't want me to mention the fight with Eightball.

I asked for a drink of water to give me a moment to think. Owens was implying that Holt sent the pictures to Eightball, thinking he'd kill Jefferson rather than Shaleena. Having a reason to frame me would make Eightball a more likely suspect and Holt like the one who set him off. How could I help the case against Holt after all he was doing to help me?

I looked up innocently hoping Owens had forgotten the question.

"So?" Owens repeated, "any reason Eightball would favor you for the frame?"

"Nothing I can think of," I lied and could see he didn't believe me.

"Well, we'll see about that," Owens said. Then turning to Holt he added, "Birmingham is not a big city. Big man; broken finger; almost surely a history of violence. We will find him and when we do we'll see who paid him to do the murder. Maybe Dr. Jefferson. Maybe Eightball White. Maybe he acted alone. I don't know yet but I will."

CHAPTER 14

WE LEFT THE ER with me in a scrub suit and disposable OR slippers. On the way downtown, Owens and Barnes were silent and I wondered what was going to happen. Wondered if I might end up in the cell where Martin Luther King wrote his famous letter.

Fortunately I never found out. They hustled me in through a back entrance and directly to a small, sterile and—thank God—air conditioned, interrogation room. I was left there alone for what seemed like a long time. I had no watch and there was no clock so I couldn't say just how long. There was a mirror on one wall through which I'm sure someone was watching. I figured they wanted to see if I acted like a man who killed a girl with a hammer. I wondered how such a man would act and hoped I was acting differently.

Maybe they thought, if I waited long enough, I'd break down and confess to whatever. Without the air-conditioning, this strategy might have worked.

Finally Owens and Barnes appeared with a large reel-to-reel tape-recorder. They went through the motions of good cop, bad cop through hours of repetitive questions.

When Owens reached for the switch on the tape recorder, I sighed audibly with relief. In the past twenty-four hours, I'd been knee-walking drunk and wish-for-death hung over. I'd wrecked a truck; broken my nose; been choked out; had the nose painfully reset; and spent the past few hours trying to talk my way out of a murder charge. There was only one reason I hadn't crashed already: the fear I'd wake up in a cell with a giant roommate with bad breath whispering sweet nothings in my ear.

Imagine my disappointment when Owens pulled a Columbo. He looked up at me just before shutting down the recorder and said, "Oh yes, doctor, just one more question."

"Sure," I smiled, just as if I'd had a choice.

Owens leaned back in his chair, got comfortable enough to ask more than one question and said, "Why did you lie about Eightball White having a grudge against you?"

The honest answer was that I wanted to protect Holt if he'd inflamed Eightball's jealously with the pictures. I obviously couldn't admit that. Nor could I deny the ER incident from the previous year. I had thought that, since no charges were filed, there would be no record. Obviously I was wrong. There was a record and Detective Owens, or maybe that idiot, Barnes, had found it. Barnes was certainly grinning as if he had been responsible. I just sat there looking confused until Owens said, "Did you have a fight last year . . . in the ER?"

"Oh yeah!" I snapped my fingers as if I'd just made the connection. "Of course I remember the fight. I just didn't connect it with the name Eightball." Actually that had been true when Holt first told me about Eightball and Shaleena. The name sounded familiar then, but I hadn't been able to place it.

"Well, that's understandable," Barnes interjected sarcastically. "It is a real common name. I know several Eightballs my own self."

"It's true," I said, looking Owens in the eye. And, since it was about half true, I thought he might buy it.

"Maybe there is some truth to that," Owens said. He was better than a polygraph. "But here's what I think. I think you and Dr. McDuff would prefer that I concentrate on Jefferson. You don't want me to get distracted with Eightball and his gang of dope-dealing killers."

Owens looked at me and I looked away and he knew he'd called it right. It had occurred to me that if Jefferson went to prison, I had at least some chance of getting back VA privileges. If Eightball was convicted, that didn't do anything for me.

"It doesn't really matter," Owens said. "We'll find the big man with the broken finger. He will tell us who hired him . . . if it was Eightball or if it was Dr. Jefferson. He will tell us and then we will know. Meanwhile, Dr. Logan, you are not to leave Birmingham. Is that clear?"

I took a deep breath and exhaled with my eyes closed. "Crystal clear. And . . . thank you for . . ."

"For not putting your Yankee ass in jail?" Barnes spat. "Well don't get too damn thankful because that might-could still happen and you'd be in jail now if it was up to me." Barnes stormed out of the room.

I looked at Detective Owens and this time he looked away. I thought about the wig and his bad skin color and hoped my cancer concerns were unfounded. If Owens got sick enough that Barnes took over . . . I still might see Martin Luther King's old jail cell.

It was after 9 PM as I wearily slid into a patrol car for a ride home. Just as we were about to pull away from the curb, Barnes came running over. He slammed a beefy palm down on the hood and pulled the door open.

"Get out," Barnes ordered the uniform at the wheel. "I'll take him."

"But, uhh . . . Detective Owens said . . ." the uniform objected.

"Owens' days are numbered," Barnes said. "You'll be dealing with me for a long time. Now, get the fuck out of the car and go get you some coffee or something."

The cop got out and Barnes got in. I was in the back seat wishing I'd hitchhiked.

Barnes drove silently around the city and, after a while, I was pretty sure he wasn't headed for my house. I asked where we were going but got no response. Eventually Barnes stopped the car in a deserted downtown alley. It was lined with garbage cans and dead-ended against a brick wall.

Barnes pulled me out of the car and slammed me up against the end of the alley. It was hard to resist fighting back but, what was I going to do? Beat up a cop? Even Owens wouldn't help me if I did that.

A couple of shots to the gut bent me over. Then Barnes straightened me up. He pressed his forearm against my throat and shoved me back up and into the brick wall. He tried to hold me off the ground that way, but wasn't quite tall enough to do it. Looking down at the top of his head, I lifted my feet and did a pull-up on the arm that pinned me. This kept the pressure off my throat and forced him to bear my weight. My larynx was protected by wrestler's neck muscles. I thanked my coaches for them because they were all that kept me breathing. As it was, the pressure was uncomfortable but caused no serious problem. With my full weight hanging on his forearm, Barnes tired quickly.

When he let me down, he slammed me back against the wall again and said, "Now, I want to hear the truth, boy."

"All right," I said, raising a hand in apparent capitulation. He backed off, put his hands on his hips, and waited.

Barnes was a bully, and I knew how he had to be handled. Once a bully knows you're afraid, he only pushes harder. I had to show Barnes he didn't scare me, even if he did.

"Here's the truth," I said.

"It better be the truth," Barnes swore, "because I'll look into your eyes and I'll know if you are lying. If you are, we will dance some more and that can go on for the rest of the night. I will enjoy every fucking minute. But I don't believe that you will."

"It's the truth," I assured him. "When you were holding me up against the wall I saw it. I had a really good view of the top of your head and the comb-over just is not working. Everyone can still see you're going bald and you just look pathetic trying to hide it. Now, you look me in the eyes and tell me . . . am I lying?"

As I had hoped, it got him mad enough to try to punch my head through the bricks. I ducked to the side and his fist connected with the wall instead. His hands were quick and he wasn't used to people slipping his punches. I couldn't have avoided the blow if I hadn't known it was coming. As it was the side of his fist abraded my cheek going past it. Barnes bent over holding his hand and I took off down the alley. Passing the patrol car, I grabbed the keys and pitched them into a dumpster.

Hitch hiking, jogging and walking got me back home around midnight.

CHAPTER 15

I SLEPT LATE the next day and woke up sore and hungry. Getting out of bed was no fun at all with a badly bruised belly. I walked slowly to the kitchen with short steps, hunched over like an old man. Pickings there were pretty slim. The milk was curdled. The bread was still stale and there was a roach in what was left of some Frosted Flakes. Fortunately I still had the ingredients for my version of the Breakfast of Champions: peanut butter and butter on Hi-Ho crackers with strong black instant coffee.

Detective Owens called early to say he knew that Barnes had harassed me. Barnes denied it, of course, and Owens couldn't prove it. He said a formal complaint from me would not be alone in Barnes's file. I passed on that. It was my word against a cop's, which sounded like a loser. A complaint would probably only piss Barnes off even more.

Bo called around noon. He had nearly an hour before scrubbing on a gall bladder.

"I just got time to drive my pickup over to your place," Bo said quickly. You can have her for the rest of the day, but first you need to carry me on back to the hospital. They might let me to do this gall-bag my own self, but it ain't gonna happen if I'm late."

"Thanks, Bo. I wouldn't let you risk losing it but I do need to stock up on groceries and . . ."

"Well stock up good because this is the only day you get my truck. You can take my bike again, if you want. Keep it as long as you need it this time. It ain't much but it thumps the hell out a walking.

"Bo . . . I don't know how to thank you, man."

"Well here's what you do. I'll call when I get off tonight and you come collect me. Come right quick. I don't want to be waiting on you. Then you buy me a beer at the Recovery Room and tell me about your crime spree, including any hammer murders you may have committed lately."

"Are you only interested in the hammer murders or . . . Hello?" There was no response because Bo had already hung up.

Fifteen minutes later, I was waiting out front when Bo arrived in his pickup. It looked almost as disreputable as Looks-Rough-Runs-Good. I got behind the wheel to drive him back and could not have been happier with a Ferrari.

Bo said speculation about the murder was rampant at both hospitals. "Most folks are pretty sure you done it," he said, "but some say you were framed by Jefferson. I think it was Holt started that last theory going. There's even some think Holt's involved his own self since he talked to the cops in the ER. Ever single other theory, except suicide, has also been suggested."

"What do you think?" I asked him.

"I been hoping it was you cause I never been friends with no hammer killer before. That'd be something to tell my grandkids." Bo smiled. "But unfortunately, I know you didn't kill her."

"How do you know that?" I asked. "You think I couldn't do it?"

"Oh you could, damn sure, do it," Bo joked. "They just wouldn't a caught you." Turning serious, he added, "I got no theory until we talk – tonight at the Recovery Room when you get me."

Then we were there and he hopped out of the truck and was running for his case in the OR I hoped he would get there in time to do it. A gall bladder is a fun operation.

The first thing I did was check the Birmingham News, which had nearly ignored the story. All it had was a one-paragraph crime brief on page three. Neither Jefferson's name nor mine was even mentioned. Later I found that TV coverage was even more superficial. At first this surprised me but the more I thought it over the more it made sense.

The hospitals would obviously want to downplay the murder. So would Jefferson and his family. They would all have plenty of juice in the local power structure. Even the cops would have reason to keep the story quiet. Detective Owens would be looking for the big man with the broken finger. He would not want sensational publicity to scare the guy out of the area. I didn't much care whether the hospital, Jefferson or the police deserved the credit. The story had been stifled and for me that was good news.

After checking the newspaper, I drove to the Winn-Dixie supermarket. I used my credit card there to stock up on cheap provisions. These included the three basic food groups: Budweiser beer, potato chips and Hebrew National hot dogs. My next shopping trip would be on Bo's bike and one six-pack would be nearly a full load.

When I picked Bo up that evening, Roberta was waiting with him in front of the hospital. The three of us went straight to the Recovery Room. I was in a black T-shirt and my only remaining jeans. The other pair was downtown in an evidence locker at the police station. Bo was in dark Polyester pants with a cheap belt and a white shirt. There was no tie in sight, so it was probably crumpled in a pocket. Roberta wore loose white slacks and a silky blue blouse with a floppy collar. Her pony tail was secured with a rubber band. Her makeup, as usual, was minimal.

We passed quickly through the aquarium bar up front and found a booth in the dark dining area. I had come to trust Bo and Roberta as true friends and I shared all the facts I knew with them. I also told them Holt's theory that Jefferson hired the killer and framed me for the murder. They laughed at how Looks-Rough-Runs-Good and a traffic cop had been my salvation. I did not mention Detective Owens' suspicions about Eightball.

Roberta provided an interesting insight about Shaleena.

"It was nearly a year ago," Roberta said. "and my first rotation at the VA. I got called in around 3 AM to see a post-op gall-bag in the ICU. The patient had a high fever, abdominal pain and no bile draining from his Penrose. I parked out back and, as I was heading in, I saw Shaleena coming out. Since the patient was in the ICU, I tried to stop her and ask about the drainage. I was hoping I wouldn't have to re-open the guy and adjust the Penrose."

"Like Shaleena would know anything about a patient," Bo grunted.

"Well, like I said," Roberta went on, "it was my first VA rotation. Anyway, as soon as she got close, I could see that she was crying—crying out loud with shoulders shaking and tears and snot streaming. When I tried to stop her, she shoved me away and ran towards her car screaming."

"Screaming?" Bo asked.

"Yeah, she was screaming like, 'Stay away from me! Y'all just stay the fuck away from me! All of y'all, leave me the fuck alone! I had enough. I ain't takin' no more,' like that." Then she jumped into her car and peeled away laying rubber."

I wondered if that was the night Shaleena decided to turn the tables. Blackmailing Jefferson could have been her way out of the drug test coercion. Once it worked to make him leave her alone, she might have decided to push it. An expensive watch and who knew what other favors in return for her silence. I started to interrupt with that thought but Roberta shushed me and went on.

"That isn't even the weirdest part," she said. "I was kind of shook up and I went in through the door Shaleena came out of. That wasn't a door I'd used before. It led to the administrative wing and pretty soon I was lost. Wandering around, trying to get back to the patient care area, I saw Chris Dugan walking towards me. You know, she's the chief of nursing."

"The rug muncher?" Bo asked.

"Yeah. A moron might call her that," Roberta answered. "She was in jeans and a man's dress shirt and, as she walked down the hall, she was tucking the shirt in. Before she saw me, she was smiling. As I approached her I said, Hi. Seeing me, she nodded but stopped smiling and looked nervous.

"Around the next corner, I saw Jefferson locking the door to what I later learned was his office. He was in a wrinkled suit, with the jacket over his arm and his tie on his neck like a scarf. He turned around with a smile on his face, just like Dugan's. But when he saw me he didn't get nervous, like she did. He got mad. Demanded to know what I was doing there. He even followed me up to the ICU to make sure I had really been called in.

"Before he left, he took me out in the hall and asked a bunch of questions. He wanted to know if I'd seen anything unusual that night. 'Unusual' was his word. I had enough sense to say, no, but I'm not sure he believed me. Then he said that passing malicious gossip could get my VA privileges suspended. He pointed out that without them I wouldn't be able to finish my training. I told him I understood and I did. I've never mentioned the incident since. Not until tonight."

By nine o'clock, Bo and Roberta were hungry and decided to have dinner. They both ordered steak sandwiches and just the thought made my mouth water. But I'd burned up my credit card on groceries and was facing impending unemployment. I lied about having eaten a big meal earlier and fended off starvation with their French fries.

Roberta called her roommate from a payphone by the restrooms to let him know she'd be home late. She was just getting back to the table when Bo's beeper went off. He hurried to the same payphone, leaving Roberta and me alone in the booth.

"Have you heard from Katy?" she asked. It was the first mention of Katy that night and hit like a tire iron to the forehead.

"No," I said brusquely. "That's over. She's not coming back."

"Call her," Roberta said.

"She left a note," I said. "The note said not to call her."

"So what? We of the female persuasion do not always mean every single little thing we say in affairs of the heart." Roberta made this pronouncement in tones worthy of Scarlet O'Hara and with the back of one hand to her forehead, as if she were about to swoon. When her hand came down, she made a fist, thumped the table lightly, gave me a no-nonsense look and said, "Call her anyway, dummy."

"What's the point, Roberta? Katy thought I was wrong about Billy. She's lost her confidence in me, lost her trust in me, lost her respect for me I suppose. And today's events aren't likely to improve her viewpoint. She certainly doesn't love me anymore. Maybe she never did."

"Come on," Roberta said. "You don't believe that."

"No, I guess not," I admitted. "I know she loved me when we were in Boston. I even know just when she fell in love with me and that's what's so weird about what's happening now."

"How is it weird?" she asked.

"I nearly got expelled from med school for breaking hospital rules to save a patient's life: just like what happened with Billy. She was the nurse on duty and I was just a med student. I'll give you the details some other time but back then it made her fall in love with me. It turned her on too. She couldn't wait to get me home and into her bed that night. It was our first time and . . . but that's not the point."

"So what is the point and hurry?" Roberta prompted. "Bo will be back in a minute."

"The point is that now, with Billy, I take the same kind of risk for the same reason and I'm right again and I save a life again, but this time, it makes her dump me. Same stimulus, opposite response. It doesn't make any sense to me."

"Well, maybe it does and maybe it doesn't," Roberta said thoughtfully. "A big motorcycle or a fast sports car is a turn-on, for some girls . . . in a boyfriend. Then it becomes a selfish ego-trip after the move-in or marriage. I've seen that phenomenon before. Maybe something like that is going on here, but . . . No. I don't buy it. I've met Katy, talked to her at some resident functions and that doesn't sound like her. There's more to it than that."

Roberta seemed to think it over a bit more and then leaned towards me quickly and spoke under her breath. "Where is this note she left?" Bo was coming back and Roberta knew I wouldn't talk about Katy in front of him. Bo thought a serious relationship was one where you took her out to dinner before the one night stand.

"I want to see that note," Roberta whispered urgently. "Boys are so stupid. You probably have no idea what that note means. It could be the key. Show me the note and then we'll see."

I had the note in my wallet. For some reason, I'd been carrying it with me. I wanted Roberta's take on Katy's message but that would have to wait. Bo was back from the phone and I didn't want him to see it.

"You know Bill Clayton?" Bo asked and we nodded. He was a first year resident who was not likely to be a second year. "That kid couldn't pour piss from a boot with instructions written on the heel. I told him to call me with any problems and he had one with ever patient on the service."

Not long after that, we broke it up and Bo dropped me and his bicycle at my place. I was back to being bicycle-boy for the foreseeable future.

CHAPTER 16

JULY ENDED AS the Alabama summer steamed inexorably on into August. I might have headed for cooler climes but Owens had said not to leave Birmingham. Also, Holt had been calling nearly every day to encourage me about my future.

In his first call, he explained why he thought I still might become a heart surgeon. "Don't you give up hope now, Yankee Boy," he said. "They'll catch the big man with the broke finger. When they do, he'll point that broke finger right at our friend Jefferson."

"But what if it was Eightball that hired him? Detective Owens seemed to think . . ."

Holt interrupted me angrily, "Now I will not hear no more talk like that. It was Jefferson what hired him, and the killer will say it was Jefferson, and Jefferson will then be arrested."

"Okay, Holt," I backed off, wondering how he could be so sure. "Let's say it was Jefferson and let's say he's arrested for murder. I mean . . . that'll be great but . . ."

"But what good does it do you?" Holt finished my question.

"Yeah," I said. "Exactly. What good does it do me?" It seemed unlikely that, as I had hoped, Jefferson's replacement would reinstate me.

"When Jefferson is arrested and questioned in this murder, it will all come out about him and Shaleena. Even if he never is convicted, that should be enough to get him fired. He will lose his spot at the VA and they'll need a new chief of surgery. Now with VA salaries less than half of what they are in private practice, finding anyone decent to take his place will not be easy. It should take a year or two at least. Meanwhile, someone's got to run things. They are going to be desperate for an acting chief of surgery."

"Well that's all very interesting," I said, "but I don't think I'm qualified."

Holt just laughed. "No you are not," he said. "but you have a friend who is."

As soon as he said that, I saw where he was going. With Jefferson out, Holt could fill in as the acting chief of surgery. He'd be hired in a heartbeat and they'd be glad to have him.

"And, when I'm acting chief, Yankee Boy, just what do you imagine I'll be doing?"

"I think I can guess, Holt, but I'd rather hear you say it first, just in case I'm presuming too much," I said.

"You ain't presuming nothing, son. I will rehabilitate your record and restore your VA privileges. After that Dr. Kirkwood can bring you back to finish training in general and cardiac surgery."

"What about the CEO, over there," I asked, "or whoever they pick as the new chief of staff. They were all in Jefferson's pocket. They might not go along with having me back."

"If they want me," Holt said, "they'll have to take you. And they will. Ain't no doubt about it. But let's just keep this plan between us, Yankee Boy. Three folks can keep a secret as long as two of them are dead. And I want this kept quiet. You got that?"

I got it and there wasn't much I wouldn't have done for Holt at that point. I was glad he couldn't see me, because something was in the air and my eyes were watery and itchy. I started to thank him but he cut me off. He said he had a case waiting in the OR.

Over the next few days, I saw that I needed to have a routine. Sitting around waiting to hear from Dr. Kirkwood or Detective Owens and hoping not to see Barnes was driving me bonkers. I started exercising in the mornings and then pedaling to the hospital to study. When I'd read all the journals in the resident's lounge, I moved on to the main library. There I studied the more obscure literature and text books. I'd never had so much time for research and my knowledge was never so current. I doubted that the busy staff surgeons knew the journals as well as I did.

As the first week in August ended, along with my vacation and sick leave, I finally got the phone call I'd been hoping for. It was Dr.Kirkwood's secretary, Marge ordering me to his office.

I'd been doing my morning workout when the call came in. This consisted of sit-ups, pushups, neck bridges and such, after which I pumped furniture instead of iron. I was in my boxer shorts and covered with sweat so I took time for a shower. Then I jumped on Bo's bike and made it to the hospital in record time. Before reaching the end of my block I was again soaked in perspiration and wondering why I'd even bothered with the shower.

Marge smiled as she ushered me into The Wire's office. Dr. Kirkwood was on the phone when I came in. He waved me to a small but comfortable chair facing his desk. The call was soon over and then The Wire smiled.

"Hello, Cooper," he said. "How are you managing?"

"I'm doing fine, sir. Thank you for asking."

"This is just a formality, you understand," Dr. Kirkwood said, "but I must ask." There was a pause and then he said, "You didn't kill that girl, did you?"

"No, sir," I said. "Certainly not. I didn't kill her."

He made some notes on a sheet of paper and nodded. "If you'd been charged in the murder, I would have had to suspend you. Since you have not been charged and since I believe that you are innocent – of murder at least," he added with a smile – "what I do with you is up to my discretion."

Then, preliminaries over with, he got down to business.

"Dr. McDuff and Mr. Whitney have been lobbying in your favor. Their opinions mean a great deal to me but the discussions are becoming redundant." The Wire grinned and then looked a bit puzzled. "Most significantly, Holt says changes at the VA could be imminent. He suggests these changes could be favorable to your future. Do you have any idea as to what he anticipates?"

Holt told me to keep his plan secret but I couldn't just lie to The Wire. "Not exactly, sir," I said. "I mean . . . Sooner or later the situation there, with Shaleena's murder and her thing with Jefferson . . . eventually it's got to blow. And if, after the dust clears, Jefferson is gone . . . Well that could open up some things for me, but . . . for the moment at least . . . it all seems pretty well contained so . . ." I left it hanging.

Dr. Kirkwood nodded thoughtfully and said, "In my experience, Holt is well informed on such matters." The Wire took a sip of coffee and seemed to come to a decision.

"At the same time," he continued, "a problem on the adult heart service has reached crises proportions. It has occurred to me that you might be of some assistance.

"As you know, Dr. Morgan Walker has recently joined our staff. He comes to us from the cardiac program in Houston. Dr. Walker is taking on the main load of adult heart cases. This will allow me to concentrate on the complex congenitals." Complex congenital heart surgery deals with malformed hearts in babies and children. These are the most challenging operations and Dr. Kirkwood's special interest.

Morgan Walker was big loud Texan with leather skin and lizard cowboy boots. He wore them everywhere except the OR, where he traded them for white plastic surgical boots. Everyone else wore sneakers, which I did, or wooden clogs for the style-conscious. I hadn't seen him operate but I'd heard all about him. He was a marvelously gifted technical surgeon and an absolute bastard to work for.

The Wire took another sip of coffee. "Like his mentor, Dr. DeBakey, Dr. Walker has a . . . a demanding and impatient nature. None of the residents assigned to his service so far have enjoyed their time with him and their . . . uhh . . . displeasure has been reciprocated by Dr. Walker. At the moment, Dr. Clayton is assigned to adult hearts and it just isn't working."

Bill Clayton had been Bo's junior resident on their last rotation. Bo didn't think much of the guy and neither had others who'd worked with him. I knew that Clayton wanted to be a plastic surgeon. The consensus was that he would not achieve that goal in our high pressure program. In Bo's words, he'd have to go elsewhere to "master the mysteries of mammary enhancement." Assigning him to hearts with a perfectionist tyrant like Walker was a prescription for disaster.

"I'm not going to fire Dr. Clayton," The Wire said, "but I am allowing Dr. Walker to dismiss him. Dr. Clayton will be transferred to the Head and Neck service where he has performed adequately in prior rotations. Dr. Walker will shortly be advising Dr. Clayton of this decision. You will take Dr. Clayton's place on adult hearts for the rest of this month's rotation. You will then take what was to be Dr. Clayton's place on my congenital cardiac service. That will bring you to the end of September and the conclusion of this academic year.

"At that point, If Dr. McDuff's optimistic expectations materialize . . . well, I would love to see you finish here in both general surgery and cardiac. If Dr. McDuff's predictions are not accurate . . . Well, I'm sure you understand."

I just nodded.

Dr. Kirkwood finished his coffee and stood up. "Now, get down to Dr. Walker's office. He'll fill you in on the details."

"Dr. Kirkwood, thanks for giving me this chance. Sitting around was driving me crazy."

The Wire looked at his watch and hustled me out. "Dr. Walker is waiting and arriving late would not be an auspicious beginning."

Dr. Walker's secretary, a lean frenetic woman with dark thin frizzy hair, was at her desk typing furiously. It almost seemed as if she was trying to kill her typewriter. She stopped when I came in and gestured me nervously to a chair by the door to the inner office. I could clearly hear voices from beyond that door and thought the chair had been placed for that purpose.

". . . and the missing X-ray today was another perfect example." From conferences and a brief introduction, I recognized the voice of Dr. Morgan Walker.

"Sir, I know I brought that X-ray up." This rather high pitched response was obviously from the unhappy resident, Dr. Clayton.

"You know you brought it up?" Dr. Walker was like a cat playing with a mouse. "Well, if you brought it up, there should be no problem."

"Yes, sir, I know I brought it up. I remember it distinctly, getting it ready for you to review along with the other X-rays." Dr. Clayton's tone of voice could only be described as whiney.

"Oh, good. I am so relieved," Walker taunted. "So, since you brought it up, just tell me where it was when I asked for it."

Dr. Clayton's response was inaudible on my side of the door.

"Yes," Walker pounced. "You see that is the problem. Because you say you brought it up but, if you had brought it up, it would have been there. And yet it was not there . . . was it?"

Dr. Clayton only managed a whimper.

"But it wasn't there, was it?" Walker asked again and I could almost see him smiling.

No response from Dr. Clayton.

"It wasn't there, was it?" Walker demanded more forcefully.

"No, sir," Clayton mumbled.

"Why do you suppose it wasn't there?" Walker shouted. Then he went on without giving Clayton a chance to answer. "Do you suppose it grew legs and walked away some time after you brought it up? Or maybe it fell through a crack in the space/time continuum? Perhaps it's in another dimension now. Or did you bring it home and your dog ate it?"

Clayton remained silent and Dr. Walker went on.

"I will tell you exactly why it wasn't there." Walker said, his voice growing louder with each sentence. "The X-ray wasn't there because you failed to have it there. And, you failed to have it there for the same two reasons you have failed so abysmally to perform adequately on this service. These two reasons are that you don't concentrate and you don't pay attention to detail. How many times have I told you to concentrate and told you to pay attention to detail?" Walker paused for a mumbled response that was probably inaudible even on his side of the door.

"I have told you time and time again to concentrate and time and time again to pay attention to detail. But you haven't listened, have you?" Walker was on a roll now and didn't even bother to pause for an answer. "You just continue to ignore me. You still don't concentrate and you still don't pay attention to detail. And that, Dr. Clayton, is why you have been mediocre on this service. And that, Dr. Clayton, is why you will always be mediocre.

"Now get out and go on to your next assignment. Perhaps, on the Head and Neck service, mediocrity will be acceptable."

Clayton hurried out wiping his eyes and forgot to close the door behind him. Walker screamed at him to, "Close the Goddamned door, you idiot." He stumbled back and just barely managed to do it before fleeing. The frizzy secretary and I watched him leave and then looked at each other. She waved me over to her desk where she asked me routine questions and scribbled down the answers.

Finally she stared at me from several different angles, jerking her head around like a pigeon. I thought she was going to introduce herself but instead she said, in a squeaky voice, "You don't look like a doctor." Just then the intercom buzzed and Dr. Walker's voice said, "Next." She cocked her head towards the door and then went back to violently typing.

"I know," I said to the top of her head, took a deep breath, swallowed and went in.

There were no introductions. Dr. Walker just handed me a list of the patients on his service. He began immediately to summarize the diagnosis and current status of each one. I grabbed for the pen in the pocket of my white coat and began scribbling notes by each name.

Forty minutes later, he had gone through every one of the 27 patients. Only then did he look up and stare at me frowning.

"Any questions?" Dr. Walker asked.

"No, sir."

"Good answer," he said, "The Fellow on my service is Ken Benson. You'll alternate on-call nights with him. When I'm not around, you'll take orders from him. I don't suffer fools lightly, you got that?"

"Yes, sir." I said as Walker got Ken on the phone.

"Ken," Walker boomed over the phone, "the new resident is here. He'll meet you in the unit in five minutes. Take him on working rounds and get him started on the scut list. He's on tonight, so you're off. I'll round with the both of you sometime this evening. Don't leave before I do."

Walker slammed down the phone and started shuffling papers. After a minute, he looked up at me and said, "You still here?"

"No, sir," I said and a split second later I wasn't.

CHAPTER 17

BY THE FOLLOWING Thursday, I had been on Dr. Morgan Walker's service for about two weeks. He was harsh and demanding. The work was exhausting and the hours were worse than ever. Every morning, Ken helped Walker operate, while I did the scut list. Then I dealt with emergencies, saw consults, admitted new patients and rounded again with Ken later. Then we both rounded with Dr. Walker, and started a brand new scut list.

I didn't really mind the hard work. At least there was no time to worry about Jefferson, Barnes, or even Katy. I was totally immersed in patient care and rarely left the hospital. Without Katy, there was nothing waiting for me at home but roaches. Cafeteria food was cheap and my time off was better spent sleeping than shopping or cooking. I could stay in the hospital for days at a time and not worry about pissing off Katy. But, when I did get home, the house was dead and empty and I missed her lost love and friendship. Bicycling back and forth through the heat, what I really missed most was her car.

I also missed being in the OR, but there was nothing I could do about that. I was hoping that, on the next rotation, Dr. Kirkwood would let me assist, at least occasionally. To Walker, I was nothing but slave labor. The Wire would work me just as hard but he would also teach me. At least he would if he thought I still had a chance to finish the program.

It was nearly 3 AM on Friday when I finished Thursday's scut list. Post-ops were stable and there was only one new patient to work up. After that I might get an hour or two of sleep. Reviewing the chart at the nursing station I saw this was a high risk patient. Artificial mitral valve dysfunction with bad heart failure and multiple previous operations. Ken had written a quick note and a few basic orders. I hated waking the man up at that hour but had no choice. Without a detailed History and Physical on the chart by morning rounds, Walker would have my ass for breakfast.

The new patient was a twenty-six-year-old Samoan named Stephen Numatalulu. He had been transferred from the Naval Regional Medical Center in San Diego. As citizens of American territories in the South Pacific, Samoans had access to medical care in military hospitals. Stephen had already undergone three mitral valve replacements. The first was done by a navy surgeon and was an immediate failure. The next two were by a high-powered professor of surgery at UC San Diego. His valves worked well for a little longer, but also ended up leaking.

The reason for these failures was not a medical mystery. In reviewing his voluminous records, I saw that, prior to his first surgery, Stephen had weighed in excess of 450 pounds. Now, after three failed operations, progressive heart failure had him down to under 350. Much of that weight was retained water, rather than healthy tissue.

Stephen had been sent to us, on the Navy's dime, supposedly as a last desperate effort. The family had been told that, if anyone could save Stephen's life, we could. The truth, as admitted in the Fellow's note, was that Stephen was simply inoperable. This had been well proven three times already.

The first attempt had the best chance of success and the Navy surgeon had blown it. He had the problem of Stephen's massive size, not unusual for a Samoan. But, with that initial surgery, the tissues the valve was sewn to were still healthy. When the sutures holding the first valve pulled through, they left leaks that caused heart failure. Failure further weakened the torn tissues by making them weak and soggy.

With each subsequent operation, the tissue had more suture tears and was weaker. A fourth attempt would be pointless and almost surely fatal.

We would examine Stephen, explain that he was inoperable and send him back to Samoa. That is if he even lived long enough to get there. I couldn't help but wonder why the Navy bothered to send him to us. The family must have demanded it and, for some reason, had the juice to make it happen.

Nevertheless, I had to go through the motions. After reviewing the chart, I trudged down the darkened hallway to see Stephen Numatalulu. I turned on the light and thought, for a moment, I was Lemuel Gulliver in Brobdingnag. There were six Numatalulus in the single room. They filled every cubic inch of space. As I shuffled through they adjusted themselves around me and filled in behind me. Except for one young man in a blue blazer and slacks, all of them, men and women, were wrapped up in tent-like sarongs or dresses under loose-fitting jackets.

The head of Stephen's bed was elevated steeply. Heart failure patients have orthopnea. That means shortness of breath lying flat, due to pooling of fluid in the lungs. With the chest elevated, some of that fluid drains downward. The lungs become less soggy, which makes breathing easier.

In spite of being in the head-up position, Stephen was wheezing and gasping. Somehow he was sleeping in spite of his tortured respiration. I guessed he had been in failure so long that fighting for each breath seemed normal

Stephen's mouth hung open and his tongue protruded over a lower lip corner. We residents called this the Q sign. The Q sign was just about universally fatal. Stephen opened his eyes when the light came on, without movement other than breathing. Expanding his massive chest took all the energy he could muster.

Many Samoans and all of the Numatalulus were massive. Even by those standards the woman holding Stephen's hand was an Amazon. I sensed right away that she had to be the patient's mother. Everyone in the family deferred to her and they all called her, Momma. So did I. It was easier than saying, Mrs. Numatalulu. I introduced myself to her and the others. They spoke heavily accented English. I took a history, learned nothing new and did a physical examination.

Stephen was so wide I had to lean over and stretch my stethoscope to reach his heart with it. But his murmur was so loud the instrument was really hardly needed. Blood was gushing through gaping tears around the valve, instead of flowing smoothly through it. The turbulence roared like a swollen river through class VI rapids. With my naked ears, from the side of the bed, I could hear the harsh murmur clearly.

After the exam, I explained to the family that Dr. Walker would make the final decision but that Stephen was clearly inoperable and would be managed with medication. The news was not well received. Rather than respond directly to me, they rumbled deeply among themselves in Samoan. I could feel the vibration of their voices as much as hear them, like a sub-sonic woofer. It seemed that Momma was getting everyone's opinion before she spoke for the group.

"This medicine of which you speak," she said. "It will cure my boy?"

"No," I admitted. "At best, it will help his symptoms for a while. As long as the leak around the valve continues, he will be short of breath from heart failure."

"Without fix heart, my boy die soon," Momma said. It was not a question.

I just nodded.

I was sitting in the chair Momma had occupied until I started my examination. The next chair over had been vacated for her by one of the other giants. Momma rose from that chair and towered over me massively. Her gargantuan body bent where her waist would have been, if she'd had one. Looming above me, she placed one manhole cover-sized hand on each side of my head. I stole a glance at the single Numatalulu in Western clothing. He motioned urgently for me to sit still. I sat still.

After close to a full minute with my head in her hands, Momma backed off slowly. She pointed to me dramatically and said, "You will save my boy."

Her pronouncement set off rumblings that may have been mistaken for an earthquake.

I tried to explain to her that I was just a lowly resident. If Stephen was a candidate for surgery, I would not be the one to do it. Whatever I said drew the same response. Momma just pointed at me. "You will save my boy," she said again to rumbles of basso profundo agreement. Finally I assured them that Dr. Walker would explain everything the next day. Then I worked my way cautiously to the door as the Samoans moved to let me reach it.

Out in the hall, I was sweating freely and feeling a bit disoriented. It was almost as if I'd been through some sort of mystical experience.

Suddenly the Samoan in Western clothing came bursting from the room behind me. "Hey!" he said. "Hey, man, hang on a minute. You gotta listen."

"Okay, come on," I said. "We can talk in the conference room." I started to lead the way and had a sudden episode of vertigo. I stumbled and the Americanized Samoan grabbed me before I fell down.

He laughed and said, "So, you did feel it. I thought you would. It would be hard not to. Tavita is my Samoan name but I've been in the States for a long time. I go by Tad here." We shook hands and walked down the hall together.

The conference room was empty at 4 AM. There was a pot of coffee sludge on a table. Tad, or Tavita, got us each a cup and sat down beside me.

"All right, look" Tad said. "I know how that seemed, but I'm telling you, it isn't just bullshit. You gotta take it seriously. That old woman has . . . I know how this sounds, man, but it's true. Momma has . . . powers."

"Okay, maybe she does have powers." I wasn't going to argue with him. "But . . . I'm sorry but her son is just not operable. And even if he was operable I wouldn't be doing the surgery. I'm a second year general surgery resident on the cardiac surgery service. Between us, that means I'm lower than whale shit on the bottom of the deep blue sea. Dr. Walker will talk with all of you tomorrow and if there's surgery to be done, he'll do it. But . . . look I'm sorry but I know he'll say the same thing I told you."

Tad looked at me and nodded, his round Asian face pinched with concentration.

"Did you wonder how come the Navy paid for this trip?" he finally asked me.

"Actually I am curious about that," I admitted. "They must have known that we could only send him back without surgery or . . ."

"Or kill him," Tad finished the sentence for me. "You don't have to sugarcoat it for me. He's my cousin but I hardly know him. I hardly know any of them. I grew up in New Jersey. Never mind why. That's a long story and it doesn't matter. The point is this." He paused and thought about how to explain things to me.

"The Samoan government is totally fucked. It's half a modern democracy. The other half is ruled by various chiefs like in the old days. Momma's from a family of chiefs—like royalty—and she's also a natural healer. She's well known in Samoa and the people love her. Your State Department knows that and they do not want to insult her.

"So here's what happened. Momma talked to the US embassy in Samoa. They talked to the State Department in DC. They talked to the Secretary of the Navy. He talked to the CO in San Diego and here we are on your doorstep."

I was really tired and saw my chance for a couple of hours sleep fading. But I didn't want to be rude and I hadn't explained just why Stephen's case was hopeless. The language and cultural barriers with the other family members made that seem pointless. Maybe Tad could understand and explain it to the others. It seemed worth a try.

"All that is fine," I said. "But politics is one thing and anatomy is another. Momma could be the Queen of England and it wouldn't change anything. The mitral valve is between what's called the left atrium and the left ventricle. But really they're not on the left so much as they are posterior."

"What's posterior mean?" Tad asked.

"In this case it means deeper in the chest, closer to the back or the spinal column," I explained and went on. "The right atrium and ventricle are more anterior than they are on the right side."

"Anterior?" Tad asked.

"Anterior means towards the front of the body. In this case, just behind the sternum or chest bone." I put my hand on the front of my own chest to show him.

"To expose the mitral valve, you have to cut into and open up that posterior placed left atrium. To do that, you need to lift and move the right or anterior atrium out of your way. This is hard enough in a normal sized person with a heart that's smaller than a football.

In your cousin, exposing the mitral valve well is a cardiac surgeon's nightmare. It's been tried three times and three times they simply couldn't do it. I've read all the op notes and they all describe the same problem. Down in the depths of that cavernous chest you just can't see what you're doing. They could barely remove the old valve, much less see to sew in the new one. You can't sew accurately to what you can't see and there's no way to get good exposure. That's why the sutures keep pulling through and ripping up the annulus."

"Whoa," said Tad. "Wait a minute. What do you mean by the annulus."

"Okay, let's say the mitral valve is round," I said. "When you cut it out, you leave a round hole. If the round hole is like a doughnut hole, the annulus is the doughnut. Healthy annular tissue is tough and that's what the replacement valve is sewn to. An artificial valve has a Dacron sewing ring around its circumference. The stitches or sutures holding the valve in place go from the sewing ring to the annulus."

Tad nodded his understanding and I continued. "Stephen's chest is incredibly deep. His heart is the biggest I've ever seen. The left atrium is way at the bottom of that hole and the right side of the heart is on top of it. The mitral valve and its annulus lay in the deepest part of that left atrium."

I paused a minute to let that sink in and give Tad a chance to ask questions. He seemed to understand so I went on. "The op-notes of Stephen's other surgeons say they could never even see the annulus clearly, much less sew to it accurately. That's why their sutures were poorly placed and pulled through shredding the tissue."

"I'm an automobile mechanic," Tad said. "I know about getting exposure, as you call it, of an engine part to fix or replace it. In a car, to use your terms, the hood would be like the chest bone or sternum. Parts like the carburetor, just under the hood would be anterior?" I nodded to confirm he had it right and Tad continued.

"Parts at the bottom of engine, by the ground, like the crank case . . . Would they be posterior?" Tad asked.

I nodded again and he made his point, actually a pretty good one.

"So if you want to work on something anterior, like the carburetor, you lift the hood to do it," Tad said. "If you want to drain the oil, you don't go through the hood. You get under the car and go that way. For a posterior part, you need a posterior approach to get to it."

"I see where you're going with this, Tad," I said. "The problem is, it's a dead end. The approach to the mitral valve is already from the posterior direction. But you can't go through the spine which would be like sliding under the car. You have to go down deep to the side of the heart and then get around behind it. That is exactly what is so impossible with Stephen. The hole's too deep and then you have the entire rest of the heart on top of you. An anterior approach is what Stephen needs, but there's only one way to do that. To use your car analogy, that would be like cutting through the engine front to back with a blow torch. That would not be too good for the motor of the car and worse for the heart of a person."

"Momma says you're gonna save her boy's life," Tad smiled. "And if she says it, it is gonna happen. So, if exposure of the valve is the problem and you can't do the operation . . . I can see only one way for you to save Stephen. You *will* figure out some better way to expose the valve and tell Dr. Walker."

This was a waste of valuable sleeping time and I was completely exhausted. But there was something about the term anterior approach that was ringing a bell in my memory. "Tad, I told you there is only one way to expose the mitral valve," I began.

Then it hit me.

Dr. Walker didn't normally operate on Friday mornings so he rounded late, around seven. I begged off morning work rounds with Ken and waited for Walker by his office.

"What are you doing here?" Walker demanded as he turned the key and went in. "Why aren't you getting ready for rounds with Ken?"

"I need to talk with you about a case, before rounds," I explained. "Ken let me go and I've been waiting here for you."

I followed him into his office, where the big gruff Texan sat behind his desk and I stood in front of it. He did not invite me to sit.

"What case?" he asked curtly. "And this better be good."

"Stephen Numatalulu," I said. "You haven't seen him yet. He came in yesterday and I worked him up last night."

Walker rolled his eyes, shook his head and started cursing quietly to an imaginary man by his left ear. This is what he did when the humans around him proved just too stupid to talk to. "I know all about that case, you idiot. The Navy surgeon called to tell me about it yesterday. It's inoperable, which should have been obvious. I was just starting to think that you might have half a brain and now . . ."

"He's operable." I said. "That's what I want to talk to you about." I knew that if Walker pronounced Stephen inoperable in front of witnesses that would be it. He could never admit that a resident convinced him to change an opinion. One on one, I thought there might be a chance he'd listen to me.

"Get the fuck out of my office," Walker yelled and started leafing through some correspondence.

I came around his desk and put the article in my hand down on top of what he was reading. I'd copied the paper from the rather obscure "Israeli Journal of Cardiac Surgery."

"What the fuck is this?" he demanded, but couldn't avoid looking at it. The title of the article was, "Anterior Approach to the Mitral Valve with Excellent Exposure."

"I had a few weeks off recently, as you know," I said. "I read every heart surgery journal carried by our library. That's how I happened to see this article by Dr. Azai Greenbaum. It describes an anterior approach to the mitral valve; it will work on Stephen Numatalulu."

I thought Walker was about to jump up and try to throw me out of his office, until I said "anterior approach." He knew that could be the key to Stephen's surgery. He settled back in his chair but still refused to read the paper.

I said, "You cut right down through the right atrium and then on through the atrial septum. Then you're into the left atrium with nothing blocking access. Unlike the usual posterior approach, there would be nothing between us and the mitral. We would just cut straight down onto it through the anterior structures. Greenbaum says, when you cut through the atrial septum, the mitral is right there. Just look at the diagram."

I turned the page for him and Dr. Walker looked at the drawing. Then he looked up at me with the ghost of a smile playing across his lips. "I'll think about it," he said. "Now you go help Ken get ready for rounds. I might be a little late."

We went to see the Numatalulus late that Friday afternoon. Dr. Walker told them that Stephen's surgery could be done but it would be risky. Stephen could easily die on the table but that, without surgery, he had no chance.

Stephen was too sick to understand much of what was going on. The decision would be made by Momma. She stood up, pointed a finger at me and said, "You will save my boy."

Dr. Walker shot me an angry look. I cringed and shrugged then said, "Momma, this is Dr. Morgan Walker. He's one of the best heart surgeons in the world. He is the one who will operate on Stephen and he is the one who can save him if anyone can do it. I think you should give him the chance."

"You must help Dr. Walker," Momma said.

I looked at Walker, but he was staring at Momma. Strangely enough, he also seemed to feel her power or charisma or whatever it was. He nodded at me and told Momma that I would be allowed to help. Her round face exploded in a brilliant smile and she spoke for a while in Samoan. I noticed that Stephen was smiling too, looking at his momma. It seemed that, for the whole family, it was all decided right then and there. Momma said that I would save Stephen and so it was going to happen.

As we left the room, Walker wanted to know what I'd said to explain Momma's behavior.

"I said nothing about me or anyone saving her boy," I said quickly. "I tried to tell her last night that he was inoperable but she wouldn't listen. She just started insisting that I was going to save him. Then I talked to one of the men, a cousin of the patient. He said she's some kind of medicine woman or whatever. I don't know. This was about four in the morning and something made me listen. I was about to blow him off but then I remembered the article I showed you." I shrugged and threw up my hands.

"A medicine woman, huh?" Walker said. "Did you know I was one quarter Apache?"

"No, sir." I said, thinking that his last resident, was lucky to still have his scalp.

"My great grandmother was an Apache medicine woman." Walker said, looking at me. "And Momma there says you have to help, huh?"

I shrugged again. "Sir, I'm not going to hold you to that. I mean, maybe if I'm just in the room, able to watch or maybe if I could just second assist . . . then you could honestly say I'd helped. But I know I can't . . ." A second year general surgery resident first assisting on this tough a heart case was out of the question.

"You take the weekend off, Logan, and rest up. We'll do Numatalulu Monday morning and you'll be first assisting." Then Walker turned to the Fellow. "Ken, I'm sorry for the short notice but you're on this weekend—the whole weekend. That gives you two days to get that patient dried out, tuned up and optimized for surgery." Then to me, "You get out of here now. I don't want you near the hospital until I see you in the OR Monday morning. Don't even make Monday morning rounds. That clear? I want you fresh as a daisy."

"Sure, but shouldn't I just stay to help Ken with the . . ." I said.

"Get the fuck out of here now," Walker ordered. "You're obviously exhausted. It's actually depressing just to look at you. So get out of my sight and get yourself together. I want you at your absolute best on Monday morning. Kirkwood and McDuff keep telling me what great hands you have. Monday we'll find out.

"Now I'm not going to tell you again. Get the fuck out!"

I got the fuck out.

CHAPTER 18

I HADN'T BEEN home for a long time. A safe return required some preparation. Katy used to spray strategic areas each day to hold down the roach population. With no chemical minefield to stop them, the insect army would be advancing. I stopped on the way for a new spray-can of crawling insect killer and entered cautiously holding the weapon at the ready. After intensive spraying, the house was safe for human habitation - as long as one didn't breathe the poisonous air or touch any treated surfaces.

I stayed in the shower until the AC had been on for a while. Getting out and drying off, I headed straight for my bedroom. It was still light out but I didn't care. For me it was several days past bedtime. The phone rang before I could hit the sheets. It was Holt.

"You still awake, Yankee Boy?" Holt asked, as if he could see what I was I doing.

"Not for much longer," I said, "I got the whole weekend off and plan on sleeping through most of it." There was a long pause.

"I hate to mess with that plan, son," Holt said, "but . . . it's Billy Sugg, the boy who's heart you done. He's overdosed on cocaine; alive but in a dense coma. He's been admitted to the neuro ICU."

I knew that Billy had been discharged a day or so after I'd been fired. I had wanted to talk with him before he left, encourage him to stay off the cocaine. But then I got drunk and bought Looks-Rough-Runs-Good and then Shaleena got murdered. I'd also been barred from the VA, under penalty of death or worse.

All good excuses, but, as The Wire always told us, "Anyone can fail with a good excuse."

Now Billy was in a coma and maybe if I'd . . .

"I know what you're thinking," Holt broke into my thoughts. "There's nothing you could have done. He was an addict. Addicts OD. Heart surgery does not cure cocaine addiction. It is not your fault. And you know that."

I knew it wasn't, but it felt like it was. I'd let Billy down just like Andy. I had lost one friend to LSD and now another to cocaine; batting 0 for 2 was nothing to be proud of. My throat closed up and my eyes started stinging. I coughed and said, "I want to see him, Holt. Did you say he's in the neuro unit? How come he's at the U?" The VA had no ICU for neuro patients.

"Yeah, I made sure they took him in over here," Holt said. "I knew you'd want to see him and you couldn't at the VA. But listen, boy, you need to be ready for that big case Monday." How did Holt learn about these things? "You can't make up for weeks of exhaustion just going to bed early Sunday evening. That's why Walker give you the weekend off. Before helping with that mitral, you need to get you a few good nights of sound sleeping. You should start with a nice long sleep tonight, Yankee Boy, and see Billy in the AM."

I looked down at my unmade bed. My head was drawn towards the pillow like a dying planet falling into its sun. I was so damned tired . . .

"I need to see him now, Holt." I said. "Just to see that he's settled. Then I'll come home and get some sleep. I promise."

"And I knew you were gonna say that too," Holt said. "That bike still your only transportation?"

I admitted it was.

"Well then I'll come by and collect your Yankee ass," Holt said. "You'll kill yourself falling asleep at the handle bars, if you try coming in on that thing."

"Thanks, Holt, but I'm going to need a way to get home," I said. "I'll be okay on the bike. It's mostly downhill to the hospital and . . ."

"I'll carry you back home after you've seen Billy," Holt said. "That's the only way to be sure you won't spend the night there."

I tried to argue but Holt just told me he'd be by in a half hour and hung up.

I quickly dressed as if for work: tan slacks, white shirt, blue tie, and black shoes. Everything except the white coat. It would be bad enough if Walker caught me in the hospital, against his direct orders. Wearing jeans and sneakers like a hippie would only make it worse. But, on the way out, I felt that damn tie strangling around my neck and said, screw it. I was off duty, after all. I pulled off the tie and threw it on the floor. It didn't make me feel that much better.

* * *

The neuro ICU was different from our Cardiac unit. We had all the beds in one large room, for maximum visibility and easy emergency access. Neuro patients were not so likely to need crises intervention. Each neuro patient had a three-walled private room. The inner sides were open to a central nursing station. A curtain across that space could be pulled for privacy. The outer wall of each cubical even had a window.

Billy was supine, with oxygen cannulae in his nose. IV lines through his chest fed large central veins. There was also a feeding tube through his abdominal wall and into the jejunum. A naso-gastric tube on suction kept his stomach empty to avoid aspiration. He apparently wasn't expected to wake up and start eating any time soon. Billy's neurologist, Deepak Pandya, was tops in his field. Holt made sure that Billy would be under Dr. Pandya's care.

Dr. Pandya was looking at Billy's most recent EEG when Holt and I came in. Holt introduced me and Dr. Pandya gave me a long curious look. I knew he was thinking that I didn't look like a doctor. He was just too polite to say so and for that I was grateful.

"The EEG is nud that bad," Dr. Pandya said. "It is nud meeting criteria for brain death, but neither does Jell-O exposed to slight vibration." He chuckled at the world's oldest neurologist joke and went on. "It may seem quite hopeless to you, but such is nud the case. He could awaken at any moment or remain comatose until dying, which might nud be for years to come or might be tomorrow."

Holt and I asked a few questions but didn't learn anything more. Dr. Pandya left and I looked around feeling kind of helpless. Unlike the abnormal EEG or electroencephalogram of Billy's brainwaves, his electrocardiogram, or EKG, was completely normal. I borrowed a nurse's stethoscope and listened to healthy heart sounds. Billy's lab work was negative for cardiac enzymes and his chest X-ray was perfect. Billy's heart was fine. None of that related to his coma but it still made me feel better.

I had fattened Billy up a bit, prior to his heart surgery. That extra weight had been lost since his discharge on a cocaine diet. I remembered how light he'd been, in the VA ICU, when I lifted him onto a gurney. That was the night I saved his life and killed my future. Billy's eyes were sunk deep in dark purple sockets. The rest of his skin was so pale it was nearly transparent. His birdlike chest hardly moved as he snored through each breath. A body that snores is a body that lives, I thought. It was better than the alternative.

"Come on, Yankee Boy," Holt said. "I gotta swing by my office and then I'll carry you on home."

"How could he do this to himself, Holt?" I asked. "I just don't understand."

"We all do it to ourselves, one way or another," Holt said. "Ever single damn one of us."

When we got to Holt's office his beeper went off and he had to go see a patient. He said he wouldn't be long and asked me to wait for him. Alone in Holt's office my eyes were drawn to the big book behind his desk next to his chair. I really did not mean to snoop. I just wanted something to read until he came back. That was the only reason I started leafing through *The Count of Monte Cristo*. Well maybe not the only reason. I had been curious about that book since I first noticed it in Holt's office.

It was a magnificent and obviously very expensive tome and it lay alone, in a place of honor, on its own elegantly carved highly polished table. An old family Bible in the house of a religious friend and a huge unabridged dictionary in an English classroom were the only other books I had ever seen displayed with such reverence.

I sat in Holt's chair and took *The Count* in my hands. The cover had the sensual feel and musky aroma of butter-soft leather and the pages had the inner ivory glow of fine parchment. The book was in perfect condition but did not look new. Checking for the date of publication, I found a picture glued across from the title page. It was a black and white photograph of a pretty young girl. She was about high-school age: a real cutie. Her curly, shoulder-length hair was dark in the black and white photo, probably brunette. The hairstyle and clothing were dated.

I turned the page and saw that she'd apparently been more auburn than brunette. A lock of reddish-brown hair tied with a small pink ribbon was preserved in a wax paper envelope. The natural assumption was that it belonged to the girl in the photo.

Everyone knew that Holt had never married and had no children. Who was this girl? Why did Holt keep her image and a lock of her hair in a leather-bond copy of a 19th Century classic?

I suddenly felt guilty for even speculating about Holt's private life. I moved quickly away from the book when I heard his footsteps approaching the office. My curiosity about the girl, powerful as it was, was no match for my shame over snooping.

* * *

As he pulled up to my house, I invited Holt in but he declined, which was just as well. I was not exactly prepared to entertain. "I do need a minute of your time though," Holt said, shutting down the engine of his Ford pickup.

He half-turned towards me with one hand on the back of the seat and the other on the wheel. "Did you know that Billy had an uncle?" Holt asked.

"Sure," I said. "I met him when Billy was first admitted and how could anyone forget . . . uh . . . Tiny. His name's Tiny, right?" Tiny's image was clear in my mind: the basketball head; the broken nose and close-set colorless eyes; the massive shoulders and absent neck; the heavy slabs of beef-like muscle; the tattooed swastikas on the backs of his hands and killer's tears under his eye. But most of all I remembered that he was totally hairless.

"Tiny generally makes a memorable impression," Holt admitted.

"How do you know him?" I asked. "And what is up with the absence of hair and eye color. No facial hair, not even eyebrows, no hair on his arms . . ."

"Nary a hair on his body," Holt said. "Tiny and I, and Jefferson too for that matter, we all went to the same high school."

"What?" I asked. "The three of you . . . you were all at the same high school?" It seemed like an impossible coincidence.

"Why would that surprise you?" Holt asked. We're all about the same age and all local boys. There weren't but three high schools in Birmingham when we all come up here. It's not surprising the three of us were at one at the same time. You already heard from Owens that Jefferson's family and mine lived near each other. Tiny was there too."

That seemed reasonable, so I nodded, okay, and Holt continued.

"I was on the football team with Tiny," Holt said, "I seen him in the shower. Tiny is completely hairless ever-where and I do mean ever-where. Funny thing is I don't recall anyone teasing him about it, ever. It's some kind of genetic thing, someone-or-other's syndrome. I don't recollect the name."

"The tattooed tears," I said. "I heard the two tears under his eye mean he killed two men in prison. Is that . . .?"

"Yeah, it's more'n likely true," Holt nodded, "Tiny can be a violent man and I guess a fella does what he must to survive in prison. I wouldn't hold those tears against him too much and there is another side to Tiny. He and I were the only boys on that team that read anything but the sports pages or a comic. Believe it or not, Tiny even loves poetry. He's memorized a buncha poems. I've heard him recite some."

Then I remembered something. "The day Billy was admitted, Tiny said that I came highly recommended. Was it you that sent them to me at the VA?"

"No. No. I ain't seen Tiny in years," Holt said. But he shifted uncomfortably and his eyes slithered off left and downward. I'll never forget that moment. It was the first time I knew Holt lied to me.

"Tiny grew up kinda wild. No daddy around and his momma was the town slut. My daddy had to arrest him more than once for juvenile offenses. I tried to get Daddy to cut my friend some slack but . . ." Holt paused and looked off into his own past. "To my daddy, right was right and wrong was wrong. And wrong had to be punished—*always*. No exceptions permitted, not never."

There was another long pause before Holt went on. "Anyway it's no surprise that Tiny went on to become a criminal. Fact is, Tiny runs all the white crime in Birmingham."

"Now wait a minute. Wait a minute," I said, holding up my hands palms out. "Didn't you tell me once that Shaleena's husband, Eightball White, controlled the black crime, even from prison?" I asked.

"I'm glad you're paying attention, Yankee Boy," Holt said, still smiling. "But what is your point?"

"Doesn't it seem a little odd to you? I mean, here's Billy. His uncle, Tiny, controls white crime in Birmingham. Billy's nurse is Shaleena, who gets herself murdered, and her man, Eightball, currently incarcerated, controls the black crime." I cocked my head with a quizzical expression on my face and my hands open in front of me.

"I don't allow as how that's much of a coincidence," Holt said. "You got a white drug addict and a black murder victim. And you got Tiny and Eightball, who between them have a hand in all the drug selling and most of the murders in this town. The fact that Billy and Shaleena were related to Tiny and Eightball don't change that one iota. If anything it makes it more likely they'd both be involved somehow."

That seemed reasonable so I shut up. This was all very interesting but it was hard to keep my eyes open.

"Now," Holt chuckled. "As I told you, Jefferson and Tiny and me, as kids, all knew each other. Fact is that Tiny used to bully Jefferson something awful. Tiny cleaned Jefferson's clock on more than one occasion.

"I had some influence with Tiny, Holt said. "As I said, we played football together. In the South, that counts for a lot. And we also enjoyed reading, which was a secret we kept to our own-selves.

"I generally did what I could to stop Tiny and his friends from bothering the weaker kids, but my protection did not extend to Lloyd Jefferson. I never hurt Lloyd my own self. Daddy wouldn't permit it. But I had no call to interfere with any business Tiny had with him." Holt smiled fondly at some secret memory.

"What did you have against Jefferson? I asked.

"Him and his whole family," Holt said, "they thought they was above the law, above my daddy's law and . . ." Holt paused for a moment with a far-away look in his eye. "But never you mind about that, Yankee Boy. That's none a your worry.

"The point here is that, Tiny might-could blame you for what happened to Billy. Jefferson coulda told Tiny that you cut on the boy for no reason. That Billy found out and got upset and that's what got him back on the cocaine."

It seemed absurd to me, but if Tiny talked to Jefferson . . .

"It's possible, Yankee Boy," Holt said. "That's all I'm saying."

"Okay," I said, "so now, in addition to all my other problems, I have a tattooed, no-neck, ex-convict, hairless mutant, crime-lord, approximately the size of Rhode Island, who may think I killed his nephew. If so, he might want to kill me and we know he's murdered at least two other people. But that was in prison so I shouldn't hold it against him. Does that about sum it up?"

Holt was laughing by the time I finished. "I'm glad you find this amusing," I added, though I had to smile with him.

"It'll be okay," Holt assured me. "If Tiny threatens you or approaches you at all, you just tell him to get with me. Even though we ain't seen each other in years, I've followed his career and he knows who I am. The bond between us is still there. You send Tiny on to me and I'll get his mind right. I'll explain it was you saved Billy's life. Then you'll have you a strong friend in Tiny.

"And when he learns about that, Tiny will have to do what he can to help you."

Holt smiled broadly as if this was part of some plan that was coming together. As if Holt and I were playing a game and now Tiny had to play with us.

CHAPTER 19

THE NEXT DAY, Saturday morning, I pedaled in to the hospital and was sitting with Billy by 10. I felt better after one night's rest but sleep deprivation lingered. I tried to study the Israeli mitral valve paper but my eyes kept closing. Finally I gave up, turned off the lights and just sat there dozing. Suddenly I jerked awake. I looked around anxiously and there was Tiny.

He came in, turned on the light and closed the curtain behind him. It's hard to defend yourself sitting in a chair, so I stood up and just watched him.

"Hello, Tiny," I said, extending my hand. He completely ignored me.

Tiny went to the other side of Billy's bed and stood looking down at his nephew. He wasn't as big as the Samoans, but was still out of proportion to the small room. He seemed like a different species from the frail figure on the bed. Tiny watched Billy breathe for a while touched his forehead and took a deep breath. Then he looked across the bed at me.

"This is your doing," he said calmly.

"How do you figure it was my fault, Tiny?" I asked, more annoyed than frightened.

"I done got the story from Jefferson," Tiny said. "He didn't have the balls to face me, the little shit, but he told me on the phone what-all happened. You were the only one Billy trusted and then you used him like some kinda Guinea pig —cut on the boy for no reason. Billy believed in you. Then he found out what you done. When he lost faith in you, he lost faith in his own-self. That's why he went back on the coke. That's why he's like this."

"Really?" I said. "That's what Dr. Jefferson told you?"

"That is what he done told me," Tiny said, and started circling over to my side of the bed.

If I'd backed up a single step, he'd have been on me in a second. Knowing that, I held my ground, keeping my balance forward.

"You've known Jefferson a long time," I said. "You think he's an honest or honorable man?"

"He's always been a lying sack of yellow shit," Tiny admitted, but kept lumbering towards me. "And how do you know how long I been knowing him."

"How about Holt Mcduff?" I asked. "How long have you known him?" The question stopped Tiny about a foot in front of me. He was uncomfortably inside my space, looking down at me with a menacing expression. It was actually hard to imagine Tiny with any other kind of expression.

"I been knowing Holt and Jefferson since we all three come up together," Tiny said.

"And how about Holt?" I continued. "Do you know him to be an honest and honorable man?"

"He's Dudley fucking Do-Right. Holt is," Tiny said. "You know Holt?" Tiny tilted his hairless basketball of a head with the question.

"I know Holt and Holt knows all about me and Jefferson and Billy. Before you take this any further, why don't you ask Holt what happened. After that, if you want to have it out with me . . . you just give it your best shot. I'm not going anywhere." I got ready to go in low, under his punch, striking up at his throat, to hit the larynx. If the biggest toughest guy in the world can't breath, he can't do much to hurt you. When he clutched his throat, I'd step to the side and kick his knee at an angle. It was a good plan and plans always work, right up until the fight starts. I was ready to react, but then I could sense Tiny thinking about what I told him.

The big thug stepped back a pace and actually scratched his cue-ball head with one finger. "You think you'd have a chance if I did give it my best shot?" he asked smiling.

"I don't think either one of us really wants to find out," I told him.

"What're you doing here anyway," Tiny asked. "You're a heart doc. You ain't no brain doctor."

"I'm here because I'm Billy's friend," I said.

"Maybe," Tiny answered. "Anyway, I'll find out from Holt what the truth is." He spun around quickly and gracefully, especially for a man his size. Suddenly he was out of the room as silently as he'd entered.

I took a deep breath, sat down next to Billy and thought about the encounter with Tiny. Something about it didn't ring true. If he and Holt hadn't seen each other in years, why hadn't he asked for Holt's phone number or directions to his office? The big man acted angry enough but, once I was fully awake, my gut never felt like I was in danger. And Holt had predicted that Tiny would come by. He even predicted what he would say, about Jefferson blaming me for Billy's problem.

It all just seemed a little too pat, as if Holt and Tiny planned it together. But Holt said he hadn't seen Tiny in years. Why lie about that? Holt had said something about Tiny having to help me when he realized what I had done for Billy. Maybe my helping Billy did obligate him. But how could Tiny possibly help me with any of my problems? And if Holt wanted his help, why not just ask him? Why set up some big charade? I could make no sense of it.

Or, of course, it all could have been for real. Maybe Jefferson had set Tiny against me. In which case, Holt would straighten him out. But then what would happen?

The rest of the morning was uneventful. I cat-napped in the chair by Billy's bed and ate lunch in the hospital. I had hoped to see Roberta or Bo, but neither one came to visit. They must have been busy. After lunch, I swung by the resident's library and re-read everything on mitral valve surgery.

Before heading home, I stopped by Billy's room again and sat with him for a while. He was stable but showed no sign of coming out of the coma. I had the certain feeling that Billy was still there, floating around in those EEG brainwaves. If I could just figure some way to get his attention, something inside me knew he would wake up. The feeling made no sense but I just couldn't shake it.

After a while Sharon Bronson came by. She was the kind of girl that was easy to talk to, as Billy had prior to his surgery. Sharon was a brunette with huge soft brown eyes half hidden under thick bangs. The olive skin of her oval face was framed by waves of lustrous locks tumbling to her shoulders. Sharon had a slim but soft womanly figure. Her breasts were the kind a man wants to bury his face in.

"Did you know that Billy was a child prodigy on the piano?" Sharon asked me.

"Actually I do know that" I smiled, noting her surprised expression. I guess she thought that she was the only one in whom Billy had confided. We compared notes about his history and Vietnam experience. He'd also told Sharon about reading sheet music to drown out the sounds of battle. She thought that was wonderful but I saw another side to it.

"It seemed to me in combat you'd want to be alert to what was going on around you," I said. "not huddled up in the fetal position pretending to be at a concert."

"Have you ever been in combat?" she demanded, eyes flashing, and I had to admit that I hadn't.

"Then who are you to criticize Billy?" She defended him like a mother lion who's cubs were in danger.

"I'm not attacking Billy," I assured her with hands raised in capitulation. "You're right. I'll never know how I would handle myself under fire. But if I was in a battle, I'd want the guy next to me to be fighting not having auditory hallucinations."

She jumped up and started to storm out then turned and said, "The music in his head was not a hallucination. The notes were just so much a part of his mind, so etched into his brain that he could hear them. It's a wonderful thing, not a shameful thing." By this point her fists were clinched and she was yelling at me. Then suddenly her hands were against her face and she was hysterically crying.

I stood up and closed the curtain to the cubicle to keep her tears private. Very slowly and cautiously, I took her into my arms, trying to provide some comfort. At first she stiffened but then she relaxed pressing herself against me. We stood there for a while as my T-shirt got soaked and I told her what Billy meant to me. .

"Why would I be here if I didn't care about him?" I asked. She just shrugged and sniffled. After a while she got her tears under control but continued to hold her face against me.

"I know she said. I'm just upset." Her quiet response into my damp chest was muffled but I got the message. Just about then, the hug that started as comfort seemed to be changing. Sharon felt it too. She tilted her mascara stained face and stared up at me. Those big brown eyes floating in tears peered up from under bangs at me. Then her eyelids, with the longest lashes I'd ever seen, came down and she tilted her head back. Parting her puffy lips, and waited for me to kiss her.

God knows I wanted to. Katy had been gone for weeks and I needed to be with a woman. Not just sexually, maybe not even mostly that way. I needed that but I needed even more the soft comfort of a woman's body. Maybe a gentle woman's soul touching mine was what I really most needed.

I knew that, once my lips touched hers, what followed would be inevitable. Suddenly I also knew—God help me—I still loved Katy.

I moved Sharon gently but firmly away and she jerked herself out of my embrace. "I'm sorry," she choked out. "I'm sorry," and ran out of the cubicle crying.

I stopped on the way home for beer and chips and ate in front of the TV before racking out early. Tired as I still was, and in spite of the beers, my nerves were too jangled for sleeping. Images of breasts and big brown eyes under bangs kept me awake. I was naked on my back on top of the sheets. With his one eye, The Big Bopper glared up at me. He was furious at me for missing our big chance with Sharon. If he hadn't been attached, he would have taken off with his two suitcases. I did what was needed to get him to leave me alone and who can say it was wrong? Pleasing yourself is basically just sex with someone you love.

After that, I fell sound asleep and didn't wake up for hours. Finally the bedtime beers prompted another bodily function. Leaning my forehead on the cabinet behind the john, eyes closed so I wouldn't wake all the way up, I guided the stream by sonar.

Staggering back to bed I heard the TV murmuring in my living room. I was sure I hadn't left it playing, so someone had turned it on. I had a pretty good idea who it was and didn't want to confront him naked. Back in my room, I pulled on jeans, grabbed a new T-shirt and went to see my visitor.

Sure enough, there was Tiny Sugg in my living room at three in the morning. He was lounging in my most comfortable chair, drinking one of my newly purchased beers, munching my potato chips from a brand new bag and watching a rerun on my TV. It was the ten year old original version of Little Shop of Horrors.

Tiny didn't look up from my easy chair as I took a seat on the sofa. I reached for the bag on the end table between us and munched a few chips. They were fresh and crispy and I needed the salt so I ate a few more. That made me thirsty and I went out to the kitchen to get a bottle of coke. Tiny called after me to bring him another beer, which I did. We chuckled as Audrey the carnivorous plant demanded, "Give me to eat," and Seymour served her human snacks.

As final credits began to roll, Tiny got up and switched off the TV. He lifted the heavy easy chair as if it were a plastic cafeteria seat, spun it to face the sofa and sat down.

"One of my favorite movies," Tiny observed.

"Yeah, a real profound message," I added somewhat pompously.

Tiny frowned. "You don't think it's profound?" he asked me.

"Well, not really," I said uncertainly.

Tiny nodded. "Don't profound kinda mean like deep?" he asked.

"Pretty much," I nodded.

"Well, ain't human sacrifice a pretty deep part a human nature? I mean we seen it all over the ancient world from the Canaanites to the Aztecs and there's still these nut-cases today murdering folks for Satan. And that movie also talks about loneliness and love, and crime and punishment, and loyalty and betrayal. I am just a dumb redneck but I'd say those were all mighty damn deep – or profound - parts a human nature. But I guess a smart guy like you would know better," Tiny added and sat staring at me.

"I stand corrected, Tiny," I said. "Holt told me you were a reader. I should not have talked down to you and I won't do it again.

"That's alright," Tiny said. "You just keep on underestimating me. I love it when folks do that, especially smart-ass college boy Yankees."

"Holt said you'd memorized a lot of poetry," I said, looking for common ground. "So have I. I know . . ."

"Let's save the poetry session for another time," Tiny cut me off. "We got us other things to talk about."

"Okay," I said. "You're on. Sock it to me."

He smiled and made a fist as I laughed saying, "Maybe I could have phrased that differently."

"Don't worry," Tiny chuckled. "I got with Holt and he told me what really went down. I actually want to thank you, doc, for what you done for Billy. And I'm gonna thank you by hepin you out with your problem. Saving Billy's life was what got you in this jam and I'm gonna see you get out of it."

"I appreciate that, Tiny," I said, "but there's no need for you to do anything. I'm sure it'll all work out okay."

"The fuck it will," Tiny said. "You need my hep, doc, and you're gonna take it. It's been a few weeks since the killing. If the cops ain't found the man with the broke finger yet, they'll never find his ass. I know ever hired killer in Alabama and have employed most a them my own self, one time or another. I'll find your man before the cops get their heads outa their paper work – or outa their butts for that matter. " Tiny laughed at his own joke.

"Now, anything you want to axe me before we get started?" Tiny said. "That is anything other than what poems we can recite" His ears flushed a little pink as if he was still embarrassed about liking poetry.

"Uhh . . . did I forget to lock my front door?" I said

"Don't matter worth a fart in a shit storm if you remember or not with a piece of crap lock like you got, doc," Tiny snorted contemptuously. "Do the two words, dead bolt, have any significance to you at all?" The way Tiny pronounced "Day-ed bolt," it sounded more like three words.

I waited for him to go on, which he did. "The space 'twixt the edge of your door and the jam is damn near wide enough to fit your pecker through – not my pecker, you understand, but your average fella's pecker. There's more than enough room anyways to stick a credit card or, hell even a damn screwdriver in that space and just push open the tongue a that spring-bolt. Now, if you had you a dead bolt, that'd be a whole nother story." Tiny slapped a handful of potato chips into his mouth with an open palm, spilling crumbs all over the front of his Hawaiian shirt, the lap of his khaki pants and my carpet. I decided to be a courteous host and didn't even mention it.

"Not that any kind a lock woulda kept me out, doc," he added. "You and me, we got talking to do and we might as well get to it. First off though . . ." He handed me a $150 in crisp new bills. "That's from Mr. Rutledge. He allowed as how he was not completely honest with you about that sea-ment truck. He took to feeling real bad about what he done and he wanted you to have your money back . . . with some interest."

I was surprised to find I was just a little worried about Mr. Rutledge. "Is, uh, is Mr. Rutledge . . . okay?"

"I didn't hurt him none, doc," Tiny assured me. "I just reasoned with the man."

"Reasoned with him," I repeated.

"You bet," Tiny said, with a satisfied smile. "Most folk will listen to reason. You just got to explain things the right way." I started to ask for more details but Tiny quickly changed the subject. "And what's up with them two front doors?" he asked indignantly. "This dump don't hardly deserve but one entrance."

"You're a keen judge of real estate and a very observant guy," I said, and I meant it. The place was obviously a dump but, at night, it was not at all obvious that there were two front doors. We never used the one on the left and there was no light or mat by it.

I said, "The only reason I can imagine for the two doors is that the architect had delusions of grandeur. Maybe he thought the owner of the house would be hosting formal parties. He probably imagined men in tuxedos or formal Confederate uniforms and Southern Belles in corsets, crinolines, and low-cut gowns. I think he saw them flowing from the porch into the dining room, through the door on that side. There they would pick up fresh mint juleps and more elegant hors d'oeuvres. Then they would mingle and flirt their way along through the living room. Finally they would go back to the porch through the vestibule and the door on that end. By then, their crystal glasses and silver plates would be empty. So they would circle back through the door to the dining room and start the process all over again."

After a long pause, Tiny said slowly, "I am truly sorry I ever mentioned them two doors."

"Yeah," I said, "Well I am just surprised you even noticed the one we don't use, especially at night, with no light on it and no mat."

"I notice ever-thing, doc," Tiny said, "especially when I'm about to break and enter." He paused for a minute, thinking about the mystery of the two doors in spite of himself. "You think there ever was any fancy parties in this dump, or even in this neighborhood?"

"Actually I've had several since moving in," I said. "I'll be sure you get an invitation to the next one. But you must promise to wear your tux and not kill any of the other guests."

"All right, doc. Enough bullshit," Tiny grunted. "I need for you to tell me ever detail and I mean ever single little detail about your fight when you found the girl's body. I need to know ever-thing that went down from the time you got grabbed right up till you passed out."

I described the struggle minutely. Tiny listened carefully and asked a few questions. Then he insisted on reenacting the whole fight right there in my living room.

"Are you sure this is necessary?" I asked as we stood up.

"Just turn around and kneel down, like as if you was looking at the dead nigger." Tiny ordered.

I did as he asked.

"Now, you hear something behind you. Look back towards me and up, just like you said you done that day," Tiny directed.

As I complied, Tiny wrapped his right arm around my neck in a sleeper hold. He sunk it deep and applied it firmly but not tight enough to make me pass out. My back was against his chest and his left hand against the back of my head, forcing my throat forward into the vice of his bent right arm. Checking to be sure he was doing as the killer did, Tiny stood and pulled me up with him.

He was tall enough that my feet left the ground, but only by a couple of inches. Tiny also pulled my neck and shoulders back, but not nearly as far as the killer had. With Tiny I had the angle and leverage needed to drive the tip of my elbow sharply into his lower ribs. In the killer's grasp, dangling higher and arched more acutely backward, that strike had been impossible. Tiny didn't budge the first time I elbowed him. I did it again harder, with my left palm pushing my right fist, helping to drive the point of my elbow into his right side. It felt about as effective as striking a large rubber tire, but Tiny grunted softly and slowly let me go.

"So how was my wrastling you different from what the killer done?" Tiny asked.

"Well, to begin with, he must have been a lot taller than you," I said. "My feet were kicking about half way down his shins when he held me. You barely had them off the ground."

I'm a couple of inches over six feet and Tiny was six, four. We figured the killer had to be six foot, seven or eight.

"What-all else," Tiny prompted. "You got me a good shot in the short ribs but you said that elbow strike didn't impress our big man one bit. Now, why was that?"

"He wasn't just taller than you," I said. "He must have also have been fatter." Tiny was big all over but in a proportionate way. His shoulders and chest were massive. His abdomen was thick but not protuberant. "When you pulled back on my neck," I told him, "I was still pretty much upright and could drive the tip of my elbow back into your side. When the killer grabbed my neck it arched my body backward over his belly. That's why only my upper arm made contact with him."

Tiny thought for a minute. "Only one thug I know that much taller'n me and he is one fat bastard to boot. Doc, you can tell ever-body you know that you done wrestled Haystack Calhoun to a draw." Tiny laughed. Tiny's laugh would have sounded goofy if it hadn't been just a little scary.

"Haystack Calhoun, the professional wrestler?" I asked. Haystack was well known for his size and because he wrestled in farmer's overalls, with no shirt and bare feet.

"Naw, we just all called him that seeing as how his last name was Calhoun and he looked just like the real Haystack. He was big as him anyway or damn near and he always wore overalls. He worked for me for about five years collecting . . . well never mind about that. Last thing I knowed about him was he was in prison for . . . let's see, I think it was something like aggravated assault. Where's your phone at?"

It was 4 AM on a Sunday morning but Tiny started right in making calls.

No one seemed to complain about the inconvenience. I could only hear Tiny's side of the conversations but it seemed that everyone wanted to be helpful.

"Haystack got out about a month ago," Tiny reported. "Just before the murder. All the real bad-asses in the system, they was at Kilby, a real hellhole. It got bad enough that it's being closed down. The inmates are being transferred to the new joint, Holman. Anyone near finishing his time, they let go and Haystack was one of them. Eightball, if he don't get paroled, still has another nickel to go – that's another five years—so he's in his new home at Holman.

"Since he got sprung, Haystack never seen his PO, not once, so he's in violation. He'll join Eightball at Holman if they catch him."

"What are the chances they will catch him?" I asked.

"Not no more chance than a nigger going to an election," Tiny said. His repeated use of the word bothered me. I promised myself I'd say something when the time was right. That night, the time was not right.

"How about you, Tiny?" I asked. "You have any idea where he might be?"

"I know zackerly where his big country ass is at." Tiny said.

"Where?" I asked hopefully.

"This weekend is the bluegrass festival at Horse Pens Forty," Tiny said. "In the five years I was knowing him, Haystack never missed Horse Pens, not once. He hated most ever-thing and ever-one, Haystack did. But he loooooved his bluegrass."

Tiny got up then and shook my hand. "I'll head on up to Horse Pens this morning. I'll bring Haystack back and he will turn himself in to the po-lice. He will swear that Jefferson hired him to kill the nigger and frame you. Jefferson will be arrested. Holt will get you back in the VA and you will get to be a heart surgeon. All that sound good to you?"

"Sure," I said. "It sounds great but how are you going to get Haystack to turn himself in and . . ."

Tiny laughed. "Same as what I done with Mr. Rutledge; I'll just reason with him. That's all. He had no business no way doing crime in Birmingham without giving me my cut. If I don't get me a cut of ever-thing that goes down, what's the point of being a crime lord? That's reason enough for me to have a talk with old Haystack. I'll come by here late tonight and tell you all about it. Might be real late, but don't worry. I'll wake you up if you're sleeping."

Then Tiny was out the door and gone before I could stop him. That was early Sunday morning and the Numatalulu case would be Monday. I'd need my sleep that night and didn't really want it to be disturbed. Well, Tiny would do what he would do like any other force of nature.

* * *

I went back to bed feeling really much better. If Tiny got Haystack to incriminate Jefferson, he would at least be arrested. Then, when or if Jefferson got fired, Holt would become acting chief at the VA. Holt would get my VA privileges back and all my problems would be over. Well, all except Katy. But if I did get back in Kirkwood's program, maybe I'd get Katy back too. I fell asleep thinking I hadn't really been so dumb to pass on sex with Sharon.

CHAPTER 20

I WOKE UP again later that Sunday morning thinking about Billy's coma. I had literally dreamed up the crazy idea that I knew how to break it. The key was what Sharon had said about the music, especially Mahler, being "etched" into Billy's brain. I got on the phone and tracked Sharon down at the VA. Bertha Henshaw, the head nurse on her floor, said Sharon wouldn't talk to me.

"What did you do to that girl?" Bertha asked. "I have never seen her so low."

"Bertha, please, just tell her it's about Billy and it's important. For Billy's sake, she's got to hear me out," I pleaded.

Sharon came to the phone sounding shy and embarrassed. I made no reference to our near kiss and quickly explained my idea for Billy. Her embarrassment was soon forgotten in the excitement of making plans.

"I don't have that kind of equipment," Sharon said. "Unless you do, we'll have to buy the stuff. It should be a fairly good system to have much chance of working. That could be expensive."

"I don't have anything decent," I said, "But I do have a $150 cash refund from that truck I wrecked. That should cover most of it. If you could lay out the rest, I'll pay you back when I can."

"Don't worry about that. I make more money than you do," Sharon pointed out. "The problem is it's Sunday. Everything's closed,"

"I know," I said. "And I've got to scrub on a big case tomorrow. I'll be tied up with it all day and maybe all night. Any chance you could . . ."

"Hold on a minute," Sharon said, and I could hear her talking to Bertha Henshaw. A minute later she was back on the phone. "Okay, I've got tomorrow off. If you can get me the money, I'll get everything we need and set Billy up with it. I won't turn it on until you get there."

"No," I said. "Don't wait for me. Get it started as soon as you can. The longer Billy's in that coma, the harder it's going to be to break it. I'll get there when I can."

I pedaled to the hospital, met Sharon in front of the VA and gave her the money.

"Look," she said, folding the cash and putting it away. "About yesterday . . . I didn't intend for that to happen the way . . . I mean I'm not like that. If anything, I'm usually too shy. It was just, I was upset about Billy and you were a shoulder to cry on and then . . ."

"Sharon, it's okay," I said. "I felt the same way. It's just that . . . my girlfriend dumped me but—pathetic jerk that I am—I'm still in love with her. Once I get past that . . . if I haven't burnt all my bridges with you . . . I'd sure like to give that kiss another chance to happen." I felt a grin twist my face and hoped it didn't look too stupid.

"You may not have burned every single one of those bridges," Sharon smiled back sweetly and naturally. "First lose that silly grin. Then get things settled with your girlfriend, one way or the other. And then—when you're all done mooning over your lost love like some cowboy in a country song—then we'll see what happens."

I spent the day in Billy's room, followed by mystery meat and mashed potatoes in the cafeteria. With lots of gravy, salt and a quarter pound of butter, it wasn't half bad. Bo and Roberta happened by and joined me. After dinner, we all went up to see Billy and I told them how I planned to break the coma.

"That is the stupidest idea I ever heard," Roberta said. "It's completely unscientific and makes no neuro-physiological sense whatsoever."

"Now, that's not fair," Bo said. "It ain't the stupidest idea ever." Then with a gleam in his eye, "But it is right on up there amongst the top ten."

I changed the subject and we talked about the Numatalulu case for a while. I told them about Momma saying I would save her boy and how I remembered the new approach to the mitral.

"Fourth time around mitral valve replacement on a 350 pound land whale, with wide open mitral regurg, mostly in bad heart failure for nearly two years?" Bo summarized. "The adhesions are gonna be ferocious and the cardiac tissue like wet toilet paper. You needn't worry about exposing the valve. That big soggy heart's gonna tear while you're taking down adhesions and obese-o-boy will bleed to death before you even get on bypass."

"I hate to say it," Roberta said, "but Bo's probably right. That big mushy heart is going to be stuck to everything, including the back of the sternum. It'll be a short case if the saw cuts through the bone and into the right ventricle."

"Well, thanks for cheering me up," I said, "about Billy and the mitral valve. Don't let the door hit you in the ass on the way out."

"Ain't no door," Bo said. "Just a curtain and, if you want to throw my bike in the back of my truck, I'll give it and you a ride to your house."

I took Bo up on his offer and he dropped me off just after dark. I didn't invite him in because I needed to get to bed early. I had to be ready to first assist on the mitral in the morning.

Bo drove off as I wheeled his bike up to my front door. I normally kept it safe from thieves in the vestibule at night. Knowing I'd be back after dark, I'd left the porch light on that morning. Now it was out, which made it hard to get the key into the lock, especially while holding the screen open and balancing the bicycle. In that vulnerable moment, I heard rustling in the untrimmed bushes by the edge of the porch. Before I could turn, Barnes slugged the back of my head with what felt like a large sledge hammer.

Next thing I knew, I was waking up on the porch's tile floor. I couldn't breathe or move. Fearing paralysis from a brain stem injury, I opened my eyes and changed my diagnosis. The symptoms were due to Barnes sitting on my chest, with his knees pinning my arms down.

The malignant dwarf was short but solid as a fire plug. He was also strong as a chimpanzee and probably nearly twice as smart. The position I was in didn't offer many options. I could swing my legs up to catch his head, but nausea hit me just thinking about it. I knew I'd have to stall for time before even making the attempt. Meanwhile, he could hammer my face into the ground with his fists or elbows.

"Detective Barnes," I managed to say, "what an unexpected pleasure. Does Detective Owens know you're here?"

"Owens is in the cancer ward," Barnes smiled down at me. "He's circling the toilet bowl, dick-head. When you hear the sound of a flush, it's gonna be just you and me playing. I thought you'd want to know. Next time I see you, I'll be expecting a full confession and, if I don't' get it . . . I'm gonna deal with you just like we done with the niggers back in the day. That'll get a confession from you. I guaren-damn-tee it."

Barnes got off me and walked to the door. I fought pain, dizziness and nausea trying to sit up. He watched me with a pleasant smile and said, "Oh and don't bother filing no complaint about my little visit. I'm somewhere else right now and with a bunch a fellow cops to prove it." Then he slapped his palm with a large leather blackjack and said, "And my old friend here, he don't hardly leave no mark at all. I've proved that many a time."

"What makes you so sure I killed her?" I asked. It was a question that had bothered me from the beginning.

Barnes counted off the reasons on his fingers. "You had you a motive. You had opportunity. You was found with the victim and the murder weapon. Now, I admit there's things that don't quite fit, but there always is. And anyways, I don't really care if you done it or not. I got no love for stuck-up Yankee pricks coming down here, talking funny and acting snotty. Do you know why a Yankee in the South is like a hemorrhoid?"

I couldn't help it. I started laughing and that made me vomit. When I looked up, Barnes was gone. Bo's bike had a badly bent wheel and several broken spokes, where I must have fallen on it. I wasn't sure if it would get me to the hospital in the morning or not. I would have to buy Bo a new bike or at least a new wheel and didn't know where I'd find the money.

My head ached too much to try sleeping and I had nothing I could take for the pain. Loss of consciousness meant I'd definitely had a concussion. A cerebral contusion was likely. Aspirin would thin my blood and could cause bleeding into damaged brain tissue. Unfortunately Aspirin was the only pain med I had. Just standing up brought on nausea and vertigo, so I couldn't get to a drug store. I would just have to tough it out. I could hear my high school wrestling coach telling me not to be a pussy.

I wrapped some ice in a towel and lay down on the sofa with it my head against it. I didn't move for several hours, lying in a kind of daze. Footsteps on my porch and the sound of the front door opening forced me to try to get up. I assumed it was Barnes and wished I'd thought earlier to get some kind of weapon. I was still dizzy and fell back on the couch, just as Tiny came in.

"You okay," Tiny asked. "You don't look so good and your door was wide open. There's also a pile of puke and a wrecked bike in your entry vestibule. I hope that bike ain't your only means a transportation."

Sitting up slowly still made my stomach heave but at least I didn't throw up. "I had a visitor," I managed to say, with my head in my hands. The ice was all melted. I put the soggy compress aside and looked up at Tiny.

"One of Birmingham's finest," I said. "A Detective Barnes. I don't know his first name. We're not that close. And, yeah, the bike's my only vehicle since the truck died."

"I know Barnes," Tiny said. "Hope you didn't hurt him. He's on my payroll and cops that dirty in Birmingham ain't too common. His first name's Allison, but he goes by Al or just Barnes mostly."

"A girl's first name. Is that what he's so angry about?" I said.

Tiny laughed his goofy-scary laugh. "He use that sap of his on you? He loves that blackjack. It's made a thick leather tied tight round a big hunk a iron. Does all kinda internal damage and don't leave hardly no mark on the skin. I seen him kill a guy with it once, seen it with my own eyes. Mashed him upside the head. That's what done it. The guy didn't die right away but when he woke up next morning . . . he was deader'n Casey's nuts. Yeah, Barnes loves that blackjack."

"Thanks," I said. "That's good to know. I'll check for a pulse when I get up tomorrow. And, if that demented dwarf comes after me again, it'll be good he loves his blackjack because he is going to need a proctologist to separate him from it."

That one had Tiny nearly rolling on the floor. In addition to his knowledge of history and literature, he apparently had a good sense of humor. It was hard to believe, but who would have picked his nephew Billy as a musical prodigy? Somewhere in that family's gene pool, a shark must have gone swimming with a dolphin.

"Anyway," Tiny said, when he got his laughter under control, "I just dropped Haystack at the po-lice station. Right about now, he's swearing that Jefferson paid him to kill the nigger and frame you for it. That should convince even a bullheaded mow-ron like Barnes, it wasn't you done it."

"Will the cops really believe that Haystack just walked in and confessed for no reason?" I asked. "I know that you—uhh—'reasoned with him' to get him to do it. But the cops . . . what'll they think?"

"Well, here's what happened," Tiny explained. "Old Haystack, he was partying hardy up to Horse Pens, like he does ever year. He was wandering around drunk in the woods, looking for a place to piss, when he passed out. Next morning, when he come to, he seen he'd been sleeping it off on a fahr ant nest."

"A what?" I asked. "Did you say a far ant"

"Not a far ant," Tiny shot back. "What the fuck is a far ant anyway? I said a fahr ant."

After a few rounds of, 'Who's on first?" I finally figured it out.

"Oh," I said, "You mean a *fire* ant."

"That's what I said," Tiny repeated. "A fahr ant. Are you deef? Haystack, he woke up the next morning all covered with fahr ant bites – and they sting like a mother-fucker – let me tell you, boy. And, what with all the pain from the bites and a turrible hangover and he'd pissed himself as well . . . with all that awful traumatic experience . . . well, Haystack, he found Jesus.

"What?" I demanded. This was the story I was counting on to save my future? I hoped there was a plan B.

"Yeah, he found him Jesus and Jesus told Haystack that, to get his big hairy ass into heaven, he had to confess his sins to the po-lice." Tiny smiled. "So he went straight ahead to the cops and he done it."

"Do you honestly think that even Barnes is dumb enough to believe that story?" I asked him, holding my head with my eyes closed."

"Let me tell you something as an expert," Tiny said quietly. "The po-lice don't give a fuck why anyone confesses. They only care if he's guilty and if they can prove it. He is and they can. Turns out there's even some physical proof to back up the confession."

"Fingerprints on the hammer?" I asked.

"I done told you," Tiny said, "that Haystack's been in prison. If his fingerprints was on the hammer, they woulda matched them the day of the murder. Even Barnes woulda known it was him what done the killing. Haystack musta wore gloves when he killed the girl."

"So what's the evidence?" I asked.

"Her ear," Tiny said.

"He had her ear with him . . . at the bluegrass festival?" I said. "She wasn't missing an ear when I saw the body."

"You said one side of her face was on the ground and it had brains and blood all over it. You never touched nor moved her, so how do you know about the ear on the down-side?" Tiny asked me.

"But why would he cut off her ear?" I asked. "And why take it with him to the bluegrass festival. Why even go there, no matter how much he liked shit-kicking music? Is he really that dumb?"

"Sounds strange, I know. But Haystack claims he was only paid half for the murder. Jefferson told him he could trade the ear, at Horse Pens, for the rest a the money. By that time Jefferson would know if Haystack had followed all his instructions about setting up the frame. Also, Haystack will swear that Jefferson wanted that ear for his own self. But he had to wait a few weeks to be sure the cops wouldn't search his home for it."

"Jefferson was going to go to the festival and trade money for an ear?" That sounded a little wacko even for that asshole. Then I remembered what Roberta said Holt screamed at Jefferson after I was fired. Something about Jefferson, as a young boy, being molested by a black nanny. How he'd been sexually screwed up by that and how no girls in high school would date him. Maybe Jefferson had a thing for ears. He clearly liked humiliating black women.

"Not Jefferson, his own-self." Tiny explained. "He was prob'ly gonna send someone to . . ."

"But then someone else would know he was involved. Why would he risk that and . . . ?"

"What do you care?" Tiny snapped. "The cops will have the real killer with a part of the victim in his pocket. The real killer will confess and say he was hired by Jefferson. Jefferson will be arrested. Holt says that should be enough to ruin him. Then Holt will take his job and fix things up for you at the VA. That's all that should matter to you, boy. Don't get hung up in the details."

Tiny was getting angry and my head was hurting too much to argue. "Okay, fine. But just one more question. Umm . . . will Haystack actually be covered with fire ant bites?"

"Hell, yes he will," Tiny said with a smug smile. "Haystack ain't no sissy like your Mr. Rutlege. To reason with a hard-ass like Haystack you need you a little extra persuasion. I have found that a bunch a angry fahr ants hep the reasoning process. It works best if the reasonee is tied down naked right next to the tore up fahr ant nest. Haystack also has a sister works at a motel up in Georgia. He don't want her to start a new career in the personal service industry with a friend a mine what runs a Mexican whore house. Do you really want to hear all the details, doc? There is other reasons for Haystack to finger Jefferson. One is what I'll make happen to him in prison if he don't do it."

I assured Tiny I'd already heard too much and asked for the time. It was nearly midnight. I explained about the big case in the morning and Tiny took off. After he left, I checked my pupils in the mirror. They were equal in size and readily reactive to light. The rest of a brief neuro self-exam revealed no cranial nerve problems and no unilateral weakness. If I could tough out the pain and avoid a bleed from Aspirin, I'd probably be okay. I flushed what Aspirin I had down the toilet, so I wouldn't be tempted. Then I tried to sleep.

But sleep proved to be illusive. The bruise still hurt where I'd been hit, but that was the least of it. My entire head throbbed with a deep sickening ache that I just could not ignore. Every time I looked at the clock by my bed, I was closer to scrubbing on the mitral. The less time I had, the more anxious I got. The more anxiety, the less chance for sleeping.

I could have tried to beg off of the case. Maybe I should have. But I had a strong irrational feeling that I was meant to scrub on it. Momma had insisted I needed to help and, strangely enough, I believed her. If she hadn't said I would save her boy, Walker would already have declared him inoperable. Momma forced me to remember the article about the new mitral valve approach. Now, because of that, her son really did have a chance. If she said I had to help with the surgery, I couldn't ignore that.

But first I had to get some sleep. I had to but I couldn't.

Lying there awake, my thoughts turned to Katy. If Tiny was right and Haystack did get Jefferson arrested, I had a real chance to get back in the program. Sharing that with Katy, if it really happened, would be a great excuse to call her. If Holt replaced a disgraced or jailed Jefferson and got me back into the VA, the future we'd dreamed of and lost might be salvaged. But calling her before that happened would be pointless. I'd sound like some pathetic jerk begging her to come back.

The rest of the night was spent watching the clock tick-tock away my last chance for sleeping.

CHAPTER 21

I GAVE UP on sleep and got out of bed at 5 AM with every nerve in my body buzzing. Stephen's surgery was scheduled for 7:30. My head still ached although it was better and I wasn't too dizzy or nauseous. I wasn't hungry either so I didn't eat, didn't even have coffee. I pulled on a pair of shorts and went to check the state of Bo's bicycle. If I had to walk to the hospital, I had just enough time to get ready and make it.

Bo's broken bike was gone and, in its place, was a sleek English racer with skinny wheels, hand breaks and more gears than I knew what to do with. I was getting to owe Tiny too much. I didn't really trust him. There was something going on between him and Holt that neither one was telling me. But, as the saying almost goes, "Never look a gift bike in the spokes." So I went inside, showered, shaved, dressed and got on Bo's brand new racer.

The bike was fast and easy to pedal but I couldn't enjoy the ride. I stopped several times for dizziness and once to vomit by the roadside. These symptoms suggested a serious head injury. I was worried but not enough to give up.

In the mirror of the OR dressing room, I re-checked my pupils. Neither one was blown and cranial nerve tests were still normal. Strength and dexterity were fine in both hands. I probably just had a cerebral contusion. I'd live through the case, but would Stephen Numatalulu?

In a clean green scrub suit, in the doctor's lounge, I pulled paper booties over my sneakers and a tied a cloth cap on my head. I was carefully tucking my hair up into the cap when Ken, Walker's Fellow, showed up. He grabbed me by the arm and said, "Come quick."

Ken explained as we rushed up to see the Numatalulus.

"It's the matriarch of the family, the one they call, Momma," Ken said. "She won't let us take the patient down unless she sees you. I told her you were scrubbing on the case, but she didn't believe me. She insists on seeing you herself."

Entering the room, the supersized Samoans cleared a path to the bedside. As I moved through, they closed in silently behind me. Ken had stayed out of the room or had been kept out. It was just me and the giants.

Momma was sitting by her son. He was hooked to a portable monitor, ready for transport to the OR. I started to assure her I'd be assisting on the case but never finished what I was saying.

Momma's moon-face split with a smile as soon as she saw me. Then the smile was lost in an expression of concern. Hauling her beach-ball round body from the chair, Momma rolled massively towards me. Passive in the power of her bulk, I stood quietly as she towered above me. She took my head between her ham-sized palms, one hand over each ear, and squeezed gently. Releasing me after what seemed a long time, she spoke urgently to the others in Samoan.

She let me go as Tad, the Americanized Samoan, seemed to pop from the crowd under pressure, like a cork from a Champagne bottle. "Momma says there's something wrong with your head," Tad told me.

I just stood there. How did she know? Ken hadn't noticed and he was a doctor.

"Well, is there?" Tad asked.

"It's nothing serious. I got hit from behind last night." I reached back with my hand and rubbed the sore spot. "I've got a little headache but . . ."

Tad cut me off, talking rapid-fire Samoan to Momma. She got busy digging through a huge woven straw purse, decorated with fake flowers. She was searching anxiously for something, talking non-stop to Tad at the same time. With an exclamation of delight, she triumphantly produced a small green leather pouch. How she found anything that small, in a bag that big, was beyond me. But so was nearly everything else about Momma.

She poured some dark brown powder from the pouch into a glass of water on the bedside table. Momma handed it to me. "You drink," she said in English.

"I can't," I said. "I've got to help operate on Stephen. I can't take a chance that it would make me drowsy or . . . or affect me in any way." I looked over at Tad for help. "Tad, explain it to her. Make her understand. I can't take anything right before operating."

Tad and Momma spoke for a bit in Samoan. Then he turned back to me. "It won't make you sleepy. Your headache will go away and you won't be queasy anymore or dizzy. It'll take a while to kick in, maybe about an hour. Then, she says, you'll be 'the best that you can be.' Those are her exact words."

I almost asked if she was recruiting for the Army, but this was no joking matter. "Tad," I said. "There's no way I can take some unknown herbal concoction before first assisting. It's out of the question. Tell her I said I'll be fine without it."

Tad just smiled. "If you want to leave this room, doc, you gotta take it." He looked back at the other Numatalulus looming between me and the door. "You don't really have a choice."

I considered my chances of making it out the door without their cooperation. I wasn't optimistic but I couldn't take Momma's potion. It could affect my performance or make my blood thinner like Aspirin. That could make me bleed into my brain injury. I didn't know what to do.

"You know why they invented the .45 caliber pistol?" Tad suddenly asked me.

"Tad, this is not the time for . . ."

"You ever hear of the Moro insurrection?" Tad pressed on.

"Tad . . ."

"It was in the Philippines around the turn of the 20th century—late 1800s to early 1900s. The Samoans were part of it," Tad said, "and we Samoans are a race of warriors. Make no mistake about that. A Samoan fighter was armed with nothing but big balls and a bolo knife. The American side arm was a .38 caliber pistol."

"Tad, we don't have time for a military history lesson."

"You know what happened" Tad persisted, "when a Samoan charged a soldier with a .38?"

"Okay, okay. What happened?" I could see he was going to tell me anyway.

"The American could empty his pistol into the Samoan. It didn't piss the Samoan off. He didn't even feel it. Besides being big, we Samoans go kind of nuts in battle. A .38 just couldn't stop a howling Samoan berserker. He'd charge right in screaming, ignoring the bullets, and cut the soldier's head off. The only hand gun that could stop a Samoan was a Colt .45 revolver. Revolvers were slow and that's why the army commissioned the .45 automatic.

The model 1911 .45, designed by John Browning, became the new American military sidearm."

"So?" I said, with an impatient gesture.

"So, are you packing a .45?" Tad asked me.

At the age of about 10, I was watching TV in a dark room at a friend's house. His mother brought us glasses of what I thought was coke. It was actually milk. I will never forget the shock of drinking that milk in the dark, when I was expecting cola. My reaction to a swig of Momma's potion was just as disconcerting. In spite of its fearsomely funky flavor, I felt no immediate improvement in my symptoms.

Dr. Walker and I stood silent and intense as the scrub nurse gowned and gloved us. Then the circulator attached our headlights and magnifying glasses. Stephen was prepped and draped on an extra large OR table and even that was a tight fit. His chest was so thick we had to stand on high stools for our arms to move freely over him. He was so wide we would have to bend way over to see down into a midline incision. Operating in that stressful posture, would have our back and neck muscles screaming.

Adhesions form after every operation. After three open hearts this internal scarring was especially tenacious in Stephen. As a result, his heart was glued to everything around it. Most dangerously, the front of his heart was stuck to the back of his sternum. We had to saw completely through the bone, without tearing into the attached heart beneath. This would be the first of many potentially fatal maneuvers to follow. The sternum is usually cut down the middle with a sort of surgical jig saw. A knob at the end of the saw is hooked under the top of the sternum at the base of the neck. As the vertical blade moves up and down through bone, it is pulled down to where the sternum ends just over the stomach.

The tip of a saw like that, sliding under the sternum, would have torn into the heart stuck behind it. We used an oscillating saw instead. This works just like a plaster cast cutter. The convex belly of its semicircular blade is pressed down on the outer surface of the sternum. It oscillates and burrows gradually into the bone, from the outside inward. When the surgeon feels the blade pop through the sternum, he pulls it back before it pushes on into the heart. Blood, marrow and soggy bone dust well up around the curved blade. After pushing through the bone at one point, Walker would move the saw down a few inches in a straight line. Then he'd go through the same process again, connecting the cuts through the sternum. Push by push, the chest bone would finally be divided into right and left segments.

Getting through the bone, with Stephen still alive, was just the beginning. The back wall and cut edges of the divided sternum were still glued to the heart. Now we had to use scalpel and scissors to dissect the heart from each half of the sternum. Then, moving down around the sides of the heart we would free it from lung and pericardium.

As the assistant, I was on the left side of Stephen's supine, or chest up, body. Dr. Walker was across the table from me on Stephen's right. I used two retractors to lift up the left half of the sternum. The attached heart was then essentially hanging from it. This opened up the space for Dr. Walker to cut safely between heart and sternum. Little by little, he carefully took down the adhesions. This freed up the front of the left side of the heart from the back of the left half of the sternum. He then continued down around the left side of the heart, freeing it up from the other glued on structures.

Then it was time to free the right side of the heart from below the right half of the sternum. I assumed that, for this, Dr. Walker and I would switch sides of the table. Then I could retract the right half of the sternum and Dr. Walker could dissect under it from Stephen's left side. This would give him the best angle for looking and for cutting.

If Walker stayed on Stephen's right, dissecting under the right half would be awkward. He would have to stretch his head past the midline just to see back towards himself under the sternum. If the Fellow had been assisting, switching sides might have been avoided. Ken could have stayed where I was, on the left, and dissected under the right half of the sternum while Walker retracted. I did not have the experience to perform such a difficult and risky maneuver. At least I didn't think I did.

Dr. Walker wanted to find out. He stayed on his side of the table and lifted the right half of the sternum for me. "Let's see if you're as good as they say, hotshot," he challenged.

I couldn't say anything about my continuing head trauma symptoms. He would have had Ken scrub in for me and somehow I knew that would be wrong. I stuck out my hand and the scrub nurse slapped a scissors smartly into my palm. With the sound of that smack, I became the little man Dr. Kirkwood always spoke of: the one who lived inside the heart, in the circle of magnified vision. I don't know if it was Momma's potion but I suddenly felt fully healthy. My headache, dizziness and queasiness were gone, for the first time since Barnes' blackjack stunned me.

My only problem was I couldn't see where to start the dissection. The adhesions obliterated any semblance of normal anatomy. The distorted ball that passed for Stephen's heart was married to everything around it. There was no recognizable line of demarcation between the heart and adjacent structures.

If I cut into the heart, the massive hemorrhage would cost Stephen his life. Even if we could stop the bleeding, the sick cardiac muscle would never recover. Cases like Stephen's are completely unforgiving. Everything must go perfectly. One error leads to another and ultimately inevitably to disaster.

Then I remembered what The Wire taught about dealing with tough dissections. I just had to find what he always called the "Friendly Little Transverse Lines." These are stretch lines, between different types of tissue, created by applying tension. Traction at the right angle would make those friendly lines appear. They would show me where to cut with my scalpel and my scissors.

Trying to bring out these lines of stress, I pressed down on right ventricle and pulled it towards me. What I felt, when my fingers touched the heart, was as alarming as a diamondback's rattle.

The turbulent flow of blood, around Stephen's leaky valve, had been audible pre-op as a murmur. Now it was palpable to my touch as what is called a "thrill." A thrill from a small leak feels like a gentle vibration or buzz with each heartbeat. Stephen's thrill felt more like an obscene gushing growl. That meant that most of the blood that should have gone out to Stephen's body was leaking back around the valve instead, flowing backwards towards his lungs and flooding them. The resulting wet lungs made it hard for him to breathe, a condition called congestive heart failure.

Forcing myself to ignore these malignant vibrations, I pushed down carefully on the heart, waiting and watching. When the tension was right, Dr. Kirkwood's "Friendly Little Transverse Lines" magically appeared.

With the friendly lines guiding my cuts, I sliced and snipped delicately, feeling my way along with the knife blade and the tip of scissors. Their cold steel somehow became living extensions of my fingers. Little by little, snip by snip, slice by slice, I continued the dissection. I freed up the heart from behind the sternum and then down along the heart's surface.

Totally lost in the intensity of my concentration, time ceased to exist. At some point, I realized that my job was done. I had freed up around the right side of the heart and down towards the spine behind it.

A self-retaining retractor was placed to hold the split sternum open. Dr. Walker took over again and finished the dissection. When he was done, we straightened up and took the strain off our backs for a moment. I looked at the clock. We'd been operating 6 hours and hadn't really even started. All we'd accomplished was to get Stephen ready to go on bypass. Only then, with blood detoured around the heart, could we work on the valve deep inside it.

The scrub nurse said, "That has got to be the biggest ugliest heart in Alabama. It looks to me just like a giant ball of icky goo." She was a tall dark athletic girl, admired by us residents for her adorable bottom. Her technical skills and cool head under pressure also made her a great scrub nurse. The word was she had other talents, enjoyed by Dr. Walker outside the OR. Neither of them was married, so it was really nobody else's business.

After a minute of rest, we leaned back over and looked down into the gaping incision. A 'ball of icky goo' was really a pretty good description. Stephen's heart was a hideously grotesque caricature of what was normal. It was huge and distended from the high pressure inside it. The normally bright yellow fat, brown muscle, red arteries and blue veins were all a sickly grey. The magical rhythmic cardiac dance of life was perverted into weak irregular squirming. I wondered how such a sick heart had managed to keep Stephen alive.

Tubes were placed to divert blood around the heart through the heart-lung machine. Now we were really ready to start the crucial part of the operation.

But, instead of proceeding with the case, Dr. Walker seemed to be stalling. He was looking down around the side of the heart to the left atrium behind it.

The right atrium lies in the front of the chest, just behind the sternum or chest bone. The left atrium lies between the right atrium and the spine. The normal approach to the mitral valve is through an incision in the left atrium, way around in back of the heart, where Walker was looking. .

That standard approach had been tried three times and each attempt had been a disaster. Stephen's heart was too big and his chest too deep to work through that posterior incision. The result was that sutures had been poorly placed and tore through where the valve was anchored. These tears had created the massive leaks that allowed blood to flow backwards.

"Maybe we should just use the regular approach," Walker said indecisively. "I don't think I should try something new, for the first time, in a case as tough as this one. Maybe I should try it on a more normal heart first."

"No," I whispered quietly but firmly.

"What was that?" Walker demanded. "What did you say?"

"I said, no," I repeated, leaning towards him and whispering softly. If Ken or the scrub heard us, Walker's pride would never let him back down. "You can't possibly get decent exposure through an incision way back around there. With this huge heart pressing down from above, you'll never be able to work on the mitral. It's been proven three times already. He'll die if we prove it a fourth time. Cutting down into the left atrium from the front, through the right atrium, is the only way to do it."

I suppose I should have been afraid to talk to Walker that way, but I wasn't. Now I understood Momma's insistence that I scrub on her son's surgery. I had to be there to make Walker use the new approach. Without me he would have wimped out and she somehow knew that. I looked up and saw him staring daggers at me. In the narrow slits above our surgical masks and below our headlights, Walker's eyes and mine locked, like the horns of bull elks fighting. I knew this staring contest would decide Stephen's fate.

Walker's eyes dropped first.

"You got a lot of balls for a young punk who's never done a valve in his life," he blustered. "I ought to kick your ass out of here right now and have Ken scrub in." The Fellow was looking over the ether screen alongside the Pakistani gas passer. The room was deadly quiet. Everyone was trying to hear our whispered debate.

"But you won't," I said confidently. "Because you know I'm right. The anterior approach is the only reason you agreed to do the case, in the first place. You said he was inoperable until I showed you the Israeli paper. By the standard approach, there's no chance for success and you know that better than I do."

In spite of all my arguments, I could understand Walker's trepidation. Approaching the mitral valve through the front of the heart was a radical procedure. It required incisions cutting deep into the empty heart's very center. When the heart was full again, those incisions could hemorrhage in inaccessible places. If Stephen bled to death that way, Walker would be blamed for a technical error. Violating the core of the heart so radically was daunting. But, with a heart like Stephen's, I was sure there was no other viable option.

"You're an arrogant little shit," Walker whispered, ". . . but you happen to be right . . . this time." Then he took a deep breath and said, "Okay. Let's do it to it."

Once on bypass, the heart was stopped and cooled with cardioplegia, just as I had done with Billy. Now it could live without blood while we emptied it and trespassed inside. But this cardiac protection would only last a few hours. If we took too long and part of his heart died, Stephen would die along with it. If we worked too fast and the sutures weren't perfect, they would pull through again. Stephen might survive the operation but only to die slowly of heart failure—doomed to struggle for every breath, right up to his last one.

Most doctors spent their entire careers avoiding such dire situations. But facing challenges like this was precisely what I was obsessed with. I yearned to grapple with the Grim Reaper himself, right there in his own backyard. I had sacrificed everything, even Katy, for the chance to fight that battle.

Walker was the primary surgeon but this had become as much my case as his. Only while doing Billy's operation had I felt such exhilaration. My stomach twisted at the thought that I might never again experience it. Unless Haystack's confession got Jefferson fired, my next service, with The Wire, would be my last one.

I had dissected the right atrium from the back of the sternum earlier in the case. At that point it was full of blood, tense and quivering under pressure. Now, bypassed and paralyzed, it lay collapsed in front of us, empty and flaccid. With one bold vertical incision, Dr. Walker laid it completely open. The cut edges of the right atrium were then pulled apart exposing its hidden secrets. Its bottom wall, or floor, was also the top wall, or ceiling, of the left atrium. This shared wall divided the left atrium below from the right atrium above it. For that reason, it was called the atrial septum.

Dr. Walker's next cut went through that septum. This opened a sort of trapdoor between the two atria. The septal incision was then extended vertically in both directions, splaying the front and top of the left atrium completely apart. At this point, the entire upper half of the heart had been laid open. The result looked more like the work of an Aztec Priest than a cardiac surgeon. Dr. Walker was scared and everyone in the room could sense it.

I was starting to wonder if that Amazon witch doctor's potion had driven me crazy. Or maybe it was just lack of sleep and accumulated stress. What was I thinking, telling Dr. Walker how to operate? Now if this radical approach didn't work, it would be my fault. Here I was stepping on my own dick again and this time with spiked boots. Katy was right to run away. Unfortunately I was stuck with myself.

But Walker, at that point, had no way to go but forward. He placed traction sutures along the cut edge of the collapsed left atrium. These radiated out, like the spokes of a wheel. We pulled on them upward and outward. Suddenly our surgical field looked just like the drawing in the Israeli journal. The heart seemed to spread itself open like the petals of a blooming rose. The mitral valve lay at the center of the flower: perfectly exposed and easy to work on.

It was a piece of cake to take out the old valve and sew in a new one.

When we were done, the new valve looked as if Stephen had been born with it. Perfect sutures were buttressed with bits of felt, known as pledgets.

These would further decrease the chance they could pull through the weakened tissue.

The incisions in the atria were quickly closed, with no significant bleeding.

The heart was allowed to fill with warm blood as we decreased flow through the heart lung machine. We watched as it woke up and began to start pumping. With my hand on the heart, I could feel no thrill. There was no leak around the valve to cause one. No longer distended, the heart seemed much smaller. Its color was also far better.

What had been a quivering ball of "goo," was now a heart throbbing strongly to Life's sacred rhythm.

CHAPTER 22

I CAME TO in a darkened room with no idea where I was or how I got there. Judging by its buttons and cables, I seemed to be in a hospital bed. My eyes adjusted slowly and I was able to look around. The hospital bed was, not surprisingly, in a hospital room. The last thing I remembered was the clock in the OR. Other details came back slowly.

After coming off bypass, Stephen had done well for a while and then developed DIC. That's disseminated intravascular coagulation, a serious bleeding problem sometimes seen after open heart surgery. Stephen's blood couldn't clot at all. He bled from every tiny adhesion we'd cut at the start of the operation. There were thousands of them and each one had to be cauterized. The burnt flesh smelled like a Fourth of July barbecue. Finally we transfused enough clotting factors to stop the hemorrhage or at least slow it. But these transfusions overloaded him with fluid. Then we had to give diuretics so he'd pee off the excess. All this happened between coming off bypass and leaving the OR.

Dealing with these complications was just another day at the office.

When the surgical field around the heart was fairly dry, Walker had left me to finish up alone. It was all coming back now. It had taken all my strength to wire that massive sternum back together. Then I ran long suture lines through muscle, subcutaneous fat and skin. Finally I helped move Stephen's heavy body to an extra-wide gurney. Leaving the room I looked up at the OR clock and saw it was midnight. I remembered figuring that I'd been operating for 16 hours and then . . . That was all she wrote.

I tried to get up but fell back, weak and dizzy. I was naked except for an open-back hospital gown. It was silly but I couldn't help feeling a little bit embarrassed. I wondered if I knew the nurses who must have stripped me and put the gown on. My head didn't hurt but I felt a weird kind of confused euphoria. They must have had me on morphine or something like it.

That got me thinking about Momma's potion. It hadn't stopped me from passing out, but only after 16 hours of surgery. I hadn't eaten since the previous day and had only a few sips of water in the OR. Not bad for a concoction of tree bark and crushed plants, if that's what it was.

A blond nurse I didn't know appeared with a pretty smile and a pink stethoscope. She had a happy face button on her white coat and looked about 14 years old. "You're awake," she said and proceeded to take my vital signs. Then she checked my pupils and did a few other neuro tests. I waited silently, letting her to finish, before asking any questions.

"My name is Sandy, Dr. Logan," she said, after making a few notes. "I'm your nurse on this shift. Do you know where you are?"

"Call me Cooper," I said, "and, judging by the tests you just did, I'll take a wild guess and say . . . the neuro floor?"

"A brilliant deduction, especially for a surgeon," she smiled.

I wasn't up to a clever comeback so I got right down to business. "Okay, Sandy, so I guess I had a syncopal episode in the OR and someone found out about my head injury. How long have I been out?"

"Just a few hours," she said. "They doped you up to keep you in lala land until we knew what was up with your squash." She opened the window curtain. The dirty grey of a Birmingham dawn oozed into the room

"Did they get tomograms yet?" Tomograms were the precursors of CT scans.

"Yes, and they didn't show anything bad," she said. "No epidural or subdural bleed; just a hairline fracture of the occipital bone and some swelling of the occipital lobe. It's all consistent with a cerebral contusion."

"Thanks for filling me in." I said with a deep breath. "It's a relief to know there's no bleed. Say, that patient, Stephen Numatalulu, the one I was operating on. Do you know if he's doing okay?"

"I'll call down to the cardiac unit and find out," she said. "And I'm dying to hear why a policeman bonked you on the head. You must have been up to something very naughty." She shook a scolding finger at me.

"Who said I was hit by a cop?" I asked.

"Uhh . . . Dr. McDuff I guess. And he made me swear I'd call him the minute you woke up." She ran off to call Holt.

I wondered how Holt knew about Barnes and the blackjack. Tiny was the only one who could have told him. The Numatalulus knew I'd been hit but not that a cop had done it.

Sandy popped her head back in the door. "They were right about you," she said brightly.

"Right, how?" I asked, "And who are they?"

"You don't look anything like a doctor," she said, "Everyone says so." Then she was gone again. This just kept getting better and better.

Holt arrived shortly accompanied by Deepak Pandya, the neurologist who was also caring for Billy. I went over my encounter with Barnes and the symptoms that followed. Dr. Pandya asked me a few more standard questions. Then Holt said he had figured it was Barnes and called Owens. It seemed a bit of a stretch for him to just assume it was Barnes. I still had a feeling that Tiny had told him, but why would Holt lie about that?

"Funny thing is," Holt said. "No one seems to know where Barnes is at. The police questioned me about it this morning. Our favorite detective showed up at the station house this morning. A couple hours later, he got a phone call. Then he went out by himself and, well, he still ain't come back. Last night, around the time you say he was bashing your Yankee head in, some friends of his claim that he was with them." Holt grinned. "I guess you must be mistaken."

"He told me he had an alibi," I said. "There's no point in pressing charges, but if that prick comes after me again he's not getting another free pass. Cop or no cop." Then I thought for a minute. "You say he's disappeared?"

Holt smiled and nodded. "Did Tiny know about your altercation with Detective Barnes?" Why would Holt even suspect that if Tiny hadn't told him? Why didn't he want me to know that he'd talked with Tiny about it? What was up with those two?

"Yeah," I said. "But you don't think . . ."

Holt just shrugged and Dr. Pandya intervened somewhat impatiently. "You are having a hairline fracture of the occipital bone," he said. "There is no collection of blood at this particular moment, but you must rest yourself quietly for at least one week. You are nud to work and nud to engage in strenuous exercises of any kinds whatsoever."

I was to stay in the hospital on bed rest, bathroom privileges only, for forty-eight hours of observation. Depending on my symptoms, they might get more tomograms. Once discharged, I was to go home, stay there and see Pandya in a week. By then my rotation with Dr. Walker would be over. Meanwhile poor Ken would have the scut list to himself, just like a lowly resident. He was a nice guy but the thought still made me smile.

As the neurologist was leaving the room, I suddenly remembered Billy. "Say, Dr. Pandya, how's Billy doing?"

"You may visit him later today—by wheelchair only." He scowled and left quickly. I guessed he would have told if there had been any major improvement.

So much for my brilliant plan to bring Billy out of his coma. I assumed Sharon had tried it out and it had been a failure. Well, it was worth a shot even for my last $150. I'd have hospital food for the next two days and maybe there was something left on my credit card.

Alone with Holt, I asked for an update on Haystack's confession. Tiny had dropped him off near the police station, the night of Barnes' visit. That was about thirty-six hours ago. Haystack was supposed to swear Jefferson paid him to murder Shaleena and frame me. So why hadn't Jefferson already been arrested?

"Ain't heard nothing on that yet, Yankee Boy," Holt admitted with a worried look. "Something should happen soon. I wouldn't worry too much. Tiny can be pretty persuasive. Haystack will do like he told him."

I just nodded. I wasn't getting my hopes up until Jefferson was actually arrested. Tiny's "reasoning" techniques, aided and abetted by a nest of fire ants, made for strong motivation. But could anything make a tough guy like Haystack turn himself in and confess to murder? Tiny had threatened his sister but still . . . For all I knew, Haystack hated his sister. The choice was between himself in jail and his sister in a Mexican whorehouse. That might not have been a moral dilemma for a guy who killed a girl with a hammer. By now Haystack was probably in Mexico himself. If so, I'd be fucked more surely than his sister. For some reason I couldn't believe that Tiny would really harm her.

Holt left shortly after that and Sandy came in. She was perky as a cheerleader. "That guy you were operating on?" she said.

"Yeah, yeah. How's he doing?" I hoped that Stephen hadn't started bleeding again and the valve wasn't leaking.

"I talked to a fellow named Ken," Sandy said. "Your mitral valve's doing just dandy. He said to tell you there was no murmur, no bleeding and no heart failure. He claims you cracked your own skull just to stick him with the scut list."

I laughed until my head started hurting and she gave me something for the pain. Then I slept until the afternoon and woke up hungry. I ate my own lunch and that of another patient too nauseated for his. When Sandy came back, I told her I wanted to sit with Billy for a while.

"I have to take you in a wheelchair," she said. "You're not supposed to stand up or walk, except to go to the bathroom. Let me set it up and then I'll be right back to get you."

I couldn't see what there was to set up but there was no rush anyway. Billy in a coma now would be just like Billy in a coma later.

Eventually Sandy returned with the wheelchair and pushed me over to see Billy. He lay on his back just like the last time I saw him. The head of his bed was elevated and his eyes were closed. The only difference was that now I noticed occasional twitching. It was mostly his facial muscles and shoulders that jerked every few minutes.

Then I noticed the expensive Koss earphones on his head and the cheaper boom-box by the bed.

"Isn't it exciting?" Sharon gushed, walking in with Holt. "He started those movements right after I put on the earphones. I'm blasting Mahler's Ninth over and over again just like you said. And he's responding. Can't you see?" She was looking at me eagerly, waiting for my reaction. The music was turned up so loud I could hear it softly around the earphones.

I looked at Billy lying there twitching and tried to share her enthusiasm. I looked at Holt who shrugged and seemed to be as underwhelmed as I was.

Dr. Pandya poked his head in and said, "Well, you see there is some improvement. At least now we do have some muscular activity." There was a smile on his face but not a very big one.

I didn't want to disappoint him, or Sharon, but I just didn't get it

"What does the twitching mean, Dr. Pandya?" I asked. "Does it mean he's going to wake up soon?"

"Well, nud exactly," Dr. Pandya equivocated. "But it does somewhat improve his prognosis."

"Well, so now what are his chances, compared to before?" I asked skeptically.

"Don't you get it?" Sharon chimed in. "The movements started right after the music. That means he must be responding to it. Your idea is working, Cooper."

I looked at Dr. Pandya, who said, "Well, now, we must nud become too excited. When we turn the music off he still twitches so—"

"Well, I know it's working!" Sharon said. "I don't care what anyone else says. I'm keeping that music blaring in his ears, and he'll hear it and he'll wake up. And I don't care if I'm the only one who believes it."

She left the room on the verge of tears. I looked at Dr. Pandya.

"The movements are an improvement," he repeated. "I can nud give you a percentage. And do nud tell the young lady, but I am nud sure if the music has caused it."

Dr. Pandya left and so did Holt after saying, "Time will tell, Yankee Boy. Your last $150 still may not have been wasted."

So everyone knew I had thrown away the last of my cash on the idiotic idea.

I sat with Billy alone for a while trying to work up some optimism. Unfortunately the twitching, to me, seemed to make him look worse not better. At least before, he seemed peaceful. Now he looked like a neuro-disaster.

After a while, Sandy came in and wheeled me back to my room. They gave me something to sleep and I dozed off until dinner. I think I fell asleep again in the middle of the meal.

Then I was being shaken roughly awake with the room in near total darkness. Tiny was bent over me. His finger across his lips ordered silence. It seemed long past visiting hours. I presumed he had snuck in.

"I seen Billy yesterday morning," Tiny whispered. "That nurse friend a his told me it was you that hep'd him. Maybe he'll wake the rest a the way up now thanks to your idea about the music. After talking to her, I decided to pay you back for what you done for Billy. So I left and got the job done and now I'm back to thank you."

"What did you . . ." I started to ask but I knew damn well what Tiny did for me.

"First off, doc," Tiny interrupted. "I ain't here. I wasn't never here. You got me?" I nodded. "And second," Tiny squeezed my arm tight and whispered into my ear. "Don't you never ask me no questions no more. Not when you don't want to hear the answers."

Then Tiny was gone. I never saw him leave the room. He was just there one minute and then he wasn't. I fell right back asleep. In the morning I thought I had dreamed the whole thing. As time passed I knew the visit was real. Barnes was never heard from.

Detective Owens, again in remission and no longer circling the bowl, questioned me several times about Barnes. I told him all about being hit with the blackjack. I never lied. I just left out any reference to Tiny. This has never bothered my conscience at all. Justice is justice. It doesn't matter who doles it out. Whatever Barnes got, the bastard had it coming.

CHAPTER 23

HOLT SHOWED UP around 6 AM with a newspaper in the pocket of his white coat.

"Jefferson's been arrested, Yankee Boy," he said. "He's charged with hiring Haystack to kill Shaleena White. Extra, extra, read all about it." He tossed the Birmingham News onto my bed and said, "I gotta get to the OR. We'll talk later."

The headline screamed, "**SURGEON CHARGED IN LOVER'S DEATH**." The story took up a quarter of the front page and continued extensively inside. There were interviews with several "friends" of Jefferson and Shaleena, as well as "official sources close to the investigation." All had insisted on anonymity.

Photographs emphasized the racial and social chasm between the surgeon and the lover. Jefferson's picture seemed to be a file photo from a formal reception. He looked handsome and aristocratic in white tie and a condescending sneer.

I don't know where they got the shot of Shaleena but it wasn't from what I'd call a friend. It had been taken at a different kind of party. Her glazed eyes, slack-lipped grin and mouth-dangling cigarette left little doubt that she was drunk or high or most likely both. The long ash on her smoke looked ready to join the red wine stain on her low-cut, peasant blouse. She was waving a Chianti bottle at the camera and did not appear to be wearing a bra.

The real Shaleena, such as she was, had ceased to exist forever. That awful photo would be all of her that anyone would remember. Printing that picture was crueler than the murder itself. She could only be killed once but that image would repeatedly murder her memory.

As bad as it was for Shaleena, the photo had to be even worse for Jefferson and his wife. A smaller picture of Mrs. Lurleen Jefferson accompanied one of the background stories. She was heavy but had a friendly round face with short auburn hair in a pageboy cut. The humiliation of her husband cheating with the creature in Shaleena's photo must have been stupefying. I didn't see how she could live with it.

To emphasize the depth of Jefferson's degradation, the story began with the heights from which he had fallen. His posts as Chief of Surgery and Chief of Staff at the VA were just the beginning. Jefferson was also a Deacon at the First Episcopalian Church of Birmingham and a vice-president of the state Right to Life organization. He was a top fundraiser for George Wallace's 1968 presidential campaign. The article said Jefferson was Wallace's, "close personal friend and political adviser." Wallace, the staunch segregationist, had recently been re-elected in Alabama. Now Jefferson would be as welcome to the new Governor as a camera in a whore house.

Much of the article was devoted to Jefferson's old and distinguished family. It noted that he was arrested at, "The Jefferson estate, once the largest cotton plantation in Jefferson County."

The heart of the story read:

> According to informed sources, Dr. Lloyd Jefferson and Ms. Shaleena White have carried on a sexual relationship for at least the past year. Ms. White was found murdered three days ago. She was bludgeoned to death with multiple hammer blows to the head. Mr. Percival Calhoun, known as Haystack Calhoun, for his resemblance to the famous wrestler, has confessed to the brutal slaying. Knowledgeable sources report that Mr. Calhoun's sworn statement claims that Dr. Jefferson paid him to kill Ms. White.

The article went on to imply by innuendo that Shaleena had been blackmailing Jefferson, with threats to go public about their relationship. A "source close to the investigation," said stopping the blackmail was the motive for the murder. There was nothing about Jefferson exploiting Shaleena's drug use to force her to be his sex toy or about the involvement of Chris Dugan, the butch Chief of Nursing. Roberta had seen both of them at the VA, the night

Shaleena ran crying through the parking lot. Apparently the involvement of the hatchet-faced Dugan in the drug test cover-up and subsequent sex games was still a secret. The omissions didn't matter to me. Jefferson was arrested. Presumably he would lose his job. That was all I cared about.

Best of all, from my point of view, were the hospital related charges.

Confidential sources at both the Veterans and University Hospitals have alleged negligence by Ms. White as the cause of several patient fatalities. These deaths were then allegedly covered up by Dr. Jefferson.

Spokesmen for the Jefferson family have refused to comment on these allegations.

The patient care issues made it less likely that Jefferson could hang on at the VA. Even if he beat the murder charge, I was sure they would have to fire him. If Holt was named acting Chief of Surgery in his place, I would have my life back. My first instinct was to call Katy and tell her the good news. Now I could finally try to get her back without sounding pathetic. I resolved to do so the minute I got home and had some privacy.

There was a TV in my hospital room. I turned it on to take my mind off Katy. The broadcast news made Jefferson look even worse than the papers. An aerial shot taken from a helicopter caught him being led from his house in handcuffs. Attempts to interview his lawyers evoked only the mantra of "no-comment" desperation.

Although there was a reference to me, my name was never mentioned. Reports noted only that, "Staff members who complained about Ms. White's alleged incompetence were ignored or, in at least one case, disciplined by Dr. Jefferson." Holt had friends everywhere. He must have called in some favors to keep my name out of the story.

After dinner Bo and Roberta came by with the latest gossip. The consensus at both hospitals was that Jefferson's career was over. We agreed that, if Holt offered to fill in as Chief, he'd get the job in a minute. Bo said he'd be praying for me and Roberta made a disrespectful snorting sound.

Neither was surprised that Mahler's music had failed to break Billy's coma. They tried not to rub it in and even pretended to be hopeful.

"Well if he's moving a little now," Roberta said, "he still could come out of it."

Bo nodded hopefully and shrugged, "It could happen. Maybe the music is even helping some. If I'm ever in a coma you could try the Orange Blossom Special. If anything could reach me that would."

"Patsy Cline might actually work for me," Roberta said, adding "if anything would," as a doubtful afterthought.

They were trying to cheer me up with their kidding but I just wanted to change the subject. I told Bo all about his new bike and he ran off to admire it before evening rounds. It was Roberta's night off. She stayed and, as soon as Bo left, I knew she would ask about Katy.

"What's happening with Katy?" Roberta asked. "Have you called her, like I said?"

"No," I admitted. "I've been waiting for Jefferson to get arrested so I could give her the good news before trying to get her to come back. As soon as I get home I'm going to give it a shot. Wish me luck."

"You're going to need more than luck," Roberta said. "What you need is a clue and I doubt you have one."

"What do you mean a 'clue,'" I asked, a bit annoyed at her attitude.

"A clue as to why she really left," Roberta said. "If things had been good between you, she would never have deserted just when the *merde* hit the *ventilator*. There's got to be an underlying problem. She just used your getting fired as an excuse for leaving. Even as we speak, there are zillions of girls just waiting around for an excuse to dump their men. Sometimes they even cheat on their guys and get caught just to create one."

"Well if there was some mysterious 'underlying problem,' she might have told me about it," I complained. "What does she think I am, a . . . "

"A mind reader," Roberta interrupted, finishing the sentence for me.

I just stared at her, wondering how she knew what I was going to say.

"Boys," she said angrily. "You're all the same. The answer is yes. Yes! Yes! Yes! That's exactly what you're supposed to be. That's exactly what we want you to be, what we need you to be – a fucking mind reader." It was the first time I ever heard Roberta use the F word. She obviously felt strongly about the mind reading issue. But, as usual with female logic, what she said made no sense.

"Yeah, well you girls are all the same too: expecting us to be mind readers. Here's a news flash for you; mind reading is impossible. Why can't you just tell us what you want? Why is that so fucking difficult?" If she could drop the F bomb, so could I.

Roberta just sighed and muttered under her breath. "Look, I'm trying to help you," she finally said in a calm voice. "I'm going to tell you something about girls that not many boys understand. If you stop arguing and just trust me, you can win Katy back. I promise."

"I'm listening," I said, "but there's still no such thing as mind reading."

"Okay maybe not literally picking up psychic vibrations. That's not what I mean. I mean being able to figure out what a girl needs or wants without her spelling it out. You don't need magic. You just need to pay attention to what she does say and to how she acts: the verbal and the nonverbal clues."

"But why do I need to look for clues? Why can't she just tell me?" I insisted.

"Do you want Katy back?"

I hesitated. I didn't want to sound pathetic. But I did want to hear whatever mysterious girl-secrets Roberta was about to reveal. "Yeah, I want her back," I said quietly.

"Do you love her?" Roberta was looking right at me and I was evading her stare. Finally I let her eyes capture mine and said, "Yeah, I love her."

"Okay then, forget about why girls are the way we are. Just accept it. We aren't always going to tell you, in so many words, everything we need or want. We want you to figure some of it out. You don't have to go out and kill dragons and you don't have to be psychic either. Like I said before, you just have to pay attention. Let's use sex as an example. It's probably the only relationship thing you've ever given any thought to."

I just nodded, thinking that this could get interesting.

"Okay, well I'm assuming or at least hoping," Roberta went on, "that you're not the hop on top, missionary position, hump hump hump, I got mine hope you got yours, snore snore snore, kinda guy. I'm assuming that you like to be sure that your partner has her . . . well that she has an orgasm."

"You're blushing," I said. She was and we both laughed.

"Well do you make sure she has an orgasm?" Roberta persisted.

"Girls have orgasms?" I joked, trying to change the subject.

"I'm serious," Roberta said angrily, starting to get up. "If you don't want my help . . ."

"Okay, okay," I assured her. "I was just kidding. "There have been no complaints so far. Do you need more detail than that?"

"Do you make sure your lover cum or not?" Roberta demanded crudely.

"Yeah, I do," I said, rolling my eyes.

"Okay then," Roberta said. "So let's say, in the immortal words of the Rolling Stones, 'You're trying this and you're trying that, trying to please some girl.'"

"*Satisfaction*," I said, "Great song."

"Yeah, it's a great song but let's focus here," Roberta said.

"Right," I assured her. "I'm all ears."

"Okay, well think about how, when you're doing this and you're doing that, how sensitive you are to every nuance of how she's reacting. She might provide an occasional word or two of insight, but you don't want detailed ongoing instructions, do you? And from her point of view, if she's directing your every move, she'd be better off with a vibrator. She wants you to know her body better than she knows it. She wants you to take her places she can't even imagine. She can't tell you how to do that, can she?"

"No, but it's kind of a tall order, for every time, over a period of years or decades," I said.

"I got a little carried away," Roberta admitted. "Just make the earth move once in a while and the rest of the time she'll still love you if you just make her . . . you know." Roberta blushed again and added, "Think you can live up to that?"

"If I can't, it'll still be fun trying," I smiled.

"Okay then, here's the big secret," she said leaning towards me. "You've got to be just as sensitive when she's telling you every day stuff as you are when, 'you're trying this and you're trying that.' Pay attention. That's all it takes to be what you call a mind reader."

"Okay, so help me read Katy's mind then, if it's so easy," I said.

"I never said it was easy," Roberta snapped back. "But I've seen your Katy and I've talked to her at resident functions. We actually got along quite well. She's incredibly sexy – one those girls who give off pheromones or something. And she's also smart, tough and funny: qualities not often seen in pheromone secretors. What's it worth to have a woman like that really love you, devote herself to you and stick with you forever: not just when things get rough but especially then?"

"Alright," I said. "I get the point, but I still don't know what her problem is."

"I'll bet Katy has told you the problem in words even a boy could understand, if he just paid attention," Roberta said smugly.

"Yeah, well why don't you just tell me where or how she did that?" I asked. "I'd love to know."

"The note, Cooper," Roberta said like she was talking to a child. "You said she left you a note when she took off. If you had shown me that note the last time we talked, you'd probably have her back now."

I did remember Roberta asking to see the note at the Recovery Room. Then Bo had come back and the evening broke up before I could give it to her.

"Now where's that note?" Roberta demanded.

The note was in my wallet in the drawer of the bedside table.

"It might be in my wallet." I said a little embarrassed that I'd been carrying it around with me. I fumbled it out of the drawer and handed it to her.

Roberta unfolded the note which was stained with wallet dye around the bent edges. "It looks like you've been carrying this around since she left." She smiled at me.

"Shut up and read it," I said. "See what big revelation you can get."

Roberta read the note out loud:

I called Boston and they said I could have my old job back. We need some time apart to think where we're going if anywhere. We could have talked about it last night but you decided to get drunk instead, ASSHOLE! I want a man who puts me first in his life. You don't. You never did and you never will. Don't call me. When I'm ready to talk I'll call you.

Katy

PS - I took all but $200 out of our bank account. You can have the furniture and all the other stuff.

Roberta stood up and started banging her forehead dramatically against the wall by the door. She finally came back, sat down next to my bed and stared at me with an expression of disbelief. "Did you even read this?" she asked.

"Of course, I read it," I said.

"How many times did you read it?" she demanded.

"I don't know," I said. "Maybe just once, when I first took it off the fridge."

"Yeah, well maybe if you had read it again, when you weren't hung over, her problem wouldn't be such a big mystery." Roberta handed me the note back. "Read it again, Sherlock. See if you can detect a clue."

I read it and I was pretty sure I saw what she meant. I guess I should have read it over before, instead of just carrying it around. "Uhh . . . maybe it's that she thinks I wasn't putting her first in my life?"

"Duhhh, do you think?" I didn't really care for Roberta's tone, but I guess I had it coming.

"I didn't think she meant that literally. I thought she was just . . . you know . . ."

"Yeah I know," Roberta said. "Katy might just as well have written, 'Blah, blah, blah, blah, blah,' for all you got out of this." Roberta took a deep breath and ran her fingers through her hair.

"Okay," she said. "Sorry about the sarcasm. I'm here to help. I really am, so let's give this a little thought, okay?"

"Fine," I said doubtfully.

"Now, is it true? Is she right? Did you put her first in your life? Or was something else like your career first and Katy a distant second? Or wasn't she even close enough to be in second place?"

"Becoming a heart surgeon was first," I admitted, "but Katy always knew that. At least, I think she did. She knew what that meant to me, what it meant to both of us. It was the future we both wanted. And she knew what kind of hours I'd be working as a resident. Well not really. The residents in Boston had it easy compared to . . ."

"Stop," Roberta said, paused and went on analytically. "The day you got fired was the same day Katy took off, so there's no way to say which hit you hardest. I won't ask you that. But when you saw the news this morning, when it looked like Holt would be able to get you back in the program . . . How happy were you?"

"Well it's still not definite so . . . so I guess I'm not as delighted as I will be, if it happens." But Roberta had put her finger on something strange. Ever since reading the news of Jefferson's disgrace, I had been pretty sure that Holt's plan was working. He would get me back into the VA and that would get me the heart program. I should have been ecstatic, should have been whistling and tap-dancing and grinning like an idiot. But I wasn't. I felt better than I'd felt for some time but still was basically miserable. Was it because of losing Katy?"

"Is it just that it isn't definite," Roberta asked. She was dead serious now, focused and intense. "Is that the only problem? What was your first thought when you learned that Jefferson was arrested?"

"It was to call Katy and share it with her. Then I realized that I couldn't," I admitted.

"Now, do me a favor." Roberta was relentless. "Imagine that Katy was still with you. Imagine reading those papers and watching the news with her. Imagine going out to celebrate and coming home to celebrate better. Imagine how different it would have been.

"And most important . . . imagine knowing that you were number one in her life."

I imagined what she suggested and said, "Okay I get it. Thanks, Roberta." She squeezed my hand and stood up.

"My work here is done," she said but stopped by the door on her way out. "Call Katy soon," she smiled, "before you forget everything."

But the conclusion Roberta wanted me to reach was not so clear cut. Sure I would have been happier with Katy and my career back, but that didn't necessarily make Katy number one. I wanted them both and, with the insight I got from Roberta, maybe I could have both.

* * *

The next morning Holt wasn't operating. He came by with Dr. Pandya. When I was discharged, he gave me a ride home. I loaded the new bike carefully into the back of his pickup. Then I climbed in front with Holt.

"You gonna need you some groceries, Yankee Boy," Holt said. "I'll stop and wait on you if you hurry it up. You got any money?"

$150 had appeared in my wallet the morning after Tiny's hospital visit. I assumed he was paying me back for Billy's boom-box and earphones. Sharon must have told him what they cost. Well, Tiny could afford it better than I could.

After the stop for groceries, Holt drove me back to my place and parked out front. I thanked him for the ride but, before I could get out he said, "Hold on a minute, son."

I settled back and waited to hear what he had to say.

"I don't want you to get your hopes up too much," Holt said. "You need to understand . . . these charges against Jefferson . . . well . . . they may not stick."

"Why wouldn't they stick?" I asked.

"Well . . . it might-could a been Eightball hired Haystack, not Jefferson. You know, like Detective Owens was saying? Like he said in the ER when we all first talked about the murder? Eightball has had it in for you since you kicked his ass in the ER. And he was mad at Shaleena for cheating on him with Jefferson. So having her killed and you framed . . . That would a pleased Eightball double."

"But if it was Eightball," I asked, "why did the cops arrest Jefferson?"

"At first, Haystack must a swore it was Jefferson hired him," Holt explained. "But that might-could a been just because Tiny told him to say that. After Tiny 'reasons with' folk, they tend to do like he tells them. Problem is what Tiny makes them say ain't necessarily exactly where the truth's at."

"So now you're saying Jefferson is innocent?" I asked.

Holt's face twisted into a malevolent mask. "Jefferson ain't innocent," he said angrily and then quickly got himself under control. "He just may not be guilty a hiring Haystack to kill Shaleena," Holt continued calmly.

"Thing is, Yankee Boy," he went on, "Detective Owens had some health problems. Just lately, he's been in the hospital for a few days. During that time, with Barnes gone too, no one who really knew the case was around to grill Haystack. Haystack's statement was taken but he wasn't given a really tough interrogation. Owens responded to treatment and now he's back in action. If it was really Eightball hired Haystack– and I'm saying 'if' here - Owens will break that big dummy. And it won't take him long to do it."

"How do you know all this stuff, Holt?"

"I told you about my daddy," Holt explained patiently. "There's still some old-timers on the force who knew him. Hell, Owens is one of them. Let's just say, I have my sources."

"Well what do those sources say?" I insisted. "Come on this is my future we're talking about."

"My sources tell me that parts a Haystack's story don't hold up too good," Holt said. "Jefferson can prove he was outa town when Haystack says they met here in Birmingham."

"So, if Jefferson's cleared of the murder, does that mean I'm still screwed?" I asked.

"Not necessarily," Holt pointed out. "Even if he ain't guilty of murder, there's still the scandal about Shaleena and the cover up about those dead patients. That still **should** get him fired and, **if** it does, I can still save your Yankee ass."

It worried me that Holt emphasized the "should" and "if" quite plainly. Obviously he wasn't sure how things were going to work out. "Tell me honestly, Holt. What's your best guess? Is Jefferson going to come through this?"

"Ever since he was a kid," Holt said, "Jefferson has been a slippery bastard. He's managed to sleaze his way out a paying for ever rotten thing he's done so far. And he's done worse'n this . . . much worse." Holt had a faraway look in his eye. I didn't want to interrupt his thoughts but I had to understand this.

"So, in spite of everything that's come out, you're saying Jefferson still could hang on at the VA?"

"That's what I'm saying," Holt smiled. "But even if that happens, don't you give up hope. Don't you leave town nor do nothing crazy. That's the main thing I want to say. That's why I give you the ride home. No matter what happens, you hang in there 'till I tell you the game is over. You hear me, Yankee Boy?"

"But if Jefferson stays on as Chief of Surgery, that's it. I stay barred from the VA and my career stays over. What's there to hang in for?" I asked him.

"Just trust me, son," Holt said warmly. "Even if he gets hired on again, you never know what might happen. It ain't over, 'till I tell you it's over. Now promise you'll hang in there 'till I say so."

"Okay, Holt," I said. "I don't understand it but I'll do as you say. I promise. I'll stay in town and I won't give up hope until you tell me it's over."

It was good to get back home. I put away the groceries, had a beer and some peanuts. I thought about Holt and Jefferson and Haystack and Tiny and

Shaleena and Owens. That got me nowhere. Then I thought about Katy, and Roberta's advice to the lovelorn. That was, at least, one problem I could try to deal with.

I dialed the number for the Tufts ICU, hoping Katy had been re-hired and that she was on the day shift.

"Tufts Boston Medical Center, cardiac ICU, can I help you?"

"Hi, this is Cooper Logan, uh Doctor Logan. I'm just wondering if Katy Conner is . . ."

"Cooper," she squealed. "It's Mary, Mary Yeager. How are you? It's so good to hear your voice. Katy's here. They temporarily reactivated her old privileges. That way she can work while the credentials committee makes it permanent. It's great to have her back but . . . well . . . we were all sorry to hear about . . . Everyone thought you and Katy were so perfect together."

"Yeah," I said. "So did I and I haven't given up yet. That's why I'm calling. Would you see if she'll talk to me Mary?"

"She'll talk to you if I have to tie her to a chair and tape the phone to her ear. Just hold on a minute," Mary said.

For a long time my heart seemed to beat to the rhythm of the beeping ICU monitors in Boston. Then I heard Katy's voice in the background. "Okay, okay. I'm picking it up."

"Cooper?" Her voice was cool, if not frigid. It still sounded good to me.

"Yeah, Hi Katy." I spoke quickly to get to the point before she hung up. "Um, I know you said not to call but . . . well things seem to be looking up." I filled her in quickly on Shaleena's murder and Jefferson being arrested for it, skimming over my own involvement as much as possible.

"So if Jefferson is charged with the murder or even if he isn't, with the scandal and all, Holt could end up acting Chief at the VA, in which case I would be welcomed back there and also into Dr. Kirkwood's program. Not just for general surgery either. The Wire promised me a Cardiac Fellowship, if the VA thing worked out. So, you know, I . . . I thought maybe . . . I just thought . . . you know, that you'd like to know that."

"I'm happy for you, Cooper. I really am." Her voice sounded a little shaky. You'll be a great heart surgeon. I've always know that. It would have been such a waste if you hadn't . . . if you . . ."

That sounded good and maybe I should have just pushed on but I had to ask. It meant too much to me. I had to know for sure. "But, Katy, I thought . . . When you left you said you thought it was my fault I got in trouble and . . ."

"Oh Cooper, you should have know better. I was angry. I just wanted to hurt you. I've never stopped believing in you . . . as a surgeon that is." I thought I heard her sniffle and took that as a good sign.

"You hurt me alright. I set a new Recovery Room record for boiler-makers per hour. I think they're putting a plaque on the wall in my honor." She let out a sort of half-laugh half-cry and I decided to go for it.

"So look, baby, come back to me, will you? I really miss you. And now . . . all our plans and dreams . . . It looks like they could be back on track again."

"I don't know Cooper," she whispered. "It wasn't just your getting fired. There were problems before that and, if I came back now, how could you ever count on me? I deserted you when you were down, just when you needed me the most, like a rat deserting a sinking ship." She was crying openly by then. I pictured her standing there in tears at the central desk in the unit: all the other nurses and techs pretending not to notice.

"Katy, I understand why you left," I said, playing the card Roberta had provided. "It was my own fault and I don't blame you. If I'd put you first in my life, like it says in your note, you'd have stuck with me through anything. I know that now and . . . even probably getting back in the program . . . It's not making me happy . . . not without you." I paused for a reaction.

"Go on, Cooper," she prodded, sounding thoughtful and interested, but a little suspicious. This Roberta stuff just might work but I had to be careful.

"Well I've just finally realized that my future as a heart surgeon . . . or as anything else, baby . . . It's nothing if you're not in it. You are number one in my life. You have been all along. I've just been too dumb to know it . . . until now. Come back to me and I'll never forget it again. I promise."

"So you finally read the note," she said coldly.

"Well I read it before but I didn't . . ." Katy could always see right through me. She wasn't buying it.

"Tell me all about reading it again. Why you did it and why you paid attention this time. Everything. And don't lie to me. If you don't tell the truth I'll know and then we really will be over. If I think you aren't telling the truth, I will never speak to you again." I believed her.

"Well, I was talking to Roberta, you know her; she's a surgery resident." Katy said she remembered Roberta and I went on. "Well I was talking to her about us . . . you know, I needed to talk to someone. . . and . . . I told her about the note and she wanted to see it and I showed it to her and . . ." I wasn't sure how much more I should mention.

"So Roberta explained the note to you and you got the idea to call me and say what I wanted to hear? Is that it?" Katy demanded.

"That's pretty much it," I admitted, actually relieved to have all the cards on the table. Katy could take me or leave me as I was. Either way I'd survive it.

"Well Roberta seems to know me much better than you do," Katy said sarcastically. "Maybe I should go back to Birmingham and hook up with her instead of you."

I knew that this was the turning point. It was like standing up to a bully. I couldn't show fear. And, if possible, whatever I said should surprise her. If I could only make her laugh . . .

"Well, if you and Roberta do get it on . . . would a *ménage a trios* be out of the question?"

There was a long pause and I decided to go down with all guns blazing.

"I'll take that as a, no. Well then how about . . . you think I could watch if I'm quiet? I might even come up with some useful suggestions."

I heard what I hoped were muffled chuckles. "You have your hand over the phone," I said, "but I can hear you laughing. If you're laughing, I win. You have to come back to me. Those are the rules and you know it. It's written in The Book of Love. They just left it out of the song."

She took her hand away and her giggles bubbled across the Mason Dixon line from Boston. I pictured her laughing pixie face, wishing I could see it. "I'll think about it," she managed to say over the chuckles. Then she gave me her home number and told me I could call her there, not at work in the unit. Then she hung up.

But I knew I had her.

CHAPTER 24

TWO DAYS LATER, Haystack changed his story. He now claimed that Eightball, not Jefferson, paid for Shaleena's murder. Jefferson was released with all charges against him dropped. I was still recuperating at home, when Holt called with the bad news.

"But Eightball's in prison," I objected. "How could he have hired anyone and set up the whole frame and . . . everything."

"I told you, son," Holt explained patiently, "Eightball still runs all the city's black crime, even from inside Holman. He must a just had one a his boys approach Haystack, with payoff money and orders."

"Well none of that matters to me," I sighed. "I only care if Jefferson gets back on as Chief of Surgery. Any word on that?"

"Nothing yet," Holt said, "and it could go either way. The scandal would normally kill any career but . . . Jefferson's been over there a long time and there's lots a folk owes him favors. I'll keep my eye on things but it may be while."

"How long could it take?" I asked, hoping an end was in sight.

"It may be a few weeks," Holt said, "before anything's definite. VA wheels grind slowly and not always all that fine."

"So this will be hanging over my head for weeks," I said. "In just a few days, I'll be starting with Dr. Kirkwood. One month after that I'm dead, unless Jefferson is fired. Looks like, this horse race is going right down to the wire."

"And a photo finish when it gets there. But remember what I told you, Yankee Boy," Holt admonished. "Even if Jefferson does get reinstated, you never know what might happen. Do not give up hope and do not leave town. The finish line a this race might not be where ever-one thinks it's at.'"

Katy and I had talked on the phone nearly every day since the breakthrough phone call. She had finally caved and we were officially back together. For now, she would keep her job at Tufts. If I didn't get back in The Wire's program, I would join her in Boston. At least we wouldn't be broke, while we made new plans for our future. Maybe I'd try for an ER job in Boston. If I found one, she could stay on at Tufts. I also knew there were rural towns desperate to recruit local health care. One of them might set us up with a clinic, in return for a long-term contract. Either way I saw a future of snotty noses and lanced boils. Maybe I'd just slit my fucking throat—death instead of a life sentence.

When I told Katy about Jefferson getting off and maybe being reinstated, it didn't seem to faze her at all.

"Even if it doesn't work out, Cooper, maybe that'll be for the best," Katy said. "Then you'll know I stuck with you even when times were tough—that getting fired really wasn't why I left you."

"I know it wasn't, baby," I said, "I thought we had all that settled. Look, whatever we do, we'll do it together. That's all that really matters." I said it but I didn't really believe it and I don't think Katy did either. I was obsessed with becoming a heart surgeon and we both knew it. But, if Jefferson got back in the VA, would it really even matter? Maybe that's why the bad news about Jefferson didn't seem to upset her.

A few days and a second set of tomograms later, Dr. Pandya pronounced me well. The next day, I started congenital hearts with The Wire. It felt good to be too busy to worry about Jefferson. Pointlessly rerunning that worry-track around my brain was driving me straight to the rubber room hotel. In spite of what Holt said, I was sure I'd stay screwed if Jefferson got back in. I resolved to use my time on The Wire's service to impress him as much as I could. If Jefferson survived the scandal . . . I'd fall off that bridge when I came to it.

Billy seemed to be moving more and to be more responsive each time I visited. I often found Sharon at his bedside and she had not given up on Mahler. She kept his ninth symphony blaring in Billy's ears through those expensive Koss earphones. Her attachment to Billy had obviously gone beyond sisterly devotion. If he ever woke up, I had the feeling that Sharon would keep him on the straight and narrow. When I asked Dr. Pandya about the prognosis, he didn't seem very hopeful.

Stephen Numatalulu had been discharged. Ken told me that, prior to going home, he was gaining strength and breathing without a struggle. I regretted not having had a chance to say goodbye to Momma. Probably, on second thought, that was for the best. Her farewell hug would probably have broken a few ribs. Passing Dr. Walker in the hall, I got only a frown and a nod. I heard he was submitting a case report on Stephen to the Journal of Thoracic and Cardiovascular Surgery. Somehow I doubted that my role in his care would be mentioned.

Dr. Kirkwood's service was a Fellow's last rotation. After that, he'd graduate as a fully trained heart surgeon. Such an exalted personage was far above helping out with the scut list. That was left to me, as the resident, and Carter Whitney, the surgeon's assistant. Mr. Whitney and I had been friends since I did Billy's coronary bypass. I would never forget his story about how The Wire cried in that movie theater.

Every morning, Mr. Whitney and I started rounds at 4:15. Then I called The Wire at 5:30 sharp. This early morning telephone report terrified most residents on the service. It focused on recent post-ops, still in the ICU, and briefly reviewed each of about twenty other kids on the service. With every call, the resident would face questions about relevant issues. The idea was for The Wire to manage the cases and teach at the same time. I knew at least one guy who vomited before every phone call. Carter Whitney could predict The Wire's questions with uncanny accuracy. He also happened to know nearly all the answers.

Mr. Whitney's help was essential in prepping for those morning reports. I was glad he was my friend. As hard as I studied and as much as I learned, he often saved me from sounding like a bozo.

The anatomy, physiology and pathology of those little malformed hearts was far more abstruse than anything in adult heart surgery. I'm not even going to try to describe a complex congenital operation. Too much boring background would be needed before I could get to the good parts.

Conceptualizing the abnormal anatomy and visualizing its repair was extremely difficult, even for us residents. To prep for my report to The Wire on some specific malformation, I would first study it in books he had written. Then I would review other texts and more recent scientific articles. Each reference would have diagrams of the anomaly and its surgical correction. Often there would be more than one potential repair. I would have to tell The Wire which one I thought was appropriate. This studying took place between finishing the evening scut list and beginning early rounds—say from 1 AM to 4 AM. After all that, I usually felt ready for the morning inquisition. Other times I twisted my brain around the convoluted anatomy until my frontal lobes herniated out through my ear drums. Then I'd stuff the grey matter back into my skull and call for help from Mr. Whitney.

No, of course there was no time for sleep.

Afternoon rounds with The Wire were major productions. There were always at least a dozen people in the entourage. These ranged from medical students, nurses, techs and residents to visiting dignitaries from all over the world. Sir Brian Barratt-Boyes, who was co-authoring The Wire's new book, sometimes attended. He's still the only real live knight I've ever known. Sir Brian acted like just a regular guy . . . only quite a bit smarter. I never once saw him with a sword or in any kind of armor.

The Wire held court initially by standing at each patient's bedside. His white coat was always immaculate and his hands were thrust, elbows straight, deep into its pockets. The resident on the service stood before him and reported on each case from memory. These presentations were even more daunting than the early morning reports. The Wire would always pose at least a few difficult questions. If you blew the answers, the audience would quietly enjoy your disgrace. It provided little comfort to know that few of them could have done better.

Any statement the resident made had to be backed up with data— numbers and statistics from some study or series. "Data" was subdivided into "good data," "bad data," or the dreaded "no data." What the average person would consider proof was often "no data" to The Wire. For example, a study that showed better results with one technique than another was "no data" unless the p-value assured statistical significance. If the resident quoted the study, he had better know the p-values.

After the presentation, Dr. Kirkwood would examine the patient. Most of them were babies or young children, which brought the stress to a whole new dimension. I could not comprehend what those parents were feeling until years later, when I had my own kids. But, even back then, their fear was so thick I could almost smell it.

Surgery on these little patients was a high stakes gamble. A valve or coronary on a septuagenarian could improve quality of life and longevity. But if an elderly patient died, at least they'd had a chance to live. With a baby or child, you gave them their whole life . . . or you lost it all for them.

No medical doctor, treating patients with pills, feels the weight carried by a surgeon. A medical specialist simply tries to help. The patient may or may not benefit. Either way the medical doc has done no harm. A surgeon must place every patient at risk, in the OR. If the surgery doesn't save a life, it very well may end it. In these congenital hearts, bad outcomes were not infrequent. Without surgery their malformations would eventually be fatal. But if a child dies in the OR, the operation caused Death's visit that day.

Dr. Kirkwood explained the difference between surgery and medicine with an analogy.

Being a medical doctor is like seeing someone drowning and swimming out from shore to try to save them. That is one level of responsibility.

Being a surgeon is like throwing someone off a bridge into the water, running across the bridge to the shore and *then* swimming out to try to save them—a far higher level.

Many of the kids were terrified and you often had to hurt them to help them. Placing an intravenous line into tiny veins often requires more than one stick. Various tests and dressing changes also can be painful. Of course the children didn't understand. To them you were a monster and that made you feel like a monster. Many older kids had undergone previous palliative procedures. Now they needed higher risk more definitive operations. They were being sucked back into a recurring nightmare and you were their real life boogey man.

On his service, I came to understand why Dr. Kirkwood had cried in that theater. The pressure was unimaginable. The pain of failure threatened to be overwhelming. But The Wire once told me, "After a case, you must not permit yourself to feel despair or elation. You just learn what you can and move on to the next patient." It was good advice. Too bad I could never completely follow it. Then again, as I knew from Mr. Whitney's story, neither could The Wire.

Making a good summary of each case on rounds was one way I could help The Wire. After my presentation, he would take a chair at the patient's bedside. Dr. Kirkwood's posture sitting was just as rigidly perfect as standing. Head erect and leaning slightly back, he would cross one leg over the other. I would then hand him the chart, with a flourish, and he would review it personally.

There was absolute silence as I stood at near attention, while Dr. Kirkwood wrote his note. He always used a Mount Blanc Meisterstuck, a massively fat black ink pen, with an 18K gold nib and platinum inlay. The Wire was as precise and graceful with the Meisterstuck as he was with the scalpel. He wrote in elegant flowing lines, as artistic as any calligraphy. For a lesser man, this bedside scene would have been an affectation. For The Wire . . . well that's the way he really was.

I loved being part of it.

I swore, if I ever became a heart surgeon, I would buy a pen just like The Wire's. If I failed to achieve my dream, I would never let myself own one—not even in the unlikely event I could afford it. A Mount Blanc Meisterstuck, just like The Wire's, became my Holy Grail. Before I could claim it, God and fate would have to find me worthy.

The Wire's service was more demanding than any of the others. I worked so late, even on my nights off, that going home was rarely worthwhile. On rare nights, things were slow and the Fellow agreed to cover. Then Carter Whitney would often give me and my bike a ride home in his pickup. Sometimes Mr. Whitney would come in and we would talk. Eventually I learned his story.

Carter was born in a Baltimore slum, near the Johns Hopkins Medical Center. He never knew his father and grew up on the streets. Pimps and drug dealers were his role models. By 1944 Carter was twelve and already in frequent trouble. A black teacher saw potential in the boy and tried hard to motivate him.

"Course, I just sassed the man," Carter said. "I gave him the usual line of bullshit. Racism keeps the black man down, so there's no point in trying. The only proud black men are revolutionaries that fight the system. The rest are servile Uncle Toms, no better than slaves. Teachers are the worst. They program young blacks to be submissive servants. In the ghetto, there are plenty of excuses for failure."

The teacher happened to know a black man named Vivien Thomas. He took Carter to see him in the dog lab at Johns Hopkins. Vivien Thomas was in charge of Dr. Alfred Blalock's experimental laboratory. He and Dr. Blalock worked closely together. They were the first to devise an operation for Tetralogy of Fallot or "blue baby syndrome." The babies were blue because not enough blood was getting to their lungs to be oxygenated.

There was no heart-lung machine back then and no open heart surgery. The physiologic problem had to be solved without correcting the anatomy. Blalock and Thomas connected an artery in the chest to the pulmonary circulation. This turned the blue babies pink, made them stronger and helped them live longer. The shunt did not repair the Tets but it greatly helped their symptoms.

Vivien Thomas was the grandson of a slave. He had no education after high school. In the great depression, he was an unemployed carpenter. He was hired to clean the dog shit out of cages in Blalock's laboratory. When no one else was free to assist, the black cleanup man was eager to help. Dr. Blaylock quickly recognized Vivien's extraordinary surgical talent. Eventually Thomas was able to perform the dog surgery without Dr. Blalock. In fact, when it came to pure technical skill, he was said to be Blalock's superior.

"Vivien Thomas gave me a job in the dog lab at Hopkins," Carter said. "As head of Blalock's lab, Mr. Thomas followed progress at other heart centers. When he learned of Dr. Kirkwood's heart lung machine, he understood its full potential. Instead of just working around malformed hearts, Dr. Kirkwood would be able to really fix them. Mr. Thomas told me that was the new frontier of cardiac surgery. He told me to get out on that frontier—to make a place for myself there." Carter paused remembering that turning point in his life.

"So, I hitchhiked from Baltimore to Rochester, Minnesota," he went on, "and got a job cleaning the cages in Dr. Kirkwood's dog lab. It was important to me to start at the bottom, just like Mr. Thomas." Carter smiled and chuckled to himself.

Dr. Kirkwood recognized Carter's talent, just as Blalock had with Vivien Thomas. Carter was not the technical prodigy that Thomas was. Few surgeons are or ever have been. But Carter did have a sharp mind and steady hands. In the dog lab, he quickly learned any surgical technique The Wire showed him. Dr. Kirkwood arranged to have Carter trained as one of the first surgeon's assistants. When Carter graduated, he was hired to work with The Wire.

Carter became Dr. Kirkwood's right hand man. He helped him develop new open heart procedures in the dog lab. Then, as a surgeon's assistant, he helped apply them to actual patients. Dr. Kirkwood devised a definitive operation for Tetralogy. He wrote an entire book about that single great achievement. Helping with the cure for Tetralogy of Fallot fulfilled Carter's ultimate dream. He helped The Wire finish the job Vivien Thomas and Blaylock had started.

When The Wire left Mayo to run the heart program in Birmingham, he brought Carter Whitney with him.

CHAPTER 25

NOT ALL CONGENITAL hearts are considered complex. My most memorable case, on Dr. Kirkwood's service, was the simplest of all malformations: a secundum type atrial septal defect or ASD. The shared wall of tissue forming the floor of the right atrium and the ceiling of the left atrium is the atrial septum. In the Numatalulu case, Dr. Walker entered the left atrium through the septum to better expose the mitral valve.

Prior to birth, for embryologic reasons, an oval shaped hole or foramen in the atrial septum is normally present. It is appropriately called the *foramen ovale*. The *foramen ovale* is normally closed by overgrowth of the septum secundum. When this process fails, the result is a persistent hole called a secundum ASD.

This type of ASD is not an urgent problem. It will only cause trouble later in life if timely repair is neglected. A child may reach puberty or older before closure is needed. Relatively simple and safe to repair, this is often a young surgeon's first heart case. Billy Sugg's bypass was my first open heart but that was unusual. If I ever got another, it would most likely be an ASD.

No one knew that better than Carter Whitney. "Got a new case that might interest you last night," he said with a teasing smile. We were mostly done with rounds and on our way to see the pre-ops. Carter had been on the night before while I'd slept for once in my own bed.

Carter was mysteriously reticent about the new case. I had to interrogate him for details. The mystery patient turned out to be Madeline Ruth, a fourteen year old girl with an uncomplicated secundum ASD scheduled for surgery the next day. Madeline was a pale blond child with damp fearful blue eyes. She was truly terrified, more so than usual, and not just of the pain. In spite of all reassurances from her family doctor, cardiologist and parents, Madeline was sure she was going to die. Other than being small for her age, she had no symptoms. The indication for operation was high flow across the ASD which, in time, would damage her lungs.

Her father was an attorney and her mother a homemaker. Madeline begged them to let her go home. It clearly tore their hearts out to make her stay. Carter and I emphasized the importance and safety of the procedure, but Madeline was adamant.

"I don't care about my lungs when I get old. If I have this, I'll never get old. I wanna go home now! Mommy please!" she said, dissolving into a puddle of tears. I wondered how long it had been since she last called her mother, Mommy.

As we left, I gestured to the parents to step into the hall. Once out of the room, I said, "Of course, there is always some risk with any operation and certainly with any open heart. I have to tell you about even minimal risks but I didn't want to do it in front of Madeline."

They both nodded and the attorney father said, "Of course. We understand."

"The chances are better than 99% that she will survive the operation and do well," I said, "especially in our program." I went on to mention the small chance of infection, bleeding, stroke, or heart block requiring a pacemaker— what Dr. Kirkwood called, "the risks and imponderables of surgery."

I'll never know if Dr. Kirkwood would have let me do Madeline's operation, but that did seem to be the plan. The Fellow was in Paris representing our program at a symposium on new techniques for repairing mitral valves. While he was gone, Dr. Walker was assisting The Wire with the complex congenital cases and doing the easier ones with me or Carter helping.

After evening rounds, Dr. Kirkwood smiled and said, "You will scrub with me on the ASD, Cooper." Dr. Walker wouldn't like that. His own service included only adult patients and he was eager to improve his resume with as many congenitals as possible. If heart surgeons are the aristocrats of surgery, congenital cardiac surgeons are the royalty. Walker had it in for me since the Numatalulu case. He would hate my edging him out of the ASD. If doing the case was an ice cream Sunday, his jealousy would be the chocolate sprinkles and cherry on top combined. As it turned out, I ate crow instead.

Dr. Kirkwood passed his first kidney stone early on the morning of Madeline's operation. This condition would lead, several years and stones later, to his first time under the knife. Before that, our post-op hearts routinely got Aspirin for pain. After his surgery, Dr. Kirkwood let us treat them with narcotics. This provided support, among us residents, for the controversial theory that The Wire was actually human.

Passing a kidney stone may be the most painful experience known to medicine. It forced even Dr. Kirkwood to do the unthinkable—take the day off. Madeline had already been anesthetized when he became incapacitated. Otherwise the case might have been cancelled.

Dr. Walker would do the case, with me assisting, and gloated about it openly. He knew that, but for the ill-timed kidney stone, I would have been the primary surgeon. He rubbed it in by telling me how fast ASDs were done in Houston. Over the years, I've met several Houston trained surgeons. Every single one wanted to brag about speed. They loved to tell you just how quickly they could do any case, skin-to-skin. Skin-to-skin means elapsed time from the skin incision to the start of skin closure. An underling would place the skin stitches, so that part didn't count.

Prior to the invention of anesthesia, speed was of vital importance. The faster one could amputate a leg, the less time an awake patient would suffer. Prior to cardioplegia, or CP, speed also made heart surgery safer. Blood supply to the heart must be stopped, while one works inside it. Before CP, when blood flow was cut off, the heart would start dying. The faster one finished and restored blood flow, the less chance of serious damage.

With the advent of cardioplegia to protect the heart, speed was no longer as important. Heart surgeons focused more on perfecting repairs and less on doing them quickly. Somehow the Houston program was late in getting that message. Maybe it was because Denton Cooley was such an extremely fast surgeon. Dr. Cooley was as idolized in Houston, as Dr. Kirkwood was in Birmingham. But Cooley was a natural—effortlessly superfast and accurate. His wannabes had to work at it . . . and brag about it.

"What's the fastest, Kirkwood's ever done an ASD?" Walker asked as we scrubbed.

"I haven't seen him do one," I responded. "He usually gives them to the Fellow. Anyway, he's more interested in making it perfect than in doing it quickly."

"So how long does it take Hanley to do one," Walker persisted. "Skin to skin."

"I don't know. An hour and a half? Two hours? I really don't remember," I said.   Dr. Kirkwood would have been quizzing me on the anatomy and technique of the repair. Walker's obsession with speed made me uncomfortable.

"Cooley used to do them routinely in under an hour—skin-to-skin," Walker went on.   "Of course, that was back in the day, before cardioplegia. I've never done one in under an hour, mostly because of the CP. By the time you insert the cannulae and wait for each infusion, you've added at least twenty minutes to the case. There's no need for cardioplegia anyway with such a short cross-clamp." It was while the aorta was cross-clamped that blood flow to the heart was suspended.

Walker paused and then added, "I may not use CP today. I may just cool down as we're opening, clamp the aorta and go. Set myself a new record . . . under an hour."

We finished the scrub and, as we turned away, Walker smirked at me. He seemed to be hoping I'd argue with him as I had about Numatalulu. He'd caved on that one, and successfully used the approach from the Israeli journal. Now he was daring me to argue again, this time about cardioplegia. If he didn't back down and had a good result, that would make us even. Madeline would almost surely do fine without cardioplegia. In the short time to close an uncomplicated ASD, the heart would not suffer much damage. ASDs had been done for years under cold bloodless arrest. The results had mostly been fine back then, though the risk was a little higher. But still . . .   What if we got in there and the ASD was abnormal? What if something unexpected delayed the repair? Why take any chance to set a meaningless record?

I wasn't going to play Walker's game. If I kept my mouth shut maybe he would use CP after all. Even if he didn't, there would almost surely be no problem.

I said nothing as the scrub nurse helped us into our sterile gowns and gloves.

I said nothing as we prepped and draped Madeline's slim naked body, anesthetized and helpless on the operating table. She was pale and still as a child's corpse, with sterile green sheets for a shroud.

Walker posed with the knife before making the skin incision. "Note the time," he told the anesthesiologist. A picture of Madeline's pre-op pleading and crying popped into my mind. I have learned to respect such fatal premonitions.

Walker moved quickly and surely. He was an excellent technician. The vertical incision slid smoothly down the front of Madeline's chest. There was hardly any fat beneath her parchment-like skin. The baby-sized sternal saw looked like a toy compared to the heavy adult model. It sliced her thin chest bone like a box-cutter through cardboard. There was little bleeding as Walker divided the translucent pericardium. Clear fluid was suctioned and the little heart was exposed.

The hearts of infants and children are pristine—the colors vibrant and brilliant. Signs of wear seen in most adult hearts are conspicuously lacking. There are no "soldier's patches" from abrasions on surrounding tissue, no adhesions from old inflammation, no scars from prior infarctions and no calcifications. A child's heart to a surgeon is like a new Ferrari to a mechanic. Madeline's heart was just that magnificent, yet still perversely abnormal—like a Ferrari designed by a Sergio Peninfarina, but assembled by Willy Wonka.

Just one small flaw in construction kept Madeline's little heart from perfection. We couldn't see the defect yet, but its sequelae were obvious. With an ASD, pressures in the atria equalize, making them functionally a single chamber. Left and right ventricles both fill from that single chamber at the same pressure. The thick left ventricular wall is harder to stretch than the thin right one. This makes the left ventricle harder to distend and fill. Just imagine putting two balloons in your mouth and inflating them together. If one balloon is made of much thinner rubber, most air will go into that one. For the same reason, most of Madeline's blood flowed into the thinner walled right ventricle. This increased volume then flooded the lungs through the pulmonary arteries.

Madeline's right atrium, ventricle and pulmonary artery were grossly swollen and dilated. This consequence of excessive flow was disturbing but not really dangerous. It was high flow to the lungs that would lead to irreparable damage. Repair now was in plenty of time to avoid pulmonary problems. With the ASD closed, her prognosis for a long healthy life would become normal.

Walker immediately began preparations to place Madeline on bypass. With The Wire, we would have paused at this point to assess the anatomy. This would include direct digital palpation of the defect. A probing finger through a tight slit in the right atrium could feel the ASD's edges. An ASD is not well seen in dye studies and back then we had no cat scans. Before opening the heart and seeing the hole, only a finger could accurately assess it.

Walker failed to take the minute to feel Madeline's defect. That's why he didn't know, until too late, of its abnormal size and position.

Once on bypass, Walker cooled the heart by cooling the blood passing through it. He then poured ice water into the pericardium. When cold caused the heart to arrest, he clamped the aorta, cutting off blood flow to the heart muscle. Lack of blood flow is called ischemia. Stopping the heart this way is called cold ischemic arrest.

Cold ischemic arrest provides plenty of time to close a normal atrial defect. But Madeline's ASD turned out to be far from normal. With the right atrium open, two problems became apparent. The defect was quite large and also too close to the AV node. The AV node is a bundle of conduction tissue, like a heavy electric cable. One can't see the node and estimates where it is by surrounding landmarks. When the atria beat, a current through the node causes ventricular contraction. If the message is blocked, the ventricles just sit there waiting for it. This is called complete AV block and requires a permanent pacer. The pacemaker stimulates the atria to beat and then stimulates the ventricle. Without a pacemaker, complete AV block can be fatal.

Stitches to close Madeline's huge ASD needed big bites of atrial septum. Thin bites, taken close to the edge of the hole, would pull through her delicate tissue. Bites taken too far back could pierce the AV node and destroy it. Walker saw the problem right away and paused to consider his options.

When he held out his hand for the needle holder, I had to say something. The bigger the defect the more tension needed to pull its edges together. Sutures closing Madeline's gaping ASD would be stretched extremely tightly. Placed deeply enough to hold, I feared they would bag the node for certain.

"Dr. Walker," I said softly, "how about a patch?" Sewing in a patch the same size as the hole would mean no tension on the sutures. They could be placed close to the defect's edge keeping the node out of danger.

"I'm not wasting time on patch," Walker spat, and began to close the defect with sutures.

He took thin bites of tissue near the edge and the first two or three held without tearing. But the farther towards the center of the hole he stitched, the more distance between opposite edges. The farther the tissue had to be pulled, the more tension on the suture. Soon stitches were pulling through, shredding the ASD's margins. Each time he tried taking slighter deeper bites, he got closer to the node's likely location. Each time one row of stitches pulled through, the next bites had to be deeper. The edges of the ASD were shredding and the node was clearly in danger.

"For God's sake," I pleaded softly, "forget your record. Put in CP, cut a patch, and take your time closing this without bagging the node."

Walker went postal.

"Get the fuck out of here," he hissed. "And you will never again scrub with me."

Getting someone else to assist would only exacerbate the situation. It would also make me partly to blame for the looming disaster.

"I'm sorry. I won't say anything else," I promised trying to calm him.

"Get the fuck out . . . now!" he insisted. "And you," to the second scrub nurse, "get up here and help me."

The longer I stayed, the more he would freak out and the worse it would be for Madeline. Maybe if I left he'd put in the CP and patch it.

Leaving the O.R. stomach churning, I knew I was part of the problem. Maybe if I had kept my mouth shut, Walker would have patched it. Once I made the suggestion, his ego made that impossible. Why hadn't I seen that? My Yankee aggressiveness could cost Madeline dearly. I desperately needed to talk to someone and finally found Holt in his office. I told him everything starting with Walker's scrub sink speech about setting a record.

"What do I say to the family, Holt? What do I say to The Wire?" My head in my hands I rocked forward in the big soft chair facing his desk. "Was it my fault? If I'd just shut up for once . . . but he kept on trying to close it. The edges were shredding and the sutures were already too close to the node. I had to say something . . . or did I?"

Nearly in tears, I took my head from my hands and looked up at Holt for an answer.

"You did what you thought best and what's done is done," Holt said firmly. "You can torture yourself about it as much or as little as you want to. Won't change nothing! If you got any sense you'll skip the self-loathing and think what you're gonna do now."

"Okay," I said and took a deep breath. "So tell me, what do I do now? The father is a fucking lawyer. If I tell him what happened, he'll sue us. What good will that do?"

"Maybe the girl will be fine," Holt said. "If so, you need tell no one nothing."

"Suppose she wakes up with AV block. Suppose Walker tries to blame me."

"You put nothing about none of this on the chart, you hear?" Holt said. "If Dr. Kirkwood asks you what happened, you tell him the whole story. If Walker tries blaming you, you go to Dr. Kirkwood. As for the dad, you tell the truth but only what truth is needed. The ASD was gi-normous and close to the node and that's why she might need a pacemaker."

I looked Holt in the eye and saw nothing but steely determination. "But, Holt, I don't know . . . I don't know if I can . . ."

Holt's bushy eyebrows levitated halfway up his forehead. He said, "You want to salvage any chance at all you might-could still get to be a heart surgeon?"

"You know I do, Holt, but . . ."

"No buts, Yankee Boy. You just do like I told you."

Madeline arrived in the ICU with complete heart block. Wires sewn to her heart came out through skin to a temporary pacemaker. The pacer sensed each atrial beat and then caused a ventricular beat to follow. With the pacer turned off, or if a wire came loose, there would be no ventricular contractions. That is called cardiac arrest and would quickly be fatal. In a few days, a permanent pacer would be installed by cardiology. Those permanent leads would be more secure and Madeline would be out of danger. Until then, she needed to be watched every minute.

Walker refused to let Carter or me anywhere near Madeline. He said he'd take care of her himself and camped out at her bedside. Around four AM, he told the nurses he was going home briefly to shower. He left strict instructions that I was not to see Madeline for any reason.

When the wire came off and the pacemaker failed, the nurses were too busy to notice. An 80 year old man on the other side of the ICU had arrested. They were all at his bedside. The central nursing station was deserted.

No one was watching the monitors when Madeline flat-lined.

Decades later, doctors would demonize the so-called "malpractice crisis." Organizations like the Thoracic Surgeons Society would embrace and formalize the conspiracy of silence. They would even set up kangaroo courts to attack doctors who testified against their members. Lingering guilt over Madeline made me a bit more skeptical of the party line than most other physicians. I found nearly 100,000 deaths per year came from medical error. The "malpractice crisis" is not a crises of frivolous litigation. It is really a crisis of bad medicine, but most doctors refused to admit it.

A few doctors with multiple lawsuits are responsible for a high percentage of all malpractice awards. Surgical societies should deal with their few bad surgeons, as Dr. Kirkwood did by firing Walker. Instead, like the Mafia, they protect guilty colleagues and attack those who tell the truth about them.

CHAPTER 26

DESPITE HOLT'S ADVICE, Madeline's death continued to haunt me. Perhaps it still does but I've had to learn to live with it.

I had two weeks left on The Wire's service when I got the bad news about Jefferson. Holt caught me just after morning report, by the phone in the ICU sleeping room. Carter left and Holt closed the door so we wouldn't be disturbed. One look at his face and something inside me squeezed tight as an anaconda. We sat side-by-side on the lower bunk and he tried to break it to me gently.

"Got some sorry news for you, Yankee Boy," he said. "They won't be announcing it 'till the press conference tomorrow . . . but the decision has been made. Jefferson will be reinstated."

"But how can they do that?" I said. "I don't . . ."

"I managed to get a peek at the statement they worked up for the press. It says he's been proved innocent of any crime, which is in fact the truth. Jefferson was in Georgia when Haystack said they met in Birmingham. That discrepancy helped Owens break the big dummy down and make him roll on Eightball."

"Eightball's going to have him killed the day he checks into Holman," I said.

"Owens musta promised Haystack he'd serve his time elsewhere," Holt said.

"What about the scandal? Adultery with a nurse working under him; no pun intended," I asked.

"It was all just a big misunderstanding," Holt smiled. "Chris Dugan, their head of nursing, cleared that up. You see, Dr. Jefferson had been kind enough to counsel poor Shaleena about a little drug problem. They held the sessions late at night outa concern for Shaleena's reputation. Dugan was present at ever one a those meetings to avoid any hint of impropriety. They even have negative drug test reports to prove how well the treatment was working."

I told Holt how Roberta had seen Shaleena that night in the VA parking lot. "Shaleena was running to her car. She was hysterical, screaming, crying out of control. It was Roberta's first VA rotation. After Shaleena drove away, Roberta got lost on the way to the unit. She wandered into the administrative wing and saw Jefferson *and Dugan*. They were leaving his office wearing smirks and wrinkled clothing."

"Well those counseling sessions can be real stressful for ever-one concerned," Holt said sarcastically. "Shaleena must a made a big breakthrough that night, to have been so upset."

"Is anyone actually swallowing this bullshit?" I was incredulous. "Does Jefferson's wife believe it?"

"Wives, like the rest of us, believe mostly what they want to," Holt said. "As far as ever-body else goes, it don't really matter. That's Jefferson's story and he's stickin' to it. No one can prove those sessions weren't counseling and Bull Dyke Dugan swears they were."

I thought for a minute. "What about the body? I'll bet Shaleena's body tested positive for drugs."

Holt smiled. "Indeed it did, Yankee Boy. Jefferson was said to be 'deeply saddened.' That's how they put it in the news release. He was 'deeply saddened' to learn that she'd had her a little relapse. But that can happen and often does with any type of treatment."

"Alright, so he sleazes out of the scandal but what about the patient care issues—covering up for Shaleena's incompetence." I could not understand how he got past that.

"Oh all that never happened," Holt shook his head. "According to the hospital statement, all alleged improprieties were—Let's see; how did it go?—'investigated thoroughly and found to have no factual basis.' The investigators were all in Jefferson's pocket, but that wasn't mentioned."

"Unbelievable," I said. "If you don't mind flat-out lying, I guess there's an answer for anything." I thought about that for a while. "So I guess, at this point, it's really all over for me." I sighed deeply.

"Yes, it is," Holt confirmed. There was a long pause and then he added, ". . . Maybe."

"Maybe?" I asked with a glimmer of hope. "What do you mean, maybe? If Jefferson's back in, I'm out for good."

"Well, you never know, do you?" Holt said mysteriously. "Remember what I told you before? You don't give up hope and you don't leave town until I say it's over. You got that, Yankee Boy?"

"Okay, but I don't see how . . ." I said.

Holt got up and headed for the door. "You don't need to see how, son. You just do as I say. If something comes up, I'll call you. Ask The Wire to give you tonight off. He'll a heard about this and he'll let you. Then you stay home and wait there to hear from me."

I must have still looked dubious because he asked, "Have I steered you wrong yet?"

I thought of how he'd insisted on my sleeping in the VA ICU and how that had only made matters worse.

"Will you be home if I call tonight?" he demanded forcefully.

"I won't be going out to celebrate," I answered somewhat evasively.

"Good," Holt said, taking that for a yes. "You be sure to stay there. I may need to get with you."

I decided not to ask for the night off but, as it turned out, that that didn't matter. Late that afternoon, Dr. Kirkwood called me to his office. This time there was no sympathetic chat on his sofa. The Wire sat behind his desk and I took a chair facing it. He was all business as he curtly told me that Jefferson would be reinstated. As a "courtesy," he had been notified a day before the announcement.

"I want you to know," Dr. Kirkwood stated tersely, "that I have tried to place you in a number of programs. When the top heart centers all turned us down, I tried general surgery residencies. No luck there either. Being expelled from a hospital is a major red flag. There are just too many competing applicants with perfectly pure records. You might find a place in a third rate program but I don't think that's what you want. My advice is . . . you should set your sights on some other profession."

"Dr. McDuff seems to think that . . ." I tried to interject.

"I know all about Holt's peculiar optimism," The Wire interrupted angrily. "That was why I have continued to waste my time on your training. Now we both need to face the facts and be realistic. You have two weeks left of this residency year. You may take them off with pay. After that . . . well . . . I wish you luck in whatever field you choose. And I will be pleased to write you a glowing recommendation."

"Dr. Kirkwood," I said, "I don't mind finishing up the two weeks. If I leave early, the service will be shorthanded. Mr. Whitney will . . ."

"Mr. Whitney will have help," Dr. Kirkwood said, then cleared his throat and looked away. "The resident currently on adult hearts will be shared by the two services."

Ben Rogers was the resident on adult hearts. He would be replacing me. I felt like I'd been punched in the stomach and my face must have shown it. I could briefly see sympathy flit across The Wire's face. He recovered quickly and stood up. "There's just no point in my teaching someone who will never use the training."

He extended his hand and I shook it silently. After the shake, The Wire sat down and sighed. I stood there like an idiot trying to think of something to say.

"There's no need to say anything, Cooper," Dr. Kirkwood said gently. "I understand how you feel. It is what it is. We both have to face that."

I nodded and mumbled that I understood as well. Then I thanked him for the offered recommendation, turned slowly and slunk out of the office. I didn't even bother to try holding my head up.

It was a long sweaty bike ride, uphill, to a house that felt lonely and empty. Walking inside was like sliding into a fired up pizza oven. I got the AC going and stayed in the shower while things cooled off. Then I grabbed a beer and potato chips and thought about calling Katy. I actually picked up the phone but couldn't bring myself to dial. Telling her about it would make it even more real. Tomorrow would be soon enough for that conversation.

The phone rang as soon as I put it down. Sharon was calling to talk to me about Billy. I didn't have the heart to blow her off so I let her bubble on about how much more he was moving and responding. She was sure he would wake up soon and had already planned out his future.

Her family had connections in New York City. An uncle was a graduate of the Juilliard School of Music. As soon as he woke up and had time to prepare, she said Billy would get an audition. She was certain that Billy would someday have a career as a concert pianist.

I tried to sound excited without much success. It all seemed like her wishful thinking. I doubted that Billy would ever wake up. He was just one more of my mistakes. I had thrown away my dream of heart surgery to save him and he'd thanked me by sucking his life up his nostrils. What an idiot I was. I deserved whatever happened to me.

I finally got Sharon off the phone and then I felt guilty about that. She had obviously fallen in love with Billy—some kind of mothering complex. If he did wake up I'd be happy for them but I doubted that would happen. I was happy for Holt, who'd caused plenty of grief for his long-time enemy Jefferson. At least Tiny's "reasoning" with Haystack had accomplished that much. And I was happy for Tiny as well. His main competitor, Eightball, would be in jail until the next ice age. I was happy for Stephen Numatalulu and his Momma. I was happy for Katy who had me and her career and who didn't seem to care if I had mine. I probably wouldn't be able to keep her for long anyway. She deserved a winner not a loser and would find one after she dumped me. Everything was coming up roses for everyone except me and Madeline. Thinking of her made me feel even worse. Some get roses and some get fertilizer.

"This too shall pass," I said to myself and ended the pity party.

After a few more beers in front of the TV, I stripped to my shorts and slid into bed. I sorely needed at least a few hours of respite. It was still light out but I should have fallen asleep easily. I'd averaged only about two hours per night on Dr. Kirkwood's service. Nevertheless, I tossed and turned wide awake for hours. Then I tried my old college insomnia cure and silently recited poetry. Robert Service seemed a good choice. The clean frozen Yukon was as far as I could get from the steaming stew of Birmingham. Sleep finally came to my weary head as Dangerous Dan McGrew was pumped full of lead.

At midnight I woke to a ringing phone and the voice of Carter Whitney.

"Did you get a set?" were the first words out of Carter's mouth.

"A set? A set of what?" I was still more than half asleep.

"The pictures," Carter said. "Pictures of Jefferson and Shaleena. Just awful pictures . . . or wonderful, depending on your point of view. Look on your porch and see if there's a big brown envelope."

I turned on the porch light and checked. Nothing was there. I returned to the phone and told Carter I'd come up empty. He said, "You must be the only one in Alabama that didn't get an envelope. They're being delivered everywhere by a private messenger service. Every doctor I've talked to has gotten a set. The ICU and every floor has a set. I talked to a messenger who saw the master list of all recipients. Jefferson's wife, his church, even George Wallace; everyone who knows him is on it.

"Pictures of Jefferson and Shaleena? You mean like . . . sex pictures?" I was a little slow on the uptake.

"So you really didn't send them?" Carter asked.

"Are you serious? Where would I get pictures like that?" I said.

"Well, you were trying to get pictures exactly like that when you went to Shaleena's body," Carter pointed out. "Everyone knows all about that and Jefferson knows it too. Everyone assumes that these must be the very same pictures you went for. They figure you kept going after those photos until you finally got them. Then, when Jefferson was going to survive, you sent them out to destroy him.

"Jefferson's bound to think it was you. There's a chance he'll go nuts and come after you. When you see the pictures you'll understand. It's not just normal sex stuff. There's a lot of black leather and whips involved, with Shaleena on the painful end. I'm coming over to get you now and I'll bring a set with me. You need to get out of your house before Jefferson shows up there with a gun. Pack a few things. Make it fast and I'll take you over to my place."

Waiting for Carter, I put on sneakers, jeans and a sleeveless black T-shirt. I had a million questions. Did the pictures come from Holt? Was that why he said I shouldn't give up? Was that what he meant about the race having a different finish line? It looked like Jefferson came in first until the photos showed the race was still in progress.

But would even these pictures be enough to finally really get Jefferson fired? They would surely blow his drug counseling story right out of the water. But if it was Holt, why hadn't he warned me of possible danger from Jefferson?

Why didn't I get a set of the pictures? The answer to that one was obvious. I wouldn't need to send one to myself, and it was supposed to look like I sent them. Blackmail pictures had been the lure to bring me to Shaleena's body. Now real sex pictures, suitable for blackmail, had actually showed up. No way was that a coincidence. Whoever planned the murder and frame knew real pictures were out there. It was all set up to look like I had finally found them and used them. Haystack said Eightball planned the murder. He had no reason to lie about that. So that meant the pictures had to also come from Eightball. If he could run a criminal enterprise from jail, how hard would it be to get some pictures? The same guys who bought and sold his dope could have gotten them and sent them.

Eightball had to be the one. Nothing else made sense. He already had Shaleena killed for cheating on him with Jefferson. Now he got revenge on Jefferson by sending out the pictures. Eightball would have been in the clear if Haystack hadn't been turned in by Tiny. If not for Haystack's confession and Looks-Rough-Runs-Good, I would have been blamed for the murder and the pictures. I had reason to hate both Shaleena and Jefferson, so I'd killed one and ruined the other. Everyone would believe that but one thing still didn't add up.

If Holt didn't know the pictures were coming, why had he held out hope for my future? Maybe Holt knew the photos would come out because he had sent them to Eightball. That was Detective Owens' theory right from the beginning.

By the time Carter arrived, I had thrown my overnight stuff into a gym bag. I opened the door as he walked to my porch with a large brown envelope. He was halfway there when screeching brakes made him turn to look behind him. A white Cadillac careened to the curb and smashed into Carter's parked pickup.

Jefferson staggered out of the car bleeding from his forehead. At the end of his right arm dangled the biggest revolver I had ever seen. It was a shiny nickel plated gun with at least a six inch barrel. Jefferson wore wrinkled brown dress pants and a crumpled white shirt with a collar. Even in the uncertain light from my porch, I saw sweat stains under his armpits. His hair was wild and blood streamed down from where his head hit the windshield. His left hand pressed against the wound and he made soft mewing noises. His shirt-front was quickly soaked with blood but he didn't seem to notice. It only took a glance to see he was stark barking insane.

Carter turned towards him and extended one hand, palm out in a calming gesture. That was a waste because Jefferson never even glanced in his direction. His eyes gripped mine and held them as he came unsteadily towards me. Jefferson cut across the lawn with Carter on the path to his right. As he passed Carter, his arm extended to the side and the gun fired twice. The .357 magnum rounds slammed into Carter's sternum. They exploded out by his spine in two long scarlet spray-paint spatters. The trajectories left no doubt that the bullets had gone through the heart. I knew right away; Mr. Whitney was dead within seconds.

In the dark yard, a foot-long flame spat from the barrel with each report. The recoils jerked his hand over his head but Jefferson never noticed. Even while he murdered Carter, Jefferson's eyes stayed fixed on mine. He killed Carter Whitney as casually as if he was swatting a fly. More casually; at least you have to look at a fly to swat it.

Carter didn't fly backwards through the air, as shot people do in movies. He just crumpled where he stood and lay in a bloody heap. I might have gone to him and gotten myself killed had there been any chance of his survival. But Carter was only a blood soaked jumble of lifeless limbs and torso. His face was somewhere in the middle of the mess and I wasn't able to see it. But I didn't need to see his eyes to know; Carter was no longer behind them.

With an effort, I shook off grief for my friend. There would be time for that later. Just then I had to clear my mind and think fast if I didn't want to join him.

Jefferson came forward, jerking the gun and ordering me back towards my doorway.

"Back, back," he said in a shaky voice. "Walk backwards, through the door. Do it now or die like the nigger."

I backed away from him slowly. If he came forward faster, the distance between us would shorten. At first it did but then he slowed and ordered me to move quicker. I backed through the door to the small vestibule and he followed me in from the porch. Instead of U-turning to the living room, I backed deeper into the entry. The screened in vestibule was small, with little room to maneuver. The more we moved around in there the more chance I'd have to grab him. Jefferson may have been crazy, but he still possessed an animal cunning. He barely entered the vestibule and sized up the situation. Then he backed up into the living room ordering me to follow. He moved slowly, keeping me at just the right distance. I was close enough that he couldn't miss, yet too far for a chance at his weapon.

I followed him from the vestibule in through the living room entry. As I passed the door, I thought of slamming it shut and trying to run. Not a good idea. The door would not stop a round from a .357. Even if I made it to the porch, I'd be shot in the back seconds later. If I had to catch a bullet, I would rather do it charging than running.

Jefferson stopped a few yards inside my living room. He stood there watching me carefully as I entered. On his order, I closed the door behind me. We stood there facing each other. The porch light was still on and anyone driving by could see Carter's body. But after midnight my residential street had little traffic. If cops had been called when the gun was fired, the police would already have been there. I couldn't count on cavalry riding to my rescue.

They say, run from a knife but charge a gun. You can't run faster than a bullet. I don't know if "they" ever looked down the barrel of a .357. I don't know if "they" ever saw a body crumple to garbage like Carter's. Maybe "they" would have charged Jefferson immediately, slapped the gun away and gone right up his nose. I might have tried it if the hammer had been down, but unfortunately it wasn't. It was fully back and cocked and I knew what that meant.

I had hunted in New England with a high school friend and his father. We used rifles for deer but my buddy's dad always brought two handguns to play with. One was an army issue Colt .45, a semiautomatic. The other was a big revolver in .38 Special. During the midday break, while the game was asleep, we killed beer cans with the handguns.

I knew that, with the hammer down, it took time to shoot a revolver. The trigger mechanism had to pull the hammer back, before it could fall on the cartridge. But Jefferson had already cocked the gun and revolvers have no safeties. The slightest trigger pressure would drop the hammer and then the gun would go bang. Hammer down, I might have gone for it. Hammer at full cock, it was hopeless.

Jefferson was an inch taller than I and lean as a starving greyhound. Looking up into his bloodshot eyes confirmed that he was crazy. The slightest provocation or scare could cause a twitch of his finger. I would be dead with the very first shot but I was sure he would keep shooting. When the gun was empty, he'd probably put one final round in the chamber. That would be for himself: the only escape from his shame and degradation.

My hands were raised but only as high as my shoulders. Split seconds would matter when I made my move. The closer my hands were to his gun the better. For some reason, I wasn't really scared, not even after what happened to Carter. That cowardly crime only made me more determined to kill Jefferson.

I was also used to thinking clearly with life or death in the balance. In surgery, it was a patient's life at risk. Facing Jefferson, it was my own life. I was surprised to find that really didn't seem to make much difference. I knew how to operate and I knew how to fight, and fear wouldn't help me do either. To give in to it now was to give in to Jefferson and that was not going to happen.

I was also encouraged by the thought that Jefferson wanted to do more than kill me. If my death was all he was after, I'd be out on the lawn with Carter. There was something Jefferson needed to say before he pulled the trigger. While he delayed, I would bide my time and hope for some kind of distraction.

If I moved first, I'd have a few tenths of a second before he could fire. It would take that long for nerve impulses to travel from eye to brain and trigger finger. Any hesitation on his part would give me an added advantage. With a distraction, if I moved first and fast, I knew I could do it. If I could just get one hand on that gun, the game would be all over.

I just had to buy myself some time and hope for that precious distraction.

"Okay Dr. Jefferson," I said calmly, "you've got my attention. But why did you kill Carter Whitney. He hadn't done anything to you . . . and the truth is I haven't either."

"You ruined my life. That's all you did!" he screamed and I braced myself for the bullet. His fingers were white on the grip of the gun. His eyes on fire with hatred. I had to calm him a little or he'd shoot before he meant to.

"It seems more like you ruined my life," I said. "What do you think I did to hurt you?"

"Those idiot cops told me you were out to get pictures." At least he was no longer screaming. "They said you wanted pictures to blackmail me with." The more he talked the calmer he seemed. I had to keep him talking. I tried to inch forward but he moved back to keep a safe distance.

"They said there were no pictures but they were obviously mistaken. You got them." He was getting worked up again. "You got those filthy pictures and you used them to destroy me! But you couldn't have gotten them by yourself. I want to know who's in it with you."

He was getting wild again, stabbing with the gun and yelling. The blood from his scalp wound continued to flow but didn't seem to affect his vision. He wiped it away periodically with a fancy monogrammed hanky.

"It's that bastard McDuff and his pet psychopath Tiny, isn't it? Tell me or I'll kill you. Tell me the truth or I'll kill now; I swear it."

It seemed more likely that he would kill me as soon as I confirmed his suspicions. He wanted to know who else he had to kill to get full payback. Once he knew the answer or thought he knew it, there would be no need to keep talking.

Just then I saw movement behind Jefferson, beyond the front window curtains.

My back was towards the vestibule on the side of the porch we had entered. Jefferson faced me which meant his back was towards the other porch entry. That was the unlit side of the porch, where I had seen the movement. It led into the dining room which led to the living room behind Jefferson. The curtains were opaque but that hulking shadow could never be mistaken. It was Tiny by the unused door at the other end of the porch. He had shown on his first visit that springing the lock would be no problem. The only question now was whether Jefferson would hear him coming.

I had to make noise and delay while Tiny got into the living room behind him. I had never seen the pictures but Jefferson was sure I'd sent them. If I denied it, he would only assume I was lying. If he thought I was lying he might not bother asking any more questions. Then I would eat a bullet before Tiny could get in position.

"Sure I sent the pictures," I said, "but not with Holt and Tiny. I'll tell you who my confederate was but not if you're going to kill me anyway. If you don't want her to get away clean, we need to make an arrangement." I thought the idea of a female accomplice might surprise and confuse him. The more confused he was the less chance he'd kill his informant.

A shadow of doubt crossed his face, which was exactly what I wanted.

"Her? What do you mean, her? Some female conspired with you? Are you suggesting it was my wife? Don't you day-ah say it was my wife?" The idea made no sense at all to me but it certainly had his attention. There was no way he would shoot now; not until he was sure I was lying.

"She would nev-ah! This has been worse for her than for me! You are a liar! Admit you're lying or I'll kill you right now!" Jefferson was screaming again which covered the sounds of Tiny springing the lock. The door opened and Tiny came quietly through into the dining area. From there he passed into the living room right behind Jefferson. His gun was as big as Jefferson's and leveled at his back.

"Drop the gun, Lloyd. Then turn around slow," Tiny ordered calmly.

Jefferson was in a direct line between me and Tiny. If a high powered bullet doesn't hit bone, it will go right through a torso. If Tiny's round went through Jefferson, I would be its next target. I'm sure that's why Tiny was talking at all instead of just pulling the trigger.

As Jefferson spun to face Tiny, I dove out of the line of fire. Tiny would be free to take the shot as soon as I got clear. Still in the air, I noticed the hammer on Tiny's gun was down.

Jefferson's hammer was cocked and, with the first move, reaction time was in his favor. Those were two big advantages but he was still an amateur. Tiny was a professional criminal and I was sure this was not his first gunfight. If Jefferson turned and took time to aim, Tiny would shoot first and kill him. Jefferson could only get off the first shot if he took it from the hip while spinning. In that case, he would almost surely miss and an aimed shot from Tiny would kill him.

The only way Jefferson could hope to win was a lucky shot while turning. Maybe he realized that and took a chance but honestly I don't think so. It looked more like dumb luck and nerves pulled the trigger. The revolver nearly came out of his hand and Jefferson fumbled to hold it.

The bullet struck Tiny high in the gut and an inch to his right of the midline. The lethal trajectory flashed through my mind: Liver, hepatic veins, maybe inferior vena cava. Still in the air, I already knew. Tiny would never live to reach an OR.

I hit the ground on all fours and bounced lightly with a wrestler's balance. I careened right into Jefferson as he struggled to hold the revolver.

His finger was out of the trigger guard and his hold on the grip was slipping. I hit him like a runaway train on a car at a railroad crossing.

The revolver would have gone flying if I hadn't grabbed his gun-hand. I managed to squeeze it around the grip, trapping them both together. Jefferson was on his back with me on top for a two-point take-down. I slid up to straddle his waist and grabbed his throat with my right hand.

My left hand pinned his right hand to the ground by his head, with the gun trapped inside it. Letting go of his throat, my right fist drew back and punched his face into the carpet. If it hadn't been for Carter, at this point I might have gone easy. But I thought how lightly he'd killed my friend and I guess I kind of lost it. The image of Carter crumpling dead on my lawn blinded me with blood and anguish.

I have only a vague memory of what happened next and it isn't very pretty. Falling forward I used my momentum to repeatedly slam Jefferson's face with my elbow. I can still feel the crunch as his facial bones gave and grated against each other. With an effort of will, I stopped picturing Carter and managed to halt the mayhem.

But that didn't mean I was going to let Jefferson sleaze out of it this time. He'd already shown the power he had, by surviving the scandal with Shaleena. With his family money and influence, if he lived, I could end up in prison. I saw no need to take any chance whatsoever of letting that happen.

With Jefferson unconscious, I had all the setup time I needed. I got his limp finger on the trigger and put my finger over it. When I pressed down, his finger would pull the trigger and drop the hammer. Moving carefully, I pressed the pistol's muzzle over his heart. Then I leaned forward and down, with my chest on the butt of the revolver.

We would both have powder burns but only his fingerprint would be on the trigger. That would be proof enough of the story I would tell the cops.

"Thank God, officer," I would say as sincerely as I could. "We were struggling for the gun and it went off between us. I guess I was lucky. It could just as easily have been pointed at me." Then I'd sigh with fake relief and remorse. I'm not much of liar and Owens at least probably wouldn't believe me. But what could he do? Just like Jefferson's lies, no one alive could disprove them.

It was all set up and ready to go. All I had to do was squeeze his finger against the trigger. He was already dead. Carter was already avenged. Tiny was avenged. The patients who died because Jefferson had covered for

Shaleena could rest easy. He had come to kill me and I killed him instead. What could be wrong about that?

He was already dead.

But he wasn't.

The pistol had not fired.

The hammer was back down after the single shot and a long trigger pull was needed. This was awkward with the gun between us and our chests pressed close together.

I re-cocked the hammer and reset our positions. Now the slightest pressure on his trigger finger . . . I braced myself for the recoil that would bruise my chest and kill Jefferson. I braced myself and waited for it and . . . still nothing.

The horrible thought occurred to me that maybe I couldn't do it.

Repeatedly covering up patient deaths was tantamount to murder. He had killed Tiny. He came to kill me. Carter's death alone was more than enough cause for me to kill Jefferson. He was crazy when he killed Carter but I didn't care. He knew well enough what he was doing.

Jefferson was a flaming, leaping, cavorting, gaping, galloping murdering asshole! There was no doubt the world would be a better place without him.

Fuck! I couldn't do it!

I couldn't force myself to kill a helpless insane man. I couldn't do it even to avenge the murder of a man like Carter Whitney.

As I came to this shameful realization, Jefferson lurched up against me. The gun went off and I honestly don't know if I meant to pull the trigger. I'd like to think I finally found the balls to kill the bastard. But Jefferson might have fired the gun himself or maybe it was really an accident. I'm not a fool so I told the cops, it just went off while we struggled.

One reason I'll never know for sure is I faded out for a while. The blast and recoil drove the butt of the magnum into my sternum. I came to with a throbbing bruise on my chest and stinging powder burns. As soon as I could move, I was off Jefferson's corpse and running out front to check Carter. I didn't have to touch his body to confirm what I already knew. I choked down my grief and ran back inside to kneel beside Tiny.

Tiny was on his back in an expanding pool of blood. I tore open his shirt to find a puckered hole in his right upper belly. There was almost no bleeding from the small entry wound but that didn't make me feel better. Massive amounts of blood had gushed from the exit wound onto my carpet.

"Doc," Tiny croaked and, to my amazement, he opened his eyes.

"Hold still Tiny, I'll get help," I said, knowing nothing could help him. Tiny must have known it as well.

"No, doc. I'm day-ed."

"Tiny," I said and my voice choked up. I took his hand and he squeezed mine hard and held it.

"Jefferson?" he whispered so softly that I could scarcely hear.

"Dead," I assured him. "I killed him."

Tiny nodded and seemed to smile. He was trying to say something. I put my ear by his mouth and he whispered, "Tell Holt . . ."

"Tell Holt what, Tiny?" I asked. But he closed his eyes and was silent for a while, barely breathing. When he spoke again, what came out seemed unrelated. I thought he said, "She can rest easy."

"Who can rest easy, Tiny?" He drifted off again and I thought for sure that Tiny was gone. I felt for a pulse and he opened his eyes and spoke again, more clearly.

"It matters not how strait the gate, how charged with punishments the scroll. I was—"

"The master of my fate," I finished paraphrasing *Invictus* for him. "I was the captain of my soul."

His grip on my hand went limp. Tiny was gone. The first thug to enter Hell quoting William Henley.

CHAPTER 27

IF DETECTIVE OWENS hadn't died two months later, I would never have figured out what really happened.

By then, Holt was interim Chief of Surgery at the VA. He had restored my privileges and no blemish remained on my record. The Wire had gladly welcomed me back as a third year surgery resident.

Katy was still in Boston at Tufts, working in the unit. She said she loved me but kept finding reasons not to come down and be with me. In spite of all our history, I could see we were not really soul-mates. Katy had been right all along—heart surgery came first in my life. The long distance relationship dwindled and neither of us tried much to save it. I was too busy to mourn the loss and frankly just too damn tired. To paraphrase the Marvelettes' Motown hit, there were, "Too many redheads in the sea." Even a blond or brunette would be fine if it was a love I could count on.

I was on surgical oncology then, a service I really hated. The heart is a pump with valves to keep flow moving in the right direction. That is something I can understand. If it breaks, I can see how to fix it. Cancer is something else again, a dark enemy that fights dirty. I don't understand it and nobody seems to really know a good way to fight it.

I was seeing a consult on the medical side when the oncology resident approached me.

"Cooper," he said, "I've got a terminal patient who says he knows you."

The patient was Detective Owens. He wanted to see me and, when I could, I looked in on him. First I checked his chart and saw that he had lung cancer. It had spread all over. With mets in his liver and lungs and chest wall he couldn't be helped by a surgeon. The medical oncology guys were keeping him alive, but the end game was approaching. Owens had just been diagnosed when I first met him over Shaleena's body. Even then, I thought he looked like he might have cancer. He'd been in and out of the hospital since, with chemo and radiation. Now he was in for the final time. Death at this point would be a blessing.

He was yellow from the liver mets. His breathing was raspy. His bile-stained eyes met mine but he didn't seem to know me.

I approached his bed and said, "Hi, Detective Owens. It's me, Cooper Logan. I am truly sorry about your illness."

He winced with pain, focused his eyes and seemed to recognize me. Then he forced a thin smile, licked his upper lip and said, "Thank you for coming."

A sudden pain hit him. I helped him into a more comfortable position. Then I pressed the buzzer for the nurse and ordered a hefty shot of morphine. Owens was grateful and complained that his docs were stingy with the narcotics. "I don't know what they're afraid of," he said. "I don't think I need fear addiction."

"I'll have a talk with your resident," I said, and for some reason thought of Tiny. "I'll 'reason with him'." I added. "And I'm sure you'll see a difference." I followed through on that promise and, until Owens died, I checked his med sheet daily. There was no reason for him to suffer any more pain than necessary. The high dose morphine might have shortened his life, but the tradeoff was well worth it. So, he died after one week of minimal pain, instead of three weeks of torture.

"Did you kill Barnes?" Owens suddenly asked. The question was why he'd sent for me.

"No," I said, "but that son-of-a-bitch desperately needed killing."

"Was it Tiny?" he asked. "His van was seen at your house the night Barnes paid you a visit."

"Probably," I said, "but what the hell. Does it even really matter?"

"Just clearing my last case," Owens said and tried to work up a chuckle. It came out more like a death rattle.

A question had been nagging around the corners of my mind. This was my chance to ask it.

"When Haystack said Eightball hired him, are you sure he wasn't lying?" I said.

"Why would he lie?" Owens seemed surprised.

"Did you use a lie detector?" I persisted.

"I'm better than any machine," Owens said. "Haystack wasn't lying. Eightball might not have hired him but Haystack believed it was Eightball."

"Haystack *believed* it was Eightball," he said and his words hit as hard as Barnes' blackjack. For Owens it was just an offhand remark, the usual caveat about lie detection. But for me it was the piece that finished the puzzle.

I suddenly understood everything and confirmed it with one more question. "Haystack wasn't hired directly in person by Eightball, was he?"

"Eightball was in prison," Owens said and looked at me like I was crazy.

"Yeah but Eightball could have had Haystack come to the prison for the assignment. Or Eightball could have called from a prison phone to set things up with Haystack. But I'll bet he didn't, did he?" I asked. "Someone else hired Haystack. Whoever it was simply claimed that he'd been sent by Eightball."

"Yeah," Owens said. "Some black guy Haystack didn't know gave him the contract from Eightball. What difference does that make?" Owens asked.

I replied, "More than you can imagine."

The nurse brought the syringe. I took it and she left, but Owens would not let me give it. His cop's curiosity buried the pain. He demanded, "What are you saying?"

I dodged his question by asking another of my own. "Eightball never confessed, did he?"

"Eightball swears he didn't cause Shaleena's death. He told me he'd loved her since high school. He said he might have killed Jefferson but would never have murdered Shaleena. How did you know about that?" Owens asked, "It wasn't in the papers."

"Did he seem like he was lying?" I asked, again ignoring his question.

"Eightball seemed to be telling the truth about that, but cons are excellent liars. What are you saying?" Owens demanded. "Are you saying it wasn't Eightball?"

I had accepted that it was Eightball because Haystack said so. There was just no reason for him to lie about it. But, if he only *believed* it was Eightball, that changed everything. It had never felt right to me that such a complex plot could be set up from prison. Getting those pictures required a pro, with special training and equipment. And distributing the pictures so no one could find out who sent them wasn't easy. I could never really see Eightball setting that up, not with dope dealer punks to act for him. On the day of the murder, Owens said Holt might have sent Eightball the pictures but still . . .

Promised sex pictures of Jefferson and Shaleena had lured me to the murder scene. Jefferson, and nearly everyone else in Birmingham, was certain to find out about that. Then real S and M photos of the two of them had been released. No way was that a coincidence. The plan from the beginning was to make it seem like I had finally found the pictures I'd been looking for and used them to destroy Jefferson. But why? Was the whole point, all along, to make Jefferson come to kill me?

Eightball did have a grudge against me so he might have planned it that way, but I didn't think so. I was pretty sure I knew who it was but couldn't imagine why. Then I thought of something Tiny had said as he was dying.

"You don't think Eightball did it; do you?" Owens asked. He was an honest detective, trying to make sure he had the real killer. But he started to cough and twisted with pain. "If it wasn't him, who was it?"

I pushed the morphine into his IV, wiping out his pain along with his suspicions.

The next time I saw him was a week after that. His resident told me he was dying. He'd forgotten all about Eightball but still was working to solve Barnes's murder. "I'll be seeing Barnes soon," he coughed and whispered. "Then I'll know if Tiny was the cop-killer."

"You won't be seeing Barnes," I said. "You're going to a different place."

"You don't know me at all," Owens said with his yellow eyes burning. "There's a reason you see no family here to hold my hand while I'm dying."

"I know you well enough," I said, "to know that you won't be where Barnes is."

Then some cop friends of his arrived with Owens' long estranged daughter. They had found her just in time. A collection paid for her plane fare. Father and daughter dissolved in tears the second they saw each other.

I left before embarrassing myself, found a phone and called Holt's office.

CHAPTER 28

IT WAS SEVERAL days before Holt and I found time for an evening meeting.

As soon as I entered his office, I saw that *The Count of Monte Cristo* was missing. Before sitting down I took a framed black and white photo from his desktop. The face of a pretty high school girl smiled at me from the picture. I'd seen her before but not on Holt's desk.

"She must feel good to get out of that book," I said. Holt just stared at me.

I sat down in the big soft chair facing Holt's desk and took the picture with me. "She's pretty," I said looking at the young girl. "What was her name?"

"Priscilla Wright," Holt said with a sigh and fired up an unfiltered Camel. "So you think you know it all now, Yankee Boy? Well I'll tell you what. You don't know nothing."

"I know what you did, Holt," I said quietly and leaned to replace the picture. "I just don't know why and I think I have a right to some answers." He didn't respond and I asked, "Who is she and how did Jefferson hurt her?"

Holt blew smoke-rings at the ceiling, pursed his lips and then glared at me. Those gunfighter eyes shot daggers. Then he said, "This meeting is over."

"I killed Jefferson," I said. "I got your revenge for you. Carter Whitney died. Tiny died and Shaleena died in the process. I want to know what caused all that. You're the only one who can tell me."

Holt stubbed out his Camel, lit a new one and dragged so deep it made me dizzy. Then he puffed out his cheeks with the exhale and pulled a bottle from his desk drawer. Two shot glasses followed and he poured them full. "This is the good stuff," he said. Holt downed his with a swallow. I half-emptied mine and felt the smooth burn of Makers Mark bourbon.

Holt downed a second shot and tapped the empty glass on the table. When he spoke his voice was husky and his accent stronger than ever.

"Her name was Priscilla Wright, my first and only love but for surgery. It was a pure love, the kind you could never see the way things are now. These kids today, they are diddling each other before they got hair on it. Back then, it was different. I kissed Priscilla's lips three times all together. Those were the three high points a my life; higher than finishing med school; higher than passing my surgery boards; higher than anything ever."

Holt stared into space for a while, filled his shot glass but didn't drink it. I finished mine, filled it back up myself and asked gently, "What happened to her?"

He bowed his head and rubbed his eyes with his thumb and first finger.

"She was killt," Holt whispered, "killt dead by Jefferson." He snorted and added sarcastically, "They called it an accident—up to Vestavia Lake. We were all in high school. Lloyd's daddy had a speed boat: mahogany and chrome with a powerful engine." It took a minute for me recall that Lloyd was Jefferson's first name.

"Priscilla's daddy was long day-ed. Her momma was a drunk and a who-er. There was a place on the lake, with a floating dock, where we kids used to go swimming. Priscilla and her friends were swimming around it, diving off it and whatnot. Lloyd and a buddy a his was there too, all drunked up and showing off. They was speeding around in his daddy's boat, near the girls, trying to scare them. He claimed he never saw Priscilla in the water. He run her down, mashed her hay-ed and cut her up bad with the prop. I wasn't there. I had a part time job. I was working. She hung on, low sick, for a while but Priscilla was day-ed before we graduated.

"Lloyd bragged that he would get away with it," Holt said and looked up at me with a cold ironic smile. I could see that, even with Jefferson dead, the hatred in Holt's soul lived on. That taught me something about revenge that I have never forgotten.

"Lloyd said his family was above the law and he was gonna prove it." Holt downed the third shot of bourbon and set it down, click, on the table. "He was right. He was above man's law, even got past my daddy. But, just like in *The Count*, God's law, with a little hep, finally got him."

"Were they able to prove he was drunk," I asked. "Did they do a blood test?"

"'They' was my daddy," Holt said. "The lake was in Jefferson County. Daddy was the sheriff. It was in his jurisdiction. My daddy, he done ever-thing he could. He proved Lloyd was drunk and driving crazy. He got statements from folks who seen what he done. Daddy was very thorough. But it wasn't enough."

"Why not?" I asked.

"The first, 'why not,' is why I did not kill Lloyd back then. I wanted to but Daddy made me promise not to hurt him. He said we had to trust the law. He promised the law would get justice. That was the only promise I know of that Daddy failed to honor.

"Colonel Jefferson, Lloyd's daddy, he had the money and the power. He fixed ever-thing for his precious boy. He paid off Priscilla's momma. She dropped all charges and moved outa state. Even Daddy couldn't find her. The blood sample proving Lloyd was drunk disappeared from the po-lice station. The test results on his blood vanished from the hospital lab'atory. Witnesses started changing their stories, obviously paid off or pressured. The DA finally claimed there wasn't enough left to prosecute.

"Naturally he would say that. Jefferson's family and his was all country club members. You can't play golf with a friend and, the next day, send his boy to prison.

"I kep my promise to Daddy and never touched Lloyd my own self. But Tiny would knock his dick in the dirt whenever we had a chance at him. We used to ambush him on his way home." Holt smiled fondly.

"But the beatings weren't enough?" I prompted softly.

"Priscilla, she was day-ed," Holt answered. "And Jefferson took to being drove home after school by his momma. No, it wasn't enough and, in spite of my daddy, I would have killed Lloyd, but for Tiny."

"Tiny stopped you?" I asked. "That sounds a little out of character."

"Well, Tiny give me the book," Holt said. "We shared books and poems with each other. As I told you before, we both liked to read. That was our shameful secret." Holt chuckled. "It wasn't something either of us could admit to our rowdy buddies. That and football made us friends, the kind that last for life. We kept our friendship quiet but we have always been there for each other."

I nodded. "So, Tiny introduced you to *The Count of Monte Cristo*, and it taught that a proper revenge meant more than simple killing."

"It is the classic book of the perfect revenge," Holt said. "I studied it like the bible and Tiny and I talked about it. We saw that anyone can kill anyone for any reason. Might-could be a good reason. Might-could be a bad one. Don't prove nothing. Don't mean a thing. A righteous revenge, like it was in *The Count*, lets a man's own evil cause his downfall. If you hep that happen, you are simply heping God punish a bad person. That was what Edmund Dantes done in *The Count of Monte Cristo*. That's what my daddy done. That was his job as sheriff."

There was another long pause with Holt staring off into space. Then he lit up another Camel.

"So you bided your time for what—thirty years? What were you waiting for?" I prompted. "Compared to you, Hamlet was an impulsive man of action."

"I didn't wait much longer than Edmond Dantes," Holt said. "Even after he escaped from prison, nine more years passed before he acted. It don't matter how long you wait, as long as it's right when it happens. Tiny offered to kill Lloyd but I couldn't let him just up and do it. Things had to be set up so Jefferson's own evil led to his dying. I told Tiny the Lord would send me a sign and when it come, I would know it."

"So what was the sign?" I asked. Holt just sat there grinning and cackling strangely.

"Don't you know?" he asked.

I just shook my head.

"The sign from the Lord was you, Yankee Boy. And His will has now been done through you."

Looking into Holt's eyes at that moment I realized he was crazy. I thought of his sudden flashes of rage sometimes seen in the OR. And Roberta's story of how he went after Jefferson at the VA when I got fired. I thought of his lonely life without love, staying true thirty years to a dead girl. Devotion to patients is fine but, with Holt, it was prompted by something perverse.

"I'm not crazy," Holt said, as if he knew what I was thinking.

"What made you think I was a sign from God?" I asked.

Holt said, "There was lots a reasons. First off was you come down here and right off made Jefferson your enemy. That alone made you my natural ally. And then there was what you said about kicking Eightball's ass in the ER." He paused to see if I remembered. I shrugged with open hands and a quizzical expression.

"I had just told you how my daddy heped the Lord punish evil people and you admitted your own self that you'd done the same with Eightball. You said that was partly why you never pressed charges." Holt smiled at me smugly.

I remembered the conversation. It was when he first warned me about Jefferson, and talked about his daddy the sheriff. "Holt, I was joking!" I protested.

"You thought you were joking," Holt insisted. "But there you were, sitting in my office, an enemy of Jefferson, talking about hepin God punish evil. I knew right then that you were the sign the Lord finally sent me."

"Holt . . ." I wanted to argue, but he just pressed on with his evidence for divine intervention.

"Next, Tiny's nephew needed surgery at the VA," Holt said, "just when that would make you his doctor. Now God's got you and Tiny and me all tied up together." Holt intertwined his fingers to show the tight connection. "I needed Tiny's hep in this and, with you hep'n his nephew, I would have it."

I remembered, when Billy was admitted, Tiny said I'd been highly recommended. "But it wasn't really the Lord," I pointed out. "You had Tiny take Billy to me. Tiny had money. Billy didn't have to go to the VA. When I asked you about that later on, you said it was years since you'd seen Tiny. That was the first time I felt that you were lying to me." Holt just smiled his weird smile and I kept on talking.

"You also gave the Lord some help making me your ally against Jefferson." I said. "Staying in the Unit every night escalated my conflict with him. Your advice just got me deeper in trouble."

"And if you weren't sleeping there," Holt demanded, "what would have happened with Billy? Answer me that, Yankee Boy. Billy would have died if you hadn't been there when he bled from pulling that wire. He still might-coulda died if I hadn't been in the OR when y'all got there. Maybe I did hep the Lord, but His hand was clearly in it. And, after that Tiny had to hep us out any way I asked him."

"But you and Tiny were friends," I objected. "He'd would gladly have killed Jefferson for you."

"He would have made Lloyd just disappear, like he done with Barnes. That wouldn't count for nothing. The perfect revenge I needed would be too public for Tiny. He wouldn't risk going to jail his own self, just to satisfy my vengeance. But then he owed you big time, when you got fired for saving Billy.

Holt paused for a shot and lit another Camel. Then he continued.

"That was when the Lord laid it all out for me in a vision. I'd use Shaleena's murder and the pitchers to get Jefferson to come try to kill you. Tiny would kill him to protect you. Jefferson would die while trying to commit murder. His death would come from his own evil. That would be my righteous revenge just like Edmond Dantes."

I asked, "What if Jefferson killed me first?"

Holt said simply, "God would not let that happen."

I shook my head in disbelief and Holt snapped, "Well, He didn't. Did He?"

There was no answer to that, so I just moved on to my next question. "Did you already have the pictures by then?" I figured he must have had them.

"I had them about a year by then," Holt said. "Since the rumors about those two started. An old police friend of my daddy took them. He was long retired from the force down here and worked as a PI . . . never mind where. He said Jefferson's office was easy to rig with cameras. It had a false ceiling and false walls, all filled with soundproofing. He took them pitchers and set it up for me to send them out when I was ready. He done it so no one could ever trace who took them nor where they come from."

I said, "Then you had Tiny recruit some black guy from out of town to hire Haystack. The guy told Haystack that Eightball had sent him. That's why, as Owens told me, Haystack *believed* he was working for Eightball. But Haystack was working for you and Tiny and he still doesn't know it."

Holt nodded and smiled and then we came to a hard part for me to handle.

"So you ordered the killing of a young girl and framed me for the murder?" He caught the anger in my voice and shot back an angry answer.

"The girl was nothing but a druggy slut," he said, "and I made sure the frame would not fit you."

"She was a troubled human being, forced to have sex with Jefferson and Duggan," I told him. "And, as you pointed out in the ER that day, Looks-Rough-Runs-Good was all that saved me. If the truck hadn't died and the cop hadn't chased Haystack away before he finished the setup . . ."

"The crime scene was left just like I planned it," Holt interrupted. "Haystack's orders from Tiny were to leave no blood on you and no prints on the hammer. That's why we had him change into that clean cammo outfit. Tiny chose Haystack because the mow-ron was too dumb to ask questions. As Tiny said, he just did like he was told by whoever paid him. He was also told to let off on the choke as soon as you started to pass out. If you died, he would a gotten no more money at Horse Pens.

"Without the cop chasing you, it would just seem like some bystander run off Haystack. The way it worked out only made the story look better. It was the Lord made you buy that truck. Even you could not have been that stupid. And that's another proof God had his hand in ever-thing that happened."

Holt was sure he could make me see his plan had God's approval and participation.

"And here's some more proof," Holt went on. "You called out my name at the murder scene to your friend Roberta. And Detective Owens who just happened to know my daddy, just happened to hear you. So I got a personal invite to meet y'all in the ER. That was my chance to clear you and set the police after Jefferson. Can there be any doubt the Lord was behind it?"

I could see how, to Holt's sick mind divine intervention had been proven.

"But how did you figure this all out, Yankee Boy?" Holt asked me after lighting another Camel.

I thought for a minute, trying to work out the sequence in my own mind. Laying it out for Holt, I really understood it myself for the first time.

"With his dying breathe, Tiny asked me to tell you something. He was quiet for a while and I thought he was dead. By the time he said, 'She can rest easy,' I thought he was delusional. I didn't realize that was the message or who it was about until later."

"Well, if you're so smart, Yankee Boy, why didn't you figure it out sooner?" Holt asked.

"I thought you were behind the pictures," I said. "But I couldn't believe you were involved in the murder. The pictures went out the day before Jefferson's reinstatement at the VA went public. They destroyed him just when he must have believed that his nightmare was over. That perfect timing was no accident and you were one of few who could have planned that. I figured that, as Owens suspected, you sent the photos to Eightball. If that was true, you also could have told Eightball when to release them. Haystack said Eightball had hired him so it all held together. That also explained why you said not to lose hope, even when Jefferson was exonerated. Only you knew the race wouldn't be over until you released the pictures."

"So why couldn't you just leave it at that?" Holt sounded annoyed that I hadn't.

"I did at first, even though some things never fit that theory. Tiny supposedly deduced that Haystack was the killer and was certain he'd be at Horse Pens. Why would a fugitive, chased from a murder scene by a cop, go to a nearby music festival—especially one he was known to frequent? Nobody loves shitkickin music that much."

"You just say that because you're a damn Yankee," Hold said with a smile.

"Tiny claimed Haystack went to Horse Pens to trade Shaleena's ear for a final payment. He claimed Jefferson wanted the ear as some kind of perverted trophy. That seemed plausible since Jefferson was a freak. His kinky sex extortion scheme with Shaleena proved that. But if Eightball was behind the murder the ear made no sense whatsoever. He might have been angry enough to kill his lover but not to have someone mutilate her. Haystack swore he was hired by Eightball and why would he lie about that? But if it was Eightball the ear didn't fit and that discrepancy kept eating at me.

"The ear was always a weak point," Holt admitted. "But we needed real evidence against Haystack. The ear was definite proof that he had killed Shaleena. That made the cops believe him, when Lloyd was cleared and Haystack claimed it was really Eightball."

"But, as Owens told me, Haystack only *believed* he'd been working for Eightball," I said. "So if it wasn't Jefferson and the ear ruled out Eightball, only Tiny knew that Haystack would be at Horse Pens. He knew that because he'd arranged the murder, and the final payment."

"How'd you get from Tiny to me," Holt asked.

"Several things made it clear that you were lying about being in contact with Tiny. You sent him to me at the VA for Billy's surgery. You told him to come to the hospital pretending he thought I'd hurt Billy. And the final proof was your sending him to my house to save me and kill Jefferson. Tiny showing up in the nick of time could not have just happened. Only you knew when the pictures went out causing Jefferson to attack me. And it was only you, Holt, who could have known when to send Tiny to protect me."

"Well if you got it all figured out, Yankee Boy, what was it you wanted to ask me?"

"The only thing I didn't understand was why. And now you've explained that clearly. Jefferson's evil—attempted murder—would have led to his own death by Tiny. Then your vengeance would have been perfect."

"I'm glad you understand, Yankee Boy." Holt was nodding and smiling. His smugness made me angry.

"A perfect revenge for you maybe," I said. "But there was collateral damage. To you Shaleena was expendable but how about your lifelong friend Tiny? He didn't kill Jefferson according to plan. Where was God when Jefferson killed Tiny?"

"Tiny was my friend but he was not no angel. He lived by the sword and died by it. It's not my fault the Lord chose that night to take him," Holt said calmly.

"Well how about Carter Whitney?" I shot back. "Is there some reason why his death meant nothing? How much do you know about that man who died for your revenge?"

"I . . . I just know he worked for Dr. Kirkwood," Holt said and his self-assurance seemed shaken. "I . . . he wasn't supposed to be there. He . . . he shouldn't have meddled."

That tore it. I stood up and put my hands on Holt's desk. I leaned towards him and yelled at him. "Let me tell you who died for your vengeance." Then I told Holt all about Carter Whitney. I told him how Carter had worked with Vivien Thomas. How a poor boy had made himself part of heart surgery's story. Before I was done, Holt had taken two more shots of the bourbon. He sat looking down at the top of his desk at the picture of Priscilla.

I threw the picture across the room, came around the desk and grabbed his shoulders. I shook him. "She's been dead for thirty years, Holt. And Jefferson didn't even mean to kill her. It was a fucking accident. Is an accident worth all this carnage? Is it worth the death of another girl, a friend of yours and a man like Carter Whitney?"

Holt just sat there limp in my grasp. I let him go and backed off. He slumped in the chair looking down at the floor.

"No I don't suppose you have anything to say. Are you having a moment of insight? Do you see what you've done for the first time? Your twisted vengeance caused three innocent deaths so what kind of a man does that make you? What would your father the sheriff think of his son the killer? I'll bet your father would say I should tell the cops about your role in those murders."

That made him look up at me. "So," he said, "are you gonna do it?"

I slammed the door as I went out and walked to the Southern elevator. It took an interminable time to come. Then I got in and waited. Before the doors closed, the shot rang out, muffled from Holt's office.

I ran down the hall and barged inside. It was far too late to help him. Holt's left hand clutched Priscilla's image to his heart. His right arm dangled loosely. His gun was on the floor by his hand. His brains were on the wall behind him.

A single sheet of paper was on the desk. Three words were written on it. They were spelled out in thick black marker pen: an enigma in capital letters.

Maybe it meant that the weight of his guilt was too much for him to live with. Or maybe Holt was judging himself and pronouncing his own death sentence. Whatever they meant his final written words were:

INCOMPATIBLE WITH LIFE

May he find in death the peace that even a perfect revenge failed to grant him.

EPILOGUE

I CALLED IN Holt's death that night but told no one of our conversation. I said he had seemed depressed but refused to tell me why. I never would have ratted Holt out and I wish I'd made that clear to him. Anger over Carter's death made me want to hurt Holt but I was wrong to lay that guilt on him. It was Jefferson that murdered Carter and I killed Jefferson. Justice was done by my own hand and that should have been enough.

The case against Eightball was eventually dropped. There was no real evidence to support it. The man who hired Haystack was never found, so there was no way to prove who had sent him.

Haystack died of knife wounds in prison two years later. He was found with both ears and his tongue cut off. Revenge for Shaleena and a warning not to not to talk to cops about Eightball.

Barnes' body was never found. I doubt anyone ever missed him.

The mediocre resident, Bill Clayton, flunked out of the Birmingham program. He became a mediocre plastic surgeon with a pleasant bedside manner. He lives and practices in Beverly Hills and drives a Ferrari.

Stephen Numatalulu went on to found the Super Natural Herbal Tea Company. Momma's potions are now available worldwide at his Website.

Ben Rogers has a lucrative vascular surgery practice in Virginia. He was recently honored for his support by the Southern Poverty Law Center.

Roberta became a professor of surgery at a prestigious medical center.

Bo opened a surgery clinic near Tuscaloosa, Alabama. No one's mother will need to die there again from a ruptured appendix.

Billy came out of his coma a few weeks after Holt's death. He and Sharon are happily married and living in New York City. Billy is a concert pianist and sends me tickets when his symphony plays Mahler. I usually find an excuse not to go. That old time rock and roll soothes my soul. Classical music bores me.

Katy found another doctor and I found another redhead. True love came to me many years later but that is another story.

I finished my training with Dr. Kirkwood and became a cardiac surgeon. I duel with Death now, in his own backyard, nearly every day. Humans are mortal so one might say I always lose in the end. Maybe so, but the true warrior doesn't live to win. He lives for the joy of battle and—as Holt taught me—he never ever gives in.

FACT, FICTION AND HISTORY

I attended Tufts College and med-school, in Boston, just like Cooper Logan. In the seventies, I trained with Dr. John Kirklin, in Birmingham, Alabama. Cooper was a resident there with Dr. Joseph Kirkwood. We each achieved our common dream of becoming a cardiac surgeon.

But Cooper is not I and I am not Cooper Logan. I had two loving parents and was a fairly decent wrestler. Cooper came from a broken home and won a wrestling scholarship. Cooper is a fictional character. I'm pretty sure I'm real.

Dr. Kirkwood, however, *is* Dr. John Kirklin. Dr. Kirklin is the real life Father of Cardiac Surgery. Everything in the story about Kirkwood's career is true of Dr. Kirklin's. The only exception is the role of the fictional Carter Whitney. No one shares Dr. Kirklin's glory as Vivien Thomas shares Blalock's.

The Kirklin character had to react to fictional situations and I couldn't presume to say what he would do without his permission. Dr. Kirklin may have died in 2004, but The Wire is still out there somewhere. Rather than risk his posthumous wrath, I used the name Dr. Kirkwood.

The fictional Holt McDuff resembles a real surgeon, Holt McDowell. Both were, "Docta Hope," to many of their patients. But Holt McDuff and Holt McDowell are also very different. The real Holt was a family man and a caring teacher to us residents. His daddy was a sheriff, but as far as I know, the real Holt had no dark secrets. Everything good about Holt McDuff was true of Dr. McDowell. The dark side of Holt McDuff springs entirely from my imagination.

To a certain extent, *Dueling in Death's Back Yard* is a memoir. The rigors of my residency are honestly described and the O.R. action is accurate. Every case, except for the ASD, is based on a real patient. Looks-Rough-Runs-Good was truly my first pickup.

First and foremost, however, this novel is a work of fiction. No nurse was murdered during my training and there was no Lloyd Jefferson. The real VA chief in Birmingham was a good man and an excellent surgeon. Houston surgeons are fast but not careless like the fictional Dr. Walker. Considering my rude Yankee ways, my fellow residents treated me more than fairly. None of them was anything like the despicable Ben Rogers. Katy is also an entirely fictional character.

I have really never thought of myself as a healer. A warrior against Death has always been my self image. I don't know how other heart surgeons feel but Cooper Logan, at least, agrees with me.

Dear Reader,

My father introduced me to the Tarzan books when I was eight. I haven't stopped reading since and, from Edgar Rice Burroughs on, I have felt a personal connection with every one of my favorite authors. The idea that *Dueling in Death's Backyard* could make readers feel that connection with me is, as the kids say, nothing short of awesome. The more readers the more awesome it is so please, if you liked my novel, give it a good review on Amazon.com.

Thomas Jay Berger, MD

ABOUT THE AUTHOR

Photograph by Lolly Anderson

Thomas Jay Berger, M.D., F.C.C.P. is a Faulkner Award winning author, distinguished cardiac surgeon, adventurer, and lifetime martial artist. After training with his mentor, Dr. John Kirklin, the true Father of Cardiac Surgery, Dr. Berger won the Navy Achievement Medal and went on to start his own cardiac surgery program in a small town in Montana. His program was recognized by the Wall Street Journal as being tied for the lowest mortality in the nation for Medicare coronary artery bypass procedures. Dr. Berger returned to academic medicine as an Associate Consulting Professor of Surgery on the Duke faculty and Chief of Surgery at a Duke affiliated V.A. hospital. When trouble with his vision ended Dr. Berger's active practice career, he spent the next 8 years sharing adventures with his wife, "Red," as they sailed their 50ft ketch, Katana, from the U.S. to Trinidad and all over the Caribbean. Settled now in Miami, FL, Dr. Berger continues to train in the martial arts and boxing,, writes, and consults as an expert in medical malpractice cases.